Rules for a Pretty Woman

Rules for a Pretty Woman

Suzette Francis

An Imprint of HarperCollins*Publishers*

HarperCollins books may be purchased for education, business, or sales promotional use. For information please write: Special Markets Department, HarperCollins Publishers Inc., 10 East 53rd Street, New York, NY 10022.

FIRST EDITION

Designed by Elizabeth M. Glover

Library of Congress Cataloging-in-Publication Data

Francis, Suzette.
Rules for a pretty woman / Suzette Francis.—1st ed.
p. cm.
ISBN 0-06-053542-3 (alk. paper)
1. African American physicians—Fiction. 2. African American women—Fiction.
3. Women physicians—Fiction. 4. Atlanta (Ga.)—Fiction. I. Title.
PS3606.R365R85 2003
813'.6—dc21 2003051977

03 04 05 06 07 JTC/RRD 10 9 8 7 6 5 4 3 2 1

To Henry,
the greatest obstetrician-gynecologist I know

Acknowledgments

Special thanks to Marcia Krosner for her encouragement and literary lessons; Andrea Pedolsky; The Bitty Society, Chattanooga; Signal Mountain book clubs; fellow writers; family; and friends.

Going the Distance

Not many people run in winter. I'm one of the few choosing to change into running clothes after work. For the better part of fifteen minutes, I stretch calves and hamstrings, do a series of warm-up exercises, and head outside where the hawkish cold stings like frostbite. I run two miles in thirteen minutes, soon reaching the runner's high, glowing inside as the dusky gray turns purple. Heat from my body mixes with the dead of winter, and an occasional car whizzes by.

Along the way, I spot another runner with cold fog spewing from his nose and mouth like steam from a teakettle, his pace steady and swift. You can tell by his firm, muscular calves that running is a great part of his life, like eating or sleeping. It took years for me to reach this level of enthusiasm myself. Now I either run each day or wind up feeling miserable by night's end. It lifts my spirit like an upper, a drug I should get busted for using, natural speed. I have to do it. If asked to describe it in a sentence, I would say, Running is man's race with time. Not against time, not to save time. When I run, there is no time, time is timeless, insignificant, and my mind, like the rest of my body, is suspended in a realm of timelessness.

Ten years ago, I ran my first big race, a five-mile run for breast cancer, which my mother had been recently diagnosed with, and I made it. Not in first place, though I remember coming respectably close to the top. That was the day I met Ralph. The day I fell head over heels in love.

Two shadowed souls run ahead of me when I veer down a winding path running parallel to the main road, their bodies synchronized to the same rhythmic pace, slower than mine, but steadier, reminding me of the days when Ralph and I ran together, when his knee had not offered him quite as much trouble as now. I miss his company. I miss the smell of spring along this path where wild wisteria blooms close to the edge, now dormant, scraggly, dried-up weeds.

After two and a half miles, I stop where the path disappears inside the black woods that might as well be the end of the earth. I catch my breath while listening to stark silence, absent the nocturnal songs of a nighttime choir, hidden deep within its thickets: the katydids, crickets, frogs, as well as those creatures beyond my common knowledge, hibernating and waiting for spring, when the earth warms, an odor similar to the womb of a laboring woman will rise up out of the thickets. I think about becoming pregnant.

1

9:00 A.M.

Shaniqua Davis: 13-year-old black female, first-time patient. Weight: 189 lbs. Height: 5'6". Gravida/para—[No history of pregnancies]. Last normal menstrual period, mid-December. Birth control: none. Complaints: nausea, vomiting, tiredness, irritability. History of present illness: Mother suspects she's contracted a virus spreading through her school. School nurse recommended a gynecological visit.

"How long have you had these symptoms, Shaniqua?"

"About two weeks," Shaniqua's mother pipes up. Ms. Davis is an attractive, well-dressed woman with short, nicely cropped hair, a smooth, medium-brown complexion, and a small build compared to her overweight daughter.

"Ever felt like this before, Shaniqua?" I ask.

"First she's ever been sick in her life," Ms. Davis blurts out.

Shaniqua looks down at her twiddling fingers.

"Are you sexually active?"

"No, she isn't," Ms. Davis says, narrowing her eyes at me, arms crossed as she sits straighter in her seat as if bracing for battle.

"I'm asking your daughter," I say patiently. "I'd like to hear from her, since she's my patient." I lower my voice. "May I have a word alone with Shaniqua, please?"

"I know what goes on with my daughter, Dr. Faulkner." Ms. Davis sneers. "She's not one of those hot 'n' fast little girls running up and down the road after boys."

"Are you sexually active, Shaniqua?"

"No, ma'am," Shaniqua whispers, giving me a shifty, bug-eyed look.

I review the initial lab test in Shaniqua's chart.

Blood pressure: 100/60. Urinalysis: normal. Pregnancy test: positive.

"Um-hmmmm," I hum, focusing on the word *positive.* "Shaniqua, I know why you've been spitting up lately."

"It's the flu," Ms. Davis says emphatically.

"No," I say, "but I'd like to have a word with her alone for a moment, Ms. Davis, if you don't mind."

"I do mind, Doctor. Shaniqua's my only child, and anything that concerns her, I demand to know first-hand."

"She's pregnant," I say softly, stroking Shaniqua's hair, which grows wild and restless about her broad, dark face like tumbleweed, with a spray of half-straight strands sticking up. She is the picture of me at her age: overweight and irrefutably unattractive. Ms. Davis breathes heavily, like a bull about to charge.

"I drop her off at school every morning," she says, astounded. "And I'm home from work a half hour after she gets home in the evening. We spend every weekend together. Every weekend! She can't be having no baby."

"I didn't do it, Mama," Shaniqua cries.

"Maybe the test is wrong," Ms. Davis says desperately.

"I'm afraid not," I say, glancing down at *positive* on the lab results.

"But I wasn't sexually active, Mama," Shaniqua pleads.

Ms. Davis glances up at me, then down at Shaniqua on the exam table, as if trying to decide whom to believe.

"How'd it happen, then?" she growls.

"I don't know, Mama."

"How can you not know a thing like that?"

"I didn't do it."

"You had to do something, Shaniqua."

"I didn't move."

"Didn't move?"

"We kissed one time, Mama, and that was it, I swear."

"What're you talking about, girl? Kissing. Nobody gets knocked up from a kiss. What d'ya think I am? As stupid as you?"

"No, Mama."

"Ms. Davis, please watch what you say," I insist. "What happened, Shaniqua? Were you forced?"

"No, I just laid on the bottom is all. He did all the moving."

"On the bottom of who?" Ms. Davis snaps. "Who is he?"

Silence.

"I said *who,* Shaniqua." Ms. Davis is pacing the floor like a light-footed sandpiper, stopping now and then, her toe tapping to a beat only she can decipher. "Thirty minutes. I leave you to yourself thirty minutes a day, and you get up under some boy first chance you get. Who is he?"

"That's not important right now, Ms. Davis," I say calmly. "Our concern should be for Shaniqua's well-being. Sometimes unfortunate things happen to the best of us. We all make mistakes."

"Well, you're not having it," Ms. Davis bristles, pointing a convicting finger at her daughter. Shaniqua stares up at the ceiling. She removes her feet from the stirrups and curls into the fetal position.

"Abortion is a viable option at this point," I say. "If that's what Shaniqua wants."

"She's not bringing another mouth in my house to feed."

"I don't want no abortion, Mama."

"Well, you should've thought of that before you laid on the bottom."

"I don't want no abortion, Doctor," Shaniqua cries. "It's a sin to kill a baby."

"You're worried about sin after fornicating with a boy," Ms. Davis huffs, shaking her head disgustedly. "You're not having nobody's baby."

"Ms. Davis, you can't force her. Besides, there are other options the two of you might consider together. Adoption, being one."

"So everybody in town knows she's swollen with a baby. Thirteen years old and knocked up. Sheila Davis's little girl's hot 'n' fast after some boy." Ms. Davis plops into a chair as if the wind has just been knocked out of her, defeat loosening the tautness in her face. I empathize with her, knowing that even as large as Atlanta is, a two million-plus population, there are still pockets of small-town neighborhoods and bible-toting Southern Baptists.

"No good. Dirty. Used. What's our pastor gonna say, Shaniqua? How're we ever gonna hold our heads up in church again?"

"Ms. Davis, you've done a fine job raising your daughter alone. Shaniqua's still a good girl, probably smart in school. I'll bet she's never given you any trouble before, right?"

"Until now," Ms. Davis says, bitterly.

"Please try to remember what it's like to be her age," I say. "Being thirteen is even harder now than when you and I were kids, Ms. Davis. Teens today are bombarded with sexual images in videos . . . movies . . ."

"That's why I've brought her up in the church," Ms. Davis interrupts. "For all the good it's done me."

"Shaniqua made a mistake, Ms. Davis. But now she needs your love and compassion."

"I know exactly what my daughter needs, Doctor."

"I'm sure you do," I say, feeling depleted. I make a note in Shaniqua's chart: *Controlling, overbearing mother.* Ms. Davis sits outside in the waiting room while I further examine Shaniqua, performing the following tests: pap, gonorrhea, chlamydia, plus a wet prep for trichomoniasis, vaginosis, and yeast. I notate *normal pap* and the lab results from the other tests are, thank heavens, *negative.* Kelly, my assistant, signals the time on her watch: twenty minutes overdue for the next patient in Exam Room Three.

11:10 A.M.

Linda Jenkins: 19-year-old white female. Weight: 142 lbs. Gravida—1/para—O, return pregnancy visit. Gestation: 20 weeks. No weight gain since last visit. Urine and blood pressure: normal. Size of womb: normal.

"Everything the same since your last visit, Linda?"

"Nooooo," she groans.

"Sharp pain in the abdomen? Severe discomfort? Bleeding?"

"Nooooo."

"Backache? Sleeplessness? Nausea?"

"Nooooo."

"What's changed?"

"He's left me," she cries. "My baby's father won't marry me now."

Complaint: despondent over break-up w/baby's father

"I'm sorry to hear that, Linda. Some men can be downright heartless. But it's not the end of the world for you and your baby, now, is it?"

"I want an abortion, Dr. Faulkner."

"Linda, it's too late. It'd be illegal at this point."

"I don't want anything of his."

"You're talking about a baby."

"I don't want it. I want my life the way it was before I met him."

Kelly flips on the fetal heart monitor; mother and child hearts beat synchronistically. Linda suddenly freezes at the sound of new life, her lips quiver as she holds back the dam. She yanks the attachments from her swollen belly, the last beep barely heard above her heavy sobbing.

"I'd rather die," she cries, lamenting that the man she loved broke his promise to marry her. He lied. He should have said sooner. "He promised."

"Having a child alone isn't the worst thing in the world, Linda. There are people who can help. Thousands of couples would give anything for the chance to raise your baby. You'll be all right. You have other options."

She cries hysterically for at least five minutes, prompting Kelly to discreetly signal the time on her watch, tapping it while Linda isn't looking. We are getting behind, so Kelly silently mouths, "Other patients are waiting."

I stroke Linda's thick red hair and whisper, "You'll be fine. You'll see." Her pale blue eyes gaze up at me helplessly. She reminds me of a child who skins her knee and cries at first, her bottom lip quivering as she sucks it in, mightily trying to be the big girl. She finally pulls herself together, wipes her eyes and blows her nose.

"I wish I was dead," Linda says. The futility in her voice frightens me. I tell her about Stella Parker, a social worker friend of mine whose job it is to assist young women in trouble. I explain that Stella can help find her a safe place to live if she needs it.

"She'll be glad to talk to you. No strings attached. Believe me, Stella goes out of her way to help." I remove one of Stella's cards from my labcoat pocket, and hand it to her. "Just call her," I say.

"No thanks," Linda says, ignoring the card. "I'll do what I have to do."

5:15 P.M.

Pamela Tucker, 36-year-old black female, return patient. Gravida—3, para—2. Birth control: tubal ligation in 1986, procedure reversed in 1990. Tubal ligation in 1992, procedure reversed in 1995. Left Dr. Hammond's practice in 1996 after tubal pregnancy. I performed a tubal ligation that same year. Weight: 215 lbs. Blood pressure and urine: normal. Complaint: Desires pregnancy. Wants tubes untied for third time.

"Dr. Fowknah," Ms. Tucker drawls as she enters my office wearing the look of a woman in love. She sashays in, her hips swaying in a kind of double-heeled bounce and step, her head proudly erect and her large breasts pushed out. The purple wool suit she wears fits snug around the waist. "Did I tell you I'm getting married?" she asks, smiling, and for a woman of her girth, she sits daintily in an armchair in front of my desk and crosses a meaty pair of legs, cloaked in sheer, silk stockings. "That's why I've just got to have another baby."

"Congratulations," I say, glancing down at the chart in front of me, where I see that Ms. Tucker's name changed three times in the past ten years. She was Pamela Miller in 1992, during the birth of her first child; Jackson in 1996, during the birth of her second; and Tucker when she left Dr. Hammond's practice and first came to see me.

"Are you sure you want more children?" I ask, dismayed.

"My fiancé wants a son," she says, without hesitation.

"I've got two daughters, now all we need is a hardheaded boy to round things out." She chuckles aloud. "Larry can't wait to get started."

"Well," I say, shrugging with a broad smile, secretly appalled at the thought of Pamela Tucker wanting another child just to pacify her new man. Even more deplorable is the fact that she uses tubal ligations as her only means of birth control. "Ever consider birth control pills?" I ask.

"My insurance won't cover it," she says matter-of-factly.

"Tubal ligations shouldn't be taken lightly, Ms. Tucker," I say in a serious, warning tone. "Any kind of surgery involves risks. Something could go wrong, and invariably, something might."

Pamela Tucker says again how badly her fiancé wants a boy, and she adds with an air of confidence, her arms crossed over ample breasts: "And I want my tubes tied again after I have this baby. My insurance *will* cover that, right, Dr. Fowknah?"

"A lot of cutting you'll need to do on that one," Kelly says after Ms. Tucker leaves the office. She retrieves patient charts from my desk to file away, her blond ponytail bouncing as she checks and rechecks each name against a list. "I'm amazed at the women some men find attractive."

"You don't think Ms. Tucker is sexy?"

"Well, no, she's kinda big."

"So big women are what, then?"

"Gross!"

"Gross, Kelly? You really think that? Well, I used to be even bigger than Ms. Tucker." Kelly's mouth flies open like she's about to pop a marshmallow inside.

"No way," she trills.

"Yes, way." The shock on Kelly's face brings a smile to my lips. "I was slightly older than you are now," I say, "about twenty-four, when I lost the size of a whole person."

"Dr. Faulkner, I can't imagine it," Kelly says. "Unbelievable." She sits in a chair across from my desk. "You've been so fit and toned since the day we both started here, I remember. Three years ago, wasn't it?"

I nod yes.

"And you haven't gained an ounce. Unbelievable. What happened to make you lose the weight?"

"Well, one day, over ten years ago, I decided to go for a run in a new extra, extra, extra-large jogging suit I'd just purchased. You know, the kind made out of that shiny, papery-looking fabric. The kind that should never be worn by anyone over a size six." Kelly, probably a size five if not less, nods in agreement.

"Anyway," I continue, "I started running around an outdoor track, which I'd never done before in my life. I got all hot and bothered after circling just once, when all of a sudden I heard a whole track team come up behind me. It nearly scared me to death, like they were at my heels about to run me over. I jumped out of their way in the nick of time, and . . ." I break into laugher at the scene unfolding in my mind.

"What happened?" Kelly asks excitedly.

"I can laugh about it now, but it wasn't funny then."

"What?"

"It was just me standing there," I sheepishly admit. "Alone."

"Just you?"

"That sound was my legs rubbing together in those cheap, shiny pants."

"Ooooh, my, my," Kelly chortles. A few charts fall and splay across the floor when she uses a hand to shelter a mouthful of giggles. I retrieve a penny from the cup weighting down a few hospital notes and plug it into the gumball machine sitting on my desk—a six-inch clown does a somersault and spins around.

"Have one," I say, offering Kelly a purple gumball.

"Thanks, Dr. Faulkner," she says, taking the gumball into her mouth and chewing impetuously, her jaws moving in rapid succession, a sign that she is thinking about the time.

"I can't believe you were really that big," she says, and then glances at her watch. She retrieves the charts from the floor, quickly organizes them in her hands, and stands as if she is about to leave.

"Being fat made me think I was the ugliest woman on earth," I say, chewing a blue gumball.

"At least you did something about your weight problem," Kelly says.

"But that's just it, Kelly. Every woman is different. Ms. Tucker doesn't see herself as having a problem at all. She seems to be pleased with her appearance."

"Hmmmm," Kelly hums skeptically. "It's almost six o'clock," she says, checking the time on her watch again. "All the other doctors and nurses left an hour ago. It'll take me forever to get home."

I tell Kelly to be careful driving north because the roads might be patchy with ice from this morning. She mutters her way down the hall from my office, so that I only make out the end of what she says, ". . . now that it's too late to see."

After work, I go for a two-mile run at the coldest time of my day—night, when scarcely a soul is outside of a car or house or building of some sort, only me and a few other diehard runners. Across Peachtree Avenue, and down the path running parallel to the main road I gallop, at a steady pace, counting *one-two* over and over inside my head, on another level thinking about how much better my life would be by having a family—a husband and a child, or two.

I turn away from the dark woods at the end of the path and head home, where I shower, then settle into a sensuous pair of Victoria's Secret satin pajamas, Ralph's favorite. I'm sifting through the morning mail, when a strange envelope stands out, addressed to Ernest Hemingway. I hold it up to the light, suspecting it to be a fan letter trapped in the mail system for fifty years, but the postmark is yesterday. My dyslexic postman read the address wrong, as he so often does, delivering it to 4241 Valemont Street instead of 4241 Chestnut.

For an hour I wait to hear from Ralph before eating a microwavable dinner, and when he does not call by eight, I am tempted to page him. Ralph almost always calls by now—an understood rule we have. I lie back on the sofa and open to the middle of a book I've been reading; one I'm determined to finish, Milroad's *The Promise of Spring.* Not long after losing myself in the wilderness existence of Clarissa Montgomery, the heroine of the story, my sight weakens into a blur. I doze. The sound of the front door opening and closing startles me awake.

"Ralph?" I call out, rubbing my eyes, now clogged with invisible cotton. I hold my arm up to the lamp next to my head, and check the time on my watch: a quarter to eleven.

"Yeah, it's me," Ralph says, now standing over me, smelling tired of a long day at the office. We embrace and give each other a few light kisses.

"You didn't call before eight," I say, reminding him of our one and only rule.

"I'm sorry, sweetheart, I forgot," he says, shrugging. "I'm working on two cases, and one is about to go to court."

"I worried."

"You shouldn't have, Lenny. If anything bad happens to me, you'll be the first person called. No news is—"

"I know, but still."

"Still what?"

I hesitate to say what is on my mind.

Ralph holds me tighter and kisses the side of my face, prodding me with soft, loving whispers. *"What is it? You can tell me. Just say it."*

"Why is it that only a married woman has the right to worry?"

"Not marriage again," he groans, removing his overcoat.

"What's so wrong about us getting married, Ralph? We've known each other nine years, lived together three. I'm ready to start a family."

"Well, I'm not, Lenny," he says. Ralph hangs his coat in the entry closet, and turns to stare at the disappointment pouting my lips. He lifts my chin until our eyes meet. "Aren't we doing okay the way we are? Will a piece of paper saying we're married make us love each other any more than we do?"

"Yes, Ralph . . . I mean no. A piece of paper won't do that. But I'm not getting any younger. I'm thirty-four years old. In a few months, I'll be—"

"I know how old you are," he says, firmly cutting me off. Ralph pulls me close once more, like the day we first met, causing tingling sensations to run through me. He cups my face in his hands, when he says, "You don't age, woman. You just get prettier."

Prettier. My heart melts. He guides me down the short, narrow hallway to our bedroom. A sad foreboding feeling comes over me, like death about to happen, like the gray fog of winter looming over everything.

"Maybe Karen and Jason's wedding will change my mind," he whispers next to my ear, words that inspire me to hope. Dream. I imagine us running along a single path, going the distance, meeting at the altar. We make a trail of our clothes from the door to the bed, our restless energies collaborating in heated passion, rising and falling in waves of rapture, like animals suspended in yet another realm of existence—a breathless, frenzied titillation, where I lose myself completely, where I do not live beyond wanting to be his wife, and all but forget the gloomy warning deep down. Time has no meaning. We are together now—yes, and nothing else matters.

4:45 P.M.

Shaniqua Davis, pregnancy, return visit, ultrasound indicates 6 weeks gestation. Reason for visit: abortion counseling.

"Last time, you were adamant about keeping your baby, Shaniqua. What happened? Why the sudden change?"

"She's not ready to be a mother," Ms. Davis says abruptly. Shaniqua gazes down at her fingers. She is about twice her mother's size, the two reminding me of Mutt and Jeff—the little one snapping at the big one who could, if she wanted, knock the little one's lights out.

"I need to hear why from Shaniqua, Ms. Davis," I say firmly. "Would you like to sit in the waiting room until we finish?"

"No, I would not." Ms. Davis sneers. "I have a right to be here while my minor child is examined. I work for a law firm and I know my rights." She glares at Shaniqua, and says, "Tell the doctor what you want, baby."

"I have to think about my future," Shaniqua says, sounding rehearsed. "There's plenty of time for marriage and babies. If I have a child now, I might not get to go to college."

"You're sure this is what you want?"

"Yes, ma'am."

"Not just what your mother or someone else wants to hear?"

"No, ma'am."

"Well then, we'll talk again next week and then set it up at the outpatient center."

"Not tomorrow?" Ms. Davis asks impatiently.

"I'm sorry, Ms. Davis, I can't. But if you'd rather go to a clinic, I can—"

"No, no, no, not that," she interrupts. "I don't want my daughter up in front of a bunch of anti-abortion picketers, so one of my church members can find out about it. No, we'll just wait."

Kelly sticks her head inside my office door, her blue eyes blinking like caution lights. Before she can mouth how late it is, that everyone else is leaving, I tell her to go on home. She scatters like a mouse through a hole in the wall. "Whatever work you choose to do in life, make sure it's what you love," I say to Shaniqua.

"Otherwise, you'll spend half your life worried about the time. Always wanting the job to be over at the end of the day. Always wanting to get on home."

"You love doctoring that much, Dr. Faulkner?" she asks.

"Like air," I say spiritedly. "I'd do it for free."

While driving down the alley behind my house, I notice my carport is empty. Nothing stirs out here but the wind, no car passing through, no dogs barking—no Ralph. But as soon as I open the door, I am greeted by at least a dozen long-stem roses in a vase sitting on the coffee table with a note attached, which reads: *Lenny, I'll always love you, no matter what.* My heart dips. Ralph is a thoughtful lover. We had a disagreement about my house this morning. He wants me to sell it, and I refused. It was the first time he'd ever asked me to do something that I felt strongly against. Now roses. *He loves me no matter what.*

I think of how giving Ralph has been to me over the years, with little regard these days for how much something might cost. Last year, he said he was making up for lost time, since for years, he had been unable to afford much more than love notes or flowers from the grocery store. For most of our relationship, in fact, Ralph was either a broke, struggling law student or a damn-near broke up-and-coming attorney, before landing a job a few years ago with Ashford, Dunwoody, and Simpson. Shortly afterward, he presented my first extravagant gift, a pair of blue sapphire earrings. I prattled on about him wasting his money, and he said, "If I spend my last dime, it's worth it. I can always make another dime."

Dear Ralph. I change into jogging clothes, and head out into the cold. Ten minutes later, I am glowing inside. A horn blares when I cross Peachtree to run along an empty sidewalk. Off at a distance a trail of white lights streams through the darkness. Atlanta's continuous rush hour grows longer and longer each year—people heading out to the city's surrounding suburban sprawl; some, like Kelly, going as far away as Calhoun to the north; while others brave the traffic as faraway as Monroe to the south. Most grumble and complain redundantly, with no resolution in mind, just talk, talk, and more talk. For them, nothing works—carpooling is inconvenient, expanding the subways is out of the question. *Subways bring crime,* the naysayers stupidly assert, without a single shred of evidence. Traffic tie-ups just keep a-coming.

Ralph fervently believes it is not so bad. He said he would prefer living in the suburbs any day of the week compared to here. Not me, though. Whenever I hear of an accident on any given day of the week—a fender-bender, pileup, or a full-blown crash that causes a delay along the interstate, hours for commuters to get to work—my resolve to remain put is affirmed. City life is definitely for me.

I run faster and faster along the dirt path, legs at a long steady gait, feet striking the earth in a sound like rapid drumbeats; the stream of car lights divides the black sky—an infinite line with no beginning and no end.

There is a feeling I get when Ralph has entered ahead of me, a certain energy he gives off. Shadows loom along the far wall of the kitchen, like ghosts watching. I glance at the calendar. Thursday. Jason's bachelor party is circled in red marker. Ralph's there, wherever *there* is—he arranged this party for his best friend, and as best man, Ralph has to be there until it is over. I wonder how long before he comes home. If he were here, maybe we would have a candlelit dinner and a few glasses of wine. On nights like tonight, I look forward to lying back in his arms, every pore on my body yearning to be touched.

I take a long, warm shower; the pipes bang and rattle inside the wall, one reason Ralph wants us to move. *Wants me to sell my house.* I change into a sexy silk-and-lace nightgown, his favorite, and prepare a microwavable meal that goes down like sawdust, each bite a reminder that essential vitamins and nutrients are missing from the low-fat petrified-looking vegetables. If Ralph were home, we would prepare a meal together, him grilling or broiling meat, and me stir-frying or steaming vegetables. Cooking alone does not appeal to me. I follow the aftertaste of flavored wood chips with a glass of merlot.

Here seems colder when Ralph is gone. Seven years ago, I purchased this house at 4241 Valemont Street, a forty-eight-thousand-dollar one-story English Tudor, built in 1938 on a quarter-acre lot. It had been listed as a three-bedroom starter home, a fixer-upper, needing a little TLC. But it was a real dump, all I could afford on a resident's salary at the time. Soon after purchasing it, a carpenter friend helped me tear down the walls separating the tiny living room, dining room, and den, creating the great room in open splendor. Now I dim the lights, lie back on the sofa, and pick up *The Promise of Spring,* where I disappear inside Clarissa Montgomery's world, at the part where she discovers Charles Crow camping out on the two-thousand-acre farm she inherited from an uncle in the Sand Hills of Nebraska. I read at least fifty pages before I crash.

At eight o'clock sharp, Ralph calls, an onslaught of boisterous laughter and talk emanating from the background.

"Where are you?" I ask sleepily.

"At a bar downtown. Somewhere. Hell," he slurs drunkenly. "Jason's bachelor party. I'm calling, so don't wait up for me."

"When do you think you'll come home?"

"Late. Don't wait up."

"Is someone else driving you, honey? Someone sober? Please."

"I can drive myself," he says adamantly.

"All right, Ralph," I say, trying to sound calm. But when the line goes dead, I immediately regret that I did not insist that someone else drive him home. How does he expect me not to worry about him drinking and driving? I think about this morning, and how insistent he had been that I contact a realtor. He said, "The market's hot. We can buy a better place together in the suburbs. *We* can afford it."

I felt pressured by his reassurances that the quality of our lives would improve with extra space in a bigger, newer house. An invisible coil wrapped around my neck while he used his lawyer talk to argue his case, my throat tightening until I could hardly breathe. "I'm not ready to sell what I'm so close to owning, free and clear of a mortgage, Ralph," I told him. "I'm not the least bit interested in a suburban commute." He said,

"That's one good reason we shouldn't get married. We can't even agree on where to live."

I pluck a rose from the vase and go inside the kitchen, where a light frost partially veils the windows. I peer out at the sound of a car passing through the alley. Ralph loves me no matter what, and I love him enough to resolve our one and only real dilemma. I stick the rose in my hair and imagine myself, a blurry vision in the frosty pane, a bride. Where we live should not matter as long as we are together.

I put a teapot on the stove and wait for its whistle before sitting down at the table to a steamy cup of ginseng tea. Ralph left the newspaper open to the stock page this morning. We have a joint investment account, and I imagine him checking up on the daily values of each stock. It suddenly dawns on me that we have several pieces of paper between us—investments, a bank account, a credit card account. What difference would a marriage certificate make? Karen and Jason say we're more like an old married couple than they are; yet, they are the ones preparing to meet at the altar.

I fold the paper over and read from the front page to the entertainment section. In my mind's eye, I see slippery roads, heavy traffic, and Ralph's car sliding into a tree. I find myself pacing from the kitchen to the great room. I check the carport, the time on the stove, and light the logs in the fireplace. When Ralph and I are home alone together, this old house becomes a cozy nook for us to shed the day and escape from the rest of the world. We fit comfortably as partners, coalesce to the same tune, often read each other's thoughts. Our personalities are compatible. We both love our careers—he is on the fast track to make partner, and the only thing that thrills me more than seeing patients each day is coming home to him. If moving to the suburbs is what it will take for us to get married, I should do it.

There is a knock at the door—two quick raps followed by two bolts of thunder. My heart beats wildly. I worry about Ralph. I get up to answer the door and am relieved to find my neighbor, Mrs. Stein, standing in the doorway with her head cocked to the side, holding an envelope up to the porch light as if attempting to read its contents.

"Sorry to bother you at this late hour, Dr. Faulkner," she says.

"It's quite all right, Mrs. Stein."

"I was just going through yesterday's mail and found this letter that must belong to your . . . ," she says, handing me the envelope addressed to Ralph Griffin.

"Boyfriend, thank you, Mrs. Stein," I say, resenting the fact that she probably considers our union unholy.

"Seems the postman's gotten us mixed up again. You'd think he'd know the difference between forty-two forty-one and forty-two forty-three by now."

"He should," I agree, but then as an afterthought, I remember the strange letter. "Do you know anyone named Ernest Hemingway?"

"I received mail with that name, too. Thought it was a joke. Now, I'm curious about who he is. I'd be happy to give this Ernest Hemingway fellow the letter you received as well. I've nothing much else to do."

"If you don't mind," I say, more than happy to pass along that responsibility. A cold chill causes me to shiver slightly. "Please come in, Mrs. Stein."

"Just for a minute," she says, closing the door behind her.

I quickly retrieve the letter for Ernest Hemingway. "Here it is," I say, handing it to Mrs. Stein. "And thanks again."

"Are you moving?" she asks, before opening the door to leave.

"No, why?"

"Well, I couldn't help notice that the letter to your . . . *er* . . . boyfriend is from a title company. Not that it's any of my business, or anything. Just wondering, because you don't get thick letters like that unless there's a contract on a new house."

"We're not buying a new house," I say, glancing down at the mail from Morgan Whitfield Mortgage Title and Guarantee Company.

"Course, you being the . . . *er* . . . girlfriend would know that."

"We don't keep secrets," I blurt out, immediately regretting it.

"Not that it's any of my business." Mrs. Stein pulls her wool coat tighter and heads outside, as the wind whips and blows through her fluffy white curls. She is a short, elderly white woman, with a sharp nose and pinched expression—the love-to-get-in-folks-business type who happens to live next door.

"Thanks for bringing the letter, Mrs. Stein," I call after her abruptly.

"You haven't gotten anything of mine, have you?" she calls back over her shoulder.

"Not today."

"I'm going to report this to the postmaster," she says.

"Good. Hope he listens this time."

I watch the old woman fade into the darkness before closing the door. Ralph and I respect each other's privacy. He would never consider opening my mail, nor would I his. But here and now, I am so very tempted to do it. I consider the conversation I had with him this morning. He wants to move, there's no question about that, but he wouldn't have bought a house without telling me. I know him. I trust Ralph. We've known each other for nine years, lived together for three, and I know Ralph Griffin better than he knows himself. There. I put the letter in his mail stack on the counter next to the breadbox.

Around midnight, the wind whirs around this old house, causing it to creak in its tired old joints. I try not to worry about some tragedy happening to Ralph. I watch the clock instead—one o'clock, one forty-five, two. A piece of bark crumbles into ashes. I go to bed, falling asleep and waking intermittently.

At dawn, the gray of winter steals inside the bedroom through a pair of French windows, casting shadows that move across the walls. Red rose petals cover my pillow. I panic when the alarm goes off. Ralph is still not here. I dress for work, telling myself not to think about calling hospitals or the police, warning myself not to do it. *Ralph won't like it.* I phone Karen at Jason's apartment.

"Have you seen Ralph?" I ask, rambling on about my last conversation with him. "He was drunk, Karen. I begged him not to drive home. But he's not here and I don't know what to do. Is Jason home yet? Does he know where Ralph is?"

"Calm down, girlfriend," she says as if plucked from her sleep, her voice cracking. "He's camped out on the sofa. They just got in an hour ago."

"Oh," I say, stupidly. "He should've called me."

"Want me to wake him?"

"No, no. Let him sleep."

"I overheard Ralph say something very important before he crashed," she says coyly.

"Important? What?"

"He told Jason he plans to *do it* after the wedding."

My pager goes off. I check to find Dr. Paul Waxler's number. He was the on-call physician for my group last night. I need to phone him right away.

"Do what?" I beg Karen.

"Propose," she says.

"But he was drunk."

"So what?" she says. "I think Ralph really meant it, Lenny. He sounded so sincere, like his life depended on him proposing to you. You should've heard him."

The pager beeps again.

"I have to go now, Karen. We're still on for lunch today, right?"

"I wouldn't miss it."

Dr. Waxler's report is good news. One of my patients delivered last night. Mrs. Andrea Burke had a successful C-section. "She looks good," he says. "Everything's normal."

I visit Mrs. Burke on the maternity ward and ask the standard medical questions. Any pain? Cramping? Constipation?

"I haven't been able to do number two," she says, clutching her stomach.

"That's normal for the first day or so," I say.

"How long will I have to be here, Dr. Faulkner?"

"Until your bowels move."

"For number one or two?"

"Two." I laugh. "By this time tomorrow, I'm betting you'll have all the numbers checked off."

I get into the office and begin examining patients, all the while trying very hard to remain focused, my mind drifting like a steady whisper that promenades between each patient and thoughts of Ralph. The moment a distant phone rings, something clicks inside. The words *marry me* flutter inside my brain like butterflies. I picture myself resplendent in white, gliding down a red-carpeted isle, with Ralph waiting at the altar. Kelly prods me along from one exam room to another.

"You're leaving early today, remember, Dr. Faulkner?" she says sharply, catching me. I peer up from a patient's chart that I've mindlessly examined too long. Kelly knows me so well. "We have more patients to see."

11:45 A.M.

Julie Sherwood, 32-year-old white female, return patient. Weight: 142 pounds. Height: 5'4". Gravida/para—2. Birth control: pill. Complaints:

itchiness in vaginal area. History of present illness: None. Herpes Test: positive.

"It's easily treatable," I say.

"You mean I have a sexually transmitted disease?"

"I'm afraid so." Her face drops. My heart goes out to her. Julie Sherwood was married six years ago. I delivered her second child last June. I remember her husband being elated over the birth. And this I know with certainty, without needing proof, or witness: Julie has never, ever cheated.

"How could he?" she says helplessly.

"Well, Julie, your husband having herpes doesn't automatically signal an extramarital affair. It can remain dormant for many years. He may have contracted it a long time ago."

Julie glances up at me with hope in her eyes, and says, "You mean a man can catch it and not know?"

I ponder briefly what I would do in her situation, if Ralph had given me herpes. I do not know that I could forgive him.

"It's doubtful that Mr. Sherwood doesn't know he has something," I say, carefully measuring my words. "But the discomfort men feel varies. For some men, herpes is as mild as jock itch, for others it can be extremely painful. Your husband may never have been properly diagnosed. He needs to be treated."

She looks thoughtfully for a moment; then smiles as if forgiving her husband before he has had a chance to make an excuse.

I meet Karen at half past noon, at an Indian restaurant in Buckhead, one of her favorites. The waiter hastily asks what we want today, pursing his lips while briskly pouring water into our glasses. We order the buffet, and in a huff, he retrieves the menus from the table as if insulted that we have ordered the same as always. It is obvious to Karen that this particular waiter does not like serving us. "Never has," she says, and growls at him for being rude, rolls her eyes and shoots him her don't-play-with-me look.

"These Indians get off the boat treating *us* like we don't belong," she complains, tossing her fine, black hair, which hangs below her shoulders. Karen has a smooth café au lait complexion and, taken with her hair and sharp facial features, resembles an Indian herself. Perhaps because I have been exposed to every make and model of woman there is, I know first-hand how man-made the concept of race is; not much to do with reality when you get down to mediocre distinctions, and sometimes only a word—black, white, Indian, or Asian, and the broadest classification of all—Hispanic. Karen and I, both black women, look nothing alike, except that we're about the same height, between five six and five eight, and we wear a size eight in clothes.

"Like *we* don't know they've overpopulated half the world with the great unwashed," she adds, like a random spin on a roulette wheel.

"You're taking this thing way too personally, Karen," I say, noticing that the waiter is now on the other side of the room. "He probably doesn't mean anything."

"Like hell he doesn't." She rasps, sounding like a woman hardened by a disadvantaged upbringing, though unlike me, she was actually born to the upper crust of Black Atlanta. Karen is a walking, talking paradox—black but doesn't look it, sophisticated yet down to earth, giving though occasionally afflicted with bouts of selfishness. I remind her, before she gets too worked up, that we can eat elsewhere; there are dozens of Indian restaurants in Atlanta.

"We can always leave," I say.

"Why should we?" she snaps.

"I'm just saying, if you don't like it here, let's go."

Karen's mouth eases into a subtle smile, her countenance becoming calm and patient, her apologetic tone steeped in Southern gentility, when she says, "But Lenny, honey, the food is so damned good here. Let's just eat."

"Fine with me." I sigh. We head for the buffet table and quickly fill our plates with an array of exotic, spicy dishes—tandoori, saffron rice, curried chicken, mattar paneer—each bite sure to be a delicious experience. Karen complains that the naan bread is too hard. I ignore her. She seems uptight, probably a bad case of bridal jitters. I've seen it happen to many of my patients, who suddenly find fault with everything. We return to our seats, and I attempt to counter her mood with a little anxiousness of my own.

"What did Ralph say, exactly?" I ask.

"What did he say . . ." Karen puzzles, curling her lips between sips of coffee, holding the cup inside her delicate hands, her nails neatly filed and lightly painted with a clear sheen. A different waiter pours water into our glasses. Karen hesitates to say more until he leaves.

"Jason and Ralph were talking about the bachelor party," she says. "They mentioned our wedding and my ears perked up. I heard him say he was going to propose."

"He actually said *propose?*"

"Something like that, I mean, it was obvious that's what he meant."

"You sure?"

"Drunk men tell everything, girl." She laughs.

I laugh, too, and begin to eat with more interest, the food's aroma teasing my empty stomach. Last night, I had eaten precious little, as eating alone is not only unappealing, but unappetizing as well.

"I waited up half the night," I say.

"Don't ever wait up for a man, Lenny," Karen says disappointedly. "How many times have I told you that? Ralph will take you for granted."

"He's been acting kind of strange lately," I say. "Moody. One minute he's the most attentive lover in the world, left me a dozen long-stem roses yesterday. But the next minute, I'm left wondering whether or not he loves me at all. He should've called me back last night."

"He's acting like Jason just before he proposed," Karen says. "That's how men are . . . scared out of their minds to commit. But he'll be fine after he pops the question. You'll see. He's working up the nerve to do it."

"God, I hope you're right."

"How long have you two been together?" she says, drumming her fingers on the table, knowing the answer before I say it.

"Nine years . . . well, the first year doesn't count. We were just getting to know each other. I was in medical school: take away another three years. Residency, minus four more . . . so there, you see this is the only year that really counts."

"Even that's getting to be too long," she says, smacking her lips in that know-it-all way of hers. "You've got to start playing the game, Lenny."

"I'm the one who introduced you to Jason," I say. "If Ralph and I hadn't had that Christmas party a few years ago—"

"Two years ago," she chimes in.

"Two years." I sigh. "Now you're getting married."

"That's right," Karen says, smiling wisely. "*I* played the game."

"Now you're an expert."

"Well . . ." she begins to exult, batting her eyes, when the first waiter returns to our table to pour more water.

"Are you really ready to get married, Karen?" I ask doubtfully.

"Oh, yes." She sighs, beaming. "I can't wait for all the formalities to be over."

"The bridal shower tonight and wedding next week."

"Mother is losing her mind over every ding-dong detail. She's driving me crazy, I tell you the truth, Lenny, girl."

"You're her only child, Karen."

"God help me."

"Just think, in a week you'll be Mrs. Jason Ashby."

"Karen Roberts-Ashby, thank you very much," she playfully quips.

"Is there anything else you ladies want today?" the waiter asks abruptly.

"No, nothing else," I say, reaching for the bill.

"How much is my share?" Karen says, raising a speculative brow.

"Your money's no good today. All brides eat free."

3

Each month I am tempted to stop taking the pill and allow nature to have her way. But Ralph would resent it. Last Christmas Eve as we sprawled across the sofa in front of a fire while watching television, a sentimental Hallmark commercial came on of a baby and its parents heading home from the hospital in time for the holidays. I told Ralph I wanted a baby before my eggs are too old. "Before I'm in need of the latest advancements in fertilization technologies." He laughed as though I had intended to make a joke, without considering how ridiculous it would be for a thirty-four-year-old woman to joke about conception. Men, like Ralph, are allowed the luxury of putting procreation off for many years. They can afford to laugh about fertilization technologies. I laughed, too. It was better to laugh than to cry.

I hear the front door open and close and immediately I spring to my feet. Ralph calls out to me. He enters the bedroom and a rush of relief comes over me. He smiles. I race to hug him, his strong arms holding me close.

"Hey, baby," he says under his breath. I follow him anxiously to the kitchen.

"Ralph?" I say, as he runs water in the sink to wash his hands; the pipes screech and clamor noisily.

"Damn," he hisses, drawing up his face disapprovingly. I open the refrigerator and take out a beer.

"Have a drink, Ralph," I say.

"Thanks, I'm really tired." He leans against the sink, frowning as he opens the bottle. He takes a few gulps, and sighs. "Those crazy frat boys kept me up all night and I had to work my tail off all day."

"Why didn't you call me back?" I ask, a streak of anger taking hold of my senses. *I'm tired, too, dammit.*

"I drank too much," he says indifferently.

"Ralph, I waited up all night."

"I warned you not to, Lenny. Everybody knows bachelor parties last all night. Come on, now."

"But I worried because you drank too much."

"I told you I'd be all right."

"How could I not worry, Ralph?" I quaver angrily, close to tears. "Bad weather and drunk drivers don't mix."

He looks thoughtfully at me and says, "I don't blame you for being mad at me, Lenny. You're right, I should've called."

"I'm not mad," I say, biting back a wave of mixed emotions. He kisses my forehead, my eager fingers clasp around his neck, and I draw his lips to mine. Ralph warms me inside and out with his tender kisses. But what I really want, what I require at a moment like this, is passion. I want to feel how much he loves me. Not another note, or lovely roses, please. I gaze longingly into his eyes, and think *It's time for bed, let's go.* But he pulls back from me. I blink.

"Lenny, darling," he says, gently stroking my hair. "The pipes are old as hell. I've told you that how many times? It'll cost a fortune to replace them."

Our hot-and-heavy rapture is shot down in flames, over pipes. I exhale.

"You've got to sell this place before it's too late," he says, coming back to where we left off this morning. I suddenly remember the letter Mrs. Stein brought over last night.

"Have you purchased another house, Ralph?" I ask impatiently, the angry streak returning.

"What're you talking about?"

"This letter from Morgan Whitfield Mortgage and something or other." I nervously shuffle through the mail and hand him the thick envelope. "Is it a contract on a house?"

"It should've come to my office," he says, taking a final swig of beer. He casually takes the envelope and tosses it down on the counter between us. "Has to do with a case I'm handling."

"Oh."

"You don't believe me? Read for yourself. Go ahead if you don't trust me."

"I trust you, Ralph."

"Then why don't you sell?" he says forcefully, banging his beer bottle on the counter for emphasis. I am taken aback by the sudden strain in his demeanor, and consider what Karen said. *He's working up the nerve to ask me to marry him.* Ralph's voice softens in an instant, he gently strokes the side of my face, cooing, "We can own something together."

"I'll do it, Ralph." My throat tightens, and I add, "Later, after it's paid off. Maybe I'll rent it out for a while, and then . . ."

"Sure you will," he says testily. I follow him into the great room, where he positions himself on the sofa in front of the television, taking up the remote control like a weapon.

"I don't want this house coming between us," I say.

"Suit yourself," he grumbles, pushing a few buttons on the remote control. I wonder if he's just looking for a reason not to propose. Maybe what Karen says is true—I'm too available. Ralph relaxes with his feet propped up on the coffee table and proceeds to watch a game of basketball. I nudge his shoulder lightly with my knuckles and invite him to go for a walk. But he yawns and stretches like a groggy bear and says, "Get me another beer, baby, will you, please?"

When I return with a cold one, he tells me to walk without him. "The knee," he says, rubbing his right leg, an old excuse from an old high-school football injury. I smile instead of objecting, which is what I feel like doing. I am a doctor, after all. Walking is what that knee needs. I run from Valemont to Peachtree and back, and when I return, Ralph, who was half asleep when I left, is now gone. I find a note on the kitchen table that reads

Lenny,

I'm meeting a client this evening. Will be working through most of the night. Don't worry.

Ralph

The note feels impersonal. Part of me believes he is sending a message. I fret over missing words like *dear* and *honey* and *baby* and *love,* most of all *love.* He could have told me he had to work. It would have been simple to jot down his whereabouts and say, "Love, Ralph." And what does he mean, *Don't worry?*

There is one enormous pitfall to our living together. Only one rule: Call before eight. Other than that, I do not always know what my limitations are with him. Recently, Ralph went away on a business trip and forgot to phone home. I nearly lost my mind, called his secretary, Angela, and demanded to know where he was. He got really pissed off about it. "Stop checking up on me," he ordered, nearly snapping my ear off. But later, after he returned home, I bristled about how inconsiderate and unreasonable he had been, and he appeased me with an apology. He agreed he should have called.

On my way to the bedroom, I stop at Ralph's office door, surprised to find it closed. There has never been a reason to close doors here, not that I know of—not in our sanctuary from the world. I wonder about his late-night meeting with a client, the envelope from the title company I refused to open, and the something that isn't quite right between us lately. Is he really going to do it? Propose, and make us both happy? I try the doorknob, but it's locked. Why? Why would Ralph install a new one, with a lock? Why now? What's going on here? Is something more sinister threatening our happy home? Cheating?

No. I shake my head in denial. *No, impossible.* If Ralph were involved in a clandestine affair, I would know it. Another woman, I would smell on him. Isn't it true that the woman is always the first to know? We have instincts about such things. There are signs, aren't there? I've had more than a few patients who have ignored the obvious signs, like the husband's sudden weight loss, or his unprecedented interest in the clothes he wears. Viagra. Hotel receipts. Jewelry stores on the credit-card bill.

One patient even said her husband had become obsessed with his shoes. "He's worse than Imelda Marcos now," she exclaimed. And later, while recovering from a hysterectomy, she discovered him having an affair with a shoe store clerk.

I contemplate this as I shower, and later, as I add hot curlers to my hair, dress in black velvet and silk, and don the lovely pair of four-karat diamond earrings with matching necklace that Ralph bought me for

Christmas. That day, he placed the glittering gems against my dark, ebony skin, and said he loved me. Here and now, the weight of it feels permanent. I trust Ralph. Yes, he is an honorable, decent man. We were meant to always be together, and after the wedding, he'll propose.

4

Karen's family home is nestled in an upper-class section of southwest Atlanta. I arrive for the bridal shower at seven o'clock. Karen greets me at the door, saying, "Thank God you're here," ushers me inside, removes my coat to a nearby closet, twirls me around to this friend and that cousin, this aunt and that neighbor, this sorority sister and that fourth-grade teacher, while I exchange quick hellos, out of breath when she pulls me off to the side. She is coming unglued—bridal cold feet—and is only a few steps away from losing it completely. I know that look in Karen's eyes, a cross between uproariously happy and crazed.

"What d'ya think, Lenny?" she says, laughing.

"You're either extremely happy or on speed."

"I do need to calm down," she says, inhaling deeply.

"That's it, breathe."

The house is packed with women. I make a quick assessment of the ones I do not already know, and wonder how many are like me, over thirty and unmarried. I notice Karen's pale, obese cousin Donna sitting next to the table of appetizers and hors d'oeuvres. I met her last year at the Roberts' annual Christmas party. She was sitting in that spot then, too. I pretend to listen to Karen's conversation with an elderly aunt whose mustache twitches when she talks, while simultaneously watching Donna slide her fingers across the table surreptitiously. One fell swoop from a pastry tray, and her hand moves to her mouth. She appears to yawn, then gulps. I smile, remembering the old days when I secretly stuffed myself, while Karen laughs with three former college mates.

I decide that Donna is chairman of my single women's club, and the three women standing in front of Karen and me, her old college chums, laughing girlishly, long hair covering their slouching shoulders and arms crossed over bulging middles, are definite members, too. To my left, a smoker fidgets with her purse—her dark lips and yellow-brown teeth give her away when she smiles. "Irene, I can't believe it's you," Mrs. Roberts calls out to her and they embrace. Irene smiles again. She's wearing too much jewelry around her neck and on her fingers, and has dyed hair, the color of an orangutan's brilliant red tuft, that makes her chestnut face look older—my guess, she's fifty-something, probably divorced, an honorary member of the club.

While Karen fights to regain her usual calm composure, I imagine the rest of us single women playing a game of musical chairs, standing around the last one, furtively circling it, afraid of losing when the music stops. How many are pretending to be satisfied with how things are? Cynthia Woodrow, tall and thin enough to be considered anorexic, is a great pretender and former college roommate of Karen's. She reminds me of a cinnamon-coated weasel when she pops out of nowhere with that annoyingly high-pitched squeal of hers: "Skippy, I can't wait to tell you all about Chicago."

"Skippy" is Karen's pet name that stuck during her college sorority days, when she had a peanut butter fetish. "Sin," good old Cynthia Woodrow, manages to steal Skippy from me and whisk her off to another part of the house before either of us can object. She's a lifetime member, I'm afraid.

"Doctor, darling, we wondered if you were still coming," trills Mrs. Roberts, an attractive middle-aged woman with buttery skin and fine silver hair. She can't resist picking apart my strengths and weaknesses—I'm a doctor and I'm late. She holds out her arms to hug me. "Glad you could come, dear."

Karen's mother gives me a polite squeeze and introduces me to her sister-in-law, Henrietta, a tall, stout woman with sharp, aristocratic features. Her silver hair adorns the top of her head like a crown, her complexion powdered to be as light as Mrs. Roberts', and her thin pink lips open into a controlled smile.

"My pleasure," she says, low and raspy, extending her hand to shake mine, her long, painted nails pricking my skin when she grabs my fingers like they're the lever on a slot machine. Karen hails from one of Atlanta's most prominent black families; her great-grandfather began an investment firm back in 1906, one of the oldest and most well-established black financial institutions in the country.

"Did you attend Spelman with Karen?" Henrietta says. I notice the wrinkle above her upper lip, a dead giveaway that she's a chain smoker.

"No," I say. "I'm a few years older than Karen. I met her at J. W. Roberts and Associates shortly after beginning my internship."

"Oh, you're a real doctor?"

"Is there any other kind?"

"I wouldn't see a Ph.D. about back pain," she says, pursing her lips as if making an intelligent point. She begins telling me the history of the family business. I catch a glimpse of Karen mingling on the other side of the living room, and think about the day we met, how at ease she made me feel. It was the first time in my life I'd ever made over two hundred bucks a week. Karen had smiled reassuringly, and said, "Girrrrrl, you're at the right place now."

Before buying my house, I lived like a sleep-deprived squirrel in a shared apartment near the hospital, working the graveyard shift, around-the-clock rotations, saving most of my income. I had no understanding of how to invest it. There was no history of having extra funds in my family. But Karen explained investing in simple terms I could understand. She said, "Shop for stock the way you shop for clothes. Buy on sale and only purchase from companies you trust." She told me not to worry about the Dow Jones and not to watch the market closely. "Pay attention to what the people on top of the company do. If they sell, you sell." Not long after following her advice—in less than a year—I turned a meager three-hundred-dollar initial investment into a three-thousand-dollar down payment on a house.

Suddenly I realize Henrietta has been talking.

"My husband taught Karen everything she knows about money," Mrs. Roberts interjects. "But you already know that, don't you, dear?"

"She's the best," I say.

"Did your father teach you anything about money, Lenny dear?"

I think about when I was growing up, how my father would come home from work with cash on Friday, most he would give to my mother for running the house, some he would keep for himself to pay for his liquor, occasional crap game, or weekly dog race, and I say, "He taught me all right."

On Friday nights, Daddy would allow himself to overdo it. He would return home raising hell after losing most of his money, pick a disagreement with Mama, and eventually pass out drunk in bed, change dropping from the pockets of his dungarees like rain. My brother, Joe, and sister, Rosetta, and I would reclaim the loose change as our allowance for the week. Joe and Rosetta would spend theirs as fast as they got it—even my youngest brother, Bobby, picked up this habit when he came along in the family. But I saved my money, nearly every penny. There was something about having it that offered me peace of mind—it empowered me to have it—and made me feel less like nothing.

"How to invest?"

"No, how to save."

"I'm so happy you're in Karen's wedding," Mrs. Roberts says. She stands next to me with her hand collecting my elbow as if she thinks I might escape if she is not here to hold me in place. Her sister-in-law engages in a conversation behind us. Across the room, Karen bursts into laughter at something said and swings her head from side to side in that sister-girl way of hers.

"She's frazzled, I tell you," Mrs. Roberts says, her voice laced with Southern gentility. I remember Karen telling me that her mother had been brought up poor in Louisiana, the progeny of a maid and the wealthy, white employer who raped her. In the 1920s, it might as well have been legal for white men to have their way with black women, even if these women were married, even if they were blood related to them. Mrs. Roberts's biological great-uncle was also her biological father.

I ease my elbow from Mrs. Roberts's grasp. I understand why she is possessive of Karen. People who were powerless as children often become controlling adults.

"She's been overwrought all week," she says. "You'll watch over her next Saturday, won't you, Lenny darling?"

"She'll be fine," I say, giving Mrs. Roberts a soft pat on the back.

"And you, Lenny darling, you'll get through this, won't you? You won't let Karen's marriage come between you?"

"No, Mrs. Roberts, why would I?"

"These things happen, you know. Jealousies. Not that you would ever be that way."

"Karen's my best friend," I say insistently.

"I know that, dear, Lenny."

"I want her to be happy."

"Yes, yes, sweetness. It's just a shame you're not getting married, too." Mrs. Roberts narrows her eyes, studying me more closely. "Have you ever tried lightening your skin?"

"No, I haven't," I say, feeling a twinge of resentment towards her. I'd almost forgotten how color-conscious she is—a color-struck woman from way back when. She used to pick Karen's friends according to their color and class, until Karen came of age and rebelled against it. Karen told me that she dated the darkest boys in high school just to piss her mother off. Jason is toasted cinnamon, only just "light enough."

"You know how some men are, dear."

"No, I don't know how some men are, Mrs. Roberts," I say curtly. "I do know that I'm quite satisfied with my skin the way it is."

"Of course you are, darling." A patronizing tone. "I'm getting to be a foolish, old woman, Lenny. Pay me no mind. Karen says all the time how out of step I am. 'Get with it, Mother,' she says." Mrs. Roberts laughs as if we have shared a joke and she has not just insulted the hell out of me—no, not really. Henrietta cranes her neck like an ostrich pecking at the bits.

"What's so funny, Alberta?" she asks.

"Oh, get with it, Henrietta," Mrs. Roberts exclaims, snapping her fingers. "You and I are getting too old." They laugh and reminisce about younger days—sorority rushes, high-society cocktail parties, and the old Carlotta Supper Club. The wine steward hired by Mrs. Roberts stops in front of us with a tray of champagne-filled glasses. We each accept one. Mrs. Roberts holds her glass up slightly and whispers a toast that only Henrietta and I can hear, as if saying it any louder might jinx the plan she has in store for her daughter's future.

"Here's to keeping my daughter and gaining a son."

5

The following Friday night, I arrive home from the office later than usual. A patient, pregnant with triplets, went into shock over the news, then denial, and finally had a meltdown. Took over an hour. Kelly was beside herself. I listen to my messages: 1) Exterminator will come tomorrow at 8 A.M., 2) Karen wonders which wedding hairstyle I think she should choose, 3) Karen reminds me that the wedding is tomorrow at 4 P.M., 4) Karen begs me to bring her a sedative before the wedding, 5) Ralph says he'll be late again tonight, don't wait up, and 6) "It's ya Mama, bye"—short and to the point. Immediately, I phone my mother. At the sound of my voice, she coughs and blows her nose.

"It's past my bedtime, Lenita Mae," she complains.

"Sorry, Mama, I just got your message."

"Mm-hmmmm," she croaks. My mother is a simple country woman, distant from the niceties of the Southern culture, at the opposite end of the spectrum from Mrs. Roberts. She blows her nose again, right into my ear, and says, "I didn't mean for you to wake me up in the middle of the night."

"Well, I knew your oncology appointment was today. I just wanted to know the test results."

Mama clears her throat of a wretched gurgle, as if some nasty glutinous muck sticks to the back of it. She tells me the cancer is back, this time, in her lungs, same as she would tell that a cold front is coming through, it rained yesterday, we're having a drought—no different. I sit up in bed, my heart racing uncontrollably.

"What exactly did your doctor say, Mama?"

"It's spreading all over my body and I don't have long to get things in order."

I am too stunned to speak. Ten years ago, I was with Mama when her doctor discovered that the lump in her right breast was cancerous. I was with her again, two years ago, when the same doctor discovered a growth in the remaining one. She told him, "Listen here, Doctor, I don't want no pep talk. Just tell me like it is."

"I already called Rosetta and Bobby," Mama says, "told 'em to get over here soon as they can to pick out what they want out the house 'fore I go on to glory. You do the same, hear?"

"What'd the doctor say about chemotherapy?"

"I ain't taking no more chemotherapy so's I can sit up and die anyway, all dried up like a bald-headed chicken like your aunt Ida Mae."

"But there are new, experimental treatments."

"I ain't taking nothin' new. It's my time. My funeral's paid up. You young 'uns can come up and take what you want."

A brief silence intervenes. Mama clears her throat before saying, "Is there anything particular you wants, Lenita Mae?"

"No, I don't need anything," I say, suddenly connected to my childhood, Mama's heart beating against my ear as she rocks me back and forth, the softness of her bosom like a pillow, the smell of her sweat mixed with homemade soap and outdoors, lulling me to sleep. She coughs now, like the bark of hunting dogs trailing a scent, breaking the spell I'm under.

"Well, you take some time to think on it," she says, her voice cracking. "Anything I got is your'n if you need it."

"Thanks, Mama," I say. "But what can I do to help you?"

"Come see me 'fore I leaves the earth," she says hoarsely. I try to remember Mama as a young woman, when she better resembled the smiling picture I have of her on my dresser in her twenties, already married since the age of sixteen, the year she had my brother, Joseph Allen, who died eighteen years later in Vietnam. Mama tells me not to fret over this, that it won't be long before she's in heaven with Daddy and Joe.

"Can I bring you anything, Mama? Is there anything you want?"

"A grandbaby." She laughs with a throaty cackle.

"Oh, Mama," I say, with a knot in my throat. I think back to when I was a little girl playing outside in the backyard while Mama hung clothes out on the line, a spring breeze billowing out the sheets that tempted me and Rosetta, who is just two years older, to bound through them. Mama's strong hands would pull us back as she scolded us, and we would stop for a while, until we would forget and do it again and again. I wish it were I getting married in the morning, pregnant with Ralph's child.

"When the time's right, you'll start a family of your own," she says.

"I do want one, Mama."

"I pray on it ever' day."

"Why don't you come live here with me?" I say softly, contemplating how I might make the end of Mama's life easier. The house I was raised in, where she still lives with a wood-burning stove, tin roof, and plastered walls, is a harsh environment to have as the last stop on the way to eternity.

"I don't wanna be no burden to nobody," she says.

"You're no burden, Mama. Please, come.

"Not right now," she says, "not wit that man you got living up in there. He come inside the house one time and I bet he don't know me from Adam or Eve."

"Ralph's a good man, Mama. He'll be happy for you to come."

Mama begins a hacking, sickening coughing fit. When she stops and catches her breath, she tells me she'll think on it. "I'm going on back to sleep now, hear?" she says abruptly.

"I love you," I blurt out.

"Ah, hah," she mutters. "Call earlier next time, Lenita Mae."

"Good night, Mama." The line goes dead. Mama does not have it in her to be gracious, so that common manner words such as *please, thank you, excuse me,* and even *good-bye,* fall outside of her lexicon. She cannot help the way she comes across. She does not mean to be unkind. I know this because of her bountiful spirit that gives and gives. My mother has given most of her self away.

I find it hard to sleep through the night, drifting in and out of one scene or another with Mama. I see her on her deathbed in that tattered old house. I awake guilty of not doing enough. I close my eyes and become eleven, with Mama smoothing salve over my knees, scraped raw from a day of picking strawberries for money. Her heavy hands knead medicine into my sore spots while she tells of how my father works hard every day, how he works a double shift even when his back hurts. Daddy rides his old tractor up and down the dusty earth, digging up the soil for planting in his spare time. I turn over and he disappears. Ralph is standing over me. He peels off his clothes and climbs naked into bed.

"Baby," he whispers sexily, nuzzling me behind the ear. I pretend I've been asleep; his arms wrap around my waist.

"Ralph, sweetheart." I turn and kiss him passionately, the kind of passion that pours out from raw, painful emotions. I want to forget the conversation I had with Mama. My eyes squeeze tightly closed, and when he kisses my cheeks, his lips touch the salty wetness of tears.

"What's wrong, baby?" he says, and I tell him about Mama. We commiserate about her dying. Ralph recollects the night his father died, and he becomes all that I need in the wee hours of early dawn; his love and strength surround me like a warm cocoon. I forget my fear, that he's been on edge lately. This old house is not important anymore. I feel safe lying next to him. We are perfect for each other tonight, united, coalescing like an old, married couple.

6

Ralph and I are both in the wedding. Karen is exquisitely put together in Vera Wang elegant simplicity and Jason is every bit the handsome, lucky catch. I make mental notes of what I like and what I would change. I like the violinist serenading guests entering the chapel, that we bridesmaids wear red silk gowns that can be cut off later into cocktail dresses. I would shorten the service. The minister had way too much to say. And the taking of pictures before the reception is drawn-out and cumbersome, especially to the guests waiting outside the reception hall for the doors to open.

The reception begins with a formal dinner, followed by dancing to the crowd-pleasing tunes of an eight-piece, top-forty band. Ralph and I dance a few times together, but being best man, he is compelled to make his way around the room, something that I, as the maid of honor, have no desire to do. I am standing alone when a tall, attractive woman I recognize from Karen's bridal shower approaches me.

"How do you know Karen?" she asks, and I explain that Karen is my best friend and stockbroker.

"Oh, I see. You're the doctor I've heard so much about," she says, smiling wide, like a model or a movie star, her skin a flawless golden brown, her eyes a rare blue-green. She flings her long, luxuriant tresses to the side as she introduces herself as Mikayla Roberts.

"Lenny Faulkner," I say, envying even the sound of her name. *Mikayla* has a musical and exotic flair to it. She looks rich and pampered.

"My gynecologist is a man," she says out of the blue. "I can't see having a woman examine my body. Isn't that weird for you? Don't you ever get tired of looking at pussy?" She flings her hair to the side again, like the tail of a horse, smirking. "Huh, Dr. Faulkner?"

Immediately, I am taken aback. I open my mouth to respond, my eyes hot as torches as Mikayla turns and sashays away from me. There was a time when nothing much bothered me. As a fat child who was teased a lot, I developed a thick skin. But here I am, a few decades later, with my mouth hanging open, too flabbergasted to speak.

"Pay her no mind," Karen says, now standing next to me, a protective hand holding my arm. I watch as Mikayla leaves the ballroom with a man I don't recognize.

"Who is she?" I ask.

"My cousin, I'm ashamed to admit," Karen says. "Mikayla has a habit of offending people. I'm glad she's leaving early."

By the end of the evening, Ralph and I are together again ready to throw frilly bags of birdseed at the happy couple as they prepare to leave for their honeymoon. While driving home, Ralph tells me he has something on his mind.

"What?" I exclaim excitedly, my composure rattled. I bury my nails into the palms of my hands and look straight ahead. My view becomes tunneled by the anticipation of hearing him pop the question. I clear my throat and in a much calmer tone say, "What is it, honey?"

"I've been thinking about something for a long time."

My heart beats faster at the word *something.* He fidgets in the driver's seat, and for a protracted span of a few seconds, while I hold my breath, I expect him to pull *something* from the inside pocket of his lapel. He does not. His hand smoothes his tuxedo in place beneath his seat belt.

"We'll talk about it over dinner tomorrow night," he says. "I'm too tired to think right now. I need to get some sleep, and I have a meeting with a client in the morning."

"Sunday morning?" I say, incredulously.

"Yes, Sunday," he says, sounding annoyed with me. He pushes down on the gas as if all at once in a hurry. "It's the only time my client can meet."

"I understand." The last thing I want is to upset Ralph. We arrive home, go to bed, and Ralph falls fast asleep. I watch the rise and fall of his chest, his face aglow in the moonlight. This is the man I want for life.

He completes me. I snuggle close and listen to his every breath before drifting off. The next morning, he is gone.

I get dressed and find a note on the kitchen counter telling me to meet Ralph for dinner at our favorite restaurant.

The Purple Peach—promptly at seven o'clock.

I think about how Jason proposed to Karen over dinner. She discovered her engagement ring buried in her dessert—baked Alaska. I go through most of the day in a fog, my thoughts changing continuously from one thing to another, from wedding dresses to baby diapers. I open *The Promise of Spring* to the part where Clarissa Montgomery is afraid of falling in love with Charles Crow. She and her young daughter were abandoned by her husband years before. She is afraid to trust this part-Indian man with a mysterious past. I close the book after he finally kisses her.

Time to change for dinner. It all at once dawns on me, as I remove hot curlers from my hair, that today is New Year's Eve, the perfect occasion for a man to propose.

I meet Ralph in the lobby of the restaurant, just after seven o'clock. He smiles when he sees me. The waitress motions that our table is ready. We briskly follow her to a candlelit table for two, where the scent of fresh-cut roses permeates the air like an amorous mood. I brace myself for when he asks me to marry him. We sit and I reach for his hand on top of the table, my nails painted that certain red that turns him on. I squeeze lightly.

"I'm so glad we're here tonight," I say softly.

"Me, too, baby." He studies his menu, seriously concentrating on what selections to make, before ordering a caesar salad, porterhouse steak, and baked potato—same as always. I think how predictable this man I love can be at times. Ralph is not as adventurous as I when it comes to food.

The waitress requests my order, and without thinking I order the same. My tongue feels glued to the back of my throat, my stomach in knots. I never order beef. Ralph glances up at me, confused.

"Sure?"

I nod yes, and after taking a slow, deep breath to calm my nerves, I lean over to kiss his cheek, wanting him to feel completely at ease. I want Ralph to be commander of our ship and take the lead—take the initiative and ask me . . . ask me . . . please, ask me.

The atmosphere fills with the sweet music of a jazz quintet: piano, saxophone, bass, drum, and singer. The female vocalist does a sultry rendition of "When I Fall in Love." It is all I can do to keep from helping Ralph with the right words.

"I've been thinking a lot about us lately," he says.

"Yes?"

"You're a very special woman, Lenny," he says.

"I am?" I say anxiously.

"We've been together a long time and . . ."

"And?"

"When I Fall in Love" rises and falls in melodious riffs. I feel the right words are about to be said; Ralph is surely going to ask me to marry him—the timing could not be more perfect. He takes my hand in his, just before the waitress interrupts what he is about to say, his forthcoming proposal lost behind a broad smile. Ralph is obviously pleased and distracted by plates filled with enough steak to feed the average American family.

"Can I get you anything else?" she asks.

"No, nothing thank you," I say, on the verge of becoming annoyed. Ralph nods in agreement and begins cutting into his steak. The waitress fills our glasses with water and moves on to other customers. I wait for Ralph to swallow. "You were saying?"

"I was saying that there aren't many women in the world like you." He releases a heavy sigh as if about to unburden his chest. I expect to hear him ask me and bite my tongue to keep from saying yes before he does. "Karen and Jason are made for each other," Ralph says, changing the subject, avoiding my eyes.

"They say the same thing about us," I say softly. He sighs. I think about what Karen said happens when a man is about to propose. It's normal for him to get moody. "Jason had cold feet," she said. Ralph will feel much better after he does it. Back to normal. We will be normal soon. We eat in silence.

"I've been thinking a lot about your mother," he says, before polishing off the last of his steak. I take a few bites myself while watching him chew and swallow. I am too distracted to actually taste the food going down. "Cancer is a terrible disease. Maybe you should go down to see her for a week or two before she—"

"I plan to," I interrupt. I'm not in the mood to talk about dying. I want Ralph to talk about us. I push my plate away and watch, distracted, as the waitress clears the table.

Ralph orders dessert. I order the same. We eat with a nervous energy between us. I try to appear relaxed while picking through the apple pie à la mode, hopeful that a ring is hidden inside one of those spoonfuls.

"How was your meeting this morning?" I say, arching my brows with interest.

"Perfect," he replies.

"I'm glad things went well."

"Hated giving up most of my day," he says as if a bitter taste landed on his tongue. "I need a vacation."

"*We* need a vacation."

He smiles. "Where would we go?"

"Well, let's see," I quaver. "When Karen and Jason get back from Bermuda, we can ask them how it was, and if they absolutely loved it, we should go there."

"They'll love it," he says, grinning. My heart flutters as he finishes his pie. Ralph signals to the waiter for the check. He examines it and places cash on the table.

"I need to take a trip to the john," he tells me, standing suddenly. "Finish your dessert. I'll be right back."

While Ralph is gone, I remove a compact mirror from my purse, check my makeup, and add more lipstick—red, his favorite. I think of the first time he and I were alone together, the way he took my face in his hands, devouring it with his eyes, charming me with a few breathless kisses. "God, you're pretty" still makes my head swoon, as if the ripcord of my innermost being is released all over again, and the real me is ready to fly.

I contemplate why he is taking such a long time in the restroom. Working up the nerve to ask me. Getting just the right facial expression. Finding just the right words. I imagine him staring at himself in the mirror, mouthing what I so want to hear. *Will you, Lenny Faulkner, be my bride?*

"Yes!" I exclaim aloud, unaware that the waiter is standing over me.

"Ma'am?" he says, bewildered by my sudden outburst.

"Oh, nothing," I say, embarrassed. "I was just thinking about something. Nothing to do with . . ."

He extends his hand and gives me a sheet of notepaper.

"The gentleman had to leave. He asked me to give you this."

I take the note and slowly open it to read

Lenny,

You're a wonderful woman and will make some lucky man happy. But I am not that man. It's over between us. Please understand.

Ralph

My eyes are fastened to these words that plunge like daggers through my heart and soul. My head spins, and all I can do is to fold the paper. I fold it again and again and again. I fold it into the size of a pack of matches, stand up, and in a daze, collect my coat before leaving the restaurant, where outside in the sobering cold, reality grips me by the throat until it aches. The man I thought I knew and shared a bed with for all these years, and with whom I had hoped to share the rest of my life, has left me. Dinner, a simple note, and just like that, we're over?

7

Why did he leave me? I drift into a hard sleep, and dream of being pregnant with Ralph's child. He comes running to the hospital on the day I deliver, tears in his eyes, pleading for me to take him back. What a fool he was to leave. He suffered without me. I turn over in bed and awake with the sun beaming across my face, a stream of light undulating across the chair and night table. Ralph is gone. I close my eyes and try not to think at all.

My beeper goes off suddenly, and I squint to see that it's after eleven o'clock. I am confused. How long have I slept? I return Frank O'Connor's page. Frank is the on-call physician who covered the practice for the weekend. He tells me he was surprised to find I had not checked on two of my patients this morning.

"And your patients are getting backed up at the office," he says sharply.

"Checked on? Office?" I mumble, dumbfounded. Then it hits me that I am late. I have been known to stretch out the day, but I am never late getting into the office. "Oh, God, Frank. I'm sorry. I overslept."

He sighs disgustedly and lowers his voice. "There were complications with a Miss Moore last night."

"What happened to Miss Moore?"

"Erythroblastosis," he says. "Your Miss Moore's baby needed a transfusion and she refused to give permission."

"She's a Jehovah's Witness," I say, thinking about the results of Miss Moore's blood test. I forewarned her of the Rh factor, told her specifically that her baby would require a blood transfusion to survive.

"We had to get a court order—woke up the judge. We had Miss Moore heavily sedated and transfused the baby anyway."

"Thank God."

"No, God had nothing to do with it. According to your patient, God wanted the baby born severely handicapped." Frank pauses. "I paged you twice," he says tersely, his throat sounding parched from a long, sleepless night. His sharp swallow twangs like a dog lick. My head feels like it was hit with a bat when I try to sit up.

"Thank you, Frank," I say hoarsely. "I should've been at the office hours ago, I know. But I can't do it this morning."

"You're not coming in at all?"

"I just can't."

"Why not?"

I take a deep breath. Frank, who is senior partner of the group, founded Women's Health Choice fifteen years ago. I have found him to be an excellent physician, caring and expert in his treatment of patients. He is a man of integrity, completely without prejudice in his dealings with me as a black woman—something I had not anticipated when I first joined the group. I hate disappointing him.

"There's so much I need to do right now, Frank. I have a lot on my plate. It's personal. I really need some personal time away from the office."

"This will inconvenience your patients and the other doctors. This is not how we do things here."

"My mother's dying of cancer," I blurt out, shamefully using Mama's illness as an excuse because it sounds better than saying my lover broke up with me. Frank sighs and clears his throat.

"I'm sorry to hear that," he says. "As you might recall, my mother lost her battle a few years ago as well. It's a terrible disease."

"Yes, it is," I agree sadly. Frank tells me not to worry. He volunteers to have the receptionist reschedule most of my patients. Frank will personally examine my full-term and high-risk pregnancies himself.

"Just this week?" he says.

"Yes," I quickly affirm. I hang up the phone and languish in bed like a lump a while longer, with no appetite for food, no desire for anything other than to see Ralph again. When the pain in my head lightens, I remember his locked office and get up to investigate. It's still locked. Hope makes me anxious, and I begin to imagine him coming back home. It was a mistake to leave—the worst mistake of my life. I wrap myself in Ralph's bathrobe, sniffing his scent. I retrieve his charcoal gray suit from the closet and hold it up to the morning light, stroking the finely combed wool and cotton fibers. I whisper quiet prayers. *Dear God, I'll do anything to get him back.*

I lie down with the suit as if Ralph were in it. A knot rests in the pit of my stomach, throbbing and twisting when I think of him leaving. Love hurts worse than labor. I am sure of it. I pass the next two days lying in bed. My back and legs are sore from being in one spot too long, next to the phone. Five, maybe six times, I dial Ralph's beeper, plug in my number, and wait. But he does not return my calls. He has no intention of talking to me. I mean nothing to him, no more than a bug on his doorstep.

On Wednesday, I rise from the dead to get my hair done at a small parlor east of the city. I clean the house and do the laundry. I pack a few clothes. Make a few plans. I try not to think about Ralph. The next morning, I drive two hundred twenty-two miles south to Madoosa County, to visit Mama. The sun is brighter and closer to the earth where the land stretches flat and endlessly across this nondescript corner of Southeast Georgia. Madoosa County is a pit stop on the way to Florida, known primarily for one thing: its foul odor.

I open my car window slightly, recognizing the putrid chemicalized-wood-chip smell that permeates this town of less than five thousand people. When I was a child, my family moved from Cottonwood, Alabama, where Daddy had worked in a cotton mill, to here, where he worked at the box factory. When I drew up my face and protested against the stench, he told me, "That's the smell of money, child, so get used to it." And I did get used to it. In fact, everybody here is used to smelling like petrified cow dung. But as soon as I could, boy, did I leave it behind.

I reach Mama's small, tin-roofed house, which is close to the road but several acres away from her neighbors. It is typical of the poor, rural dwellings in this part of the country, replete with a large abandoned field on one side of the house, where crops from corn to cabbages were once harvested each year. And on the right side of the house sit a few broken-down cars, along with Daddy's twenty-year-old truck, and a rusty antique tractor.

The house has weathered gray since the last time it was painted, not long before my father's death. A pang of guilt needles my insides from seeing how Mama lives and knowing that she has never had it easy. On the occasions that Ralph and I passed through on our way to the Florida coast, we stopped long enough to catch up with Mama. Actually, I would sit in the front room with Mama while Ralph remained in the car. She would pointedly tell me I'd been away too long, then proceed to inform me about the goings-on of the neighbors, her church members who'd died, or whose daughter had a baby—usually out of wedlock.

Before saying good-bye, Mama would generally divulge that a hardship was visiting Bobby or Rosetta. There would always be a crisis. One or the other would be behind in a payment, or one of their children needed something. I would be broke by now from their picking me clean if it were not for the investments Ralph and I made together.

I knock on the door and Rosetta answers it, greeting me warmly with a gap-toothed grin and big hug, her robust body soft and cushy. I notice her eldest daughter standing behind her and wonder how much this visit will cost me.

"How's Mama?" I say softly, curious as to what state our mother might be in—cantankerously wide awake or resting peacefully.

"Raising hell with Bobby on the phone," Rosetta says as I step inside, the smell of old, rotting wood and mildew surrounding me like nostalgia. My sister chuckles and puts her fingers over her mouth, covering the spot where she lost her tooth last year when her ex-husband punched her.

"You know Mama. She ain't gonna slow down for nothin'. She's mad with that brother of ours. He was supposed to get rid of that junk out there before you come up here."

"Some of those old cars have been rusting in that same spot since we were children," I say, glancing around the small living room, which also hasn't changed for as far back as I can remember. I sit down on the sofa, which is still covered in the plastic it was delivered in when I was ten.

"The last thing Mama should be worrying about is impressing me."

"I know, Lenita Mae, but she don't want you feelin' sorry for her, is all. She wants us all to be glad she don't have long to suffer."

"This place is a disgrace, Rosetta. You and Bobby live close enough that you could be doing more to help Mama around here."

"We've got kids to take care of, Doctor, and we don't live in some big, fancy house to lavish ourselves in like some folks. And we don't make enough money to buy Mama a new house like some folks. And I ain't blaming nobody."

"I offered to buy Mama a new house," I say defensively, falling prey to Rosetta's habit of insulting me on the one hand and begging for money on the other. I remind her that Mama didn't want to leave.

"Well, you ain't never made no offer like that to *me,*" she huffs.

"No, I haven't," I say, leaving it at that. I hear Mama's footsteps, a stomp and shuffle down the creaking hallway from her bedroom. Rosetta stands taller, placing her hands behind herself, her portly figure less pronounced when she sucks in her gut.

I can almost remember how attractive she was growing up, how boys from miles around were after her. Mama used to say my sister was the pretty one and I was the smart one. We were assigned these roles from the beginning, though I was behind most of my class at the time. I was not even close to being smart. Now, Rosetta is neither smart nor pretty. She grins wide when Mama pauses at the entrance of the living room, leaning on her walking stick for support.

"So you finally made it," Mama says, squinting at me as if something is wrong with my hair, the way she used to do when I was a child, just before saying, "You need to tame them kinks on top of your head." I always hated when she spoke like that, filling me with hurtful ideas about my dark skin and hair as if God had cursed me. Without meaning to, I am sure, Mama imparted tidbits of an oral tradition that stemmed from slavery. *Stay out the sun. Comb your nappy hair. Put some lotion on them ashy, black legs.*

Deep down, I know my mother never meant any harm. She did not mean for me to be scarred by low self-esteem. I understand it all now. I have rationalized the whys and what fors. She never learned any better from her own upbringing. But knowing this intellectually does not lessen the pain of recollecting what it felt like as a child.

Mama sits down in her big easy chair and looks askance at me. "You ain't half bad to look at no more," she says.

"What?"

"You growed up better'n I thought you would," she says. I smile and thank Mama, because this is as good a compliment as I can ever expect. When I ask how she feels, she grunts and says, "Good 'n' bad." She gazes out the front room window, training her sights on my car.

"Glad you didn't bring nobody wit you. I ain't in the mood for no company."

My throat tightens; Ralph's departure has drained me empty. I wish he were sitting outside in the car, insulting my mother by refusing to come inside.

Bobby comes over later in the evening with his short, stout wife, Barbara, and their three boys, all under the age of five. The boys are unclean, with snot staining their faces. They are wild and undisciplined by parents who ignore their unruly behavior as soon as they sit down at the kitchen table to eat the hearty meal Rosetta has prepared. A meal, by the way, that could feed a small army, complete with fried chicken, ham, mashed potatoes, collard greens, and cornbread—enough cholesterol to last a lifetime.

"Mmm-hmmm," Bobby hums his approval and is first to dig in. Rosetta's eldest daughter, Chili, grumbles that her boy cousins get on her nerves, the boys grabbing from the table like their daddy. Rosetta's youngest daughter, Tabby, pops Bobby Junior in the back of his head, telling him to sit down and shut up. I hold my breath waiting for Barbara to get angry, but she stuffs her mouth with mashed potatoes, and for once, says nothing—she looks the other way.

"Settle down, boys," Bobby says, all at once hopping up and reaching for his belt. The boys sit, frightened for a split second, then the two sharing the same chair try to elbow each other to death. I want Tabby to smack their hard, bony heads.

"What'd your daddy say!" Barbara snaps at them. The boys stop and eat a few bites, waiting for the adults to forget them. There was a time, not so long ago, when Barbara would have blown up at anybody correcting those boys. She helped turn them into little monsters, and now they've finally worn her down. She gives me a defeated, deadpan look and says, "Be glad you don't have young'uns to tend with every day."

I shrug, trying to imagine what my life would have been like had I not left for college. Maybe I would be as big as Rosetta and Barbara, waiting for the next meal to feel good about myself, using food as a sedative to calm my nerves. I watch the two women stuffing themselves, and at the end of the table, Bobby eats with his mouth half open. He sounds like a pig at the trough.

"Mmmm, boy, this is good eatin'," he bellows. A shame, I think, that Bobby never pursued any higher aspirations than our father. He was a bright student in high school; his teachers all urged him to go to college. But I remember how adamantly against it he was when I begged him to give it a try. He was accepted to Morehouse College, and offered a full scholarship to boot. My father, however, convinced him to stay home, telling him he would be better off working at the box factory. "You can earn more than teachers," he told him. Now my brother is like our father, afflicted by the same low self-esteem, same lackluster life. He makes ends meet. Bobby prefers to sound as ignorant as the people around him.

"So," he says, chewing and talking simultaneously, "how long you gonna stay?"

"Until tomorrow," I say.

"Figures," he snaps, rolling his eyes at me in disgust.

" 'Least she helps me out when she do come," Mama says, temporarily silencing my brother, who will need me before I leave, I guarantee it. After dinner, we sit around the table as Bobby and Rosetta retell old childhood stories that seemed funny when we were young. They howl and slap their knees, doubling over now and then at something they say, causing Mama to break into a wretched, throaty chortle.

"Lighten up," Bobby says, slapping me on my back when I don't join in. My heart is breaking without Ralph. I ache in places no one here can imagine. My siblings continue to take turns poking fun at other people's misfortunes—at the woman who lost her wig in church, at the drunken neighbor who was found, wrapped around a telephone pole, by the sheriff one morning, at the uncle who left his teeth in a jar at his mistress's house. My father's sister, Aunt Reba, was so fat she had to be weighed at a truck stop, and when she died, her family had to pay for two plots and two coffins. This might have been hilarious, if not for the fact that it was true. A small army of men had to squeeze through the doors of Waycross Baptist, hauling my aunt's enormous casket like a flat of timber on its way to the chip mill. Her final resting place was the size of a crater.

"That was the biggest affair I've ever been to," Bobby jokes, he and Rosetta howling mercilessly over our dead, fat aunt. It isn't funny to me in the least. There, by the grace of God—and my own perseverance to run for my life—go I.

"Sticky's back in the joint," Rosetta says, now bantering about our cousin, Thomas, who got the name Sticky because he is a thief. Rosetta gets a great deal of perverse satisfaction out of telling that Sticky has been to prison so many times, they've named a cellblock after him. She cracks up, laughing and spitting through the hole in her teeth, the place she self-consciously covers with the fingers of her right hand. I think of a man whose youth was wasted behind bars, and find nothing to laugh about.

"And Roly Poly here ain't cracked a smile," Bobby says, motioning toward me with his head. He and Rosetta tease me about the days when I was so fat, I couldn't bend over to tie my shoes. My nephews latch onto "Roly Poly." They begin to chant, "Roly poly, puddin' and pie." I try to ignore them.

"Lenita Mae used to say, 'Tie my shoes, Rosa, I'll give ya a piece of candy.' Sittin' up on the sofa, big as all get-out."

Rosetta and Bobby break into giggles over it, as does Bobby's plump wife. The teenage girls eye me closely as if looking for the girl I used to be. They all laugh as if I have no feelings, as if my feelings have never counted. I realize I have become an institution to them, a place to go for money, a place they must insult in order to build themselves up a notch or two—a place, not a person.

Steam rises inside me. I could scream at them that Ralph is gone. At any minute, I could stand up and tell them to all go to hell. But they would probably laugh at that, too. A tear glides down the center of my cheek. I have forgotten how to toughen up and let insults roll off my back. This is the consequence of living in a polite society, where the unkind word may be implied but left unspoken. Their laughter soon falls flat and they see I am human after all.

I feel abandoned by Ralph; my mother becomes a stranger, an old woman picking at her plate, her appetite and interest in living all gone. Between robust Rosetta to beer-gut Bobby, they've managed to open an old wound, the hurt still festering inside me. I wipe my eyes with a paper towel, used for a napkin.

"Well, she ain't big no more. . . . *You is,*" Mama says sharply to Rosetta, sitting up stoically in her seat at the head of the table. She coughs and spits bloody phlegm into her handkerchief, reminding us all of her imminent mortality. She folds the red-stained cloth and uses it to wipe the sides of her mouth.

"Look at you two, big as buffalo rump wit nerve enuff to talk."

I burst into laughter for the first time in weeks. It feels like a hard cry, almost painful, yet cleansing to the spirit.

"Didn't I tell ya," Rosetta says, grinning wide. "Mama ain't slowed down for nothin'. Always gots something to say."

Rosetta laughs at our mother who rolls her eyes and coughs. Bobby slaps me on the back and says, "We're just funnin'. No need to take it personal."

"I know," I say, acknowledging to myself how ridiculous it was to let them get under my skin. I have grown away from these people and from this place that once held me like a cage. I am here and not here.

8

After Bobby and Rosetta leave with their families, Mama insists that I stay the night.

"There's a motel on the outskirts of town," I say, thinking how Mama's house is too small, with only three rooms—a living room, a kitchen, and a bedroom. When I was a child, this tiny dwelling seemed all we needed, big enough. The one bedroom had a wall of quilts running down the middle, with my brothers sleeping on one side and my parents on the other. Rosetta and I slept on the pullout sofa in the living room, our clothes and personal effects stored in wooden crates stacked in the coat closet.

"It ain't fancy like you done got used to, but it's clean," Mama says proudly.

"I'll stay, thank you, Mama," I say, choosing not to argue with her about something as trivial as where to lay my head, not when Mama is sickly and months away from dying. I sleep in bed next to her, on the same bed she had when I was a child, maybe the same mattress underneath. The scent of cancer seeps through her pores, and I touch skin hanging on bones that used to be strong and healthy, now frail from being eaten alive. Mama moans and coughs pathetically in her sleep.

When I was a girl, I craved the long, wavy hair that Mama used to have before chemotherapy turned it into a soft, gray mesh. I gently stroke what feels like the fuzz on a baby chicken, cottonlike. Mama used to have what folks around here called *good hair.* Rosetta inherited it, while the opposite was passed down to me from my father's side of the family—nappy hair with a buck-wild personality. As a grown woman, I have been meticulously concerned with my hair, with ridding its naturalness because I grew up being told how bad it was. I used to pray for God to make it right. Of course, *He* never did.

Since meeting Ralph, I have not missed a single weekly hair appointment. My shoulder-length tresses are either permed, deeply conditioned, blown straight, or hot curled, so that when I leave the salon, it bounces and swings. To look at it, one would never know how willful it really is. But now Ralph is gone. Like my hair treatments, he was only temporary after all. I think about all the hours I've spent sitting in salons, or sitting at home waiting for Ralph—all the years it might add up to.

Mama whispers prayers in her sleep that drift over my head like the cooing of a dove. Tomorrow I will begin again. Tomorrow will not hurt as much as today.

The next day, I help Mama by cleaning up around the house. I make a list of things to do, and start by calling a neighbor plumber to come out and repair the leaky fixtures in the kitchen and bathroom. A neighbor carpenter repairs a hole in the floor next to the bathtub, but when I ask him to paint the house, he says, "I don't do no paintin' for nobody. I'm too old."

"I understand," I say, "but do you know of someone young enough to do the job?" He shakes his head emphatically, telling me there's no one he'd be willing to count on.

"You know young'uns today," he says disgustedly.

I circle *painting* on my list, and look through the pitiful Madoosa County yellow pages for a towing company. There are two, but this morning, neither Jebb nor Ronny is willing to haul away the old, useless vehicles sitting abandoned and scattered on the lawn. They're busy. What a joke. Finally, I try to convince Mama to come to dinner with me in Valdosta. She reminds me that she doesn't eat from folks she doesn't know. "Don't know where folks' hands have been," she says.

Rosetta and her daughters come over and we eat the leftovers from yesterday's big supper. Mama eats very little. She nibbles and draws up her face when she swallows. She tells Rosetta that the ham dried out overnight and the leftover collard greens taste flat.

"Ain't my fault," Rosetta says, pulling herself up from the table to get another helping of ham and cheese macaroni, beginning the process of eating another meal, only chewing a few times before gulping it down.

"If they paid you for eatin', you'd be rich by now," Mama says.

"Leave me alone now, Mama," Rosetta chuckles between chews. There was a time in her youth when she hardly ate anything at all. She was sixteen, with a slender, petite figure, a body that was the envy of most of the girls we knew.

Rosetta had a car and a boyfriend named Junebug. He was mature for his age. He had a full mustache and a big Afro. He would stand on the front porch and pick out his hair before coming inside the house. Once, Junebug overheard Mama comparing him to a gnat with bushy hair. I felt sorry for him. He looked down at the floor like his feelings were hurt. But he willingly came back for more insults, because he absolutely worshiped Rosetta. Junebug thought the sun rose for my sister. But the day Rosetta got pregnant was the end of him. Daddy threatened to bash his head in with a baseball bat, and Junebug, who feared him more than he loved Rosetta, never returned.

Rosetta lost the baby when she crashed her car into a large, stately oak tree that used to thrive in the front yard. Now she wipes her mouth with a paper towel and burps. I cannot help feeling sorry for the way her life turned out. Rosetta dropped out of high school and lost another baby. She married a man who beat her. She has two daughters to care for. Rosetta is stuck.

"How's that cute boyfriend of yours," she asks, "what's-his-name, the lawyer?"

"Ralph's fine," I say, sickened. I think about the years I have wasted waiting to marry him, and all the dreams I have deferred.

"When y'all gonna get married?"

"That ain't none of your business, Rosetta," Mama says throatily. "You needs to find a man yourself."

Rosetta laughs and shakes her head, saying, "Told you she ain't changed a lick."

"I might climb Kilimanjaro this year," I blurt out.

"Where's that?" Rosetta asks incredulously.

"It's the tallest mountain in Africa."

"Africa? And what's-his-name's going, too?" Rosetta burps and places a hand over the missing tooth.

I shake my head no. Giving up my dream of climbing Mount Kilimanjaro was one of those sacrifices I made to be with Ralph after finishing my residency, when I wanted to travel, and work with poor, needy women in other countries. He threatened not to wait for my return. It is futile to think of what might have been.

"He's letting you go?" Rosetta burps again.

"He doesn't have a choice."

I spend a final night with Mama. We sit in the front room, like old times, and she tells me about the goings-on in Madoosa County. The daughter of a girl I went to school with is having her second baby—out of wedlock.

"Girls these days don't have a lick of shame," Mama says. "And you remember that boy who used to tease you when you was a big, little girl? Timothy Moore's old bad boy from across the way?"

"I don't."

"Well he's growed up to be a right responsible fella. He's divorced now and been asking 'bout you."

"Oh."

"Not that you'd ever be interested in the likes of him."

"Not in the least bit, Mama."

"And you know Charles Duncan," she says, stopping to catch her breath.

"Sorry, Mama, I don't recall him either."

"Alice's husband, Lenita Mae," Mama says, pointing in the direction of the kitchen. "You know, they lives over yonder."

"I don't remember them," I insist.

"He died peacefully in his sleep last week," Mama says, sadly.

"I'm sorry to hear that."

"That's how I wants to go," Mama says, wistfully. "Real peaceful-like." She coughs and spits and continues telling about people I no longer know, until the sun moves behind the clouds and a dark shadow fills the room.

"It's gittin' past my bedtime," she says. I help Mama up on her feet and the two of us dress for bed. In just two days, I have grown accustomed to the smell of rotting wood and the stench of Madoosa County. The woeful aroma of cancer seeping through Mama's flesh has become elusive. It comes like an unexpected breeze, reminding me of death. Mama weakly climbs into bed, and I crawl in beside her.

"Good night, Mama," I say. "I love you."

"Uh, huh."

I awake glad to see Saturday. I am more than ready to go home. I miss having my own space and my own things. I miss seeing my patients most of all. Bobby and Rosetta come over, and together, we go through Mama's things—a house of mediocre furniture, decaying, plastered walls, and loose floor boards. The only item I want is the picture of our family hanging on the wall above Mama's bed, taken before Joseph Allen went to Vietnam. In it, Daddy wears the only suit I ever knew him to own. Mama is expressionless, dressed in her Sunday best, holding the infant, Bobby, on her lap. Rosetta's a beauty. Her shoulder-length hair is flipped at the ends, and the dress she has on is tight enough to show off her petite figure. And then there's me, the fat little girl stuffed in the middle, who hated herself more than anyone else could.

"Look-a-here!" Rosetta exclaims, noisily going through Mama's meager jewelry box that contains earrings, rings, and necklaces never worn, most of them purchased by me. On the bottom is my old diary from fifth grade. Rosetta opens it and lets out a howl.

"Rules for life," she laughs. I snatch it from her.

"It's mine," I whine, like a hurt child.

Bobby pulls me aside and I try listening patiently to his ridiculous diatribe about a business venture he is involved in, something I could profit from by making an investment.

"I'll think about it," I say, tightening my grip on my old diary.

"What's there to think about, 'Nita? It's a win-win sit-ation, the way I see it. You see what I mean?"

"No, I don't," I say, knowing from experience that I would get more return on money flushed down the toilet.

"Look here," he says, "I guarantee you'll get your money back."

"Well then, that sounds like a much better deal," I say sarcastically. I place our family picture in a box I've cushioned with old newspapers and put my old diary on top.

"I tell you what, Bobby," I say, now wanting him to disappear. "Since you already owe me over ten thousand dollars, just take some of that money and invest it for me. When the money rolls in, you can pay me back."

"I'm short this week," he says.

"Figures," I say, sealing the box with duct tape. I carry it outside, the tattered screen door banging shut as Bobby follows me to the car. He says how hard his life is right now. And I think how hard it always will be until he learns to manage the money he makes. I picture him sprawled across his bed Friday nights, like Daddy used to do, his pockets emptying of change, money his sons scrounge for on the floor.

I am tempted to say, "You're just like our father, Bobby Lee." But I don't. His ego bruises easily. I carefully place the box inside the car, then go around to the driver's side and open the door to remove a checkbook from my purse. I write a check for two hundred dollars.

"It's for the boys," I say, handing him the folded check. His brow is knit with disappointment.

"I'll think about the other," I say, like an excuse, even though there's not a prayer in heaven that will make me give him money to invest. He hops into his red truck and waves to me. I wave back. There are no thank-you's in this family.

"Lenita Mae," Rosetta calls out, sweet and syrupy.

"Yes?" I say, watching her shift from one foot to the other, the way she does when she's about to ask for something big.

"You know Chili's birthday's coming up."

"Yes, I know."

"She don't ask for much. She'll be seventeen."

"Mmmm-hmmmm."

"She's been wantin' a car real bad."

"A car!!??!!"

"She don't have no mama who makes a lot a money like some folks who can afford to buy her a car. I do the best I can wit no help from her daddy." Rosetta's voice quavers and she breaks down in tears.

"Give me a break, Rosetta," I say under my breath. I've grown tired of this performance. She does it every time I come home. Always, she cuts up when I am ready to leave.

"If you can see your way clear toward helping," she says, wringing her hands and shifting her weight from one foot to the other, like she's about to pee.

"No," I say. "I will not contribute to the delinquency of your daughter. She does not need a car to get away to places you don't know about."

"Chili's a good girl," Rosetta says defensively.

"She had an abortion last year," I say curtly, the words slipping out like a slap across Rosetta's face. She looks at me stunned. And I feel a stab wound in my gut from how wrong I was for saying it.

"I shouldn't have said that," I say remorsefully.

"You damned right," Rosetta says in angry spurts. Her hands go to her hips and her eyes buck, fixing me with a bloodthirsty stare.

"Like you so high and mighty 'cause you went to college. When you was young enough to have babies."

"What do you mean?" I say, astonished. "I'm still young enough."

"Maybe," she says dubiously. Her eyes narrow and she grins slyly like a cat about to pounce on a bird, like she knows a secret.

"Women over thirty have babies all the time," I insist.

"Even ones who cut their inners all up, Doctor?" Rosetta says perniciously, aiming her words at my secret place. I feel shamefully naked, found out. How could she know? How could anyone know? I went to great lengths to hide it.

"You think I don't know what happened back then? You think I couldn't figure out why you was rushed to the hospital? The doctor told Mama you lost a lot of blood. I knows what makes a woman lose a lot of blood."

"You don't know what you're talking about."

"I know one thing," Rosetta says, shaking her index finger at me. "My daughter might've had an abortion, but she wasn't the first one in the family, now, was she?"

I am stunned into silence, feeling like the biggest hypocrite ever. Lower than the low. Rosetta always manages to make me feel guilty of something before I leave. She leans back against my car and folds her arms across her chest, staring into space. Her lips tighten as if what she is compelled to say must wait for me to speak first. The sky darkens suddenly and the smell of rain coming wafts through the air.

"Looks like a storm's on the way," I say uneasily. Rosetta sighs impatiently but says nothing. The last time I was here, she made me feel guilty for not visiting Mama while she underwent chemotherapy. Now I am guilty of judging her daughter for having done what I am too ashamed to admit. I think of Ralph and ache all over.

"We don't have no car no more," Rosetta says when she hears my keys jingle. She straightens and faces me with a dour expression. "The transmission broke and I don't have enough money to fix it."

I glance around the yard at all the broken vehicles that were never fixed.

"How much does it cost to fix the transmission?" I ask, expecting a lie.

"Three thousand at least," she says.

"Then have your mechanic send me the bill and I'll pay it." She leaves with a scowl downing her lips, angry that I have not been my usual gullible self. I know no rebuilt transmission costs that much. Hell, a new one is about half as much. Rosetta only thinks of Rosetta when she sees me, never expecting that I might have problems of my own. She would never stop to wonder whether or not I am happy. I throw my bags into the back seat and return to the house for the last time.

"Mama, come stay with me," I say, rubbing her bony back. "In the end, you'll need hospice care. There's no such help here in Madoosa County."

"I can't stay there when you ain't married," she says.

I hesitate before telling her about Ralph and me. Emotions rise up in back of my throat and I swallow to hold back tears.

"We aren't together anymore," I say, trying not to sound bitter.

"Say, what?"

"Ralph and me broke up, Mama. It's over."

Mama gives me a cockeyed glance as if she doesn't believe me at first, then she looks down at the floor and taps her cane.

"I never did like him no how," she says. "He looked sneaky." She stares searchingly into my eyes and tells me she knows all about men like Ralph. "Just after one thang: your pocketbook."

"He earns a good living, Mama."

Mama looks down and taps her cane on the floor again.

"If I do come, Bobby can bring me up there."

"That'll be fine," I say, before it hits me, the thought of living with my mother again after all these years. It won't be easy. Part of me wants to impress her with how great my life has become, that in spite of having been an ugly, fat child, I've grown up to become a desirable, strong woman. I want her to sleep in my house that she has never seen, to relish the soft cotton sheets that smell as fresh as the beginning of spring, and know how purposeful my life is—even without children. I want Mama to look around my yuppie neighborhood as we drive through it and say what she has never been inclined to say: "I'm proud of you, Lenita Mae, you done good. I love you."

9

When I arrive home, I know immediately that Ralph has been inside the house. His scent hangs in the air like pine after Christmas. He left my mail on the kitchen counter and a short note saying

Lenny,

I took what belongs to me.

Ralph

It slips through my fingers as I run to the bedroom and fling open the closet doors to find that his side is empty. It feels like death, the final nail hammered into the coffin of our relationship. I go through the house, room by room, exploring what other parts of him are missing. My furs are gone, the jewelry he gave me over the years, taken, and paintings we paid for together lifted off the walls, leaving light, square spots behind.

I imagine Ralph pilfering my things, and I see red—red dress, red roses, and blood. He stole everything worth anything to me. Even my heart feels stolen. I phone Karen, just back from her honeymoon. My lips tremble when she answers the phone.

"How was your trip?" I say, an uncontrollable quiver creeping into my voice.

"Lenny," she says, sounding concerned, "I just heard about you and Ralph. I'm so sorry. I never thought he would do such a thing."

"Well, he did," I say with feigned stoicism. I have never been a whiner, and even with my innards torn to shreds I find it difficult to express my pain.

"How are you holding up, Lenny?" she says softly. I break into a soft whimper as I relay the gist of what happened. I am standing in the great room staring at the bare walls, my voice rising against my will, telling Karen how Ralph came into my house while I was away and took not only his personal belongings, but also every gift he ever gave me.

"I can't believe that!" she says, astounded.

"Believe me," I tell her. "It's true."

"What a jackass he turned out to be! You just wait 'til I see him again."

"You know where he is?" I ask, before pleading with Karen to tell me. "I have to talk to him."

"You don't wanna know, Lenny. Trust me."

"He's with another woman, isn't he?"

"Yes."

"Who is she?"

"I should've known better, Lenny," she laments. "They were right under my nose and I couldn't see it."

"Who? What?"

"Mikayla."

An image of the stunning beauty comes to mind. I picture Mikayla tossing her gorgeous mane, smiling and scheming behind my back, saying through her perfect white teeth, "Pussy doctor."

"Your cousin?" I ask incredulously. Karen moans. "But how, Karen?"

"I feel like such an idiot," she says.

"How did they meet? When?"

I picture Karen's "know-it-all finger" tapping against her chin. I imagine her eyes growing rounder in surprise as she suddenly figures things out.

"I don't know when it started. I was out of the office a lot, planning the wedding, and somehow, Mikayla wiggled her way into helping Ralph with a few investments without telling me. I didn't find out until yesterday, when she said she'd be handling his account from now on."

"But I trusted *you* to handle it, Karen," I say sharply. "Not her. Not the cousin you don't even like."

"Lenny, I'm sorry."

"HOW COULD YOU?" I scream.

"I never would have . . . I. . . I . . . I didn't know . . ."

"The goddamned wedding," I say angrily, cutting her off. "The world had to stop for that day, right, Karen? It's always about you, isn't it? What

Karen wants. What Karen needs. Well, let me tell you something, this is my life you've messed around with, my goddamned future, and my whole world crashing down around me, so I don't care how sorry you feel, okay? I don't have it in me to forgive you either."

Karen bursts into tears. "God, I can't believe this happened."

"Where's he staying, Karen?" I ask pointedly.

"He bought a . . . a . . . a house."

"He's bought a house?" I exclaim, the words burning my cheeks. I picture Ralph holding the letter from the title company in his hands, calmly lying. *It's for a client. Should've gone to the office.* He tossed the envelope down in front of me, like a gauntlet, daring me not to trust him. What a bodacious liar. Why didn't I open the letter?

"Where does he live, Karen?"

"It's not a good idea for you to go there, Lenny."

"WHERE?" I yell.

"Lenny, please, no."

I lose what control I have left, and scream, "GIVE ME THE GODDAMNED ADDRESS, KAREN!" And she does.

I decide against going to Ralph's house tonight. I am too angry to face him. I might do or say something to regret later. Instead, I open the box I took from Mama's house containing the framed picture of our family and my old fifth-grade diary. The picture feels heavier somehow. I scan the empty walls in the great room for the right place to hang it, but there are too many square spots left on the walls from Ralph's pillaging to decide. I place it on the floor next to the fireplace. Maybe it should go above the mantel, maybe not. I open the diary with its yellowing pages and curl up on the sofa to read about the girl I used to be.

On the first day of school in September 1977, I wrote

If I was dead nobody but Mama would miss me.

A few pages back, Billy Moore, the boy Mama now says has been asking about me, had come up with a chant that caught on faster than a forest fire on a dry summer day:

Poor ol' Meaty Lenita, ate so much her legs couldn't keep her. She fell down on her big, fat butt and stayed until she lost her gut.

I remember him now—Billy Moore's drawn-up, little-boy face, his sharp tongue, and the way he liked pushing me in the soft of my back. I remember the names he and others hurled my way: "Two Ton," "Bertha," "Fat Mama," "Roly Poly," and the one that stuck the longest, "Meaty Lenita."

On Christmas day of that same year came the words

I wish I was a ghost.

I remember that, too. There was nothing I wanted more than to disappear. I hated going to school. I especially hated having to squeeze inside one of those tiny all-in-one desk-chairs. It was nothing less than a daily torment. So I feigned every illness in the book to try to stay home. But Mama was smart enough to make me go anyway. She told me I couldn't stay home unless I was either dead or dying. She told me to "pay those young'uns at school a no never mind," and to "shut 'em up" by being the best at everything.

But it was my teacher, Mrs. Drake, who took me aside after school one day, and said I had the potential to either be great, or be a great failure. She made the difference. "You're an intelligent girl, Lenita Mae" were words that inspired me. I survived off the fumes of her kindness. Finally, by March of the next year, I had had enough of Billy Moore. I made a set of *Rules for Life,* and my daily entries took on a confident quality.

One of these days he'll eat my dust. One of these days he'll wish he was my friend. One of these days, I'll forget who Billy Moore is.

I smile at the thought of Billy Moore asking about me now, and me not knowing him from the nearest stranger. Following the rules helped me change my circumstances. During that spring of 1978, I found a purpose: the citywide spelling bee. I wanted to win it. At the time, I was not particularly gifted as a speller. You might even say that I started from a deficit by having parents who were barely literate themselves. But I had determination, and that proved all I needed.

I followed my *Rules for Life:*

1. Early to bed, early to rise,
2. Study every morning and every night,
3. Always raise my hand first,
4. Read as much as I can,
5. Be on time, and
6. I won't let nobody ruffle my feathers.

I won the class bee, then the school spelling bee, and after I won the citywide, people began to see me differently, especially the other students. Suddenly, I was bigger than a fat girl. Billy Moore was forced to leave me alone and most of the teasing died down, just as Mama had predicted. A sense of pride wells up inside me as I recollect the dedication it took for me to transform myself. I had recited my *Rules for Life* every morning, until following them became a habit. I rose to the top of my high school and college classes, and got through medical school without a hitch.

Nothing could stop me. My fate changed its course like a rocket barreling into outer space, aiming for the moon but passing it, preferring instead the distant and the unknown. I was intent on succeeding. Now I have more than I grew up wanting: a great career, a home almost paid for. I look around at the bare walls, the feeling of loneliness ascending over me. I have everything I need, except people I can trust. Yet, I am not defeated. No, I will be the captain of my own ship from now on.

On the first blank page of the diary, I notate the date and write new *Rules for Life.*

Rule 1.

I will not allow ANYONE to control me.

10

10:48 A.M.

Christina Dennis, 28-year-old white female, return patient. Weight: 130 lbs. Height: 5'11". Gravida/para—0. Last normal menstrual period: February 13. Birth control: abstinence. Complaints: extreme pain and cramping in abdomen. Can't work through the day without doubling over. Excessive bleeding during menstruation. History of present illness: Patient is being treated for endometriosis.

Christina Dennis, tall, thin, smart, and very cosmopolitan, brought a list of questions for me to answer. She sits across from my desk, occasionally running a hand through her short, dark hair, moussed and shiny, likening her to a raven, reading aloud, ticking off what I have answered sufficiently and taking exception to what I have not, according to something written about in a magazine or a book. I think about what Mama used to say about me. *A little bit of knowledge can be a dangerous thing.*

Christina crouches slightly with pain as she reads, grimacing now and then when the severity of it becomes greater, her big, blue eyes shutting and opening behind a trendy pair of small, square-lens eyeglasses. She is one who knows just enough about everything to extend her visit into overtime. However, I do not argue with Christina; she is in the mood for a debate. I am not. When she pauses to catch her breath, I say, "That's all very well, but I wonder who's funding the study."

"What difference does it make?" she says.

"None, if you're the drug company pushing the drug."

She reads an excerpt from a recent article in an alternative medicine magazine on endometriosis. I check my watch; her time is up.

"Christina, I would love to discuss this issue with you on a day when I'm not quite so busy. I've explained all I know about treating endometriosis. For three years, we've tried nearly everything, including two laparoscopy procedures. You refused anti-hormone treatments, remember?"

"Those drugs cause cancer," she says.

"But the pain medicine isn't working," I say, thumbing through her chart.

"I'm informing you of other alternatives," she says indignantly.

"And as soon as your class is accredited, I'll take the course, Dr. Dennis," I say, emphasizing *doctor* to make my point.

"I have a right to ask questions without being insulted." Christina licks her index finger and turns to the next page; this woman is prepared to go the distance. She grabs hold of her waist with one hand, squeezing as if to stop the sharp pain, and reads another question. I glance at the time once more, and decide to be conciliatory.

"Of course you have a right to ask questions," I say. "And I apologize for being disagreeable, but do try to see my point. After utilizing the medicines that you would accept for the past three years, your condition has gotten worse. The endometriosis has advanced throughout the pelvis. I recommend you schedule an oophorectomy if you decide against the hormone treatment."

"Take out my ovaries? Why is it when we women have a problem with our reproductive organs, the best solution is to cut it out? But when a man, God forbid, has a problem with his organ, every effort is made to keep it intact."

I rub tension from my forehead. The world's social ills will not be solved today.

"Christina, you're bleeding heavily and you've complained of having severe cramps for over a year. You can't work a full day without doubling over in pain. I don't have anything left to offer except the medication or the surgery."

"I have more questions," she says.

"Just leave them with me, please," I say, before she gets started again. "I'll take a look and get back with you."

* * *

11:50 A.M.

Shaniqua Davis, Pregnant, 9 weeks gestation. Weight: 179 lbs. Reason for visit: Abortion.

I have terminated hundreds of pregnancies over the years, but this one I do not feel right about. On her last visit, Shaniqua sounded rehearsed when she said she wanted an abortion. I glance at her chart and notice she has lost ten pounds. Is the weight loss related to morning sickness, or her mother? When I enter the room, she turns on her side into a fetal position.

"It's not too late to change your mind," I say softly.

"A baby will get in the way of my future," Shaniqua says, sounding just like her mother. I tell her to lie on her back and put her feet in the stirrups. When Kelly flips on the suction machine, Shaniqua begins to quake and sob aloud. She turns on her side and draws up her body. I notice thick welts riddled up and down her back. She flinches when I touch her sore spots.

"Please don't kill it, Doctor. I've been praying on it every day, and last night, a voice told me not to do it. I think God's telling me not to kill my baby, Dr. Faulkner."

"Well, even if God isn't telling you that, you don't have to have an abortion if you don't want one."

"Mama won't like it," she cries.

"Are you afraid of your mother, Shaniqua? Did she beat you last night?"

"No, ma'am," Shaniqua says. "I fell in a briar patch."

"This wasn't caused by a briar patch, Shaniqua," I say. Shaniqua wails like the child she is—too young to be a mother. I turn off the suction machine and tell her not to worry. "It's fine that you changed your mind. You have that right. You will always have that right."

Seeing Shaniqua like this brings back the day I attempted to give myself an abortion. I was a sophomore in college, raped a few months earlier by a boy I'd just met. I was grateful that the gynecologist taking care of me after I almost died never told my parents.

I tell Shaniqua to get dressed, and I meet with her mother inside my office while she does.

It doesn't go well. Ms. Davis threatens to sue me for malpractice. "You tell her she has to go through with the abortion. I'm paying you to get rid of it," she says.

"I don't perform abortions on girls who don't want them, Ms. Davis."

"I wanted it and I'm her mother."

"You are not your daughter, Ms. Davis," I say.

"I know what's best for my daughter, Doctor."

"That's not enough."

"What do you mean, not enough? I gave her life. She's mine."

"Shaniqua may be your daughter, but she is not your property. She should obey your rules, but she shouldn't be abused when she doesn't."

"I don't abuse her. I spank her when she needs it."

I say, "I must warn you, I have to report any suspected abuse to social services."

"I'm getting out of here," Ms. Davis says, snatching up her purse. "I'm raising my daughter according to the book. God will judge me, not you." Kelly enters as Ms. Davis brushes past her. She tells me I have patients in Exam Rooms Two and Four.

I phone caseworker Stella Parker in between examining patients and report the bruises on Shaniqua's back.

"Is there any way Shaniqua can be removed from her mother's care immediately," I say, quick to add, "at least until after the baby is born?"

"Did she actually tell you that her mother beat her?"

"No, as a matter of fact, she said she fell into a briar patch. Can you imagine her saying that? It sounds like she lifted the excuse out of a fairytale."

"Unfortunately, Lenny, there's not much I can do unless there is evidence of abuse. The only thing I can do is to visit Ms. Davis and let her know that she is being investigated."

"You think a visit will be enough?"

"Sometimes it helps. I'll tell her that Shaniqua is required to visit you regularly as part of our investigation."

"What if she objects, Stella? She gets free legal advice whenever she wants."

"Do you think she'll want any lawyer she works for knowing she's being investigated for possible child abuse?"

* * *

4:45 P.M.

Susan Jenison: 32-year-old white female, return patient. Gravida/para—0. Weight: 161 lbs. Height: 5'8". Last normal menstrual period: February 10. Birth control: none. Complaints: Infertility. History of present illness: Patient has not used birth control in six years. Lab results for husband's sperm samples: Motility is abnormally low.

Mr. and Mrs. Jenison sit anxiously across from my desk. They remind me of college students waiting for the results of their midterm exams. I glance down at Mrs. Jenison's chart and tell them both I know the source of their infertility.

"I know it's not me," Susan Jenison asserts, sitting straighter in her seat. She glances accusingly at her husband whose shoulders slump when she adds, "All the women in my family are fertile. My sisters each have no less than four kids. I should've been pregnant on our honeymoon, but . . ."

"But, what?" snaps Alan Jenison. "I'm doing *it* wrong?"

"You're not doing *it* enough."

"Twice a week is not enough?"

"I told you what Ellen said."

"Your sister's a quack chiropractor. She's no doctor. If I want advice, I'll listen to a real doctor." He looks at me, and says, "Doctor Faulkner, whose fault is it, mine or hers?"

I sit back in my brown leather chair behind my large, imposing mahogany desk, which is here to render in the minds of my patients a sense of my importance and authority. However, in this case, these two need to lighten up. I take a penny from the weight cup and insert it into my acrobatic clown gumball machine.

"Have one," I say, looking from the meek, pale husband with thick glasses and thinning hair to his overbearing, overweight wife with rosy cheeks who can never be wrong.

They both accept in unison, a yellow gumball for Susan, and a pink one for Alan. I take a red one into my mouth, rolling it around on my tongue before chomping into it. I can sometimes tell a lot about a woman by the way she chews. Susan Jenison has a hard, desperate bite, with her lips slightly parted, a tiny pop escaping. I want her not to be right about her husband. In fact, I want her to be dead wrong, but she isn't. I glance down at the patient's chart again before I speak.

"In situations such as this, it's nobody's fault, Mr. and Mrs. Jenison. There is no right or wrong way to bring about a successful pregnancy. Mr. Jenison has live sperm. The problem is the way they move. They swim in circles instead of going straight for the ovaries."

"See, I told you. You're just like your brother."

"What d'ya mean? Andy has a son," says Mr. Jenison.

"Yeah, but something's wrong with that boy. Anybody can see that. He runs around in circles and makes himself fall out on the ground. It's the sperm doing it to him."

"That's nonsense, ain't that right doctor? Little Andy's two, that's what two-year-olds do. They run around."

"Not my son," says Susan Jenison, indignantly.

"You don't have a son, yet."

"No thanks to you."

As this moment heats up with Mr. and Mrs. Jenison hurling acrimonious comments at each other, I am tempted to say maybe God knows best, that some couples ought not have babies. But I know the pain in each of their faces. It is a pain I relate to more and more with each passing day. It is an unjust hurt that festers around the heart like a tick on a dog, sucking away at me, sucking away at Susan and Alan Jenison. I pucker and blow a bubble until it bursts.

"Oh, my, Dr. Faulkner," Susan Jenison exclaims, as I scrape away my gum mustache. She gives a nervous giggle and attempts to blow an even bigger one. Alan Jenison tries, too. Before long, they are more focused on who can blow the biggest bubble than on his sperm. They are able to laugh at themselves, until Mrs. Jenison checks the time on her watch. It's almost five fifteen when the tension between them returns.

"Mr. Jenison, your sperm is healthy," I say, hesitating as I watch relief come over him. His shoulders swing back. His chest is out and he smiles as if vindicated.

"There are options available to you . . . to remedy this problem. One option may be to inject your sperm farther up inside your wife's vagina. It's probably your least costly solution."

"But what if the child runs around in circles?"

"Then you'll be lucky it's healthy," I say to Susan Jenison, who sits back in her chair, hands clasped over her stomach, lips pursed together. I refer them to Dr. Mason, an infertility specialist. When they leave my office, I plug another penny into the gumball machine. It's been a long day.

11

At home, I take a long run. Fresh air flowing inside my lungs gives me peace of mind and takes me outside of myself. But afterward, when I return to my lonesome, empty house and my footsteps echo from the great room to the kitchen, I decide that the time is now to face Ralph. I take a long drive to southwest Atlanta, park my car in front of his new home, and wait.

My hope is that all my questions will be answered. I want my things back. I want to know why he left me. I deserve to at least know that. His new two-story contemporary stone-and-cedar house sits quietly back from the road. I think of how he wanted me to sell my house. What a fool I would have been if I had, left on the street without a clue. Across the street, a car wheels out of its driveway, backing frightfully close to mine before whizzing by. An ache grows deep inside my chest when I think of Ralph and Mikayla together. A broken heart surely must hurt as much as labor. No one could survive more pain than this. It is not humanly possible.

I get out of the car and numbly approach the door. I ring the doorbell, and when Mikayla appears, my body implodes with rage. If I had a gun, I would shoot her. I want to claw her lovely eyes out. I want her dead.

"Can I help you?" she says, smiling, perfect white teeth gleaming. She is slightly taller than me.

"I'm here to see Ralph," I snarl.

"Well, I'm sorry, but he's not home yet."

I open my mouth to curse her to hell and damnation and say any manner of foul language that might come to mind, but my lips quiver, and nothing comes out.

"Why don't you go on home, Doctor," she says dismissively, smiling victoriously. "If Ralph wants to talk to you, he'll call."

I slap Mikayla. The brevity of shocked silence dividing us makes time stand still. My hand pulsates from the heated connection to the side of her face. I had not planned to do it, no premeditation, or justifiable intention. She holds her face with both hands, her mouth open, and I feel a small measure of relief, though if I had had a gun, she would be dead.

"Gooooo," purges out of her. "Before I call the cops."

I quickly head for my car and go home.

The dishes are stockpiled in the kitchen sink, germinating fungus. A collection of clothing covers a chair in the corner of my bedroom like an eerie figure in the darkness, haunting me at night. I have not slept through the night since Ralph left me. I have not bothered much with my appearance. Yesterday, I went without deodorant, just forgot about it, until I smelled myself while measuring the size of a patient's uterus. I could tell by the alarmed expression on the patient's face that she smelled it, too.

Damn Ralph for doing this to me. Damn him for all the years I have waited, all the years I have loved him unconditionally. It is unfair, damned unfair that he has taken up with another woman. Just like that, I'm out and she's in. What did I do wrong? I pick up the phone and press the glow-in-the-dark buttons to page him, and leave my number after the beep. I have this feeling that once he tells me that he doesn't love me, I will finally be free of him. The ache will vanish forever.

My heart races, palms become sweaty as I dial and anticipate. But of course, nothing happens. The bastard hasn't the decency to call me back. Hours pass and I hate him and I love him and I want him back, desperately. I wrestle the night with Ralph constantly on my mind.

The next morning, his secretary, Angela, tells me she will give him my message, same as yesterday, and the days before that. When I phone her at noon, she gives a frustrated sigh, and I know that Angela has grown tired of giving me that same tired-ass line. Instead, she says, "He doesn't want to talk to you, Lenny."

"But, why? What have I done?" I break into tears. Poor Angela. I feel her uneasiness through the line. She says how sorry she is.

"Just tell Ralph I hate him," I whimper.

"Really?" she says, surprised.

"No, not really," I say. "Tell him to call me. It's important."

I am in bed when suddenly my pager goes off. I phone Mrs. Henderson back. She tells me her contractions are three minutes apart, and I urge her to get to the hospital. I dress in a snap, hurrying there myself. When I finally reach her, Mrs. Henderson is lying on her side in a fetal position, her face blanched as she screams at her husband and the nurse and me. The nurse yells for her to stop pushing.

"Everything's going to be all right, Mrs. Henderson," I say calmly, as her eyes close tightly. "Looks like you're ready to have a baby."

There is no acknowledgment of what I've said. Her mind goes blank while her body dances with pain. The nurse and I pull her to the end of the bed and wash her vulva with soap and water. I feel for the position of the baby's head, push apart the lips of the vulva, and see the scalp protruding through the vagina, the wrinkled skin of the vulva stretching so tight that it shines, ready to crack open.

If there is enough time, the skin around the vagina will loosen and we can avoid a large episiotomy or laceration. I try holding the baby's head inside with my fingers. Mrs. Henderson pushes against my force, crying, "I can't help it." We press against each other until finally the head thrusts forth, popping through the opening so fast that the skin rips. A tiny face peers out at the world.

"Hello, Little Chicken," I sing, using the bulb syringe to suction mucous and blood out of the nose and mouth.

The baby gasps and begins to whimper as its airways clear. Mrs. Henderson knows I'm distracted and takes full advantage; she does not try to keep from pushing. She has a contraction and shoots the baby out. I block the infant girl's descent to the floor with my knees, grabbing her slippery waist, pulling her close. I feel the baby I was to have with Ralph—dark, curly hair and creamy, brown skin. I feel the spirit enter her tiny body, away from her mother for the first time. It warms my fingers, and touches my soul.

"Mr. Henderson, you may cut the cord," I say to the new father, whose face suddenly lights up. I hand him a pair of surgical scissors, pointing out where to cut the umbilical cord, and he nervously complies. Gently, I clean away what remains of the baby's birth, swaddling her tightly in an infant's blanket.

Mrs. Henderson anxiously reaches for her new daughter and I carefully hand her over. She cuddles her baby girl to her swollen bosom. Mr. Henderson tells his wife how wonderful she is. This scene touches me deeply. The spirit of this new life hugs my heart, and I take in the natural beauty of husband, wife, and child. There is no better place to be than here, at the epicenter of creation, as a mere witness to the miracle of life, when the question of a God is answered. Yes, there is a God. There has to be. I feel better because of it, stronger, and transformed into someone bigger than a woman mourning the loss of the man who left her. Ralph is unimportant here.

12

The next morning, Karen phones before I leave for work. She has not slept well since we talked.

"I haven't slept," she says hoarsely. "I feel responsible for everything. I've missed you so much, girlfriend."

"Is that why you've called?" I ask coldly.

"Lenny, I asked Mikayla to give me your account back last night," Karen says. "It doesn't look good."

"What do you mean?" My blood burns as it courses through my body.

"He redeemed the account last Monday," she says, the stress in her voice alarming me. "He cashed in, Lenny."

I drop the phone. The weight of this news suddenly presses against my chest and I can hardly breathe. My head swells. I rush down the hall to the room Ralph used as his home office, a myriad of dreaded possibilities clogging my mind. What about all the money I've handed over to him? Once a month, like clockwork, I've forked over half my salary: sixty-four hundred after-tax dollars each month. I multiply three years and three months of figures together using the calculator on top of his desk—over two hundred and fifty-five thousand dollars invested, and now missing.

I open his desk drawers in search of information on the account—bank statements, any evidence that shows where my money might be—but the drawers are empty. His diplomas and license to practice, which had been honorably displayed, have vanished, their empty hooks left behind on the blue marble wallpaper. How long had he planned this? I rush back to the phone. Karen is calling for me.

"I want my money!" I scream hysterically.

"I know, Lenny. It's your money. You've worked too damned hard for it."

"Why'd he do this to me?"

"He's lost his mind between his legs," Karen says contemptuously. "But he won't get away with it. I'm meeting with my father this morning to discuss this mess. We'll get to the bottom of everything." She hesitates, before saying, "There's just one more thing, Lenny."

"What else!!??"

"The account was listed as Lenita Faulkner *or* Ralph Griffin. That means he didn't need your signature to legally liquidate the account."

"Damn him!" I cry, angrier with myself for being a fool. It was Ralph who had insisted that either of us have signatory over the account in case the other was unavailable for an emergency. I went along because I wanted to trust him, even though my internal red flag waved fitfully for me not to do it. I discounted the panic I felt back then as a control issue I have with regard to money, deeming it an undiagnosed paranoia of some sort, a fear of losing everything and becoming as helpless and unworthy as I had felt as a child.

"I should've had more sense," I mutter. At the time Ralph asked me to sign the papers, I had a vision of my father's change rolling around on the floor. I signed over part of my right to know because I did not want my fears to affect my relationship with Ralph. I was afraid of losing him.

"You couldn't have known he'd do this," Karen says. "Meet me for lunch today, Lenny, please. I'll know more then."

"All right. The Taj Mahal?"

"Yes, and don't worry, Lenny. Keep the faith."

Faith. I am put off by the word. I had faith that my relationship with Ralph would lead to matrimony. I had faith that Karen would carefully manage my investment account. Yet she said *faith* as if it made sense—as if somehow, this will save me in the end.

13

9:00 A.M.

Rania Amin, 47-year-old Asian female. Weight: 108 lbs. Height: 5'2". Gravida/para—1. History of present illness: ovarian cancer. Surgeries: oophorectomy and hysterectomy. Complaint: hot flashes.

"How long have you been having hot flashes, Rania?"

"Just a few months, Dr. Faulkner."

"How often?"

"It's unpredictable. Sometimes I wake up in the middle of the night soaked through. And sometimes I break into a cold sweat right after I get to work in the morning. There have been times when I've gotten so wet, I've had to go home to change clothes."

"I'll prescribe a medication that should help."

"I'm not really complaining, Dr. Faulkner. I'm grateful you found the cancer in time to save my life." She rises from her seat and places a basket of cookies on top of my desk. "I baked them last night just for you."

"Rania, you've discovered my weakness," I say, biting into one of the exotic, sweet cookies. I hum how *deeelicious* it is, and a few minutes later, I meet her in the exam room across the hall.

"Tell me something good this morning," I say gingerly, while putting on a pair of latex gloves.

"Well, Doctor, my life has a whole new outlook since the cancer," she says, wistfully. Her large, black eyes glance up at the ceiling. She takes a deep breath and relaxes. I notice that her complexion has regained its smooth maple color, made blotchy after three bouts of chemotherapy.

Kelly hands me a speculum from a warming drawer. As I glide the heated instrument into the vagina, Rania stiffens, then relaxes immediately, her feet propped into colorful kitchen mitts that shield her feet from the cold, metal stirrups.

"Nothing bothers me anymore," she says. "The hot flashes seem minor compared to almost dying. It really changed my perspective on things."

"Is that right?" I say.

"Yes, Doctor. You see, a year ago, I was worrying about the C's my daughter was making in school. Bhavna's a smart girl and I knew she could do much better. I was angry with her all the time. But then you found the cancer and that stopped me."

"How did it stop you?"

"Well, I stopped worrying about the small things. Life is worth a whole lot more when you're on the verge of losing it." Her eyes tear up as she smiles bravely at me.

"That's a lesson we can all learn from," I say.

"What about you, Doctor?" she asks, her eyes becoming bold and curious. Kelly clears her throat and checks the time on her watch.

"Me?" I ask, shrugging my shoulders.

"Do you have good news?"

I take a minute to contemplate an answer, and consider my mother's cancer, the bare walls in my house, and how much Ralph has stolen from me. "You're my best news of the day, Rania," I say.

She chuckles, and says, "Then you need a little more life, Dr. Faulkner."

11:45 A.M.

Tammy Silas, 34-year-old white female. Weight: 120 lbs. Gravida/para—2. Last normal menstrual period: February 18. Complaint: last visit palpable thyroid enlargement. History of present illness: Patient denies heart abnormalities, hyperactivity, abnormal weight loss, and insomnia. Referred Pt. to her internist for follow-up on enlarged thyroid.

"Tell me something good, Tammy," I say, making conversation to help put her at ease. The last time she was here, she refused to remove her boots. I notice a pair of running shoes in the corner, below a stool holding a neatly folded jogging suit.

"I've just gotten a divorce," she twangs nonchalantly.

"That's good?"

"Leaving Will Silas was the best thing I've done in years, Doctor. He never had time for the girls. Always had something more important to do. Always had me waiting to serve him. Now he has to take the girls every weekend. Can you imagine? I have free baby-sitting every weekend."

Tammy laughs under her breath. I feel around her neck, checking for swollen glands. On her last visit, she was showing symptoms of hyperthyroidism. I examine her eyes, the back of her tongue, her complexion, which looks healthy—an attractive peachy color, her girlish face shaped by dark, short hair. She is in excellent shape. I lean over to glance at her chart. She weighs a hundred and twenty pounds, sixty-four pounds lighter than last year.

"You've lost a dramatic amount of weight, Tammy," I say, before pulling the drape sheet above her knees. Kelly hands me a speculum. "What happened?"

Tammy smiles sheepishly, and says, "Losing a husband sure took a load off. Remember how I used to wear boots to hide my fat ankles?" She glances thoughtfully up at the ceiling. "I learned a big lesson, Doctor. Will Silas was a selfish, *demanding* son of a bitch. I don't know why I stayed as long as I did. I let him control me. I'll never let anybody do that again."

"You're not the only one learning that lesson, Tammy, believe me," I say.

"Well, I'll be damned if I ever have to learn it again."

On my way to meet Karen, I contemplate what Tammy said about her husband. My mind replays a few scenes with Ralph telling me what to do, him telling me what to wear, and how to decorate my house. Victoria's Secret was all for him. And he controlled my money. He stole it. An invisible rope coils itself around my neck, tighter and tighter as I recollect Ralph's insistence that I sell my house. I almost agreed to do it. If Ralph had asked me just once more, I would have sold my house and lost everything.

I think about my girlish *Rules for Life* and how driven I became to achieve—an eleven-year-old girl on a mission, with an ounce of tenacity. Nothing could stand in my way. What happened? What happened to the young woman who lost the size of a person off her hips? I imagine myself transforming into a lioness, the roar in me coming out, as I maneuver up Peachtree Avenue.

I hate you, Ralph Griffin! Why didn't I know who you were sooner? Why couldn't I see? My eyes sting with tears, the left lane becoming a blur. What should I have done? What can I do to keep this from happening next time, if there ever is a next time? *Ralph, you may have wasted my good years, but one of these days, you'll eat my dust, and I won't remember who you are.*

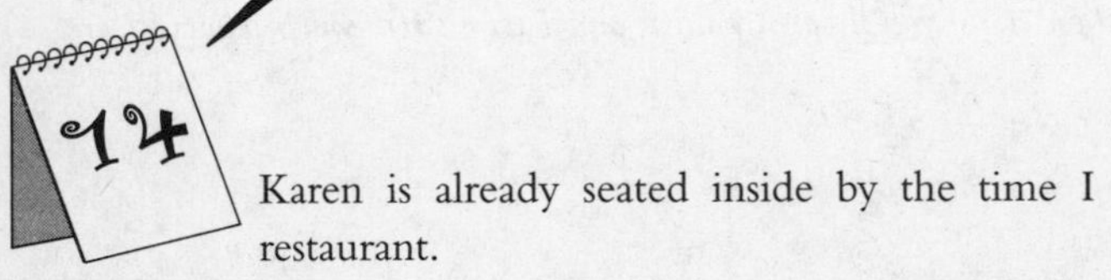

Karen is already seated inside by the time I reach the restaurant.

"I'm on my period," she whispers as soon as I sit down, glancing about to insure absolute privacy; that no one I know is in earshot. Menstruation is one of those secrets that most women keep from the public. They pretend not to have periods. I hear about periods day in and day out. Women are comfortable telling me it lasted too long, or it was too short; some say how irritable it makes them, others become too sentimental. A large number of women have severe pelvic pain, while a smaller number have no problems whatsoever. The Indian waiter plops our water glasses down on the table.

When he leaves, Karen says, "Jason wants me to get off the pill. I'm scared."

"Most women are, the first time they plan to get pregnant, Karen." I feel a pang of envy at the thought of her and Jason starting a family. In my mind's eye, Mrs. Roberts is holding me by the elbow, saying *Jealousies.* Karen's eyes swell with tears.

"I don't think we're ready for a baby yet," she cries.

"Then don't have one," I say testily. "I didn't come here to hear about babies, in case you've forgotten. I get enough of that at work. You said you have information about *my* account that I trusted you with."

Karen nods, wiping the corners of her eyes with a napkin, quavering, "You're right, Lenny. It's not about me. I have to stop being so goddamned selfish."

"Self-absorbed."

"Yes, and I want us to be best friends again."

"When hell freezes over."

Karen's eyes tear up again and she begins to sob full throttle. Immediately I regret my anger towards her.

"I didn't mean that," I say, placing my hand on hers, squeezing gently. "It's just gonna take time for me to heal from this."

"We'll get through it, won't we?" she says pitifully.

"We'll try."

We opt for the buffet and get up to select our foods, but neither of us has much of an appetite.

"You'll need to be healthy when you get pregnant, so eat, Karen."

"Ooooh, noooo," she cries.

"Calm down, Karen, breathe."

We sit, and while picking distractedly at our food, Karen reaches inside her purse and hands me a large white envelope.

"It's a record of your account activity over the past three years."

"Huh?" slips nervously from my lips as I scan down each page, making mental notes that only my paychecks were deposited each month.

"Ralph was supposed to deposit as much as he could afford," I say, feeling every bit the total idiot. "I didn't expect him to pay much the first year we lived together—not just getting out of law school. But for the past two years he's been working for Ashford, Dunwoody, and Simpson, I thought he was contributing as much as me. I assumed he had."

"Lenny, I'm sorry, I thought you knew what he earned. Jason helped Ralph get in the door of that law firm, but he had to start on the ground floor."

I stare blankly. *Up-and-coming attorney, Mr. Soon-to-be-partner*—part of me is slipping through the floor.

"This could've happened to any woman," Karen says reassuringly. "Any woman."

"How much did he make?" I choke.

"Not even a third of your salary."

"I should've known that. I should've looked at the statements. He always took care of the business end and I was satisfied with being told everything was all right."

"He's a bastard, is all," says Karen as she slaps the table with the open palm of her hand. "Don't blame yourself."

"We were together all those years. How could I not know?"

"Women are bamboozled by men more often than you think, Lenny," she says.

I notice the account value. The Newton stocks soared over the past two years, and even with the recent decline, Ralph managed to make a hefty profit. He cashed in just shy of two million dollars, without contributing a single penny.

"The check was mailed," Karen says.

"What? What did your father say this morning?"

"He's as angry as I am, girl. He says Ralph gives all men a bad name." Karen pushes her plate of half-eaten food away as if an act of defiance. "You had a joint account, Lenny. Daddy says our hands are tied. I don't know what else we can do."

"Then I'll do something," I say, fuming. "He won't get away with taking my money. I won't go down without a fight."

"We'll fight him together," Karen says as if sharpening her claws, ready to pounce. I think of a conversation I had many years ago while confined to a hospital bed, almost dead from the botched abortion I had while in college, when two dear college friends stuck by me. Laura Ruth Harris and Venita Perry kept telling me we'd get through this thing together. I was lucky to survive, lucky to have good friends. I want to trust Karen again. I have to trust her because I cannot get through this alone.

"We'll beat Ralph Griffin at his own game."

1:15 P.M.

Shaniqua Davis, prenatal visit. Weight: 176 lbs. Complaints: weight loss, nausea, and vomiting. History of present illness: prescribed medication for morning sickness on first visit.

"I'm glad you've decided to bring Shaniqua back to see me, Ms. Davis."

"I didn't know I had a choice," Ms. Davis huffs, sliding back in her seat against the wall, scowling at me. "That social worker threatened me with a court order."

Shaniqua gazes up at the ceiling, her feet shifting nervously in the stirrups.

"Turn over for a minute, please, Shaniqua," I say. "On your side, please. That's it." I examine her back and legs for more marks. The old ones have healed. "Very good. On your back, please. We're going to have a look at your baby, okay?"

"Yes ma'am, Doctor."

Kelly lifts the drape sheet and spreads a gel over Shaniqua's stomach. She flips on the ultrasound machine, and before long, I get a clear image of the fetus. I measure its head, stomach, and legs to determine whether it is growing properly.

"There, Shaniqua, take a look," I say.

"That's her?" she says.

"Well, I can't determine the sex yet, but it looks like you're carrying a thirteen-week-old fetus." I notate next to *gestation, 13 weeks.*

"I don't want no boy."

"You should've thought about that before you opened your legs," Ms. Davis snaps. "It's too late for that now. You'll get what God thinks you deserve."

"Ms. Davis, *please,*" I say.

"Nerve enough to add another mouth to feed."

"That's how she looks in real life?" Shaniqua asks, ignoring her mother's comments.

"Almost," I say.

"She's gonna have a big head like that?"

"The baby will be a little top-heavy for a while. We all start out that way. Even as toddlers, most of us look like we belong on a Charlie Brown special. Just remember, Shaniqua, as long as you take your vitamins and eat nutritiously, you shouldn't have any problems having a healthy child."

"I'm sick every morning. I can't keep nothing on my stomach. Not even the vitamins."

"There's a lot you won't like about being knocked up," Ms. Davis says. "You've made your bed hard. You didn't listen to me, so don't expect any sympathy."

I glance down at her chart and notice that I had previously prescribed medicine for her morning sickness.

"Are you taking the medicine I prescribed before or after breakfast?" I ask.

"It's my prerogative as her mother to approve any drugs you prescribe, Doctor. And I don't want her taking anything for morning sickness." Ms. Davis stands and puts her hands on her hips. She glares as if slapping me might bring her some pleasure. "Shaniqua needs to know that having a baby ain't meant to be easy. She needs to suffer so she won't be so anxious to go chasing hot and fast behind a boy again."

"Ms. Davis, please try being supportive," I say. "Besides, it's not good for her baby that she can't eat and take her vitamins. Shaniqua's lost nearly ten pounds already, when she should be gaining. You *do* want a healthy grandchild, don't you?"

Ms. Davis turns away from me, her arms crossed in stubbornness. I tell Shaniqua that peppermint tea has been known to help morning sickness. "I'll have a talk with Ms. Parker about it. I'm sure she'll find a way for you to have a cup each morning at school."

Before I leave the exam room, Ms. Davis rolls her eyes at me, and says, "I have nothing more to say to you, Doctor."

After examining patients in Rooms Two and Four, I phone Stella Parker to tell her about Shaniqua's morning sickness, that her mother is preventing her from taking medicine for it.

"I'm so angry at the power this woman holds over her daughter's head that I could scream. *Really,* Stella, the mother is as mean as a snake, and she doesn't show an ounce of affection for her daughter."

"I'll have a talk with her," Stella says. "I believe Ms. Davis wants to be a good mother. Most mothers do. She just doesn't know how."

"So it's all right for the baby to suffer?"

"No, of course not, Lenny. I'll have a talk with Ms. Davis and reason things out."

Kelly signals to me from the doorway of my office, impatiently tapping her wristwatch and mouthing the words *getting behind,* like I'm either too deaf or too dumb to know what she means.

"How about lunch next Wednesday?" I say to Stella.

"Sounds great," she says. After hanging up, I examine ten more women before my last patient of the day.

* * *

4:25 P.M.

Lula Brown, 81-year-old black female. Gravida—8, para—6. Post-menopausal. Weight: 168 lbs. Height: 5'3" Last menstrual period: 1972. Reason for visit: routine pap.

"When was the last time you and Mr. Brown got down to Possum Creek?" I ask. She giggles, bashfully holding a hand over her mouth the way Rosetta hides her missing tooth. Possum Creek is what she calls her vagina. I notice that hers is becoming dry and cracked.

"Been a long time, Doctor," she says in that West Indian singsong of hers. "Jimmy's been having trouble with his fishing pole."

I ask her if Mr. Brown has been to see a doctor about it.

"No, he tain't sick or nothin' like dat, Doctor," she says.

"There might be a medical reason as to why he can't go fishing, Mrs. Brown," I say.

"Or maybe I'm finally too old to bait da' hook," she says wearily.

"We all get old, Mrs. Brown, but never too old to bait the hook."

She giggles again.

"You get Mr. Brown to see his doctor as soon as possible, will you please, Mrs. Brown? Could be that the medication he's taking for his blood pressure is keeping the fish from jumping."

A short while later, when she is about to leave, Mrs. Brown comes up to me with her arms wide open. It's been a long day. I sink into a warm, soft hug. Old women seem to know the medicinal power of hugs. She tells me I looked like I needed one.

15

"Looks like chopped liver," says Kathleen, the surgical assistant standing next to me as I cut away at Mrs. Jackson-Miller-Tucker-Jones's scarred Fallopian tubes. She and the other assistant shake their heads in dismay that a woman with two kids would voluntarily untie her tubes for the third time because her new husband wants a son. I tell them that the patient may be unconscious, but she isn't deaf.

"Plain stupid if you ask me," says Kathleen.

"Fifty bucks says she'll never get pregnant again," says Gloria, an older, stout assistant, with a slight mustache above her upper lip. She leans over and suctions blood from the surgical field.

"Somebody turn the heat down, *please,*" I say, perspiration forming beneath my surgical cap. The new, young nurse in charge of the instruments temporarily leaves the room. The temperature cools shortly after she returns. We have been at it for over an hour.

When I have cut away as much scarred tissue as possible, I begin the process of reattaching the tubes. A half hour passes, and when the tubes are joined, I inject ink through a catheter placed inside the uterus, then test to see that it comes through the Fallopian tubes. We wait a few minutes for a minuscule amount to seep out. The uterus contracts and causes a blockage. My guess is that these tubes have already seen their last hurrah, that there won't be any sperm squeezing through this pinhole anytime soon. Gloria is probably right that Mrs. Jones will never get pregnant.

I clean up and return to my office, but before I meet with my next patient, the receptionist places a message on my desk. It is from Ralph. I imagine him standing in the doorway of his house with Mikayla, laughing at me. I phone his office and Angela tells me to hold while she transfers my call. I hold my breath and try to remain calm, so wanting him to say he is sorry. *There's been a terrible misunderstanding. I want to come home.*

Angela returns to the phone.

"I have to take a message. He had to rush to court," she says.

"Really?"

"Yes, really. This time he really does want to talk to you about . . . something. He said it's real important."

There goes that word again, that *something* that sends a chill down my back. I hang up and begin examining patients.

11:20 A.M.

Lydia Foster, 31-year-old white female, return visit. Weight: 148 lbs. Height: 5'6". Gravida/para—3. Last normal menstrual period: Birth control/pill. Complaints: foul odor. History of present illness: none.

Mrs. Lydia Foster is in Exam Room One, where a putrid odor permeates the atmosphere. Kelly, who enters ahead of me, draws up her face, muttering *damn* under her breath. She sniffs around the patient's clothes like a beagle after foxes and glances up, baffled by the pervasive stench.

"You all right, Mrs. Foster?" she asks.

"I stink down there," replies Mrs. Foster. Her bleached hair, teased high on top of her head, gives her the look of an old-fashioned country-western singer. She blushes, making her salon tan appear darker against the white paper gown draped over her body. I tell her to put her feet on the stirrups and she reluctantly complies. When she does, a funk like a dead decaying rat stings my nostrils. I slip on a surgical mask. Kelly does the same, and I lift the sheets, exposing a reddish irritation around the vulva.

"Did you use tampons during your last menstrual period?" I ask.

"No, ma'am. I use Stayfree's."

I slide on a pair of surgical gloves and insert the speculum inside the vagina, which tenses, then loosens as its delicate tissue responds to the warm, steady pressure. I peer through the speculum and notice two round objects blocking the entrance to the cervix. I can't imagine what they might be. I remove the speculum from the vagina, hand it to the nurse, and finger inside the vagina. A vision of Mikayla pops into my head and I hear her say *Pussy Doctor.* I touch two hard objects that are round and slippery. I get my thumb and third finger around one and manipulate it out, then go back inside for the other.

Two silver balls roll around in my hand.

"Mrs. Foster?" I say, bringing the balls forward so she can see them, too. "What on earth are these doing inside you?"

Blushing beet red, she says bashfully, "My husband wanted me to use them when we did it once."

"Oh, my God!" exclaims Kelly.

"Just the one time," says Mrs. Foster. "About a month or so ago."

I explain that her odor was caused by an infection she developed from having the balls inside her vagina.

"It's Mother Nature's way of telling you that things don't belong up there. If you must have . . . things in there, try not to forget them next time."

"Yes, ma'am, Dr. Faulkner."

When Kelly and I leave the exam room, she whispers, "I've never smelled anything as appalling as Mrs. Foster in my whole life, Dr. Faulkner."

"Well, I have," I say, remembering the first time I smelled Madoosa County, how I drew up my nose, hating the stench, and I consider telling Kelly what my father told me. *It's the smell of money, so get used to it.* But I don't.

When the office closes for lunch, I phone Ralph again. Angela tells me he hasn't returned from court yet. She's not sure when he'll be back, and of course, she will give him my message. I leave the office and meet Stella Parker at a café across the street.

Stella wears little makeup. From a few feet away, her skin appears to be flawless and milky-white, her overall appearance crisp and clean-scrubbed. With her short, blond curls, she resembles a Swedish dairy maid. Stella and I have been friends since my residency days. We've worked together on cases ranging from child abuse to teen runaways. She removes a manila folder from her briefcase and places it on the table next to her salad.

"I've met with Shaniqua Davis a few more times," she says, her genteel Georgian tongue like a trickling stream. She opens the file and jots down the date.

"And?"

"She swears her mother has never laid a hand on her."

"So, what now? Do we wait for something serious to happen?"

"That may very well be the case. I've seen Ms. Davis's short fuse ignite."

"I fear for the pregnancy," I say.

"I've told Shaniqua that if she's ever beaten to call me. I might be able to get her into a home for teen mothers."

"But Stella, she'd have to agree to give up her baby, wouldn't she?"

"Not officially. These agencies would never tell her that outright, though. Most of them are sponsored by adoption agencies, religious organizations, or private individuals wanting desperately to adopt. They would tell her there's no room at the inn before telling her the truth."

"Shaniqua wants to keep her baby," I say.

"Thirteen-year-olds don't know what they want, Lenny," Stella says. "If she's adamant about raising her child, I could get her into a shelter."

"A shelter's the best you can do?"

"Yes, if there's space. There's not much out there for girls who want to keep their babies. And quite frankly, I don't know that there should be. I mean, we don't want to encourage teenagers to raise children they aren't prepared to care for by themselves."

"We don't want the children of these unprepared mothers to suffer because of it."

"It's tough, Lenny. There are apartments all over the city occupied by single teen mothers who receive government assistance."

"Are most doing okay?"

"The girls I'm assigned to are inadequate as parents. They don't have a clue as to what it takes to raise a child today. How to budget the little money the government gives them so there's something left for food and diapers by the end of the month. And some children only know a few words by the time they reach two: *no, sit down, shut up,* and *stop it.*" Stella takes a bite of her salad and stares gravely into space while she chews.

"Aren't there classes these girls can take?" I ask.

"There aren't enough qualified nurses to teach them."

"So the best Shaniqua might hope for is a shelter?"

"Where her emotional needs will not be met and questions she might have about her body won't be answered sufficiently. You won't find nurses at the shelters, believe me." Stella retrieves a pen from her purse, and asks, "You didn't happen to notice any outright signs of abuse during Shaniqua's last visit, did you?"

"No," I say. Stella makes a few notes in Shaniqua's record.

"It's a shame," she says ruefully, slipping the envelope back in her brief case. "There's no place a girl like Shaniqua can go to get the support she really needs."

"A place," I say, thinking about my own grim search years ago that brought me to the end of my rope, when I plunged the end of a coat hanger deep inside my womb, coming within seconds of death.

"I wish there was at least one place in all of Atlanta that provided the kind of support girls who want to keep their babies need with sufficient parenting classes, among other things. A model home that shows all the others how to do it right."

"A place," I repeat, wishing I had enough money to start a home for girls like Shaniqua. I think about all the money Ralph took and invested. How rich he has become at my expense. When I finally face him, eye to eye, and in a place inconvenient for him to escape, I will demand my share. I consider the message he left, and the *something* he wants to discuss with me. *Something,* perhaps, that I desperately wanted to hear before he left. Or maybe he wants to be fair after all.

16

4:20 P.M.

Linda Jenkins: 19-year-old white female, return visit. Gestation: 34 weeks. Weight: 149 pounds. Urine and blood pressure: normal. Size of womb: normal. Complaint: lack of sleep, lack of enthusiasm for her unborn child. No provisions made for the baby's homecoming, undecided about whether to place baby for adoption. Indication: depression.

After examining Linda Jenkins, I ask her how things are going. She gives a woeful shake of her head and says, "Not good at all. Everyone treats me like I'm a pariah, or something. I'm the same on the inside. No one wants to see the real me because of this thing growing inside me."

"Your child," I say, attempting to encourage Linda into thinking of her baby as a living being.

"I just want things the way they were, Dr. Faulkner. Before Randy abandoned me and his child. He walked off into the sunset while I'm stuck carrying something I don't want anymore."

"You're not stuck, Linda. You have options." I remind Linda of the card I gave her during her first visit, when she wanted an abortion and was too far gone for me to help her. "There are people lined up behind every baby who needs a home. Stella Parker can help you find a couple you'll like."

"So I can worry about her for the rest of my life, always wondering if I've done the right thing." Linda's face reddens as she sucks air and swallows as if holding back what else she has to say. "No thanks, Dr. Faulkner. I'm stuck, and there's nothing more to it."

"Well, I hope you make peace with your decision before the baby comes, Linda."

It is a quarter to five when I finish examining Linda Jenkins. Kelly hands me a message before she leaves. She is in a pleasant mood. We finished on time today. I head for my office to read the message from Ralph requesting I meet him at the North Wilshire Club around seven o'clock. A feeling of hope scatters my sensibilities. I race home to freshen up and change into the best of what I can find: a tight, black dress cut a few inches above my knees, sheer black stockings, and a pair of spike heels.

The doorbell rings, and I squint through the peephole at my neighbor, Mrs. Stein, standing on the porch holding a letter in her hand. She waves the letter in the air before I open the door.

"Something has to be done about that dimwit who keeps giving me your mail," she croaks. "Postmen were dependable in my day, through rain, snow, sleet, or shine."

"Yes, ma'am, they were," I say, eyeing the letter.

"This afternoon, I saw the young man who used to live here."

She knows Ralph has moved out. She probably watched him through her bedroom window, the day he came to haul his things away.

"He came by and asked me if I had any of his mail." She studies my face. "He knocked on my door and scared me to death. I told him I didn't have anything that belonged to him. I told him I had in mind to call the police. This letter here," she says, handing me the envelope, "has your name on it, Dr. Faulkner, not his."

"You're right, Mrs. Stein, and thank you," I say. She casts her eyes up and down the length of me, staring uncomfortably long at the shortness of my skirt. I strain to smile when she looks up at me again.

"I think I'd change my locks if I were you," she says. "He would've gotten inside your house if I hadn't stood in my doorway watching him, I'm sure of it."

"Thanks for your advice, Mrs. Stein," I say, getting annoyed. The last thing I need tonight is a nosey, old neighbor telling me what to do. I watch her slowly descend the steps of my porch and vanish into the shadows of the frigid evening. I close the door and glance briefly at the envelope, before tossing it onto the kitchen counter with the rest of today's mail.

On the way to the club, I get a page from the hospital and pull onto the shoulder of the interstate to answer it. A nurse informs me that I have a patient in labor. I remind her that Dr. Waxler is on call. She says the patient specifically requested me. I ask for the particulars on the patient: How many centimeters dilated? The fetal heart rate? Blood pressure? I ask for the position of the baby's head. The nurse can only tell me about the patient being three centimeters dilated. She had not fully examined the patient, which pisses me off to no end. I wait for her to verify that the fetal monitor strip is normal.

"You're new at this, aren't you?" I ask tersely.

"Yes," she quavers. "It's my first day on the job."

"Another doctor would've blasted you for this," I say. "So be prepared next time. Finish examining the patient, then call if there's a problem."

After hanging up, I arrive at the club twenty minutes late. The auburn-haired receptionist trills, "Can I help you, ma'am?"

I inform her that I am here to meet Ralph Griffin. "Is he waiting for me in the bar?"

"Mr. Griffin left a while ago," she says, smiling politely. "You're Dr. Faulkner?"

"Yes," I choke out.

"He asked me to give you this." The receptionist hands me a note.

Lenny,

You're late, as usual. I'm not surprised. This habit of yours is the reason I left. You take my time for granted. I can't be with a woman whose work is more important than our relationship.

Ralph

My face feels brutally slapped and anger burns like simmering coals that settle in the pit of my stomach. Ralph had no intention of meeting me tonight. He's tricked me once again. I dressed and rushed out here to be made a fool, jerked around like a love-starved puppy on a leash. He called, and I jumped at the opportunity to see him. Just like that, I forgot all about my *Rules for Life:* 1. I will not allow myself to be controlled by anyone. What good are rules if I'm not going to remember to abide by them?

"He didn't stay very long, ma'am," the receptionist says. I scan the lobby for the slightest clue that Ralph might still be here. Maybe he watches me from a dark corner, quietly amused. My blood turns to fire, ravaging my soul. I hate Ralph truly. I'm all at once consumed by enough hatred to kill him. I imagine myself turning into a hungry, vicious Doberman with teeth as sharp as razors, and the expression on Ralph's face when he sees that I am prepared to chomp into his behind turns frightful. I smell blood. His eyes bulge and he takes off, and I run after him, faster and faster. He won't get the better of me again. I hate him so. I won't be the fool next time.

I smell Ralph's scent in the kitchen as soon as I arrive home, where my mail has been rummaged through and scattered carelessly about on the floor. He trampled through like a horse crossing a muddy puddle. Ralph is a callous, self-centered, egotistical coward. Wish I had caught him here.

I notice that the refrigerator was left partially open. There are a few drops of beer leading to the back door, proof that he was in a hurry. I pick up mail from the floor, from various spots along the countertop, the stove. Nothing seems to have been opened. I wonder what he's looking for.

I open the envelope Mrs. Stein delivered tonight, which happens to be my credit-card statement. The hairs rise on the back of my neck as I study it. Just when I am beginning to believe matters can get no worse, *Whammo!* I'm smacked broadside once again.

My knees go weak at the sight of a tremendous, mind-blowing balance, fifty-seven thousand dollars and change, and a minimum payment the size of a monthly mortgage. I flop into the nearest chair. This cannot be right. I rarely ever use credit. It simply goes against my nature. I glance down the list of recent purchases and notice jewelry bought in places Ralph traveled to last month, when he had a so-called business trip, prior to his leaving me—gifts I never received. And to top it all off, the brazen coward bought tickets for two to Switzerland.

I imagine myself standing on a railroad track, frozen in place at the sight of a train steadily heading my way. My heart races wildly. The train whistles eerily into the night. I am alone in this world. Here and not here.

17

I phone the credit card company to cancel my card, then change into my winter jogging suit, and head out into the frosty night air, my breath unsteadied by rage and fear. *I will get through this* becomes my mantra as I sprint like a spastic antelope down the path running parallel to the road. After a mile or so, I break into my stride, churning at a swift, steady pace.

The chill disappears and I'm at the summit. I could stay here forever, all night long. I check my watch when I reach five miles from home. It is after ten o'clock. I turn around to head back. My ankles begin to ache, so I walk. I walk quite a ways down Peachtree, past shops and hotels, past trendy, new restaurants. I find myself wondering how many times my credit card was used around here. What did I buy Mikayla from this shop, or that jeweler?

Once home, I shower and wash my hair, change into flannel pajamas, the kind Ralph hates and ridicules as frumpy. My hair dries into soft ringlets that shape my face and hang to my shoulders. If Ralph were here, I would've spent an hour getting ready for bed, blow drying and straightening my hair, pampering my face and body with fancy concoctions that soften and sweeten my skin. More hours wasted trying to please. In the morning, I'll phone a locksmith and have new locks installed.

I slide into bed and open *The Promise of Spring* to where Charles Crow helps Clarissa and her daughter manage the ranch she has inherited, mending fences, roping steer, and driving cattle to and from Clearwater Pond, on the other side of which lives her enemy, Angus Adams, the man who lusts after her land. Clarissa and Charles Crow make love for the first time, at night, in a field of clover, where fireflies twinkle like stars overhead. I set the book on my nightstand, turn off the light, and stare blankly at the pitch blackness. *Is this all there will ever be?*

I reflect upon the past nine years, critical mating years, now wasted years that can never be recaptured—I was twenty-five when I met Ralph, a senior in medical school, when I thought I had all the time in the world to think about marriage and babies. In my mind's eye, I am waltzing around the last chair in the single women's game, feeling the desperation of other single women around me, each of us expecting the music to stop at any minute. We are waiting for Mr. Right, the Charles Crows of the world to come along and rescue us from living alone. We are waiting for our real lives to begin.

He's after one thang. My mother's voice crashes into my thoughts like a thunderous downpour. *Never trusted him. Sneaky eyes.* My stomach tightens. I should have known the real Ralph. I should have learned his income before he moved in with me, that he spent well beyond his means. Why was I so afraid to ask the tough questions? Why didn't I demand to know more? Ralph was a handsome, debonair man whose sweet nothings took possession of my heart from the start, his true nature invisible to me, as cunning as a cat tracking its prey. I saw what I wanted to see in him, heard what I wanted to hear. When Ralph told me I was pretty, I believed it meant he loved me.

I turn on the light, retrieve the diary from my nightstand, and write under today's date:

I tried to be what Ralph wanted me to be. I changed everything about myself to please him. Everything. What happened to the little girl who won the spelling bee? The young woman who lost over a hundred pounds? The good doctor who wanted to reach the top of Kilimanjaro? What happened to me? I forgot what made me, me.

I am Dr. Lenita Faulkner, a woman who can dare to ask the tough questions, take chances, and accomplish her goals.

I flip forward to the note page where I am starting my new *Rules for Life* and add

Rule 2.

I will only change to suit myself.

18

The phone rings. I answer holding my breath, afraid of hearing Ralph's voice.

"Finally. I been trying to call you all morning."

"Bobby?"

"Yeah, I'm on my way with Mama," Bobby says as if about to deliver a truckload of firewood. I am relieved to hear his voice. "I need directions to your house."

I give Bobby directions, and after we hang up, my heart sinks. I think of how sick Mama is, that she is not long for this world. I fill with regret over not visiting her more often, and for lacking the capacity to eliminate her suffering.

Here I am, a doctor, trained to treat and cure, expected to always be able to do it; yet, there is nothing I can do to save my mother. She is a woeful-looking figure, growing steadily weaker, a mere shadow of the strong, big-boned woman she once was. Perhaps, had I borne a child by now I would feel less guilty. Mama would have another grandchild to feel blessed about.

I hop out of bed and begin to clean the house for Mama's arrival. I vacuum and dust and polish. I do laundry and wash the dishes that are piled high in the kitchen sink, and when I'm done with that, I mop the tile floors here and in the two bathrooms. The guest bath had belonged to Ralph. I notice he took a collection of fluffy white towels that we both favored. It is useless to wonder why he bothered with those, considering all the other things he plundered from the house.

I clean the toilet bowls and sinks, scrubbing away the remains of

Ralph's last shave. He left his prized marble-handled razor next to a bottle of aftershave. I think of him a month ago, one morning before shaving, his stubble pricking my cheeks and neck, as he loved me inch by inch, tickling. He laughed because I laughed, and giddiness gave way to goose bumps all over my body. I drop the razor in the trash can, wondering how much it cost me, how much he audaciously charged to my credit-card account to have the very best, my mind racing between the scene in our bed, a foreplay of carefree laughter, to the scene at the Purple Peach, his cowardliness, my heartache, a note saying it is over. How long ago had Ralph planned to cheat me? A year ago? Or was it three years ago, when he first moved into my house? *My house.* I wipe the mirror clean until I see myself undeniably clear. *I will get through this. I will get through this. I will get through this.* I roll clean, white, less-expensive towels to place inside the built-in shelf next to the tub. *I will get through this.*

The framed prints and paintings I had stored in the attic, the ones hung in the house before Ralph moved in with me—the ones he said had no style—I use to cover the light bare spots perfectly well. I hang the picture of our family, before Joe died, over a bare hook in Ralph's office.

A thought occurs to me as I begin to dust the furniture in this room, my bedroom before Ralph moved in: It is larger than the space Ralph and I shared, and far more appealing. He needed the extra space to accommodate his things—a king-size bed taking up the middle of the room, the antique armoire with a twenty-four-inch television set stored inside it, a large bookshelf loaded with law books, and an enormous oak desk sitting conspicuously in front of a pair of French doors.

I polish the oak desk, remembering the day Ralph and me made love on top of it, when he was passionate and easily aroused. I was a distraction, he had said, and I was foolishly flattered. I complied with his request for the extra space by moving my things to another, smaller bedroom. I stored my desk and bookshelf in a room the size of a closet.

My dust rag becomes a weapon, each stroke wiping clean a place he may have touched. I know he brought *her* here. I imagine Mikayla's face, her big, pearly teeth and long, luxuriant hair, and I yank the bed sheets off, replacing them with fresh, clean, lemon-scented ones. Shortly after two o'clock, I phone Karen to commiserate about Ralph's latest crime against me.

"He ran my credit card up to the max," I say, boiling over it.

"I'm coming over," Karen says, and quickly adds, "There's something I have to tell you that can't wait."

"What is it now?" I say, dreading more bad news.

"Jason and a friend are in the kitchen right now, Mother. We're about to have breakfast together, so I'll see you in about an hour?"

"Ralph's there, isn't he?"

"Yes, Mother, that sounds like a very good idea."

"Ask him why he's done this to me."

"Can't just now, Mother."

"Ask him how he's able to live with himself."

"Not now."

"Then tell him he's messed over the wrong woman this time."

"Good-bye, Mother."

The doorbell rings. I hurriedly put away my cleansers and wash my hands before racing to open the front door.

"It's 'bout time," says Bobby.

"The wind cuts right through the bones up here," says Mama hoarsely as she totters inside the house, glancing wearily about as I help her out of her overcoat. She *tap-taps* her cane next to me as I guide her from the tiny foyer to the den.

"Real nice place you got here," she says, sitting down on the sofa.

"Thanks, Mama, I want you to feel at home."

"Aaaahh, haaa."

"Can I get you anything to drink?"

"Naw, nothing for me."

Bobby removes his jacket, tosses it onto a chair, and picks up the remote control. He sits next to Mama and turns to a basketball game.

"What you got decent to drink?" he says.

"Juice, milk, tea, coffee . . . a few beers."

"Beer sounds about right," he says matter-of-factly.

"Mama, can I get you anything?" I say. Mama coughs and spits into her stained handkerchief, catches her breath, and shakes her head no. She grimaces through the pain swelling the cavity of her chest, a hand clutching between her absent breasts.

"No, nothing," she says. Mama seems thinner since I last saw her. She squints her eyes, looks above my forehead, and says, "What happened to your hair?"

"I'm trying a new natural style, Mama," I say, patting my chemically relaxed air-dried hair. "It's easier to wear. I just wash and go. Lots of models wear their hair like this in the fashion magazines."

"Ah, huh," she says like she doesn't believe me. "I liked it better the way it was."

"Wanna lie down, Mama?" I say, not wanting to hear another negative comment about my hair.

"Lord, yes," Mama sighs, eyeing my new 'do with suspicion. She has no idea how many compliments I've gotten from patients and other doctors, people of all sexes and colors, some who can't help touching it to see how soft it is. Mama will probably never understand what it feels like for me to finally appreciate the natural tendencies of my hair. She might die convinced it's just plain ugly.

I help her ease onto the king-size bed in the guest room and elevate her head on two soft pillows. I think about my Indian patient, Rania Amin, dying of ovarian cancer when her perspective changed. "Nothing bothers me anymore," she had said. I try to remember how serene she was when she said it. But I find myself thinking about Ralph and how much I hate him, how much I want him to suffer.

When Karen arrives I introduce her to Bobby, now laid back on the sofa like he owns it. She extends her hand, and Bobby, being the consummate country bumpkin, gives her an empty beer bottle and says thank you.

"Nice meeting you too, Karen," he adds, guilelessly. "Bring me another cold one, will you?" Bobby places his hands on his large, round belly, returning his attention to the television. Karen's smile flattens, her eyes widen as she stares at the bottle I remove from her slender fingers, telling her to pay him no mind.

"He was born a pig," I say.

She laughs as if relieved and we retreat to the kitchen. I sit across the table from her.

"How's your mother, Lenny?" she asks.

"She's here now, to live until she dies. Bobby brought her a little while ago."

"I'm so sorry, Lenny. How terrible for you," she says regretfully, "with everything else you're going through."

"It certainly can't get any worse."

Pensiveness shadows Karen's face, when she says, "Ralph came over last night."

"With her?"

Karen nods yes. "It was awful. I told Jason I don't want them in my house. They aren't welcome. I said if they stay, I go."

"What happened?"

"You called me at home this morning, didn't you?"

"Yeah, but Ralph was there, too."

"He came over with some lame excuse about needing to talk to Jason about a case."

Bobby enters the kitchen in search of more beer. I point him to the refrigerator and he stands with it open, cooling the entire kitchen while poking around inside, humming ludicrously, finally yelping, "Yessah, yessahree bub."

After he gets another bottle and leaves the kitchen, Karen says what she came to tell me.

"Ralph hasn't cashed the check, yet," she says. "It was mailed here. My dimwit cousin forgot to change the address in the system when she liquidated the account. The check should've arrived a few days ago."

"So that's what he's looking for," I say.

"Ralph was here?"

"He went through my mail last night, pretending he wanted to meet me at the country club. I was there while he was here."

"God, he's lower than a snake."

"He didn't find anything, though."

"He didn't?"

"My mail was at my neighbor's house by mistake."

"Did you get anything from our office?"

"I don't think so." Immediately, I go to the stack of envelopes on my countertop and carefully shuffle through them. "No, nothing's here."

"Well, you've got until Monday morning to find it," Karen says, excitedly.

"Why Monday morning?"

"If you don't deposit it first thing Monday morning, the check will be canceled. Mikayla requested that a new one be reissued to their new address."

"But it's my money."

"I know," Karen says, "but to get the money back you'll have to prove he set you up and intended to steal it."

"That's exactly what he did, isn't it? I should sue him."

"Lenny, a case like this could drag on for years."

"I don't care how long it takes. It's my money." I slump into my chair across from Karen.

"I'm with you, Lenny. If you wanna sue Ralph, fine. Let's do it."

My head begins to throb as I glance down at the balance on my credit-card statement. I feel stupid, and stupider. "God, I hate him so much, Karen. He charged over fifty thousand dollars on my credit card."

"He what?" I slide the statement across the table and allow her to see for herself. Karen's mouth forms an empty hole. "How, Lenny? How?"

"When Ralph first moved in with me, I ordered an extra card in his name."

"Oh, no. You didn't."

"It seemed logical at the time," I say, defensively. "Ralph did all the shopping. I thought he divided the expenses every month and paid off the charges. Of course, now I know he didn't earn that kind of money."

Karen taps her bottom lip with her finger, and shakes her head in utter dismay. "This is unbelievable. Well, if it makes you feel any better, my father fired Mikayla before she left the office Friday."

"Not a second too soon."

"Don't worry, Lenny, we'll find that check."

"Well, it's not here," I sigh, shrugging my shoulders. "Just nuisance mail and a few bills. One envelope is addressed to a neighbor I've never met. Kevin Ellison."

"Kevin Ellison?" Karen repeats, puzzled. "Any chance he might have your mail?"

"There's only one way to find out."

We walk past a few houses up Valemont Street until we come to a gray, tidy-looking, two-story Cape Cod, complete with a white picket fence. I imagine a perfect family living here—a wife and two children, a boy and girl. A waft of frosty air whips through our hair and across our faces; we walk faster to the front door. Karen rings the doorbell.

The door opens and standing inside is an incredibly handsome man, the color of Melba toast, his short hair dark mixed with specks of gray. He wears a knit top and a pair of jeans that fit with precision over his muscular frame, and his dark penetrating eyes startle me when he glances from Karen to me.

"Are you Kevin Ellison?" I ask.

"Yes, that's me," he says, eyeing the envelope in my hand.

"Then this belongs to you," I say.

He smiles, and says, "Thank you very much." Karen nudges me in the back. I am afraid to open my mouth again. I don't know what to say.

"My friend here, Lenny, is looking for mail of her own," Karen blurts out. "She thought you might have gotten hers by mistake."

"Well, I've been out of town for a while. It's possible I have it."

He opens the door wider. "Please come in."

I take a look around. The furniture in the living room is nice, masculine, with black-and-white framed prints on army green walls. A black leather sofa stands out in the center of the floor, a lacquered baby grand piano shoots out of a corner. A single red silk orchid sits majestically in a slender glass vase on a glass table by the window.

He puts the mail down, and shrugs—nothing.

"Thanks anyway," I say. "I hope it wasn't too much trouble."

"No trouble at all. I've seen you run past my house a few times," he says. "I've wanted to meet you." His eyes narrow handsomely as he stares deeply into mine. I look away to the red orchid. "Lenny, it's been a pleasure." He extends his hand, giving mine a warm, friendly squeeze. I retract from his touch. It reminds me of Ralph and the money he stole from me, the reason I am here.

"We'd better be going," I say abruptly.

"I run myself, sometimes," he says, turning his head toward the window. I admire his profile; he has the nose and bone structure of a Greek god.

"The only running I do is to my car when it rains," Karen says. He smiles without taking his eyes off me.

"Would you go jogging with me in the morning and maybe grab a cup of coffee afterward?" he says.

"I'd love to," I say, without hesitation.

"Well, that's wonderful. How about eight o'clock?"

"Fine."

I attempt to exit the front door, but it jams, and he reaches around me to firmly pull it open. I catch a faint whiff of his cologne, the scent of flora along a path that winds through the woods on a warm spring afternoon. I am almost afraid to smell more of him.

Once outside, Karen nudges me harder in the back.

"You don't waste any time," she says.

"We're running. Big deal."

"I hope Ralph sees you with that beautiful man."

"Karen, please," I say, only mildly objecting. Nothing would please me more than for Ralph to see that I am over him.

By the time we reach my house, a man is ringing the doorbell. He turns to watch us as we amble up the driveway. Clumps of brilliant reddish brown tendrils peek out from beneath his dark cap. He uses a white envelope to shade his eyes against the sun.

"May I help you?" I say a few feet away.

"Does Lenita M. Faulkner or Ralph R. Griffin live here?" he asks, bringing his hand down to his side. He sports a poorly managed beard, patchy reddish-brown hair that drapes past his chin.

"I'm Dr. Faulkner," I say, taking a few cautious steps forward, Karen following close behind. He steps down from the porch and meets us halfway. I panic at the officiousness of his tone, wondering what other evil Ralph may have committed in my name. Bill collector? The IRS? FBI? The visitor looks from Karen and then to me. Oddly handsome, the eyes.

"I'm finally at the right place," he says, breaking into a soft chuckle like a boy trapped inside a man's body—a man's voice and sad puppy-dog eyes.

"Right place?" I stare into those deep, dark eyes curiously.

"I read the address wrong a little while ago and wound up at a house a mile down the road," he says. "There's no house number on your mailbox, Doctor."

"Why are you looking for me, sir?"

"Well, Dr. Faulkner, I received this letter in the mail a few days ago."

He hands me the envelope posted from Karen's brokerage firm and says, "I'm sorry for not delivering it sooner."

"That's it!" Karen squeals excitedly.

"Oh, my God, I think so," I say, nervously. I read the sender's name aloud, needing to hear it, "J. W. Roberts and Associates."

"That's it!" Karen squeals louder. We hug each other tightly, bursting with the thrill of victory, a jumping dance in place.

"This is it!"

"I can't believe it," Karen trills.

"There is justice in the world." I hold the envelope against my chest. The neighbor man says something we do not hear, and turns to leave.

"Oh, thank you . . . er . . . Mister . . . er," I say, unsure.

"Ernest Hemingway," he says, stopping.

"You're a real person?" I ask, astonished, recollecting the letter that erroneously came to my house addressed to him months ago, the letter Mrs. Stein later delivered. "I mean, your name is really Ernest Hemingway?"

"The last I checked," he says, smiling.

"I'm Karen Roberts-Ashby," Karen says, extending her hand to shake his. "What name did your mother give you?"

"Ernest Hemingway," he says matter-of-factly. "It's true, though no one ever believes me."

"But why?" Karen asks, as if there has to be a reason worth further exploration, a point to his name.

"I suppose she wanted me to aspire to become like the great man himself."

"Are you?" I say.

"No, unfortunately. I teach high-school English."

"Your mother was close enough," I say. "The two disciplines go hand in hand, don't they?"

"Not necessarily," he says, lifting his brows, his amiable smile vanishing like a flame blown from a candle. There is mystery behind his eyes. Looking into them is like diving into a lake at night when the air turns ominously wet and chilly. There is much more to Ernest Hemingway than can be seen. Still waters.

"Thanks for bringing this letter," I say. "It means a lot."

"Glad I could help," he says, pulling a pair of leather gloves from his pocket. His hands are more rugged than one would expect of a teacher, dry and slightly weathered, with calluses on each knuckle. Working man's hands, like my father used to have. More mystery. He slides his hands inside his gloves and says, "Have a nice day, ladies."

"Good-bye, Ernest Hemingway," Karen and I say in unison, watching him leave.

"The money!" Karen trills, now beside herself with an urge to actually see the check. We race inside the house to the kitchen, and I rip open the envelope and pull out the check, laying eyes on my new fortune.

"One million, seven-hundred, fifty-two thousand dollars . . . Is this true? Is this right? It's mine? My God, Karen! All mine!" I hold the envelope to my chest, dazed. "Karen?"

"All yours, girlfriend, let's celebrate this momentous occasion in style," Karen says. She retrieves a bottle of champagne from the pantry, pops the cork, and fills two wineglasses. "Here's to my newest millionaire client and best friend."

"Oh, Karen, I can't believe it. What a roller coaster we've been on today. I feel like I've just been given my life back."

"And what a life it's going to be, Lenny, ol' girl."

19

I leave the house to meet Kevin Ellison this morning. He smiles when he sees me coming up the road.

"You remind me of a schoolgirl," he says, examining my hair with an amused glint in his eyes, a giant puffball bound by a band in back of my head.

"Haven't heard that line before." I laugh lightheartedly.

"I don't do lines," he says calmly, bending and stretching his legs. I stretch my hamstrings, wondering what it would be like to be bundled in his arms. We jog slowly at first and pick up speed at the parallel road. Near the end of our run, where the path meets Peachtree, he asks, "Ready for a coffee break?"

"I can't this morning," I say, briefly explaining my situation with Mama, her cancer; that Bobby is returning to Madoosa County. "I don't want to leave her home alone this morning."

"I understand," he says softly, giving me a look that undoes me completely as we walk down Valemont Street. His arm casually brushes against me. When I trip over a crack in the sidewalk, he catches me against his strong body, his arm light around my waist, my heart beating so loud I can hear it.

"Can we do this again sometime?" he asks, pausing momentarily in front of my house.

I nod yes, my voice stuck in back of my throat.

"Until next time, then," he says.

I nod yes, and wave, speechless. Kevin walks like a surefooted panther, in long, steady strides, as in the description of Charles Crow in *The*

Promise of Spring; and I am Clarissa Montgomery, an independent, adventurous woman, afraid of falling in love again.

Bobby is standing in the middle of the kitchen drinking a small glass of orange juice. His clothes are wrinkled from sleeping in them overnight, his face unshaven, and hair matted to the sides of his head.

"Time to hit the road," he says, reaching inside his pocket to pull out his wallet, which he immediately opens to find himself coming up short.

"Took more 'n I thought to bring Mama all the way up 'ere," he says. "Gas ain't cheap. I needs some mo' cash to get back."

I ask how much he needs and he looks up at the ceiling, mumbling a series of figures as if he's got a computer stuck up inside that half-empty brain of his, finally saying, "Three hundred dollars."

"Three hundred dollars?" I say incredulously.

"Wit the cost of gas so high 'round here. Plus my tires is worn down in front. . . . I mo' have to git new ones on the way home."

I consider my newfound wealth in judging the precariousness of my brother's circumstances. Bobby will never change. He's a natural-born taker. I decide to help him once again; same as I have done since he was a boy. He drives me to an ATM a few blocks away. When I stop to get the money, he rolls down his window and tells me five hundred would be better in case of an emergency. I pretend I don't hear him. I attempt to withdraw enough money for Bobby's trip home, but my request is declined for insufficient funds.

I check and double-check the balance of fifty-two dollars. There should be thousands in this account. I feel like another of my buttons has just been pushed and all the crap I've endured for the past few weeks comes flooding back: the cowardly note Ralph left me, all the things given as gifts and taken away, betrayal, cheating, the credit card, and now, money from my checking account missing. I kick the machine and hurt my big toe, right away seething with pain. *Holy crap.* I curse myself out for being such an idiot. Hit my head on the glass wall when I bend over to rub the sore spot on my foot. *Bastard.* I take a few long breaths before exiting the booth with only fifty dollars and a balance slip in hand.

"Sorry, Bobby," I say, embarrassed. "Looks like somebody beat me to it."

"What d'ya mean? Somebody done took yo' money?"

I imagine Ralph leaning back on the sofa with his arm extended for me to fetch him a beer. He uses the other hand to push buttons on the remote control. I rush to the kitchen and grab a cold one on a warm, sunny afternoon. He reaches and I pour it over his head, his mouth opening with beer suds dripping down his face, down his pristine white shirt, his designer tie, his tailored suit.

The caught-napping expression on his face causes me to suddenly burst into laughter. I'm standing here, outside of an ATM booth after finding out I've been robbed, and I can't stop laughing. Bobby scratches his forehead and eyes me suspiciously. He says, "Did whoever it was take a lot?"

"Almost all of it," I say, a giggle tickling the back of my throat.

"How much is almost?" he says, and when I say what's left, Bobby tells me he'll take it. He gets out of his car and reaches for the last of my checking account without an ounce of concern for me. He snatches the fifty and hops into his car.

"You gonna be fine walkin' back to yo' house, won't you 'Nita Mae?" he asks selfishly. "And tell Mama bye for me. I'll keep in touch."

"Why don't you tell her yourself?" I say. He revs his engine.

"Naw, I can't stand seeing Mama suffer no mo'," he says, closing his door, waving a hand before taking off without a final farewell to Mama, the woman who brought him into the world, fed him, and changed his dirty diapers. He drives off as if her suffering would be made less by his immediate absence. Bobby is a selfish man, in the same bastard league as Ralph. My father's tall, thin sister, Aunt Cleo, the woman I resemble most, accused my mother of spoiling him rotten when he was a boy, especially after Joe died. She told Mama, "You'll have a mess on your hands when he grows up with his feet still planted under your supper table."

I watch his car disappear around the next corner and I turn to jog back home. I will not miss seeing my brother after Mama dies. When her body is burned and the ashes buried in the same plot with my father, I doubt that I will visit him or my sister again. I feel emotionally drained when I'm around them, with all their negative tales spinning like spider webs through the air, trapping me like a fly before I'm eaten alive. We have nothing in common; our worlds are completely different. Even their language is becoming foreign to me. I am the First National Bank to Bobby and Rosetta, and to me, they are people I have been obligated to endure.

* * *

Mama is propped up in bed listening to gospel music on the radio. She strains her frail vocal chords, humming. I sit at the edge of the bed and wait for the song to end.

"Bobby's gone, Mama. He told me to tell you good-bye."

"I hope you didn't give him no money."

"A little," I say, hesitantly.

"I give that boy plenty before we come up 'ere, 'Nita. He was born holding his hands out to the world," she asserts, in the same way she said Joe was born to do something important, Rosetta was born pretty, and I was born ugly but smart. Mama struggles to clear her throat, wretchedly hacking as if the walls of her chest were filled only with dust and little air. She spits into the stained handkerchief kept next to a growing collection of used and unused cloths.

"Bobby's to get my life insurance after I'm gone. I give Rosetta the house." Mama's hand pats her chest as if drumming a rhythm twirling around in her head; her dark, doleful eyes stare blankly. I think of all I've done for her over the years, the money I've sent home, the clothes and jewelry I've bought, the new house I offered to buy her after her second mastectomy. Despite all my doings, I am still the child overlooked, the one expected to fend for herself, the girl with hand-me-downs instead of new, the teenager who walked instead of getting a car, the ugly one who needed to be smart, the smart one who never needed as much as the pretty one.

"Your brother and sister ain't ne'er satisfied," Mama says, coughing mucous and blood into another handkerchief. "Thank God for giving me my grands. Having my grandbabies is worth more than all the money in the world. They's the future."

"What about me, Mama?"

Mama gazes discerningly at the top of my head. "When you was born, I took one look at them tight little curls and said, 'Lawd, that child's gonna have some bad hair.' Used to take forever to braid that stuff ever' morning. Ne'er did think it'd grow past your shoulders, long like it does when you wear it straight. I likes it better straight."

My brain splits in half. Mama convulses out a nasty chuckle. She is an ignorant woman, born of ignorant people, been ignorant all her life, and simply cannot change. She won't change. I have learned to listen for what she means and dismiss half of what she says because she does not know when she is being insulting, and absolutely intends no harm. Still, it hurts like hell to be the lesser child.

"You'll die, Mama, and you won't know who I am," I say.

"Did I say something wrong?" Mama says, mindful that a sobering silence has swept over me. " 'Cause you know I ain't never meant to hurt nobody, 'Nita."

"I know that, Mama. It's just that if I were dying, the last thing I'd want to leave my daughter with is how bad her hair used to be."

"Well I kinda likes what you done to your hair, anyway."

"Thanks, Mama, but it's not about my hair."

"You gets used to it after a while, I reckon."

"I reckon," I say resentfully, though fully aware that it is useless to be offended by Mama, like holding a grudge against the wind, rain, or any other natural element. I twiddle my fingers through the tangled tendrils of my hair, rubbing a lock of it against my cheek. My attention shifts to the picture of our family on the wall next to the bed, a few feet away. Sadness comes over me when I think back to the day it was taken. I feel Mama's eyes bore past me, each breath expiring more audibly.

"Why did I have to pick strawberries so young?" I ask.

"We needed the money and I wanted you to learns to work hard."

"Why not Rosetta? She was the eldest?"

"She weren't dependable as you," Mama says, "Rosetta was better at cookin' and housework."

"My knees used to kill me."

"Your daddy's back hurt like the dickens, but he never complained," Mama says, her voice growing weaker with each word, her face becoming sodden and empty. I remember the day my father planted ten rows of corn after putting in a full day at the box factory, his face and back wet with perspiration.

"You're right, Mama, Daddy never did complain." I wipe moisture from Mama's brow. My father did not complain because the taste of liquor dulled his sensibilities. Mama was never able to piece the two sides of him together. The drunk, abusive side was always forgotten the morning after, suppressed, unmentioned.

Mama's breathing steadies after a while.

"I'm glad you wanted the picture," she says, the fragile rise and fall of her chest causing me to feel helpless. Even with my new fortune, I can do nothing to make her life more meaningful or enjoyable. There isn't enough money in the world to make her days any less painful. I follow her gaze back to the picture, a young mother with skin as flawless as butter, Bobby clinging to her bosom, one daughter with swollen knees, the other just beginning to blossom, a husband wearing the only suit he would ever own, a son just weeks before he dies.

"I like how you put it close so's I can see," Mama says.

"It's the best thing you could've given me, Mama."

A reticent smile slips over her face. I make a conscious decision to permanently put aside my childish grudges, those deep-seated animosities held hostage too long. I want the spring to hurry up and come so Mama can see the pink dogwoods bloom outside the bedroom windows, when this part of the earth finally settles closer to the sun, and the windows open to the garden scents of the lavenders and jasmines and lilies.

"You wanna watch the television now, Mama?"

"That be's fine," she says wanly.

Mama's spirit is thick inside the room, weighing me down as I lumber across the floor to open the doors of the armoire. I wonder if her spirit is slowly leaving her body, if she will die before spring. As I reach for the remote control, I notice a framed picture of Ralph and me, taken at a New Year's Eve party only a few months ago, nestled in a set of law books on a shelf above the television.

I take the photograph in hand. We appear to be happy. In fact, there is not a single trace of discontent etched in his face, no sign that he was secretly planning to leave me, no clue.

"Is that *him?*" Mama asks, pronouncing *him* like there's a bad taste in her mouth.

"Yes."

"Why keep it if'en he's out yo' life?"

"I don't know, Mama."

"Think of the devil and he'll appear, remember that."

"Oh, Mama."

"Well, God willing, when I gits to heaven I'se gonna work hard to finds you a man you deserves."

"What man do I deserve, Mama?"

"The Lord rewards hard work, that's why I wanted you to works hard, Lenita Mae. Wanted you to have what-all I couldn't. I wants you to have a man that won't take his hands to you and makes a decent living and ain't afraid of no hard work. You deserves a honest, decent man that can looks you in the eye."

I take the picture of Ralph and me to the kitchen, remove it from its glass frame, and tear it in half, splitting the two of us apart. Before tossing him into the trash can, I ask Ralph's face, "How can you sleep nights?" I think about how different my life might have been had I followed my dream of working in remote areas of the world, Third World countries, places where women suffer most. Who knows what difference I might have made in the world? I go to bed and open my diary, slip what's left of the photograph into the fold, the picture of me, before writing

Today I'm a millionaire with enough money to do anything I want. But I don't know what to do with it. I'm almost thirty-five—too old for fairytales and long white dresses. Why didn't I live out my dreams? Why did I give Ralph the power to stop me? Where in the world would I be if I hadn't?

I cannot afford to have another man coming into my life, lording his love over me like a snake charmer.

Rule 3.
I will follow my dreams.

20

Before going in to the office, I make rounds at the hospital and then head straight to the bank, where I close out my old account and open new ones before depositing my million-dollar-plus check. McCoy Tyler, the branch president, comes out to meet me. He gives me a limp, little lady handshake, and would like to personally explain all the investment services the bank has to offer. His nasally tone is patronizing, and he wears a toupee, a cheap one.

"Thanks, but I have to get to work," I say. "So I don't have much time. As long as my money's safe, I'll leave it here."

"Oh, it's safe all right, Dr. Faulkner," he says, practically salivating over the interest and fees he'll earn investing my money. Like a fox waiting outside a chicken coop. He reminds me of Angus Adams, the man after Clarissa Montgomery's land in *The Promise of Spring,* when he says, "Guaranteed." I feel as if I am standing at the checkout counter of a pricey boutique, preparing to pay for an assortment of things I do not need, I do not deserve. My innards grow numb. I feel guilty—here and not here. I sign forms that open a savings account, a money market account, a certificate of deposit, and an interest-bearing checking account.

"Call if you need anything," Mr. Tyler says. "Anything at all."

I leave the bank and arrive at my office at half past nine, in time to treat a bad case of vaginal warts in Exam Room Two and discover an ominous breast lump in a patient in Exam Room One.

* * *

10:15 A.M.

Kristie Loftus: 24-year-old white female, first-time patient. Weight: 142 lbs. Height: 5'8". History: First gynecological examination. No abnormalities noted.

I smile reassuringly while lifting the sheet that covers her breasts and do a double take. They point to the ceiling like tits on a mannequin, obviously tampered with, enormous for her small figure. I press and feel around her nipples, which have been stretched to maximum capacity. How comfortable can implants be, really? She flinches and I know, not very.

Giving a breast exam to a woman packing hefty saline sacks is like playing with a set of water balloons. I feel for lumps, and her breasts spring back into place each time I firmly press and rotate my fingers. In my personal opinion, implants turn healthy, young women like Ms. Loftus into playthings, sex objects for men to fantasize about—big tits and a tight butt. Vacation Barbie.

I casually ask Ms. Loftus how long she's had them.

"Two years," she says, adding that Dr. Miller informed her that implants would not affect breast-feeding after she has children.

"Of course, Dr. Miller tells all of his patients that."

"I can, can't I?"

I pull the sheet over her shoulders, retreat to the other end of the table, and say, "You can, Ms. Loftus. The only problem comes when your breasts fill up with milk. They enlarge tremendously for most women. The breast tissue stretches, and after nursing, this tissue will sag over the implant."

"What does that mean?"

I tell her to imagine a lumpy mountain.

"Oh, no!"

I think about how men come and go, but that what happens to a woman's breasts lasts forever. With her feet placed on the stirrups, I begin performing a pelvic exam. Her first. I study closely the outside skin, which is smooth and unblemished with no evident sign of irritation; then push back the labia for a better look at the vagina and the cervix. I notice that her hymen is intact. Ms. Loftus is a virgin. She tells me she's getting married in June.

Kelly hands me a speculum, and I tell her to get the smaller one. I ask Ms. Loftus if she is planning to start a family soon.

"Yes," she says, sounding unsure.

"Have you and your fiancé considered birth control?"

"No, Doctor," she says, blushing a dangerous shade of pink. "God will bless us with as many children as we need."

I am tempted to say that God blessed her with as much tit as she needed, but that didn't stop her from adding improvements.

"If I nurse my babies, Dr. Faulkner, can I have the lumps taken out later?"

"That's something you'll need to discuss with your plastic surgeon, Ms. Loftus. I look for abnormalities and diseases, not aesthetics."

"Oh," she says disappointedly. Kelly hands me the K-Y jelly, and I smooth it over my fingertips before pushing them inside Ms. Loftus's vagina, feeling for the bladder, the Fallopian tubes, the ovaries; she moans as I check for any masses, abnormal tissues, swelling. I remove my fingers and pull the drape sheet down between her legs, glimpsing a youthful innocence in her eyes, idealism about how the world really works. She has not had enough experience to determine whether this man she hopes to marry is who he appears to be. Is he ready to be the husband she wants and needs? Will he be there for her after five or six babies come along? Hell, does she even know whether she will be?

Too bad it would not be appropriate to advise Ms. Loftus that even being with a man nine years won't guarantee that she will know him well enough. I remove my gloves, telling her she can get dressed now. After exiting the exam room, I make a final note in her chart, and contemplate how little we both know about men.

4:45 P.M.

Clara McAllister: 54-year-old white female, return visit. Weight: 178 lbs. Height: 5'10". Complaint: persistent headache. History of present illness: In March 1999, patient was referred to me by Dr. Geoffrey, her internist of less than a year. After treating her menopausal symptoms, I attempted to refer her back to Dr. Geoffrey, but he requested that patient never return to his practice again. In April 1999, Dr. Wiseman refused to treat patient's headache after two visits. Between May 1999 and December 2000, a total of eight physicians have refused this patient continuity of care. During last visit she complained of headache and constipation.

Mrs. Clara McAllister, an educated, upper-class woman, is antagonistic—at times contentious—bordering on the neurotic. She's an overall pain in the butt. Last week, I recommended she take an enema for the constipation and headache she was having. "Drink plenty of water," I told her. Now she tells me how her bowels are moving just fine, but her head is pounding.

"My insurance company paid you to stop this pain," she complains, rolling her eyes, which are withered from lack of sleep. She then does what comes naturally, piques like a sword, and strikes where it hurts.

"I'd have gone to another doctor, if I'd known you couldn't fix a simple headache," she sneers.

"I can only do the best I can, Mrs. McAllister," I manage to say evenly. "But if you'd rather see someone else, then—"

"Oh, I bet you'd like that, wouldn't you, Doctor?"

"No, Mrs. McAllister," I lie.

"Can't you see I'm suffering?"

"Yes, and I'm trying to help you." With Mrs. McAllister, there is always something wrong that requires an immediate remedy. The time before her last visit, she had trouble sleeping. And the time before that, she was depressed after her daughter left for college. Mrs. McAllister wants a magic pill. She admitted during her first visit that she was not put on the earth to suffer one iota.

"How long must I suffer before you do something?" she says indignantly.

I don't answer that. I tell Mrs. McAllister to open her mouth and I check the condition of her teeth, ruling out cavities and abscesses. She has perfect white teeth that gleam. In fact, what amazes me most about this patient is her fastidious attention to the details of her appearance. Her hair is perfectly highlighted, nails manicured to match her lipstick, makeup done no matter how badly she might feel. And she dresses to the nines, expensively put together from head to toe. I feel for thyroid gland swelling around her neck and use my otoscope to peer inside her ears. Nothing unusual.

"When was the last time you had your eyes checked, Mrs. McAllister?"

"Recently," she scowls.

"So your eyeglass prescription is up to date?"

"Of course. My head hurts, not my eyes."

"Just ruling out problems," I say calmly, while making a few notes in her chart.

"Any changes to your diet?"

"No."

I examine the way Mrs. McAllister sits, suitably upright—no slouching, no muscle tension. She's the type to stay on top of things, always on time for her appointments, does what is prescribed—even douches before coming to see me, usually with some flowery scent like "A Summer's Meadow" or "Spring Rain." She scrubs and perfumes and powders every nook and cranny of her soft, plump body, ridding it of its natural womanly scent.

Something inside Mrs. McAllister's head must be causing the headaches—a small tumor, blockage, fluids—but before referring her to a neurologist, I need to have a look for myself.

"I'm going to send you for a CT scan, Mrs. McAllister. I need to rule out tumors and vascular problems in the brain."

"Tumors . . . cancer! My God, I live a healthy life. Nobody in my family has ever had cancer."

I tell her I didn't say a thing about cancer. "At this point, the CT scan is just a technicality."

She tells me if she has brain cancer, I've been paid to catch it in time.

I pick up the history of the MasterCard account and run my finger down the list. It drags me under a dark cloud. Perfume from Paris really pisses me off. All the times I told Ralph not to waste his money buying me such extravagances. *His money.* What a joke. An image of Mikayla wearing my fox comes back to me, and I want to smack her again. I stack the list on top of the unopened mail and unwrap a bouquet of yellow roses I picked up today from a florist shop across the street from my office. Mama's favorite. I rinse and clip the stems, stick them in a large, crystal vase, and take the sweet arrangement to Mama.

"What's got your tail hanging from a fence post?" she asks, sensing the fury burning inside me. I can hardly retain the wall between us that protects her from my pain. I admit to being tired, and nothing else. But Mama has the instincts of a fox. The day I almost died from the botched abortion, she tried to contact me at my dorm room. Velma Johnson, my roommate, lied, telling her she didn't know where I was, but through persistent prodding, Mama was able to reach me at the hospital. She said, "I dreamed you was laying on the bottom of a clear, blue lake with a hawk circling over. I knew you weren't long for this world."

I put a jazz CD on the stereo before sitting on the edge of Mama's bed. A rendition of "My Funny Valentine" plays, mood-stirring jazz impressions surrounding us like sheer, tapering veils. The sensuousness of the crooner touches me deeply, his voice resonating like a sad memory. Haunting emotional exchanges between voice and instruments. As we listen, I notice the way Mama watches my face with piteous regard.

"Thinking about him?" she says softly, with dust in her throat.

"Yes, Mama."

"You needs to git on with your life, child. You need to git somebody else to think about."

The phone rings as I prepare for bed. Karen.

"Ralph came here after work this evening," she says anxiously. "Raging about that money, girl. He yelled at me in front of my husband. Said he knew I had something to do with you getting that check. I'm so upset, Lenny. He's threatening to take you to court."

"What?"

"Jason made him leave."

"How low is he willing to stoop?" I ask myself. "I can't believe I used to think Ralph was the perfect man for me. No one on earth could've said anything different. I wasted all those years loving him."

"You haven't wasted anything, Lenny. You just gave him more than he deserved."

"That's all behind me now. I'm getting on with my life."

"I'm worried about you, Lenny. Ralph had this crazed look in his eyes. I've never seen that side of him before. There's no telling what he might do. You've got to be careful."

"Don't worry, I'll be fine," I say reassuringly, sliding into bed, exhausted from a long day at the office.

"Well, if you need me . . ." she says.

"I know."

21

9:00 A.M.

Shaniqua Davis, 22 weeks gestation, prenatal visit. Weight: 183 pounds. Complaint: pain in abdomen, gas, and bloating.

"Does it hurt here?" I ask, gently pressing above the abdomen, her pregnancy progressed to an obvious size.

"No."

"Here?" I press both sides.

"No."

"You're supposed to hurt," Ms. Davis snaps. "Having a baby is not supposed to be a picnic."

"What about here, Shaniqua?"

"Ouch," she cries at the force of my hands below her abdomen.

"Here?" I press against her pelvis bones.

"Yeah, it hurts!" she shrieks.

"Your pelvic bones are loosening up to accommodate your growing baby," I say.

"It feels broken."

"Like your head," Ms. Davis peals from her seat in the corner of the room. I glance back at her, a silent grimace taking hold of my face, while I wait for her mumbling to end. She rolls her eyes and purses her lips tightly closed. I tell Shaniqua that her pelvic bones are going to widen even more.

"So the baby can make his way down the birth canal and out through your uterus."

"Ugh. How big will the baby be?"

"Between nineteen and twenty-two inches," I say, measuring with my hands extended. "From five to eight pounds. He could even be bigger than that, you know. You've gained eleven pounds since your last visit."

"Ugh. You mean *her,*" Shaniqua says. "I'm having a baby girl."

"Well, we can find out today," I say, signaling to Kelly to prepare for an ultrasound. She smoothes gel over Shaniqua's belly, and flips on the machine. Before long, the fetus appears on screen. I examine the image from a series of angles, until evidence of the sex appears. Sometimes what appears to be a penis might actually be a shadow. But when the fetus opens its legs, spread-eagled across the screen, I know it's a boy.

"Congratulations," I say. "Looks like you're having a healthy baby boy."

"I didn't want no boy," she says.

"Too late to place an order now," Ms. Davis gripes.

"It hurts when I walk," Shaniqua says, her mother's voice dissipating in thin air. She groans about the pain in her abdomen.

"That's normal," I say.

We watch the fetus move about the screen, kicking his legs and arms in a fit of jerky movements. Shaniqua's heartbeat races congruently with her son's, almost indistinguishable in strength, a primitive, steady rhythm. Kelly pushes the copy button that captures the image on film. She hands it to Shaniqua before turning the machine off.

"You're sure it's a boy, Dr. Faulkner?"

"Quite sure," I say.

"Are you ever wrong?"

"Once."

"I hope you're wrong."

"Let's hope he's healthy."

"I can't stand the smell of fish and mayonnaise and collard greens. Milk and chitlins make me sick."

"What about the peppermint tea? Do you get to drink it at school?"

"Yes, Doctor, and I can eat when I drink that stuff. But it hurts to bend over. I can't hardly stand to walk through the halls at school."

"You might try wearing a girdle around your hips, not around your waist, you don't want to squeeze the baby."

"I feel like I walk funny. I can't help it. A friend of mine at school laughs at the way I walk. Why does it hurt so much? Can't you give me something for the pain, Doctor?"

"You might change how you sit and the way you lie in bed. A little Tylenol could ease the pain." I sigh when Ms. Davis warns me against prescribing anything for her daughter. Kelly taps her watch and silently mouths, "Time to go." She cleans Shaniqua's stomach and puts away the instruments used during the exam.

"Why can't I stand the smell of French fries?" Shaniqua asks.

Teen mothers: No matter how many times I remind them that what they experience during pregnancy is normal, they expect me to instantly make it go away. Shaniqua is gaining an adequate amount of weight, so I'm not worried about the baby's health, or hers. Besides, it is normal for a woman's appetite to decline at certain times during pregnancy, as her sense of smell heightens, a spell of nausea sometimes waiting around each corner—the school cafeteria, her refrigerator at home, the bakery she passes on her way to my office, and the seafood department at the grocery store. Shaniqua tells me that she craves peanut butter. I tell her peanut butter is a good source of protein.

"But I can't stand some things I used to eat," she says.

"You're supposed to suffer." Ms. Davis bristles.

"I wish I was having a girl," Shaniqua moans.

"The sex of the baby won't matter after you deliver, Shaniqua. You'll fall in love with your son. I see it happen all the time."

"I had a name picked out for a girl," she says.

"There are plenty of boys names to choose from," I say, notating the size of the fetus's head and limbs in the chart.

"Tabitha. I like Tabitha for a girl."

"Shaniqua, are you ready to be a mother?" I ask.

"Huh?"

"If it snows in August," Ms. Davis hisses.

"Do you really want this child, Shaniqua?" I ask directly.

"I'm keepin' it," she says. My heart sinks. Here lies another thirteen-year-old statistic, another child having a child. When I ask why she wants to keep her baby, she says, "Because it's mine."

"You'll stay and finish school?" I ask.

"Yes, ma'am, Doctor."

"Go to college, too?"

"Yes."

"Any more questions, Shaniqua?"

"My stomach still hurts," she says.

Kelly signals Exam Rooms One and Four with her fingers.

11:45 A.M.

Linda Jenkins, return pregnancy visit, 36 weeks gestation. Weight: 152 lbs. Complaint: Depression.

Linda Jenkins frets over not wanting her baby. Her long, auburn hair is fashioned into a girlish ponytail and she wears an oversize Emory sweatshirt with blue jeans, the way any coed might.

"Have you gotten in touch with Miss Parker?" I ask, expecting to hear that she has. But she bats her large, green eyes in bewilderment, as if I have not previously given her one of Stella's business cards and urged her to call.

"She can help you, Linda," I say, reaching inside my white lab coat for another card. She takes the card and stares blankly.

"Have you had any pain with urination? Any discharge? Bleeding?" She shakes her head, dismally denying any adverse symptoms; but when I ask if the baby is moving normally, her fresh, homespun face drains of its color. I wrap my arms around her when she bursts into tears, gently pulling her close, telling her to calm down, relax, it's going to be fine. She sobs quietly and lies back on the exam table. Kelly hooks her up to the fetal heart monitor. She stiffens at the sound of her baby's pulsing heart.

"There's a wonderful couple waiting to adopt this child if you can't care for her when she comes. You aren't stuck, Linda." I urge her to focus on giving this baby a good start in life. "Remember to take your vitamins and eat well."

The baby's heart pulsates with a strong, steady rhythm. Linda sucks in her next cry and says what a jerk the baby's father turned out to be. I measure the size of her uterus and tell her I understand what she means.

"Jerks come in all sizes, ages, and colors," I say.

"I'm scared I won't be able to give her up," she says, desperately.

"When the time comes, I'll help you get through it, don't worry. It's all right to change your mind. Having a baby's not the end of the world."

Before Linda leaves, she tells me she should've had an abortion.

The rakishly cold winds seem to wash through me as I attempt to jog this evening, with darkness patched with gray fog, and slivers of ice waiting along the side streets. It isn't safe out. After slipping a few times, I grind to a much slower pace, prudently walking to Peachtree and back. When I arrive home, I follow my dreams and gather the nerve to call Kevin Ellison, hoping to know him better soon.

"I look forward to running again," I say to his answering machine. I picture him flying somewhere exotic this evening, over white sandy beaches and blue-green waters. He's been a pilot for over ten years, he told me. He's been all over the world, even stood at the base of Mount Kilimanjaro.

I look in on Mama, expecting her to be asleep, her breathing spastic and unpredictable. She calls to me and motions weakly with her hand toward a place on the edge of her bed. I sit and take hold of her bony fingers.

"A man called while you were out," she says faintly.

My heart beats faster. I think of Ralph.

"Did whoever he was leave a name?"

"Annie didn't 'member no name," she says, grunting to clear the clog in her throat. "She said he sounded drunk."

"Maybe he was in a good mood. Annie could be wrong."

"She knows a drunk man when she hears one. And I do too. I was married to one for twenty-seven years."

"Oh, Mama."

"Annie said he sounded right pitiful-like."

I envision Ralph sitting at a bar, downing drinks with his boys, becoming an obnoxious rebel, and calling my house to raise hell. I had put my life on hold, waiting for his career to take off, waiting for him to be ready to start a family. How dare he call my house now, after all he has put me through! Mama's hand goes limp, her eyes closing as she sleeps, air struggling to enter and exit her watery lungs.

"You'll never hear from that insufferable bastard again," I whisper. "He'll rue the day we met when I'm through." I go to my room, and lay across the bed. I am tempted to phone Ralph and tell him off. But I don't. I take out my diary to get him off my chest.

Ralph Griffin used my fear of losing him to his advantage. I was desperate and he knew it. He knew I was willing to wait my whole life for him. I waited for my real life to begin, a baby and a husband. But I may never have a family of my own. I may be as much family as I will ever have. And for now, that has to be enough.

Rule 4.

I will never again put my life on hold for a man!

22

Annie, the hospice nurse, comes each day from eight to five thirty, making sure Mama eats and bathes, that she is not in pain, that her last days will not be wretched. She is a short, stout woman as dark as me, with a tuft of gray hair pulled back into a natural, coarse bun. Mama took an instant liking to Annie. She enjoys her company. They watch the same soaps and both enjoy the gospel hour. "She's not uppity and trying to be more than she is," Mama says every now and then, her way of saying she does not feel insecure around Annie.

Before she leaves the house this evening, Annie tells me that Mama would not eat today.

"Is that unusual?" I ask.

"Not under the circumstances," she says, "but it's a sign that she might be giving up."

The thought of Mama dying is a kick to the chest. The front door closes behind Annie, and I melt onto the sofa with my overcoat hanging on me like a cape, utterly exhausted. I cannot think straight. My mind races with the things that need to be done. I need to get something to help Mama eat. I need to eat myself, pay the bills, clean the floors, the toilets, do the laundry—bury the memory of Ralph. I page Ralph's beeper. I'll offer to split the money with him if he calls back. Fifty fifty is more than fair.

Hours pass. I am cleaning the kitchen when I hear a knock at the front door. I hurry to answer it, startled to see Ralph.

"You called," he says, walking past me. My mouth becomes parched. I'm at a loss for words.

"Why'd you do it, Ralph?"

He glances around the room as if searching for something he forgot to take.

"I should've told you what I was going through," he says downheartedly. "I loved you so much, Lenny. I never meant to hurt you."

"Then why, Ralph?"

"I always felt last with you," he says, inhaling deeply. "Your patients came first, then your family, friends, and if nothing pressing came up, there was me . . . dead last."

"That's not true and you know it. My whole world revolved around you."

"It's funny how you always had time to see a patient or attend a conference or even meet your friends for lunch, but not me."

"Ralph, I . . ."

"Not once did you ever take a day to spend with me," he says, pointing his index finger like a sword. "There were nights when you were on call and I'd sit in front of the television staring at space. You don't think I was lonely?"

"I loved you more than anything, Ralph. You never said . . ."

"Said what? I'm alone in this relationship? Can we please be together? Can we make love more than twice a month, if we're lucky?"

"You cheated, Ralph. Don't turn this around on me like it's my fault."

"After years of being in last place, when a beautiful, young woman opens the door and says come in, only a fool stays outside in the cold."

"Why'd you pretend to love me? Why'd you lie for so long? Because you wanted my money? My house?"

"I did love you, Lenny. I didn't plan to fall in love with Mikayla. It just happened."

"Nothing just happens, Ralph."

Ralph caresses the side of my face with his hand. He leans close and kisses my cheek. I gaze into his eyes, indifferent to me now, devoid of all sincerity. Mikayla worked on our account over the course of this year. But Ralph had been looting from me years before that. I pull away when he attempts to kiss me again.

"You took back every gift you ever gave me. Gifts, by the way, that I paid for. Overcharged a fortune on my credit card account, and emptied my bank account. You're nothing but a low life, Ralph. Nothing but a thief."

"I didn't take anything I didn't deserve," he says adamantly.

"Deserve?" Part of me wants him to turn back into the same old Ralph and explain it all away, but the better part of me is reminded of his cheating and lies. "You deserve to go to jail."

"If you hadn't pushed me, we'd still be together," he says pointedly, now squeezing the back of my neck.

"Stop it!!!" I yell and he releases his grip.

"All your talk about marriage and babies," he says, his hand sliding clumsily down my arm. Suddenly, I detest his touching me; his face sends an annoyance impulse to my brain telling my ears not to listen.

"Get out, Ralph!"

"What were you going to do, Lenny? Have a couple of kids and expect me to nurse them while you attend your patients?"

"You know I'd never have done that, Ralph. You said you weren't ready and I respected your wishes. Sure, I wanted to marry you. Of course, I wanted us to start a family." My eyes tear up and the dam breaks against my will.

"I warned you not to push me," he says, standing briskly. He begins to pace the floor in front of me, his voice spastic and breathy. "None of this would've happened if you hadn't pressed me."

"Congratulations on your engagement to Mikayla, Ralph," I say. "Seems you didn't need any pressing to do it. Hope you have a long and prosperous marriage because you'll not be honeymooning on my dime. Now get out, before I call the cops."

He looms over me like a foreboding shadow, and says, "I want my money."

I dry my eyes on the back of my hand, and yell, "Get out!!!!"

The evil inside Ralph spurs him on to brand-new indignity when he reaches down and grabs me forcefully by the shoulders.

"I guess you thought I'd crawl on my knees and beg for my money. Make no mistake, it's mine, all mine."

"Let go!" I yell, trying to break free from his iron grip.

"I want my money," he sneers.

"Your money!?" I push Ralph and send him stumbling into the coffee table. He grimaces, trying to steady himself.

"Who managed that damned portfolio? Me!" he bellows, beating his chest like an ape. "I made it worth something."

"You used *my* money, Ralph, and you would've cheated me out of my house, too, if I'd been stupid enough to sell it."

Ralph's gaze turns cold and callous. Karen was right in her description of his dark side. He takes a few menacing steps forward as if getting ready to strike.

"I was the one who took care of this old broken-down place. I earned at least half its worth, and most of that money you took belongs to me," he snarls, leaning forward, his face inches from mine.

"Lenita Mae!!!" Mama calls out, wretchedly. Ralph stands bolt upright, and I take advantage of this opportunity to give him my best shot, a swift kick between his legs, the pointed toe of my hard black boot connecting to the most delicate part of his manhood. Ralph grabs himself, stoops over. His face contorted, mouth open, while his body spasms and gyrates silently, like a toddler well popped on his bottom for bad behavior.

"Dammit to hell," he mutters, two octaves higher. Ralph is afraid of me now. I am stronger than he must have imagined, stronger even than I believed myself to be.

"Get out, Ralph," I say, seething. He collects himself and tries to stand upright, but cannot fully do so. He reminds me of a trapped rat, dragging himself to the door, trying mightily to escape. I follow him, and when he steps outside, he turns to face me.

"I'll see you in court, Doctor."

I slam the door.

When I enter her room, I see that Mama's eyes are dark sunken holes that seem to light when she takes note of me, her gaze shifting from the television.

"Are you all right, Mama?"

"What was the ruckus out there?"

"Nothing, Mama."

"It was *him*."

I retrieve a bouquet of fading roses from the night table next to her and go into the bathroom, where I add water to the vase. Tomorrow, I'll get a whole new bunch of bright yellows. My hands tremble when I reenter the bedroom and I try to concentrate on steadying them.

"Don't never allow no man to hit you," she says weakly.

"I won't."

"If he does it once, he'll do it again."

"Yes, Mama." I remember the last night my father came home drunk, shortly before I entered high school. He picked a fight with Mama over how much money she put aside to spend on Christmas, and Mama, who said we deserved a lot more than she could give us, ignored him at first. But when he pushed her against the wall in the living room that particular night, something snapped inside her. Rosetta and I exchanged surprised glances, adulation for Mama, who finally stood up to him. Mama filled with mounting rage from all the years she took his crap—all the years she had allowed him to boss her around—pushed back. She hurled her fist, and in one rope-a-dope broadside punch to his face, Mama knocked him out.

I follow her gaze to the large French windows behind Ralph's old desk, where the frigid temperatures continue to hold back the spring.

"Rosetta called, says she wanna come see me first Saturday of the month if that all right wit you."

"Mama, this is your house as long as you're in it. You don't have to ask."

"Good then, 'cause I told her to come anyway."

I sit on the edge of the bed, the gloominess of winter taking hold of my spirit. Mama lifts her frail hand to rub my back. An immense sadness takes shape inside me. I am perilously close to tears. When she dies, I'll be alone.

"I want you to be happy, Mama."

"Lenita Mae, I'm just thinkin' the same 'bout you."

"You were?"

"Prayin's mo' like it. I been praying for the Lawd to let me come back after I'm dead and buried, just one good time so's I can pick out the man you deserves."

"Oh, Mama." I burst into tears.

"Don't cry 'bout it," she says hoarsely.

"I love you, Mama."

"Aaah, haah," she says thickly, pinching back her emotions. The gentle hand on my back falls to her side and I recall the day the news came of Joe's death; it was the first time I ever saw my mother cry, losing the hard veneer that holds people at bay, her heart sullen and broken in places that never healed.

* * *

The doorbell rings. I amble down the hall from my bedroom, hesitating at first to open the front door, not wanting to lay eyes on Ralph again; but when I do, Mrs. Stein is standing in the doorway holding my mail.

"I think what we ought to do is stop doing the postman's job," she says in her nasally drawl. "Perhaps, if we start forwarding mail back to each other, he'll start getting it right the first time."

"You think?" I say, accepting my mail.

"It just might work," she says optimistically. Mrs. Stein stands on her tiptoes and cranes her neck to see around me. I step aside, allowing a view of the great room, the entrance to the kitchen, a partial view of the dining room.

"I saw a large white van parked at your house a few weeks ago. I wondered what it was all about. A nurse comes here every day at eight o'clock."

I hesitate to respond, suddenly remembering that I happen to live next to the nosiest woman in the universe. Mrs. Stein knows more about the comings and goings of my household than I do, and she won't leave without an answer.

"My mother's staying with me. She's dying of cancer."

"I'm so very sorry."

"It's all right, Mrs. Stein, my mother's prepared."

"Please let me help you," she says kindly.

"Help, how?"

"When Mr. Stein was dying of cancer ten years ago, I read to him a little each day, and he actually looked forward to it. Let me read to your mother from time to time. I bet she hasn't had a single friend to visit."

"No, she hasn't," I admit, considering that Mama has left her home of twenty-plus years, children and grandchildren, the friends who kept her company, especially her fellow parishioners from Wayside Baptist. Mama now lacks what makes us solidly human. She has no real intimacy, no companionship aside from Annie and me. But even so, I cannot imagine her being accepting of this sweet, well-intentioned white woman. In fact, I know Mama will flat-out refuse to have Mrs. Stein sit next to her deathbed, reading from time to time.

"When can I start?" Mrs. Stein says eagerly. She tells me that on Tuesdays and Thursdays she is usually available. I haven't the heart to turn her down.

"Next Thursday," I say dubiously, and Mrs. Stein agrees to come, planning to arrive before Mama eats her lunch.

"Mr. Stein always ate better after a good story." I notice a gleam in her eyes, anticipation that her good deed will be welcome. I hope Mama's unbridled tongue does not offend too severely.

A car stops in front of my house. I strain to see a shadowy figure get out. In the twilight, he hovers around my mailbox. The thought of a pipe bomb exploding spurs my imagination. The mysterious man gets back inside his car and drives away.

I worry fitfully throughout the night. I think of the sinister look in Ralph's eyes when he shook me by the shoulders. I should call the cops right away. I should. But I can't. I imagine my cousin, Sticky, locked up for the rest of his life and the thought of Ralph in prison stops me.

The next morning, I dress and head directly for the mailbox, preparing to die if necessary. I stare at it briefly, heart racing, my hand finally reaching nervously forward. I freeze, quickly scanning the sidewalk for any branches downed by the last big ice storm. At the edge of my drive, I retrieve a long, sturdy stick, which I use to tug open the mailbox and poke inside.

Terror takes hold of me. The stick bangs against the metal walls. I jump. Nothing happens. I peer inside to see a stack of envelopes bound tightly together by a rubber band, a note folded neatly on top.

Dear Lenny,

I took the initiative to number your mailbox. Hope you don't mind. I thought it might help the postman better find your address. The attached mail came to my home while I was away.

Sincerely,
Ernest Hemingway

On the back of the page, he has written his address and phone number. This kindness of his, the gold letters neatly pasted to the outside of my mailbox, renews my faith in humanity. I call Ernest and leave a message on his answering machine, inviting him for lunch soon, "on Saturday, I'm free."

I was willing to die rather than get Ralph in trouble, willing to blow up like an old casino along the Vegas strip. I stack the mail on the kitchen counter and go to my bedroom, where I retrieve my diary. Annie trills hello as she passes my door en route to see Mama.

"Morning, Annie," I say automatically, before writing.

No man is worth dying for, especially not Ralph Griffin. The next time he shows his face around here, I'll call the cops. I have to look out for me. I'm too damned important.

Rule 5.

I will not risk my life to save anyone's reputation.

23

Throughout the day, I worry. I have a security system installed, and a couple of weeks pass uneventfully. Mama gets neither worse nor better. Buds begin to form on the dogwoods, the tips of tulips crest above the frigid earth. I wonder if Mama holds on for Rosetta's sake, if seeing my sister one last time will give her the peace she needs to finally let go of this life. One evening, I tiptoe quietly past her bed to the bathroom, where I cut back the stems on the fresh yellow roses I purchased on the way home from work.

"Rosetta called this afternoon," Mama says weakly as I place the roses in a vase on the table next to her bed.

"She's still coming in the morning, right?"

"Naw, she can't. She's having problems with that car again."

"That's too bad," I say, seething underneath like a smoldering fire. Rosetta should be here. The least she can do is be here when Mama dies. *I will get through this. I will get through this.* I go to my room and change into jogging gear.

"I'll be back in a few, Mama," I yell, double-checking the security system before heading outside. I take off down the street, but within seconds, a voice calls to me. Kevin. Dear, sweet, sexy Kevin joins me, and the two of us run in perfect synchronicity. I needed something to distract me from Mama dying, someone to hold my hand and listen. We walk hand in hand after a five-mile run, and he seems genuinely interested in how bad my year's been.

"That Ralph's a jerk," he says. We stop in front of my house, his handsome face aglow from the full moon, and his dark, dreamy eyes seem to see through me, waking my hotspots. He homes in for a kiss, a tender, succulent lip-locking kind, heat from my body mixing with the heat from his, my body greedily yearning for more. I fear I might have an "O" without the requisite amount of foreplay, fully clothed, right here, the two of us standing in the street.

"Forget about Ralph," he says breathily.

"Ralph who?"

We lock lips again.

"Good night," he says. I nod and wave.

At lunch the next day, Karen and I discuss my windfall.

"You need to take most of it out of savings and invest it," she says, insisting. "It might as well grow, because you'll never spend a dime of it."

"Not true."

"Some charitable foundation will inherit a fortune one day," she quips. I laugh at that, even though it might be true. I laugh because the beginning of spring lightens my heart. Kevin is on my mind.

"It's good to see you happy again, girlfriend," Karen says. "Must be a man."

"How can you tell?"

Karen smiles in that know-it-all way of hers, and says, "I'm a woman."

The same Indian waiter who always serves us whenever we come to the Taj Mahal plops our water glasses down on the table, and Karen cuts her eyes at him when a few drops wet her hand.

"I've had it with you," she growls. "Get me the manager."

He is taken aback by her sudden anger. His black eyes enlarge when she repeats, "Get the manager."

"Please, miss, there's no problem."

"Oh, yes there is," Karen snaps. "You're rude."

"Please, miss, what can I do to please you?"

"Never wait on me again."

He lifts his hand, signaling to a waitress, and I recognize my patient, Rania Amin.

"Rania?" I say, surprised.

"Dr. Faulkner, I'm so happy to see you," she says.

"I didn't know you worked here."

"Now I do, Doctor. I had to leave my other job because I take too much time off. This is my husband, Nader."

"You're the doctor who saved my wife's life?" he asks, astounded.

"Yes, Nader," Rania says. "I'm alive because of Dr. Faulkner." They exchange a few quiet words. He glances down at Karen.

"Dr. Faulkner and Miss, what can I do to better serve you?" he says solicitously.

Karen settles back in her chair with a satisfied expression on her face. She glances at her menu, and says, "I think I'll have the buffet."

"And you, Doctor?"

"The same."

"Everything you want today is on the house," he says. "I couldn't be there to thank you when my wife had her surgery. So this is my thank you."

We get our food, the usual spicy aromas surrounding us with warmth and pleasure as we sit and eat.

"What were we saying?" Karen says.

"Saying?"

"Before you made peace with the Indian subcontinent," she says.

"I don't remember."

Karen taps her bottom lip. "Oh, yeah, I remember now. Your new man."

Mama yells "Fire!" in her sleep as the burglar alarm peals clamorously around us. I dash into her bedroom, still half asleep myself, barefoot and out of breath.

"It's just the alarm, Mama," I say. She sniffs for smoke.

"I don't mind burning up myself, I'm ready to die—but not you, Lenita Mae."

A lump forms in my throat. This is as close as Mama might ever get to saying she loves me. I turn off the alarm in the kitchen. I know instantly that Ralph has been here. I can feel it. He's after my money. I jump when the phone rings, and cautiously answer it. A representative from the security company is on the other end of the line, wanting to know if there is a problem.

"Yes, there's a problem," I say, breathlessly. "I've had a break-in."

"Is the perpetrator still on the premises?"

"No, I don't believe so." The idea that Ralph might be hiding somewhere inside causes me to shiver.

"A police officer will be there shortly, ma'am."

I hang up and rush to reassure Mama. I tell her the security system is faulty. "It went off by mistake."

"Get a dog," she says hoarsely. "They don't go off 'less there's something to bark at."

When the cops arrive, I am tempted to tell them my security system is faulty and put this matter to rest. But I think of Rule 5, *I will never risk my life to save anyone's reputation,* and I stop myself. They quickly search the house and discover that the intruder broke a glass pane in my back door. A bloody trail leads to my foot, and broken glass is scattered across the kitchen floor. My foot stings when I remove a piece lodged in the bottom. I feel as violated as the day Ralph stole my things. What was he planning to do tonight? I tell the officers I suspect my former boyfriend.

"He threatened me a few weeks ago," I say. They write up a report of this incident and give me a card with their names and precinct information on it. There is no evidence that it was Ralph. No witnesses. Any of his fingerprints could have been made long ago.

"Call us if he comes back," an officer says.

"We'll pick him up, then," says the other.

I shudder at the thought of Ralph returning. There is no telling what he is capable of doing. After the police leave, I bandage and clean my hurt foot, before sweeping up the broken glass. A zest of cool night air seeps through the empty pane, and I get angry. I patch over the broken pane with cardboard, and get even angrier. The next time—if there is a next time—I won't wait for evidence. I won't wait for the police to say there is none. I will do whatever the hell I have to do to protect myself and my mother.

4:45 P.M.

Clara McAllister, return visit. Complaint: chronic headache.

Mrs. Clara McAllister sits straight in her seat, expectantly.

"You should know what's causing my headaches by now," she says tersely. I consider that if her last internist hadn't barred her from his office, I would be done with her by now.

"You're right, Mrs. McAllister. I should know, but I don't. All the tests have come back negative. There are no tumors or bacteria or disease causing your headaches. We've ruled out allergies. Sometimes women get menopausal headaches, but the neurologist you saw suggests . . . ," I pause to choose my words carefully. "He suggests that your symptoms could be psychosomatic."

"You think I'm crazy?"

"No, no, Mrs. McAllister. I'm not saying that at all. It's just that I've noticed a pattern with you. Every time something stressful happens in your life, you get sick."

She sits back in her seat and draws her hand up to her forehead, holding it in place.

"What's going on at home, Mrs. McAllister? Your daughter's gone away to college. You and Mr. McAllister getting along okay?"

She sighs deeply and shakes her head. "No," she peevishly admits, "we're not. Winston came home one night two months ago and said he wasn't happy. No other explanation. He packed one suitcase and left. He left like he had been planning to do it for a long time."

"It's unfair," I say. Mrs. McAllister begins to weep.

"I know what you're going through," I whisper. "I've been there."

"After twenty-four years," she cries, shaking like an erupting volcano. She bursts into a fit of rage, accusing her husband. "He's ruining our lives. The bastard left me for a younger woman."

I lean over my desk and hand her a box of tissues.

"I've loved that man most of my life," she says bitterly. She rips tissues out of the box and presses a wad against her eyes. How stoic she usually is, how tough and snappy her tone of voice that easily insults or threatens. It feels weird seeing her vulnerable side like this—almost scary. I never expected us to have something in common.

"I thought we were happy," she says, taking a deep breath. "Winston never said a thing. I kept thinking he might come back, come to his senses. But the divorce papers arrived this morning."

"I understand. I'm so sorry this has happened to you," I say, immediately regretting it. People like Mrs. McAllister have a strong disdain for being pitied. She would rather live her whole life suffering in silence. She straightens in her chair, her body stiffening into its usual regal stance, like an aging upright piano with keys going stiff. She holds her head proudly and tells me that her headache has gone away. I plug a coin into my bubblegum machine, hoping that the spinning, flipping clown will brighten her mood. It doesn't. She stares at the gumball I offer her with disdain.

"No thank you, I'm fine now," she says coldly. She glances at me, suddenly flushed pink with embarrassment.

"You need to see a therapist, Mrs. McAllister," I say assertively. "You've been under a great deal of stress lately. You need someone qualified to help you get through it."

"Well," she huffs, "you don't expect me to pay for coming down here today, do you? You could've given me that tidbit over the phone."

The next morning, after saying good-bye to Mama, I find a dead parakeet on my doorstep with a noose around its neck and a note stuck to it that reads:

Watch your back, Dr. Fucker.

I bite back a scream, not wanting to upset Mama, or Mrs. Stein. Is it possible for Ralph to be as perverse as this? I examine the handwriting closely, especially the *F.* Of course he did it.

After retrieving a shoebox from inside the house, I place the yellow bird inside it and, while holding it in my hands, try to decide what to do. Is this evidence? Do I call the cops? I get in the car and drive directly to Ralph's office, with no idea of what to say or do.

Angela eyes the box and me with suspicion.

"Tell Ralph I'm here to see him, please."

"May I ask what it's about?"

"He'll know," I assert, holding the box tighter.

"Mr. Griffin's in an important meeting right now," Angela says, "and I don't know how long it'll last."

"I'll wait," I insist.

"Please take a seat, then."

I watch twenty minutes pass. Kelly should be climbing the walls about now.

"Can't you go in there and tell him I'm here?" I ask, raising my voice.

Angela glances up at me from her word processor, shrugs her shoulders, and says, "He's in an important meeting."

Without another thought, I walk right past her desk and storm into Ralph's office.

"Ralph, I believe this belongs to you," I say, tossing the shoebox on his desk. The top flies off and the poor deceased bird rolls out. Shock spreads across Ralph's face. He really is in the middle of a meeting. His client's face turns an indignant beet red.

"Was this supposed to threaten me, Ralph?" I ask, sternly. "A dead bird, you sick bastard?"

"Ralph?" the client says, brushing two stray yellow feathers from his gray pinstriped suit.

"Andrew . . . this . . . this . . . is crazy, and she's . . . she's insane," Ralph stutters.

"Insane?" I hiss, reaching across the table toward him. "Don't play with me, Ralph. I don't like playing games."

"Angela!!!" he calls out, jumping back.

"Here, Mr. Griffin," Angela says, stunned.

"Get security."

I leave before I am made to leave.

* * *

Ralph stops his car in front of my house as I arrive home from work. He rolls down his tinted window, wearing sunglasses on an overcast day. I go over to him, saying, "You're not welcome here."

"If you keep my money, things will get ugly."

"I'm not afraid of you, Ralph Griffin," I say, shooing him away like a pesky fly. "Go, before I call the cops."

Ralph removes his sunglasses, glaring at me. I do not recognize him anymore. There is not a trace of what I knew of him left—only the slightest resemblance to the man I loved so dearly. He's a stranger.

"I'll sue you if that's what it takes," he says.

"Go right ahead," I retort. "I have a mind to do the same to you." Ralph starts the engine of his car. I follow his gaze to my neighbor's front porch, where Mrs. Stein has come out to get a better look. He pulls away from the curb and mutters *bitch* under his breath, a verbal slap from a man who had once been so tender and kind.

"Is he bothering you again?" Mrs. Stein calls out as I head up the driveway to my house.

"Not anymore."

25

The following Saturday morning, I lace up my running shoes, head outside, and stretch before taking off down the street. Ten minutes later I am coasting along contentedly, high on life, with no adverse preoccupations cluttering my mind. No worries. At the quarter-mile mark, in front of a cedar-and-stone house, I turn up Chestnut Road and head toward Peachtree. Within seconds, I hear the sound of racing footsteps behind me. Kevin flew to Japan this weekend, so I know he is not following me. I speed up, and whoever is following me speeds up, too. Blood rushes to my forehead; a new mantra twirls inside my panicky thoughts. *I will not live in fear. . . . I will not live in fear. . . . I will not live in fear.* I stop to turn around, and freeze.

Glare from the sun obscures his face; I squint with my hand above my eyes to better see, holding my breath. I make mental notes: average height—five-eleven to six feet, weight approximately 180 pounds, white T-shirt and a pair of blue jeans. Copper-colored hair peeks from beneath a black Falcons cap. He continues toward me, and the beard gives him away.

"Ernest?"

"Yes, I beg your pardon, Lenny," he says, catching his breath.

"Why are you following me?"

"Lenny, I was gardening when you ran by, and remembered your invitation to lunch today."

I notice a cluster of purple tulips in his other hand.

"Oh, yes, Ernest," I say, "I appreciated you so much for numbering my mailbox. You were so kind to do it."

"No bother, really," he says, smiling pleasantly, then, as if an afterthought, he offers the tulips. "Please indulge me by accepting these. I planted many more than I intended."

"Of course," I say, taking the flowers to my nose and sniffing their mild perfume. We stare at the tulips twisting slightly in my hand, this way and that—an odd, rich purple, almost drinkable. Fluid-looking, like miniature cups of grape juice. "Thank you, Ernest, I've never seen purple tulips before."

"A new hybrid, actually," he says, "I wanted them to bloom earlier, but they didn't turn out in time." Ernest has handsome dark features, lightly golden skin, with a few freckles on his nose. His copper hair makes him unusual—though it could use some reshaping, and he could stand doing away with his beard altogether.

"In time for a competition?" I ask, curiously. "I've heard how cutthroat they can be."

"No, no," he shakes his head, "I grow everything for pleasure only."

"Oh, *everything.* An English teacher, and a botanist, too."

"Just a man who appreciates nature," he shrugs, smiling amiably, as he begins to back away from me. "If you're still interested, Lenny, I'll be happy to join you for lunch."

"Have a cup of coffee with me now, Ernest," I say impetuously, and when he hesitates, I add, "There's a Starbucks just a few blocks away."

"Sure, thanks for asking."

We walk there, passing the Saturday-morning bustle of trucks and cars along the way, and a shop I know from my credit card statement whose name bugs me every time I see it: *Rowan Jewelers.* The line inside Starbucks is short, and when it is our turn, Ernest requests a large cup of water for my purple tulips. We order cups of coffee and seat ourselves next to a window, with the tulips as our centerpiece.

"How's Mr. Griffin?" Ernest asks good-naturedly.

"You remembered his name," I say, impressed.

"Well, I've gotten several pieces of his mail . . . your mail, and I haven't forgotten that one envelope with both your names on it. You know, the one that made you and your girlfriend jump for joy."

"We didn't jump," I laughingly refute.

"Leap, then." Ernest smiles again briefly, then sips his coffee and purses his lips. "Mr. Ralph Griffin, right?"

"Yes, he left me."

"I'm sorry, Lenny," he says, removing his cap. His hair glistens like coils of copper, springing forth invitingly. Part of me wants to reach out and touch it.

"I've moved on," I say.

"You make it sound easy."

"Well, it wasn't."

"A broken heart never is," he says. "Everybody expects you to move on, but it's like a wound that has to heal."

"You speak like you've had experience."

"I lost my wife," he says somberly.

"How long ago?"

"She died of cancer a year ago."

"How terrible for you, Ernest." My heart dips when I think of what he said about the tulips. They didn't turn out in time. I think about Mama holding on for Rosetta. "It must be devastating."

"Amy was my life," he says. "We moved here three years ago. She was diagnosed last March, and by the end of June, she was dead."

"How are you coping?"

"I stay busy, but . . ."

"But?"

"It's difficult to come home every day, surrounded by reminders of my wife. I haven't been able to touch her things yet. Move them anywhere, I mean." He leans back in his seat and sighs. "I don't know why I'm telling you this. Forgive me for being depressing."

"No, Ernest. You're not at all. Please, tell me about her."

"You're being kind."

"No, I mean it. Tell me, please."

"Well, Amy was such a marvelous woman, Lenny. What can I say? I think you would've liked her. She was very talented, a superb artist. She could do anything she wanted—even made her own clothes, like a professional designer, and taught herself to sail a twenty-eight-foot boat."

"Definitely, I would've liked her," I say.

"She was really something." He sighs wistfully. "Amy took me sailing across the Gulf of Mexico from Pensacola to Cozumel two summers ago for my birthday, before we knew she was sick."

He shakes his head despairingly.

"If I'd only known then," he says. The pain I remember seeing in his eyes the day we met reappears.

"I understand," I choke.

"I could've done more. So much more."

"My mother's dying of cancer, and I feel the same way. There's nothing I, a doctor, can do to make her live longer. Absolutely nothing, except to make her as comfortable as I can."

"Helplessness and guilt."

"Yes."

The sun fades briefly. I stare down at my fingers as they circle the rim of my cup. Ernest clears his throat and says, "I hope your mother doesn't suffer long."

"Thanks Ernest, I hope the same for you."

26

By the middle of April, the dogwoods are in full bloom, like a celebration of life. Karen missed her period last month and is well on her way to starting a family. My old roommate, Laura Ruth, writes that she is having a baby in November, a third child. She cut back her hours at her private practice to two days a week. *For the sake of my family,* she writes. This morning, I glance at the enclosed photograph of her good-looking family: husband, Earl, and daughters, Kimmerly and Kara, and fill with want. In my mind's eye, Laura Ruth is holding my hand after my abortion, reassuring me that I will have children when it is the right time. "Our kids will grow up together."

I send Laura Ruth a note:

Dear Laura Ruth,

Congratulations. I hope this one is a boy. Your children will likely be grown before I have the first one. You're so lucky to have so much.

Love,
Lenny

11:45 A.M

Karen Roberts Ashby: 32-year-old black female, pregnancy visit. 3 weeks gestation. Gravida—1/para—0. Last menstrual period, February 3. Birth control prior to pregnancy: pill.

Karen is my last patient before the lunch break. It amazes me how readily new mothers bond with an image on a black-and-white screen, a frequency of sound waves bouncing off human tissue, creating the shadow of a form they thrive on, hope for, and want to cuddle in their arms.

"Can you tell what the sex is, Lenny?"

"Not yet."

"Well, it has to be a boy."

"Has to?"

I give her a cup of orange juice. "Have you thought about any names?"

"J. Samuel Roberts Ashby if it's a boy. Estelle L. Ashby for a girl."

"J for Jason, of course?"

"And my father's as pleased as punch to finally have a namesake. Sammy."

"A regular song-and-dance man," I laugh, "or daughter. And she'll be named for?"

"Jason's mother," Karen says, curling her lips to add, "the L's for Lenita. We'll probably call her Lenny."

"Oh, Karen," I choke, tears stinging my eyes. "I'm so honored. You're a wonderful friend. You really are."

When I finish examining her, Karen and I leave together for the café across the street. I have less than a half hour to eat. We sit in a booth near the door.

"We bought the house," Karen says dejectedly.

"Which house?"

"The one around the corner from Mother and Daddy."

"There are worse places to live, Karen."

"No there aren't," she gripes. "Lenny, I hate to go home now. I'm starting to resent my husband as much as I do Mother. I feel trapped."

"It's normal to become emotional during pregnancy."

"Emotional, my eye. I've always wanted to get away from home. Can you imagine what it's been like to know where you'd go to college, what you'd grow up to be, the kind of man you'd marry . . . all before you entered kindergarten?" Karen begins to sob quietly.

"No," I say. "I can't. My parents didn't care whether I went to college or not. They didn't have the money to send me. I left home because I had a chance to do it."

"Oh, Lenny, I'm sitting here feeling sorry for myself, rattling on about nothing. I'm being selfish again."

"No, you're a woman about to have a baby, girlfriend. There's nothing selfish about that. You need to put your foot down with your mother. She controls you because you let her, just like I allowed Ralph to control me."

"He came to the house yesterday," she says as if suddenly remembering.

"What now?"

"I wouldn't let him in the door. Jason had to go outside to talk to that bastard."

"What'd he want?"

"He's hired some top-notch attorney to sue you."

"You know, Karen, if he hadn't been so cruel and dishonest, I'd have given him most of the money. Honestly, I would've. But the way he treated me, like I was a piece of litter on the sidewalk to be stepped on . . . I won't give up a dime without a fight."

Karen removes a business card from her purse. "Take this," she says, handing it to me. I study the unfamiliar name, J. Paul Anderson, Attorney at Law. "Jason highly recommends him."

"Jason?"

"He says the way Ralph's behaving makes him sick."

"Thanks," I say, staring at the card, gray with burgundy letters. I trust Karen, but I don't trust her husband. He and Ralph are best friends. This could be a setup, a tactic for Ralph to legally take everything. I put the business card inside my purse.

"By the way, I received an invitation to your baby shower," I say, secretly amused. "You're not even showing yet, Karen. Whose idea was it?"

"Mother's," she sheepishly admits. "I told her it was too early. I don't need a shower. She and Daddy have completely furnished the nursery already."

"You gave in."

"Like a fool. You know how I hate confronting Mother. She cries and I can't take it. I'm her only child. It's easier to let her do what she wants."

"I've never been to a first-trimester baby shower before."

"Lenny, you've got to be there."

"Wouldn't miss it," I say cheerfully, even though I would rather suck raw eggs than sit around with a group of women ogling over baby sweaters and blankets. I would rather jump naked into the chilly waters of the Atlantic and count to a hundred. I would rather give Ralph half the money. But I think about the fact that Karen is my best friend in the world since my friends Laura Ruth and Venita Perry moved north, and I would walk through fire to save her, I would jump in the lake, and short of kissing Ralph's behind, I will endure the torturous baby shower.

27

Rosetta does not visit as she promised. Months have ticked by. Now she claims her rebuilt transmission has broken down.

"Take it back to the shop," I command. "There has to be a warranty on repair work that cost over fifteen hundred dollars."

"There ain't no warranty," she says lackadaisically.

"Any idiot would've made sure before paying them the money," I say. But Rosetta says nothing. I sense her hurt feelings in the stony silence between us, and I regret belittling her. I think of my newly acquired wealth and how badly Mama misses her favored daughter.

"If you can manage to get down here, Rosetta, I'll buy you another car."

"Sho 'nuff?"

"Yes, I'll do it," I say, amazed at how Rosetta always manages to get what she wants in the end.

"Then I'll hop on a bus tonight."

Rosetta's bus arrives promptly at ten the next morning. Rosetta waves as soon as she spots me standing at the gate. I watch her meander into the tiny station, taking her sweet time, intentionally pushing my buttons. We exchange an awkward hug. She looks a mess. Rosetta is grossly overweight and busting at the seams of a matronly print dress, her wavy hair slicked back into a country bun, and she smells like a stale pack of cigarettes.

"It ain't as cold as Bobby said it was gonna be," she says, pulling at the thick, brown sweater she wears. She stares disapprovingly at the sleeveless white tunic I wear over a pair of black Capri pants.

"Didn't know doctors dress as common as all that," she says.

"Doctors are people, too," I retort. I point in the direction of the car. "I'm parked over there." Rosetta carries a brown paper shopping bag, which I assume contains snacks and a few magazines.

"Where's your luggage?" I say, and she lifts the bag and tells me this is it. She climbs into the passenger side of my old Toyota Corolla, tossing her brown-bag suitcase into the back seat.

"Can't believe you still driving this old thing," she sputters.

"Old Faithful drives like a dream, and it's paid for," I say, sliding into my seat, starting the engine and speedily leaving downtown, shifting gears and whizzing through traffic to get home. I wonder if Rosetta regrets wasting years being pretty when she should have focused on being smart. To think I once wanted to be just like her. I would've pulled teeth to have her hair and lighter skin. When I was a teenager, the only boys who were nice to me were the ones who wanted to make it with Rosetta.

I pull into the driveway of my house, which she has never once visited, and glance at her. She pretends to be bored and unimpressed.

"When we gonna look at cars?" she says, indifferent to everything except herself.

"As soon as you make Mama feel damned special that you've come here just to see her, that's when."

By evening, when the sun begins to fade, Mama wakes from a long sleep. She gazes up at the humbled face of Rosetta, who shakes her head in disbelief at the change in our mother. Mama is weakened beyond what is humanly imaginable. I take small comfort in seeing my sister crumble and break down in tears.

"This ain't no time for cryin'," Mama says faintly, her voice barely audible. Her eyes look famished, resolved to whatever happens next.

"How're my grandbabies?"

"Fine mostly, Mama. But they gots so much they needin' right now. We barely makin' do. The old house ain't sold just yet. So money's tight."

Mama says nothing.

"Things costs a lot more these days," Rosetta wheedles. "I don't know how we'll be able to make do."

"You even gets my social security check, Rosetta. There ain't no excuse. You and Bobby need to live in your means."

Rosetta grins wide, covering the gap in her teeth with her hand, and says, "Mama's still raising hell."

But Mama does not cackle or even crack a smile. She strains to catch her breath and says, "What I'm tellin' you is the truth, Rosetta. When I die, ain't nobody gonna come 'round to wipe your butt clean no more. You gots to get things right, child. For them grands, you gots to do it."

"I am, Mama," Rosetta insists. Mama lies back and closes her eyes, the drip from the IV bag plugged into her arm louder than the rise and fall of her chest. I put a Mahalia Jackson CD on the stereo next to her bed, light a scented candle, and signal to Rosetta that we should leave.

Rosetta gets down on her knees and prays fervently over Mama—a combination of The Lord's Prayer and the gospel song "I'm Going Up Yonder To Be With My Lord."

The next morning, before I go to work, Mama is awake, sitting up in bed as if invigorated somehow.

"Mama?" I say. The distant gleam in her eyes frightens me. Her lips move with silent words spewing nervously from them. She reaches out to me, and when I wrap my arms around her, she squeezes me close, her frail body enlivened with resilience.

I follow her gaze to the French doors, and wonder if she is overcome by the sight of the fully bloomed dogwood, pink and billowing in the fresh breeze that stirs it. The windows are open. A cheerful scent of spring blows inside. I wonder who opened them. Did Annie open the windows this morning, or in the middle of the night?

"God spoke to me when that white lady read the Bible the other day," she says in a voice clearer than on the day she first arrived. "Spoke to me this morning, too."

"What'd God say, Mama?"

"She says she sent me an angel, and that angel is you, Lenita Mae. She says you was sent to be my angel and I ain't once said thank you for nothin', not once."

Sobs rise up inside Mama from deep inside. She grabs me around the neck, her parched lips pressing against my face like sandpaper.

"Thank you, baby, for all you done for me. I loves you so much, Lenita Mae. So don't go feeling bad about me passing. I'm looking forward to it. I can't wait to see Joseph. He's waitin' for me at the pearly gates."

"I love you, too, Mama," I whisper, as her body goes limp, her eyes roll back in their deep, dark sockets, and her breathing stops. She is dead at 7:42 A.M. I use a tissue to wipe her last tears away and remove the IV from her arm. "I'm no angel, Mama," I say as I glance around the room, as lavish and comfortable as I could make it. The vase next to her bed contains a dozen or so purple tulips from Ernest. The sight of them brings me to tears.

A warmth begins to flow through me, pulsing rapturously at the very center of my being, all around, hugging me tight like the spirit of new birth trickling through my fingers, touching my soul. I know it is Mama's spirit saying good-bye.

28

My mother's dying wish was to be cremated and for her ashes to be buried in the same plot as my father's. She did not want much fuss, not a lot of handwringing and wiping tears and feeling sorry. She wanted the pastor from Wayside Baptist to say a few words of prayer for her entrance into Glory. Mostly, Mama looked forward to death. I recall her saying not long before she died: "I can't wait to see Joseph. He's waitin' for me at the pearly gates."

I think of my brother reuniting with Mama, and an image of them embracing after all these years gives me a sense of peace. But more than that, there is a part of me mended, now made more whole because she finally admitted that she loved me.

"What we gonna do, Lenita Mae?" Rosetta wails vociferously. She suddenly becomes like a wild bull, charging from the kitchen to the great room, thunderously stomping her feet before finally plopping into a chair. Her hands shoot up in the air, her head rears back, and she screams, "MAMMMMAAAA! Oh, God, Mama . . . Mama . . . Jesus Christ . . . what we gonna do?"

Mama would have scoffed at my sister's behavior. She would have told Rosetta to stop carrying on. "Why don't you sit down and cut it out?" she might have said. I wait for Rosetta to snort and catch her breath between squeals before I speak.

"Calm down, Rosetta," I say sharply, my sense of peace now gone. She bawls like a baby. I phone the hospice and give the time of death. Saying Mama's name numbs my throat. Buelah McKinsey Faulkner, dead at age sixty-six. I'm here and not here.

"Lord have mercy," Rosetta squeals, before flopping back in a chair, and finally piping down. She covers her face with her hands like a child who is afraid to face me. My heart dips. What are we now that Mama is gone? I think how I wanted this moment to be the end of our sisterhood. I sit across from Rosetta, remembering when we were children. We were innocent, sweet little girls who loved each other. The clock from the kitchen ticks away each minute, sounding louder somehow, like an urgent reminder that time is running out. Yet, an eternity seems to pass while we wait.

The doorbell rings and I get up to answer it, glancing briefly back at Rosetta, whose eyes begin to tear-up again.

"Come in, please," I say, inviting two dark-suited, nondescript black men from the funeral home inside.

"Let me say how sorry we are for your loss," whispers one discreetly, as if keeping the secret that Mama is dead. "We'll do everything we can to make things easier for you and your family."

Rosetta stands, raising a hand in the air, as if giving testimony in court, exclaiming, "Lord, help me."

I lead the men past her to Mama's bedroom. They size up what is left of Mama. I wait outside the room while they zip Mama into a body bag, and then remove her from the house. I watch as they ease the bag on a gurney into the back of a hearse.

"What'll I do without Mama?" Rosetta remains slumped in the chair while I stand by the window. "Mama's gone, what'll I do?"

"Hush, Rosetta," I whisper. What we both feel is the same sorrow I sense from babies when I take them temporarily away from their mothers, the same lonesome, pitiful whine, and the same quivering bottom lip. I stand over Rosetta, her mouth gaping open in agony; the missing tooth like a dark hole she has forgotten existed.

"We'll get through it, Rosetta," I say, reaching my arms around her broad shoulders. Her large body quakes as she weeps against my neck.

"It's all right," I say. "We'll be fine."

"We will?"

"We're still a family, Rosetta," I say, contemplating the fact that Mama's death cannot so easily undo the ties that bind us together.

"Lord, yes," she agrees, settling down again. "But what about Bobby?"

I contact Bobby on the phone and he breaks down crying.

"Oh, God. Mama, I . . . I . . . I'm sorry," he stutters. "I should've come on back . . . I . . . I . . . I should've done right by you, Mama."

"Bobby, we'll get through it," I say, as he blows his nose over the phone line like a honking goose. I remember something my father's sister, Aunt Ida Mae, said about Bobby and Rosetta after his funeral: "The worst young 'uns always show out and cry the loudest over their Mama or Daddy's corpse."

"I'll get Barb to write up Mama's obituary," Bobby says.

"That's good," I say. "Be sure to mention Joe, and tell folks not to send flowers . . . They can send money for cancer research."

"Ain't that what killed her?"

"Yes, Bobby, that's the point."

"Yeah, well, I'll head over to the house and get rid of all the junk," he says, all at once bursting into an uncontrollable sob.

"God, Mama's really gone."

"She loved you so much, Bobby," I say. "You were her little boy. Her precious jewel."

On Tuesday, after working half the day, I take Rosetta out to test-drive a used 1998 Toyota Corolla, telling her how dependable it is. "The transmission in a car like this is superb," I say.

"New cars last longer," she says.

"Not always," I say. "All the kinks have been worked out of this one. It's a finely tuned machine."

She takes my word for it and drives it off the lot all the way home to Madoosa County with her brown bag luggage in the back seat. I return home to an emptier house than when Ralph left me. I'm motherless and completely alone. I close the door to Mama's room and plop down on the sofa for a long while, staring blankly. I thought I would be relieved after she died. I thought I would not feel as deeply for Mama as I do. My heart aches as I remember her heavy hands shooing Rosetta and me away from the billowing sheets as she hung clothes in a crisp fall breeze, or even in winter, when the tips of her fingers were like clumps of ice. On the coldest days, she ironed the lining of my coat to make it just a little warmer, just a little more protection against the winter. I see Mama braiding my hair, prattling on about the texture, smoothing it back from my face, and gazing into my eyes to say, "One of these days, you gonna be somethin' else, child."

There is a knock at the door, and I shuffle over, half expecting to find Mrs. Stein.

"Ernest."

"On my way to work yesterday, I noticed a hearse leave your driveway. I thought about your mother."

"She died."

"I'm so sorry, Lenny."

"Come in, Ernest." He enters and takes a seat next to me on the sofa. I feel unglued, part of me coming apart.

"Can I do anything to help?" he asks.

"Hold me," I say, my lips quivering. Ernest wraps his arms around me, awkwardly at first, before I sink into the side of his neck. His scraggly beard. The smell of herbal scented soap. His rough, gardener's hands tenderly caress my face. My eyes fill with tears as he whispers, "It's all right, Lenny. I'm here." Inside, my body quakes from losing the woman who brought me into the world, and I sob off and on for what seems like hours before falling asleep. When I awake, I am lying with my head in Ernest's lap. His eyes are closed. I wonder where Kevin is, if he is back from Taiwan, if he knows I need him. Ernest gazes down at me, smoothing my hair back from my face.

"I'm here as long as you need me," he says.

I head for Madoosa County with the urn carefully stored in the trunk of my car. The smell of the box factory seems worse than ever in the poorest section of town, the side where I grew up. The tiny church swells with warm bodies, relatives and friends fanning themselves against the stagnant air. Reverend Johnson, a short, dark-skinned man with a deep, sturdy voice, speaks of how Mama loved the Lord. She worked tirelessly in the church. She was a loving wife and mother. The minister uses words like *selfless, kind,* and *forgiving.*

I start to nod off briefly, imagining Mama hanging clothes out on the line. In another memory I am asleep and Mama shakes me awake, telling me to be hardworking like my daddy. I hear the strawberry-picking truck as it rounds the corner, and I hop up and run for it. I am a girl, no more than ten. Somebody has to bring in extra money, since Joe died. Somebody has to be dependable. *Be the first one there,* Mama says, church bells ringing next to my ear. *Be the best,* she calls out, the urgency in her voice spurring me to run faster.

"It's time," Rosetta says, nudging me into opening my eyes. She is standing over me with her hand outstretched, and I reach for it. Bobby is on my left side, helping me up. We take Mama's ashes out to the cemetery in back of the church and place the urn in the plot next to my father's grave. Bobby says The Lord's Prayer and Rosetta sings "I'm Going Up Yonder." I tell them that before Mama died, she heard God speak to her.

"She was at peace," I say, as warmth trickles through me, surrounding my heart with the feel of Mama's weak arms embracing me. "She's with us, I feel it."

"Me, too," Rosetta says.

Bobby cries, "I promise I'll do right, Mama." His body slumps against me, and we grip each other tighter as if letting go too soon will be the end of us. We talk about better days, when Joe was alive, before Daddy began to drink heavily.

"Remember how Joe would ride us on his bike?" Rosetta asks. "Down to the duck pond, o'er that big hump in the road, so's we'd almost fall off, laughing and carrying on."

"Yes, and I remember how he used to take us fishing. We'd catch baby carp and he'd make us throw them back."

"I couldn't even do that, caught the hem of my dress one time."

We laugh at Rosetta tugging at the back of her dress to demonstrate.

"I don't remember him," Bobby says. "I remember the way his things smelled."

"Daddy got right with the Lord just in time," Rosetta says. "After Mama almost knocked out all his teeth, remember?"

Bobby and I nod in agreement.

"He gave up all that drinking and sho' 'nuff turned his life around."

"They're all together now, like us," I say, tightening my arms around Bobby and Rosetta, not wanting this bond to break.

29

As soon as I arrive home, I call Frank O'Connor. "I'd rather be busy," I say.

"You've just buried your mother," he says. "You should take more time."

"Work keeps my mind off things."

"I understand," he says softly.

"Anything I should be aware of?"

"No, so far the evening's been quiet."

"I'll take over from here, Frank. Good night."

We hang up. I change into a pair of soft blue scrubs. The air is cool with the windows open. I pull back the covers of my bed and slide between the sheets. When I stop listening for the clock ticking on the table next to my bed or the distant hum of the refrigerator in the kitchen or the natural, rhythmic harmonies of the night creatures outside—I descend the final level of consciousness. Soon I am whirling around in darkness, and when the light comes, Mama is standing in the center of a circle of red and yellow roses. She is holding a clock in her hand. The alarm goes off and she frowns, reminding me that it is time for work.

You gonna be late again if you don't git, she says, the ringing next to my ear. Mama shakes me by my shoulders. *Hurry up, Lenita Mae, before the strawberry truck gets here.* The strawberry truck comes at first dawn before the dew has time to dry. I hop in back with the rest of the early pickers and we spend the day bent over, crawling around in the stifling heat, our knees and knuckles bruised and sometimes bloody.

The alarm rings louder and louder; I am snatched unmercifully awake, eyes half closed and cottony, barely cognizant of my beeper or the fact that I am being paged.

"Oh, crap," I blurt, squinting to make out the phone number on my pager. It's the hospital emergency room. I phone the attending nurse.

"Who is she?" I ask.

"Linda Jenkins," the nurse says. "She's critical."

"Jenkins?" I say drowsily; then it hits me who the patient is. I hang up the phone and quickly get out of bed, snatching my purse, keys, and stethoscope. My Toyota reaches the hospital in record time. The emergency room is hectic and overcrowded. It takes me a few minutes to find out what happened.

Linda had been unconscious and bleeding when paramedics arrived at her college dorm room. They started an IV, and here in the emergency room, the patient was given several units of blood. An emergency team of doctors and nurses worked efficiently to stabilize her, and when she regained consciousness, she told them she was my patient.

"We paged you right away, Dr. Faulkner," says the ER physician, Dr. Benjamin Chaffey, a tall, thin man whose eyes appear as small specks behind his bottle-thick glasses.

"Where is she now?"

"In the operating room with Dr. Spindell."

"The vascular surgeon?"

"He's repairing vessels in her arms."

"What's wrong with her arms?"

"She slit them," he says, checking his watch for the time and pressing his lips firmly together.

I am too stunned to say more. Why would she do it? Kill herself, and for what? I cringe at the thought of a young woman with so much life ahead of her wanting to kill herself. Why didn't I make sure she made contact with Stella?

Dr. Chaffey rushes off to his next case. I enter the OR suite just as Linda is being wheeled into recovery. A nurse from labor and delivery is evaluating the fetus.

"Dr. Faulkner?" Linda says sluggishly, dazed by the surroundings. She is a child rediscovering herself with bandaged wrists, an IV line taped to one arm, me standing over her concerned about her health.

"Why didn't they let me die?" she moans, breaking into a series of long, helpless sobs.

"Calm down, Linda, we'll get through this together. Remember? You know I won't allow you to suffer, don't you? Don't you trust me, Linda?"

"Oh, God, I just wanna die."

The nurse glances up at me, worried from reading the strip spilling out of the fetal heart monitor.

"The baby's EKG doesn't look good, Dr. Faulkner," she says. I notice Linda's blood pressure going up.

"Administer magnesium sulfate," I say to the other nurse assisting me. Linda could have a seizure. She is weak from all the blood loss, the pallor of her skin sallow and sickly.

"Oh, God, noooo," she moans. Linda draws her legs up toward her abdomen. She is in labor. I time her contractions: Fifteen minutes apart.

"Hold on, Linda." I put on a pair of surgical gloves and moisten my fingers with K-Y jelly before inserting one finger, then two fingers to measure the dilation of her cervix. An hour passes and she does not progress beyond a two-centimeter opening.

"Help me, please!!!" she cries sharply. Her contractions are constant and intensely painful. I order an epidural.

"Try not to push," I tell her. "It's not time."

"You don't want to cause a tear before you're dilated," cautions Dr. Liu, the anesthesiologist. She tells Linda she will feel a slight sting.

Within minutes Linda feels no more pain. She closes her eyes and whispers, "I wanted to die, but I didn't want to hurt the baby."

"The baby will be fine," I say soothingly. Another hour passes and Linda's blood pressure is back to normal.

"The baby's having decelerations, Dr. Faulkner," a nurse says, examining the monitor strip. The baby's heartbeats are slowing down. "Should we take her in for a C-section now?"

"Not yet," I say. "She's lost a lot of blood and might be too weak right now. But prep her."

"Her contractions are two minutes apart now, Doctor."

"Cervix still holding at three centimeters."

I glance at the monitor strip's jagged, cascading line. Linda is breathing steadily. Her swollen eyelids are closed; her hands are clasped together on top of her belly mound. Some of the pink has come back to her complexion. A half hour passes. I want her to be strong enough for a C-section, but if I wait too long, she and the baby might die.

We medicate Linda to slow the labor, but in spite of our effort, she begins to push involuntarily an hour later. The opening of the cervix is still too small for a normal delivery.

"Should we start the C-section now, Doctor?"

"Not yet." I am afraid to cut into Linda. A series of "what if's" flash like flood warnings.

"The baby's heart rate is dangerously low," the labor-and-delivery nurse says with more urgency in her tone.

"All right, let's prepare for a C-section," I say. The assisting nurse preps the patient. A big, burly nurse breezes inside to assist the delivery. Her plump hands caress Linda's arms.

"You'll be fine, young lady," she says, reassuringly. "Just hang in there."

"I will," Linda says tiredly. "Dr. Faulkner's here." The tension in her face relaxes into a tranquil resolve, as orderlies wheel her back into the OR.

I cut in a fourteen-centimeter single lateral line above the pubic hair at the skin fold, down to the rectus muscle—the six-pack, if you aren't pregnant and happen to work out like crazy. I begin the intricate process of entering the abdomen. This is where I notice unusually large amounts of bleeding, blood perking up from all over, like mineral springs, only terrifyingly red. I worry about the patient outcome, but at this point I must move quickly to get the baby out.

I carefully strip the bladder off the lower uterus and cervix, and make a lateral incision between them, slicing through muscle the feel and color of salmon, down to the amniotic sac, where the baby is visible, a toy alien inside a plastic bubble. I cut through the sac, relieved to see the baby's color isn't blue.

I drop the instrument on a tray and extend the incision with my fingers to push on the uterus and guide the baby's head through the opening. I pull this small, weak infant from its mother, gently holding it in my hands, the feel of its warm spirit sifting through my fingers like the wind, its body turning from ash white to pinkish. It is a girl. I suction out her tiny nostrils and she gurgles. The labor-and-delivery nurse wipes tears from her eyes.

"It's a shame the mother almost killed it," she says.

"We hurt ourselves when we're young," says the other nurse.

The infant's chin quivers with the faint sound of a soft breath escaping her tiny, pink lips. A neonatal unit team, summoned earlier, is ready to whisk her away for emergency care. But before handing her over, I rouse the patient for a look.

"She's beautiful, Linda, see?"

"Oh, God," she cries out. "She really is." Her eyes become glassy orbs that scan the newborn entirely, taking in the number of fingers and toes.

"She'll live, won't she, Doctor?"

"Of course," I say, trying to sound confident. I quickly pass the baby to one of the nurses on the neonatal team. Half the room leaves with them. As I prepare to close the womb, I realize Linda is oozing from every incision. I call for several units of blood.

The nurse anesthetist hustles in with a larger IV line, which she inserts into Linda's arm. We give her platelets, whole blood, plasma, fluids. The bleeding continues as I work to repair uterine blood vessels. Blood spills from the uterus, where the skin is cut, at the place where the bladder was separated, and at the IV site. It bubbles up like newly tapped oil.

I begin to sew up the uterus. Suddenly, Linda's heart rate drops. Her face drains of all color.

"She's in shock," I yell.

"Her blood isn't clotting, Doctor," says an assisting nurse.

"Blood's everywhere," the nurse anesthetist says, panicking.

"Stay with us, Linda," I yell. "I promised we'd get through this together."

The nurse anesthetist pages Dr. Liu. The emergency attending physician flies into the OR just as the patient goes into cardiac arrest. A fluorescent green line flattens out across the screen of the monitor.

"All clear . . . all clear," Dr. Liu says, as she prepares to initiate coronary pulmonary resuscitation, or, in other words, to use a defibrillator, a pair of paddles that act as giant sparkplugs, to recharge Linda's heart. Dr. Liu mounts Linda's chest with the paddles, and a bolt of electricity causes her entire body to quake. The monitor hums; then slowly it begins to beep. There are no less than eight of us working to bring her back to life. I feel like I am standing outside the crematory waiting for Mama's body to completely burn. She made me promise this before she died, afraid that her body would be shipped off to a lab and used for experiments. I waited for the metal door to open and a tray of ashes to slide out of the huge oven. Yes, I gave the mortician the nod that I was satisfied. I was numb, like now, watching a movie of myself.

A moment later, another flat line. Again, the emergency team uses the defibrillator to jumpstart Linda's heart. The heart beats briefly, then a flat line drones across the screen. Dr. Liu glances up at the emergency-room head.

"Are you ready to call it?" she says.

"No," I say. "Please, don't." The team continues to massage the patient's chest. But there are no more beats, only a flat line and a constant hum that seems to blare inside the otherwise silent room.

"Are you ready now?" the doctor says, perspiration dripping down the sides of her face, her eyes unblinking through her spectacles.

"Yes," I say quietly. The emergency specialist checks her watch and announces the time. At exactly 3:08 A.M. I am standing at Linda's pale feet, which will never walk the earth again. The room clears and I am alone. It suddenly strikes me that she seems alive, her eyes closed as if in sleep. She seems dead and alive simultaneously. What cruel irony that she felt this way for months.

Blood covers the front of my scrubs and is tracked all over the floor, as if an explosion has gone off. Linda's belly is still open. I push the skin back in place. My nostrils fill with the raw, sanguine odor that permeates the room. I break into tears. This isn't supposed to happen in obstetrics—not really—and especially not to me. I have never lost a patient before, never thought I would.

The events leading to Linda Jenkins's death replay in my mind over and over. *What could I have done to save her? She must have taken a ton of aspirin—that's what caused the bleeding. What could I have done? How could I have known?* There is no burden heavier than feeling responsible for someone's death, a mother taken before her time. A motherless child. Nothing prepared me for this, no class in medical school taught me how to deal with death.

I cover Linda's body entirely with a bloody sheet, and wonder about the man who dumped her. Does he know what harm his actions have caused? Will he regret that she hurt enough to die? Suddenly, I am paged from labor and delivery. There is no time for mourning or feeling pity. Another patient has arrived. Another emergency.

30

After Linda Jenkins's death, I perform another emergency C-section, and later enter a vacant on-call room, the place where doctors go to rest and recuperate at the hospital. I remove my bloodied clothes and crawl between stiff hospital sheets, naked except for a black bra and panties, utterly exhausted. But just as I am about to drift off to sleep, a nurse shakes me awake, telling me I have a patient three centimeters dilated, first pregnancy, no late decelerations, and her contractions are five minutes apart. She could be in labor for hours, more than enough time for me to shower.

I peek outside the door. There isn't a soul stirring. The doctors' corridor is uncommonly empty, and my attention turns to the muffled sound of a television left on in one of the other on-call rooms farther down the hall. I hesitate briefly before making a fast break to the women's locker room, clad only in my underwear, preferring to leave the bloodied scrubs behind. I'm racing along, planning to brush my teeth, take a quick shower, and change into a pair of clean scrubs, when a door abruptly opens. The sound of a TV commercial blares out into the hallway. Someone is watching me. I look straight ahead, and just as I am about to disappear inside, I hear the chuckle of one of my male colleagues, then the words, "Timing is everything."

Embarrassment whips across both cheeks. I shower and dress in a hurry. While brushing my teeth, my pager goes off. The hospital emergency room. When I phone back, I am told that Linda Jenkins's parents are there. The parents who sent their beloved daughter off to college are waiting to be told she is dead. The thought of it makes me nauseous. This isn't supposed to happen in obstetrics. Young mothers aren't supposed to die.

Before heading to the waiting room, I make a detour to the neonatal unit, something deep down compelling me to know the baby's condition. She is one of five unnamed, one of two girls, the only one with a dead mother. I look closer and notice her skin tone. I understand part of Linda's dilemma in the face of this tiny, innocent creature. She is not going to be white bread and red-haired, like her mother.

I have to be strong and deliver the news every parent fears. I try imagining what they'll be like. Linda Jenkins seemed alone in the world. Her unnamed baby is fighting for her life in an incubator.

I near the waiting room, my footsteps echoing through the empty corridor. I open the door, and find the room is full of people who quiet as I enter. Most of them have auburn hair and pale skin, like Linda's. My feet freeze in place, and I am stuck in the doorway. Linda belonged to all of them. Her entire family has come to be told. My throat becomes parched and constricts. A woman with cropped silver hair approaches.

"You're Linda's doctor?" she says.

"Yes," I say, stepping into the room with leaden feet, extending a hand to shake hers. The waiting room door startles me when it bangs shut.

"I'm Dr. Faulkner."

"I'm Linda's mother," she says. "We took the first plane out of Salt Lake City late last night after we heard about the accident." She takes my hand in both of hers, rubbing instead of shaking. She has soft, big hands that I imagine scrubbing Linda's back in a tub full of soapy water when she was a girl, or combing her long, auburn hair into pigtails, or teaching her to pray.

Mrs. Jenkins takes a deep breath and introduces me to the others. Her husband is short and lean, like Linda. When he shakes my hand, he has a strong, firm grip. He sits, next to his wife, and they both look up at me.

I move around the room, listlessly shaking the hands of Linda's four brothers and two sisters. I am here and not here. After the introductions, the room hushes again.

"How is she?" says the eldest sister apprehensively. She is older than Linda and only vaguely resembles her sister, her expression pinched. She looks the way I felt hearing Mama tell me that the cancer had returned. Before I can answer, she says, "What happened?"

I swallow hard and say, "I've been Linda's obstetrician for only a few months. A physician from her school referred her to me. She came thirteen weeks pregnant."

A collective gasp circles the room.

"Pregnant?" says the mother, staring down at her hands, clasped together on her lap.

"She came into the emergency room this morning." I hesitate and glance at the faces around the room, my heart pounding wildly. "She had slit her wrists."

Mrs. Jenkins weeps softly; her husband wraps an arm around her.

"Is she all right?" says one of the brothers impatiently.

"I'm sorry to tell you that Linda went into cardiac arrest at about three o'clock this morning."

Silence.

"We tried all means to resuscitate her." My eyes water and knees become weak. "She had lost an enormous amount of blood. We worked on her for nearly an hour. I'm so sorry, Mrs. Jenkins."

"But she's our baby."

"Wanted to come south instead of staying home and going to B.Y.U."

"We should've kept her home with family."

Their eyes become reproachful towards me.

"She delivered a healthy five-and-a-half-pound daughter," I say optimistically, before realizing how insensitive I must sound. Nothing can make up for the loss of Linda. I wish I could disappear.

"She's dead? My baby's dead?" The father crumbles into his wife, sobbing. There are tears and questions and anger all around me.

"I'm so very sorry, so sorry," I say, like a babbling idiot, my voice quivering.

"We must pray for Linda now, Papa," says Mrs. Jenkins. They pull themselves together and form a circle, linked together by their faith and crossed hands. The father signals for me to join in and when I do, he prays aloud for God's forgiveness of their daughter's sins and for Linda's eternal life.

Afterward, her eldest brother, whose hand I am holding, says, "I taught her how to ride a bike. Seems like yesterday."

"I thank God for the privilege of sleeping next to Linda as we grew up together," says the shortest, younger sister. "She made me feel safe."

"I'll miss her at my wedding," says a woman almost the spitting image of Linda.

"No one could sing as sweet," says another brother.

"She was a precious gift," her father says.

One of Linda's sisters cries out, "She's gone. I can't believe she's gone." Reality sets in and spreads around the room. Grief covers their decorum like a thin veil.

In the course of a few minutes, the room begins to settle down to occasional sniffles.

"I'm so sorry this happened," I say, searching for the right words. "Linda was a good person. I'll miss her."

"The baby's healthy?"

"Yes, Mrs. Jenkins," I say. "Linda had not intended to harm her daughter. Deep down, she wanted to keep her."

"We don't give our babies away," says Mr. Jenkins.

I wonder if this is really true. What will life be like for this child who changed from ash white to pale rose, and then to light brown, with dark, curly hair? What happens when more of the father's DNA prevails within this child as she is raised in Utah? What will they tell her about herself? What will they tell the neighbors? I tell them I believe the father to be either African American or Hispanic—expecting a change of plans. But the few who speak up say it doesn't matter. The sister with the pinched look says, "As soon as she's ready, we're taking her home."

A nurse pushes the door open and tells me that the patient who came in at three centimeters is now five centimeters, her water has broken, and her contractions are now one minute apart. Time to deliver. Timing is everything.

When I get home and step out of my scrubs, the emptiness inside my bedroom seems drastic in comparison to the bustle of the hospital. I grieve over losing Mama and Linda Jenkins. I see Linda's face all around me, pale and sickly. I feel sick and alone, with no one left to comfort me. I cry until my eyes ache. The phone rings and Ernest Hemingway leaves a message on my answering machine. "Lenny, I hope you're okay." He hesitates before adding, "Let's get together soon."

I want to answer him, hear a voice, and talk out my feelings, but instead, I take a shower and focus on the sound of pulsing hot water against my skin. It hurts to think about what has happened. My skin is raw by the time I put on a robe. Just as I am about to get into bed, the doorbell rings. I find Mrs. Stein holding a basket of fresh baked goods.

"I'm glad you're home," she says, surveying the pink flannel robe I'm wearing. "Hope I didn't get you at a bad time."

"No you didn't," I say, feeling like crap warmed over. I'm sure I must look as bad as I feel.

"Well, I've been wanting to bring you something since your mother passed." She hands me the basket, saying how sorry she is.

"Thanks, Mrs. Stein," I say, "It's good she isn't suffering anymore."

"She was so proud of you," she says. "Told me how hard you worked at everything. She bragged about the money and presents you sent her. She said you never forgot her birthday. You were a good daughter, Lenny."

"Thanks for all the times you read to Mama from the Bible."

"Oh, I didn't read from the Bible," she says matter-of-factly, "I read from the Torah, and your mother saw a vision of an angel."

"Did you see anything?"

"No, nothing at all. But I believed your mother when she said she did. I felt the presence of something divine." There is a glimmer in Mrs. Stein's eyes when she says, "Your mother said you were her angel."

"She must have been delirious."

"She seemed perfectly clear to me. With all you did for your mother while she was alive, you're an angel in my book, too."

A warm feeling flows through me, like when I stood with Rosetta and Bobby at Mama's grave, like when Mama died in my arms. I invite Mrs. Stein inside for tea, and the two of us sit in the kitchen where we share the cinnamon rolls and biscuits she brought.

"So, how's the young man who used to live here? Still scratching at your door?"

"No, he's found what he wants *elsewhere.*"

"*Elsewhere.* I see. Well, I didn't much like his attitude. And he was vulgar to bring women to your house while you were away."

"I'm glad I didn't know it at the time," I say, thinking how this would be the perfect occasion to tell Mrs. Stein she watches my house way too closely. But instead, I say, "It doesn't matter now. He's history."

"You've got another fellow?"

"Just a friend for now. I'm getting to know myself better."

"Getting to know yourself?" she says with a slight chuckle. "That's a popular theme these days. My daughter had to *find* herself a few years ago.

She divorced her first husband because of it. You'll have to meet my Sonya." Mrs. Stein takes a sip of tea and sighs, rolling her eyes toward the ceiling.

"When I was young, most women knew who they were," she says. "We were wives or mothers or teachers or secretaries, not much compared to nowadays. But we were enough, somehow."

"What about now, Mrs. Stein?"

"Now I'm old. I know more than I'd like to know about myself."

I laugh and so does she.

"How many years were you married?" I ask.

"We celebrated our fifty-fifth anniversary before he died. Ezra was a wonderful man, the very best. My Aunt Gertie chose him for me."

"You're lucky it worked out."

"Luck had nothing to do with it, I assure you. Women like my aunt were expert matchmakers. They didn't make mistakes in putting young people together. They used their brains like love scientists."

"Come on, Mrs. Stein, love scientists?" I quip.

"Yes, it's true," she says, defensively.

"Really, now."

"I just think what a pity young people today depend on themselves."

I follow her gaze through the kitchen windows and glimpse flower boxes that had sat empty all winter, now overflowing with white petunias and pink impatiens. Mrs. Stein pours herself another cup of tea. She reminds me of a patient, Mrs. Gleason, an elderly widow who spends most of her time at home alone.

"When did you come to America?" I ask.

"Oh, you don't want to hear that old story." She shrugs.

"I do, really, please."

"Well, let's see," she says, putting a finger to her bottom lip, tapping, like Karen just before a know-it-all answer. "I was thirteen when my family left Poland before the war and settled in New York. I didn't even speak any English then, but now my relatives tell me I have a southern accent."

She chuckles softly to herself. "Ezra never lost his Polish accent. Most of our neighbors here couldn't understand him."

"He moved to New York at the same time, before the war?"

"Oh, no," she sighs sadly. "Ten years passed before I saw Ezra again. He lost his entire family during the Holocaust. We married and moved here to Atlanta, where he taught chemistry at Morehouse College."

"That must've been quite a change for both of you."

"It was difficult at first, with no family so far south, but we managed. Raised our children as best we could. Atlanta was a big, country town back then. Very unsophisticated. Segregated, you know."

"Indeed I do."

"Yes, well, like I said, we managed. Sonya and Randolph, my children, are doing just fine. She's a lawyer and he's a cardiologist."

"You must be proud."

"I don't hear from them as often as I'd like, but, yes, I am proud."

She covers her mouth to yawn, sleepily. I want to know more about her life in Poland, and what happened to the relatives she left behind.

"Time for bed," Mrs. Stein says, standing abruptly, ready to go home. I check the time on my watch, surprised that an hour and a half has slipped by.

"Thanks for stopping by," I say, reaching out to her, arms extending for a mutual embrace.

"I can always use a hug," she says.

"Me, too," I agree.

31

I rouse from sleep and check my pager. No calls. I feel gloomy inside from thinking about death, Linda Jenkins, and Mama. It makes me both sad and angry to know that Linda tried to take her life because the man she had hoped to marry left her. Why is it that we women convince ourselves that our lives are less important without *him?* When Ralph left me, I thought I might die from the pain it caused me. I lost my mind. Why did I allow myself to suffer? Ralph did not suffer one iota. The father of Linda's baby is probably busy making out with his next victim. I write in my diary that the only difference between Linda Jenkins and me is that I survived and she didn't.

It's only by the grace of God that I didn't die from a botched abortion when I was Linda Jenkins's age. My life would have ended as a student. I would have missed out on becoming a doctor, owning my own home, and having a best friend. There are so many things I want to do, so many places to go. I am free to dream. There, by the grace of God, go I.

Rule 6.

No man is worth suffering over.

Spring is the peak season for birth, the vernal equinox, when nature blooms, the time of year when hearts open beneath a brighter sun, when love and hope collide. I wonder if Kevin is back in town. I open my bedroom window; outside is pleasant, not too warm, with a light, steady breeze wafting through the tops of the trees. I dress in a pair of running shoes, shorts and T-shirt, head out to the street, and begin jogging. I hear footsteps running behind me. It is tempting to look back, but I don't. I turn up a side street and the person behind me does, too.

I jog onto Peachtree and so does my follower, down a side street that leads to a jogging path. I pick up the pace, running full throttle, face fixed in racing grimace, head back, heart pounding. A man ahead of me speeds up when I run around him, two women step aside to allow me through, down a hill where the paved path becomes dirt, through a wooded area where the shade cools my face. I see Mr. Jenkins bury his face in his wife's neck. What else could I have done?

At the end of the five-mile path, just before reaching the street, I stop to catch my breath, turning to face the footsteps trailing me.

"Hello, Doctor."

"Kevin?" I say, startled. "I had no idea you'd be home."

"I've missed you, Lenny," he says.

"I'm glad you're . . ." I begin to say, when suddenly the turbulence twirling around inside me, just beneath the surface, boils over, and I am overcome with grief. I break into a series of uncontrollable sobs.

"It's all right, baby," he says, taking me in his arms. "Don't worry. Everything works out in the end."

Other joggers pass by as we hold on to each other. An eternity goes by.

"My mother died and I had a patient die during a C-section," I tearfully admit. "I keep thinking I should've done more."

"You did the best you could," he insists, catching hold of my hand as we begin to walk slowly home. He has no way of knowing that I did my best, but hearing him say it brings me some solace.

"I lost a close friend in a plane crash once," he says, as we cross the street. "And blamed myself for a long time because I let Cleave go up in my plane alone, just before sunset. My instincts said not to—a thunderstorm had been forecast—but Cleave wanted it badly, and I didn't object strongly enough."

"How long did it take you to get over Cleave's accident?" I ask weakly.

He sighs and puts an arm protectively across my shoulders as we proceed down Valewood Street towards my house.

"A long time," he says at the foot of my drive. He puts a hand lightly around my waist and a rush of electricity shoots through me. Is it sadness in his eyes, or lust? He kisses me gently, his tender longing soothing to my soul.

"How about you coming to my house for dinner tonight?" he asks.

"Yes," I say.

"I grill mouthwatering seafood."

"I'll eat anything."

"So will I."

"What time?"

"As soon as you get there."

32

Stella and I sit next to a window inside a café across the street. I am about to begin eating lunch, when I notice a woman shielding her face with a large tan envelope in her hand as she crosses the street. The envelope is her only protection from the unforgiving sun, and instantly I think of my mother baking in the wrath of late summer while planting or picking weeds or hanging the laundry out to dry. Nearly three months have passed since Mama died. In a way, it seems much longer. Even Linda's death is moving steadily behind me. I don't see her face appearing, gaunt and helpless, in my dreams anymore.

"Lenny?" Stella says, bringing my attention back inside the diner. "You won't believe what happened this morning."

"What?"

"Shaniqua's school contacted my office this morning. A teacher reported seeing cuts all over her arms and legs."

"What happened?"

"She wouldn't say at first. I had to probe harder to draw the truth out of her. She said she did it to herself. Used a razor after her mother left for work."

"But why, Stella?"

"Her reasons make no sense, Lenny," Stella says gravely. "She's emotionally unstable."

"But what happens now?"

"Since she's a danger to herself, she's now going to be in the custody of Child Protective Services—a colleague is seeing a judge right now. We can hold her for three days, at least. I don't think Ms. Davis understands that her daughter has a very serious problem. She thinks Shaniqua's acting out rebelliously. She said her daughter is just trying to stay home from school."

"What can I do, Stella?"

"She seems to look up to you, Lenny. You might be able to get at the root of her problem the next time she comes in for a visit. Getting her to talk may help a great deal."

"The root of her problem is her mother."

"Which we can't change."

"Are you Dr. Lenita Faulkner?" A woman interrupts, and I recognize her as the one I had seen a moment earlier crossing the street.

"Yes," I say, observing beads of sweat on her forehead. She is an overweight black woman wearing a snugly fitted suit, but neat. She smells sweet with an expensive perfume, one that might cost as much as forty bucks an ounce at a department store. I notice a large diamond on her marrying finger when she hands me the envelope and tells me it is a summons to court.

"A summons!" I yelp, as the woman turns to leave.

"What is it, Lenny?" Stella asks.

"Ralph. I can't get rid of him."

"That's too bad."

"I'm getting a lawyer," I mutter, sliding the envelope off the table and onto my lap. "Just when I'm beginning to recover."

"Recover?"

"I had a patient die during a C-section last month," I say, sighing heavily.

"I'm sorry, Lenny."

"She was a pregnant college student named Linda Jenkins. She tried to kill herself."

"How sad," Stella says, shaking her head piteously. "Linda Jenkins, you say?"

"Yes, I tried to get her to call you, but she wouldn't do it."

"But she did call me, Lenny," Stella says. "Linda Jenkins was asked to leave her dormitory this semester because of her pregnancy, and she needed a place to stay. Unfortunately, there were no openings at any of the group homes."

"But I thought you said there was always room for a girl who didn't want her baby and wannabe parents lining up to help her."

"She wanted to keep it, Lenny. At least, that's what she told me. If Linda Jenkins had agreed to adoption, believe me, there would've been a much nicer place for her to stay. All I could find for her was a shelter."

"That's terrible, Stella," I say, distressed. "It's wrong."

"That's the way things are and there's nothing we can do about it."

"Nothing?" I remember what Stella said about there being no adequate facility for girls who want to keep their babies, no place these girls can go to become properly trained mothers, no nurses. "You said what this city needs is a place that does it right. Remember, Stella?"

"Yes, I do."

"A model for the others to follow."

"Yes, got any ideas?"

"I'm willing to put up seed money for a home like that, Stella, if you'll agree to run it."

"But you'll need to put up a lot of seed, Lenny," she says.

"Think a million will help us get started?"

"A million? Why, yes, if you've really got that much seed."

"That's what this is all about," I say, holding up the summons. "When we get this home off the ground, I'll thank Ralph Griffin for his contribution."

Stella hesitates, the look of surprise crossing her face like a tidal wave. Then, all at once, she breaks into a wide smile.

"You're serious about this, aren't you, Lenny?" she asks, and when I nod yes, she says, "Well, you've got yourself a deal."

We shake over soup and salad.

The next day, I phone Paul Anderson's office.

"Jason Ashby referred you to me," I say.

"I've been expecting your call." His voice is calm and reassuring. Instinctively, I don't trust him.

"What do you know about my case, Mr. Anderson?"

"Only what you decide to tell me," he says. I tell him everything: how all the money invested was mine, that Ralph stole my jewelry, pictures, and drove my credit card up to its limit.

"He even tried to get me to sell my house," I say.

"Sounds like a charming guy," he says sarcastically. "I'll be happy to take your case."

He transfers my call to his secretary and she makes an appointment for me to see him the following Tuesday morning. I cannot afford to be deceived. I know how attorneys operate. I lived with one for years. Secretly, I plan to record our meetings, keep track of the actual time, and stay on the subject. I will not pay for frivolous talk that has nothing to do with my case. And I definitely will not pay for legal advice that steers me away from keeping the money. The minute Paul Anderson encourages me to give Ralph his fair share I will walk right out of his office.

After a full day of examining patients, I go home exhausted. This lawsuit business is beginning to wear me down. I cannot stop thinking about what might happen if Ralph wins. What happens to the home for pregnant girls if I cannot deliver the money? I am greeted by a spring bouquet of fresh-cut flowers on the porch outside my front door, along with a note from Ernest Hemingway.

Dear Lenny,

Just thinking about you. If you need a friend, please call.

Yours truly,
Ernest

I put the flowers on the night table next to my bed and prepare a warm bath. Time loses its grasp on me as I doze off in the tub. Before long, I am climbing to the top of a mountain. I see every rock and scrub and minute insect with such clarity that I am compelled now and then to stop along the way. The sky is the bluest blue; a hawk calls urgently as it glides on the wind above my head. My mother's voice calls out like a song, telling me to be first. And bells peal from the valley, their sound resonating in my ears as I reach the top. Kevin is standing above me. I call his name and he smiles his perfect smile. He reaches for my hands to help me up. But when I let go of the rope, he lets go of me. I am falling when suddenly the doorbell rings, wresting me awake.

It is twilight and my body is pimpled all over from the cold water. I am shivering and hurriedly tie on my robe before answering the door.

Peeking first, I see a man's face cast partially in shadow. He smiles and I know him. I open the door and explain why I'm dripping water on the floor. Kevin scoops me up in his arms and swings the door closed with his foot. He carries me to bed and removes my robe. He gently rubs the goose pimples from my arms and chest and tells me I shouldn't bathe in cold water. I forget about the dream. Kevin has been patient with me. We've only kissed up until now. We make love and I smell liquor on his breath. His tongue is sweet. His eyes are glazed and sexy.

In the morning, I listen to him snore as rain pours from the sky. This will be a perfect day to languish in bed. Kevin is here and I'm not on call. When he wakes, he blinks, looks briefly confused by my presence. Then he smiles at me. We get up and prepare a breakfast of eggs and toast and coffee. He retrieves the newspaper from the front porch and we retreat to my bed, where we eat and watch television and read headlines. By noon, he is thirsty for beer. He finds the ones Ralph left behind acceptable. He drinks all four bottles and tells me he's falling in love with me. His eyes are as glazed and sexy as last night, and I can't resist wanting him again.

After Kevin leaves to ready himself for the next day's flight to Indonesia, I phone Ernest Hemingway and thank him for the note and flowers he left me. "They mean a lot to me," I say.

"I know what it's like to lose a loved one."

"Let's get together for coffee tomorrow," I urge.

"I can't, Lenny. My dad was put in the hospital last night. So, I'm flying up to Cincinnati in the morning."

"I hope he has a full recovery," I say.

"Coffee when I get back," he says.

"Let's."

33

On Tuesday, I meet Paul Anderson in his office. There is something familiar about him, but I cannot place how or where. He is tall enough to have played basketball in college. I flip the switch on the tape recorder inside my purse and note the time to be 9:15 A.M. He looks like he could be a good friend of Ralph's. *One of his boys.* I imagine them golfing together or teaming up with the other *boys* to sit around watching a game of basketball.

"Did you play basketball in college?" I blurt out and bite my tongue. He tells me no, and I guard my lips from going off course again. Unlike with doctors, time is money for lawyers. I could stand on my feet for eighteen hours and still receive the same managed-care fee.

"I brought all the records I have," I say quickly.

"Very good," he says, reaching for the materials in my hands. He studies each sheet and places them neatly into two stacks on his desk. He shuffles through a few bank statements and explains the battle that might be ahead of us because I shared a joint investment account with Ralph. He says that even though I can prove Ralph did not contribute directly, I may have a hard time proving that his involvement with the account was in bad faith. The account quadrupled under his management.

"Have you ever met Ralph?" I say.

"Yes," he says without hesitation. "In the courtroom."

"So, he's not a friend?"

"I wouldn't offer to take your case if he was."

"Thank you," I say. A big part of me does not trust him yet. He is clean cut in appearance, wears wire-framed glasses, and his office is modest compared to Ralph's, though neat and orderly. His law books are arranged alphabetically. The framed picture that sits on his desk with its back to me is probably of his wife and children. He's a "family-type" man with all the trappings of honesty and decency. I thought Ralph was family material, too, when I met him.

"Give me a few days to review your case, Dr. Faulkner," he says. "I'd like to research a few things before we get together again."

9:00 A.M.

Angelina Finley, 22-year-old Hispanic female, first-time patient, Weight: 115 lbs. Height: 5'2", Birth control: none. Last menstrual period: June 11. Urine test is positive for pregnancy. Complaint: Nausea.

"Mrs. Finley, it looks like congratulations are definitely in order. You and your husband are going to have a baby."

"Oh, this is wonderful news, Doctor. I can't wait to tell Phillip. He graduated from West Point two years ago, just before we got married, and he's finished his tour of duty in Japan. This is our first baby!"

"Sounds like you have a bright future ahead of you," I say. Kelly flips on the ultrasound machine. I explain to Mrs. Finley that I verify the age of the fetus by measuring its head and limbs. "Since your last menstrual cycle was two months ago, I expect the fetus to be between six and ten weeks."

"It would have to be," she says. The image of the fetus appears and I measure it—the size is approximately fourteen to sixteen weeks.

"Are you sure you've only missed two periods?" I ask.

"I don't remember, Doctor. Probably not. What do you think the date I conceived this baby should be?"

I take out my pregnancy calculator and count from fourteen weeks ago to the probable month of conception.

"Between April and May," I say, "and you can expect to deliver between January and February." I make a note in her chart, changing the date of her last menstruation.

"Oh, no," she says, slumping into her seat. She covers her face with her hands, and cries out, "It can't be."

I make the mistake of asking if there is a problem. Of course there is a problem. She is my patient. Therefore, there has to be a problem, and hers just happens to be a whopper. Her husband was out of the country for the entire months of April and May and the first part of June. He could not have fertilized the egg.

"What am I gonna do? He's waiting out there."

"You have two options, Mrs. Finley. You can be honest and confess the truth. But if you need to keep up appearances, or if you're worried about how your husband will react, you can pretend the baby's premature. Only you can decide what is best for your family."

Angelina Finley's mental wheels turn, her big brown eyes blinking nervously. She stands, and before leaving, she says, "I'm having a baby with my husband, and if it comes early, there's nothing we can do about that."

I examine three more patients before noon. On my lunch hour, I induce labor in Jessica Worley, then grab an apple from the doctor's lounge and head back to the office, where Shaniqua Davis is waiting in Exam Room Two.

1:25 P.M.

Shaniqua Davis, routine pregnancy visit, 32 weeks gestation. Weight: 197 lbs. Complaints: Gas and indigestion. Still has trouble walking. Mild contractions.

"Sometimes my stomach feels squeezed and the baby can't move and I just hold my breath 'til it stops. Am I about to have this baby, Dr. Faulkner?"

"No, you have a little while yet, Shaniqua," I say.

"Before my birthday? It's the twenty-second of October."

"Could be around that time," I say.

"I hope it comes for my birthday," she says.

"That's about the only present you'll be getting," Ms. Davis gripes.

"I don't care 'bout presents. I just wanna stop feeling like I'm out in the rain," Shaniqua says.

"Out in the rain?" I ask.

"Like an alley cat," Ms. Davis says. "Catting around in the rain."

"Ms. Davis, *please.* I'm talking to your daughter, this is *her* examination, not yours." I look down at Shaniqua and ask, "What does out in the rain feel like?"

"Like I can't feel nothin' but cold and wet."

"Like you're sad, Shaniqua?" I say.

"Mighty sad, Dr. Faulkner. I'm stuck in a cloud."

"Is that why you've been cutting yourself?"

"Like you don't have an ounce of sense in your head," Ms. Davis says.

"Ms. Davis, I have to ask you to leave."

"I have a right—"

"Yeah, yeah, sue me. Now go, please, before I call security."

"Shaniqua!" she yells.

Shaniqua turns to face the wall.

"Quickly, Ms. Davis. You may wait in the reception area."

Ms. Davis rolls her eyes and storms out of the room, muttering, "I work for a law firm. I know my rights."

I examine the size of Shaniqua's womb. Her stomach hardens and she bites her bottom lip. I measure the size of her uterus, two weeks of growth since her last visit, for a combined total of thirty-two centimeters in thirty-two weeks. I notice the cuts on her thighs.

"Tell me more about how you feel when you're sad," I say.

"Like I'm on an island in the rain. With nobody there but me. And when I cut myself, I just wanna make sure I'm alive."

"You were doing this every day, before your stay in the hospital?"

"Sometimes."

"Well, Shaniqua, we're finished with your exam. Everything looks normal. Baby's normal. So now I'm going to have a word with your mother."

"Yes, ma'am, Doctor."

I leave the room and say to Kelly, "Tell the mother to meet me in my office."

Ms. Davis saunters in with her hands parked on both hips.

"You didn't have no right," she says.

"Your daughter has a very serious emotional problem, Ms. Davis."

"Only thing wrong with her is her big, embarrassing belly."

"Shaniqua is suffering from depression," I say, my voice deeper than usual as I tower above the petite woman, with my arms crossed, postured to finally tell her off.

"Depression? That girl's not depressed. She's just trying to get attention."

"It isn't normal for a healthy teenage girl to cut her flesh the way your daughter has. If she's really trying to get attention, I think you'd better give it to her, because depression is a serious illness, with serious consequences."

"What do you expect me to do?"

"I expected you to take her to a therapist months ago. It's covered by your insurance. But you didn't. Now, I'm going to give you a prescription for an antidepressant that she can take while pregnant. And I expect you to get it filled today."

"What if I don't," Ms. Davis says, frowning, a tired, dazed look in her eyes.

I hesitate, then add, "The last patient I had with this type of depression killed herself."

My pager goes off. Kelly will have to arrange for a few patients to be rescheduled, I tell her, before rushing off to the hospital to deliver Mrs. Worley's child.

The baby is crowning, and the patient pushes spontaneously. Mrs. Worley is the kind of over-forty first-time mother who gives me hope that I still have time to beat the biological clock.

"Hold on, Jessica," I say to the patient. Her body has a life of its own. It convulses and spasms. She screams that she can't help it.

"I can't make it stop," she shrieks.

"You're doing fine," I say. "Remember to breathe through the contractions." Her silver-haired husband repeats what I say. We both tell her to slow down.

"I CAN'T!

"Calm down, Jessie," says Mr. Worley assertively. This is a mistake most husbands make the first time. A man's normal tone of voice during labor is annoying to most women, as unnerving as the sound of a chalkboard being scratched. One woman told her husband not to open his mouth for a week. Mr. Worley counts each breath the way he learned to help out in Lamaze class.

"Relax, Jessie, breathe," he says, with measured calmness.

"I'm trying!"

"Hold on, sweetheart. Cleansing breaths."

He rubs her forehead and hands, the two places every husband should leave alone. There is only one place a woman wants to feel her husband's touch during labor. She wants a strong, heavy hand pressing and rubbing away the pain in her lower back. But Mr. Worley caresses the side of her face and tells her to breathe through the next contraction.

"Go to hell, you bastard!!!!"

Mr. Worley retreats from his wife's clutches. The crease between his brows deepens and his face goes red as if he's just been slapped.

"Now push, Mrs. Worley, push."

The baby rockets out in one final thrust. With the baby out, Mrs. Worley's disposition changes instantly. She coos with outstretched arms for her new bundle. Her husband who is now leary of her becomes the love of her life. She pecks his blushed cheeks full of kisses, and when he is sure she has been exorcised of the devil, he kisses her back with the baby between them. They are a happy family because she is happy. I am reminded every single day that women suffer from selective recall and short-term memory lapses. Mrs. Worley tells me it was not so bad. "I think we can do this again."

My pager goes off. It is Kelly from the office telling me I'm running behind.

34

In September, I read to the end of *The Promise of Spring,* finally discovering the mystery behind Charles Crow, the man Clarissa falls in love with, the part Indian who helps to build her ranch––the bastard child of her dead uncle. Like Angus Adams, Charles Crow wants the land, but he believes it is his birthright. And so it goes: Clarissa faces my same issues—betrayal, betrayal, and more betrayal. Yet, in the final scene, after Charles Crow is arrested for the murder of Angus Adams, Clarissa decides to wait for him, *however long it takes.*

Disappointed, I close the book and toss it under my bed. Why did I waste my time reading about a woman more foolish than I? Waiting. I scoff at the notion. I check the time—eight o'clock. I go to the kitchen, make a cup of tea, and wait for Kevin to arrive. There is a pattern to our lives together. Kevin came that first Friday night that we made love and stayed until Sunday. Two weeks later, he brought his clothes and beer, and now I expect him at any minute. My life is on hold and I am waiting instead of doing. Here I go again, giving in to my desires and lusts, Clarissa Montgomery, breaking rule 4. *I will never again put my life on hold for a man.* The dream I had of climbing to the top of a mountain to reach Kevin comes back to me. He let me fall. What if Mama is sending me a message from the other side? *Get out while you still can.*

After Kevin comes, we have dinner, and later rent a video. We end up at his place—in bed.

"We should've gone out to a movie," I say. We're lying on our sides facing the window.

"A movie?" he asks, sleepily, his hand clinging to my waist, his breathing heavy, smelling of beer.

"I wanted to see that movie, you know the one."

"The one." He sighs.

"About the Congo, Lumumba—you know, the one about him being killed."

"Mmm-hmmm."

"The art film at Garden Hills."

"Yeah, next time."

"You said we'd go tonight."

No answer.

"Kevin?" I say softly. He does not respond. Kevin is fast asleep. I turn to face him, noticing every detail of his features by the moonlight. His handsome face has lost some of its luster for me, and not because he is unkind. While home, Kevin opts to live a somewhat sedentary life. He travels every day and prefers to idle when he is not flying hither and yon. I have been voluntarily stuck for too many years with Ralph. I am ready to travel and see some of the world myself. There is no reason why I should not.

I get up and quickly dress, while he lies there like a lump. Not the hunk he used to be. Not the man who used to jog with me. I go home and mope. I notice a message from Karen on my answering machine. "Lenny, please prescribe something. I just want to sleep until the baby comes."

I return her call at half past eleven.

"Lenny, where are you?"

"Home. I left Kevin asleep in his bed."

"Is the honeymoon over already?"

"I like him, I mean, he's a nice guy. But I'm bored."

"Don't get me started about being bored. Bored is when you grow up and live one block from your mother. Bored is when the biggest kick in your life is a pint of Rocky Road ice cream. Bored is when your husband prefers to caress the remote control."

"Karen, you're right. I shouldn't have gotten you started."

"I need something, Lenny, I mean it. I can't sleep."

"Are you still drinking coffee?"

"No more than two cups a day."

"Stop! You're pregnant now. Your hormones are changing. Don't drink any more."

"I love coffee," she says. "You know that."

"Do you want to sleep, or not?"

"Yes."

"Then, count your blessings that you married a man you love, you're having his baby, and the only real problem in your life, namely, your mother, you can resolve as soon as you put your foot down."

"And what about you, Lenny? How're you going to resolve your problem?"

"You mean Kevin?"

"Yes, the boring one."

"I'll stick to my rules."

"And which rule covers him?"

"Rule four."

"Four?"

"It has to do with putting my life on hold for a man. I won't do it anymore."

"Your life?"

"The great one I'm going to have."

Two weeks later, I am asleep when Kevin, back in town again, rings the doorbell. Drowsily, I welcome him in and we head straight for the bed. His pores reek of alcohol. We begin to make love, and just when I am warming up, ten minutes later, he collapses next to me. Quarters, nickels, and dimes fall out of his pants and roll across the floor. He becomes the image of my father.

"Kevin, get up," I say sharply. His eyes, which had seemed glazed and sexy before, are bloodshot now. He blinks.

"What?"

"You drink too much." I remember Mama saying that she lived with a drunk for twenty-seven years.

"I work every day. So what if I have a few on the weekend?"

"That's not the point. Look, my father was a high-functioning drunk who took care of his family. He worked hard every day."

"So, you think I'm a drunk?" Kevin's words are slurred.

"After a few drinks, my father was actually fun to be around for us kids, playful and animated. But as evening turned into night, he drank to extreme, and a darker side of his personality would come to light. He'd be vulgar and threatening, hurling expletives at any of us in his sight, striking out primarily at my mother, especially on weekends."

"I'm not your father, okay? I'm not vulgar, and I've never threatened a woman in my life. Have I ever threatened you?"

"I'm not saying that, Kevin."

"No? Then what're you saying?"

"I'm just saying you need to watch it. Alcoholism is one of those diseases that can creep up on you. And no, you've never threatened me. I know you're not my father. But . . ."

Kevin is snoring, loud, then louder.

Damn him. I turn over and bury my face in the pillow. In the morning, I nudge Kevin awake. He squints as if trying to focus his eyes.

"Lenny?" he says, sounding unsure of his whereabouts.

"You want breakfast?"

"Sure, fine."

I bake blueberry muffins from a box, scramble eggs, and make a fresh pot of coffee. I bring a tray to Kevin, who is now sitting up in bed reading the morning paper.

"Mmmm, good," he says, like Bobby. After breakfast, I kiss the side of his face.

"Let's go for a jog, honey."

"Not this time," he says. I count the number of times on one hand that we have jogged together since we met. I run five miles, and when I return home, Kevin is parked in front of the television drinking a beer. He looks weak and I pick his faults apart in my mind. He needs a haircut. His gut is beginning to hang over his pants. He needs a bath.

"Did you pick up any beer?" he asks.

"No," I say, heading into the kitchen for bottled water. My warm, moist face cools from opening the refrigerator door. I stoop to retrieve a bottle of water and when I do, I notice a can of beer. I close the door and drink the water.

"Can you run down to my house and get a six-pack, please, baby?"

"No," I say disdainfully when he gazes up at me with his bloodshot eyes. "I won't get you any more beer."

"Come on, baby, please. Don't be mean. Bring me a beer."

"Get it yourself."

"I'm watching the game."

I walk to the living room and stand in front of the television set. "I want us to go to Hawaii for Christmas. And I want to hike Kilimanjaro next spring."

"Been there," he says indifferently, "and it's no big deal."

"Well, it's a big deal to me."

We lock eyes. The crowd roars from the television set.

"Step aside, Lenny, please. Make yourself useful. Get me a beer."

"I won't fetch beer like I'm your pet poodle."

"You're not much fun today, are you, sweetheart?"

"No, I'm not, Kevin," I snap. "You drink too much."

"It helps me forget," he says, tiredly.

"Forget what?" I ask, and before he sighs heavily, hesitating to answer, I recognize it in his eyes. Guilt. Kevin's best friend crashing his plane. I pity Kevin, but I cannot wallow in the bottle with him. I won't. I have no more time to waste.

"We don't feel right together anymore," I say, as evenly as possible. "I think it's time for you to go."

"Are you asking me to leave?" he asks, completely befuddled.

"Yes, I am," I say firmly. Kevin rises from the sofa and glances at me as if he is being punished. I say nothing as he buttons his uniform and picks up his pilot's cap. *I solemnly vow to uphold the rules.* Kevin mumbles good-bye between opening and closing the front door. I have no regrets in ending us. Something powerful has happened inside me. I am in control. I thought this day would never come, when I, Lenita Mae Faulkner, would break up with a handsome, desirable man. But I have done it and it feels just right.

In my diary, I write

I'd rather be by myself than with a man who sits around gulping down one can of beer after another. I am not a waitress, and my home is not a bar.

Rule 7.

I will never again go fetch the beer.

35

It is damp and chilly at the crack of dawn. I start out in a jogging suit on a five-mile run along the path running parallel to the road, where the scent of surrounding flora and the earthiness of raw dirt commingle beneath the morning dew. A rabbit briskly crosses my path. Leaves are just beginning to turn red and yellow. I slow my pace to better appreciate the natural surroundings that I usually take for granted: the call and response of birds overhead, the sound of crickets, frogs, and katydids communing in the thickets, and wild wisteria in bloom along the edge. Within a half hour, I am down to a tank top, with my jacket wrapped around my waist.

I run past Ernest Hemingway's house and he calls out to me. I stop to smell the last of his roses. Ernest knows the names and derivations of more plant species than I knew existed. He has created a sanctuary for monarch butterflies that stop here during their great northward migration each spring. And several odd species of birds flock to the small woods behind his house.

We sit on an arched wooden bench beneath a wooden gazebo he designed and built himself in the shape of a Buddhist temple. He designed the Japanese garden that surrounds us, complete with a pond full of giant goldfish and bordered in stone and exotic flora. He said it reminded him of that part of his childhood spent in Okinawa, where his father was stationed during the Vietnam War.

"My brother was killed in that war," I tell him. Joe's death has been long enough ago to talk about without feeling sad. I do not feel uneasy about mentioning my eldest brother anymore.

"How old was he?"

"Nineteen," I say. "Joe had planned to become an architect." Ernest listens as if there is more to my story I might divulge. He seems to enjoy for a moment the sounds of birds and insects and trickling water in his garden. "Joe liked building things, too, Ernest. He would've liked what you've done back here."

"This is where I leave the rest of the world behind," he says. He looks at me when I do not answer, and adds, "It doesn't hurt so much to think about Amy here."

"I understand."

"It only took a year to build everything. I built it for Amy. She really liked sitting out here. She'd close her eyes and listen to the sound of the water. And after we knew she was going to die, she said, 'Heaven should be this perfect.' "

"You must take great comfort in knowing that, Ernest," I say. "You made Amy very happy."

"I tried."

I close my eyes and try to imagine what heaven might be like: the slow, steady trickle of water, whispery breezes wafting through trees, tweeting birds, and the movements of tiny insects. I don't look up when I hear Ernest's footsteps as he heads toward his house. His back door opens and closes. I take several deep breaths, before the door reopens. I glance back to see Ernest returning with a book.

"I have something I'd like you to read," he says, handing it to me.

"*Lessons of the Lotus,*" I read.

"A Buddhist monk friend of mine wrote it."

"Really, Ernest? I've needed something new to read. Something unromantic. Something real. Thanks."

"I found it helpful," he says.

"Helpful I need," I sigh, opening to the middle of the book. *Forgiveness.* "This was a hard year for me, too, Ernest. Ralph leaving and looting me, Mama dying, and now, Kevin."

"Kevin?" he says, as if trying to remember.

"A pilot I met. He didn't last long enough to be worth mentioning."

"Any relationship is worth mentioning if it bothers you, Lenny."

"Kevin doesn't bother me. Being alone does."

"I know what you mean."

"Then let's have dinner tonight," I say awkwardly. "I bet you haven't eaten out since she . . ."

"No, I haven't," he says.

"I bet you haven't had a real friend since you moved here."

"Not until now."

Around six o'clock, Ernest arrives and takes me to a soul-food restaurant in the middle of town. The people who own the Corner Grill know him.

"Professor," the waiter, a short, stubby, dark-skinned man calls out to Ernest. "Glad to see you back again, man. Been a long time, ain't it?"

"Over a year, Old Man," Ernest says.

The waiter seats us at their best table, next to the only window. We order glasses of wine, and take a few minutes to examine our menus.

"Old Man," Ernest says, "what's the special?"

"Baked trout and garlic potatoes."

"Lenny, have you decided?"

"The special sounds nice," I say.

"Two specials, Old Man."

"So be it."

"How do they know you so well?" I ask curiously, as more of the mystery of Ernest Hemingway unravels.

"Amy and I came here a lot."

"Oh." I glance around this old place. A hint of mildew permeates the spicy air. Most of the diners are white and I cannot help wondering why. We are close to the side of town where most of the people are poor and black. Where the crime rate is higher.

Ernest lights the candle in the middle of our black linoleum tabletop. "Old Man" brings our food, and from the first flavorful bite, I am addicted. In the corner of the room next to the smoke-filled bar, three musicians set up to perform: one on keyboard, another on drums, and the most senior of the trio in front of the mic with his guitar.

"That's Sammy Goldfinger," Ernest says, nodding toward the older man, who belts out the blues and causes the audience to erupt. Ernest crosses his right ankle over his left knee and leans back in his seat as if quietly meditating, curling his lips discreetly into a smile when the guitarist riffs above his head or behind his back like Jimi Hendrix.

The performer pretends to eat the strings of his guitar and some people get up to dance in place, while Ernest listens intently. His foot bouncing on his knee is the only thing that gives his love of the blues away. He sips one glass of wine very slowly and when the band finishes the set, he turns to me, asking, "Are you enjoying yourself, Lenny?"

"I've never heard live blues before."

"Most black people don't come out to hear their own music. We don't support our own traditions."

"I'm guilty," I say sheepishly.

He blushes, nervously plucking at his beard, and says, "Forgive me for preaching."

"You're forgiven," I joke, and he laughs. His teeth are straight. As a boy he probably wore braces. Ernest is conservative in his movements, formal—a perfect gentleman, part of a dying breed. He stands and helps me from my seat. We leave for home. Ernest parks in front of my house and walks me to the door.

"Thanks for putting up with me tonight," he says.

"Thanks for putting up with *me,*" I parrot.

We laugh and Ernest awkwardly kisses my cheek. I take his bearded face in my hands, breathing his breaths, wanting to kiss him fully, but afraid of jeopardizing our friendship. I do not want to lose him. He kisses my forehead, and my hands fall to my sides.

"Good night, Ernest. I had a wonderful time."

"We'll have to do this again," he says, stepping away from me. "Good night."

Once inside, I take a deep breath and close the door, listening for Ernest's footsteps as he makes his way down the driveway to his car, a lonely, woebegone sound, like a train taking off down the tracks. We are both like wounded animals finding our way home in the dark.

9:30 A.M.

Karen Ashby, 26 weeks gestation. Weight: 158 lbs. Complaint: fatigue.

Karen tells me that she has finished decorating her son's room.

"Maybe now you can get the rest you need," I say.

"Cynthia Woodrow is coming to town next week to host another baby shower for me. I told her not to do it. I wish Mother hadn't given us that shower so early in my pregnancy. I've gotten way too much already. Mostly pink."

"You can always give to charity," I say.

"Mother would die if I did that."

"You can save the pink for when you have a girl."

"I don't even want to think about that possibility. Why do women go through more than one pregnancy? Do they forget what it's like?"

"Most of them do."

I measure the size of her womb and listen to the baby's heartbeat.

"Everything's good in Pleasantville," I say, patting her fat belly.

"You think he'll come before Christmas?"

"I doubt it. I'll bet on that mid-January due date."

Karen sits up and says, "Jason is beside himself with pride and can't wait to hand out cigars." I think about what Ernest said about African traditions and realize how mainstream we all are. Men do not hold their sons up to the moon or plant placentas in sacred places. They do not pass down their oral histories or hold manhood ceremonies for their pubescent sons. In so many homes in this city there are no fathers around to teach boys to be men.

"Your son will be one of the luckiest boys in the world," I say.

"I know," she says, beaming, lightly rubbing her belly. A knot grows in my throat. I may never find the right man to love me, and I can live with that, but I still have an emotional need to have a child.

"Let's have lunch today," Karen says.

"Can't," I say, "I have other plans."

"A new man?"

"No, a special project I'm working on here at the office."

"Oh," Karen says skeptically. She knows me so well. I hate making excuses to avoid her. But the bigger she gets, the more her conversation revolves around the baby. He is not even here yet, and she speaks as if her fetus has a personality. *The little bugger wouldn't settle down last night. He loves hearing classical music,* or *He hates it when I eat onions.*

"How do you like Paul Anderson?" she says before I leave the exam room.

"Well, he hasn't asked me to settle with Ralph yet, so I guess I'll keep him as my attorney."

"You're going out with him, aren't you?" she asks.

"No, Karen. Our relationship is strictly professional."

"Let me know how it goes," she says, leaving me with the impression that she had intended more than attorney-client privileges between Paul Anderson and me when she gave me his card.

Paul Anderson seems to be an impeccable professional. I study him closely as he greets me with a fleeting smile and firm handshake. I remember Karen's remark about him being a good man. I take mental notes of the striking features of his dark face, his broad, determined chin, his nose that flares out deliberately, reminding me of a picture of the Greek god Zeus. His eyes are both serious and inscrutable. He offers me a seat, and I sit across the big desk from him. I feel like a patient waiting for a diagnosis.

"I've met with Mr. Griffin's attorney," he says, then clears his throat. "Your client wishes to settle for forty percent of the profits."

"What do you think I should do?" I say, expecting him to advise a settlement, at which point, I plan to walk out the door.

"I think settling at this point would be premature. I've done a little digging into one of your investments . . . Newton Industries. And I find it hard to believe Mr. Griffin was lucky in picking an obscure technology startup. That company has recently filed for bankruptcy. How did he know when to buy and when to sell?"

I shrug from sheer ignorance.

"So what if he bought and sold at the right time," I say, confused. "Ralph does most things on time."

Paul Anderson's face tenses. He clasps his hands together as if about to squeeze the life from something when he asks, "How much do you know about Newton Industries?"

"Nothing," I say.

"Good," he sighs, leaning back in his chair.

"What do you mean, Mr. Anderson?"

"There was no legitimate reason why Mr. Griffin purchased that much stock from an upstart company."

"But lots of people bought into the high-tech industry hoping for the next big Microsoft to emerge," I say. "Obviously, Ralph was no different."

"But most investors don't quadruple their money in one year and sell their stock two days before the company they've invested in files for bankruptcy."

"What are you saying?" I ask, dreading the answer.

"Mr. Griffin's law firm has represented Newton since its inception," he says while studying papers from the package his secretary gave him. "I'm willing to bet the company was Mr. Griffin's client."

"So what?"

"So if the FCC investigates they might find him guilty of insider trading."

"And if he's guilty?"

"Insider trading is a federal crime. He'd go to prison."

"Maybe that's where he belongs."

"If he handled the legal work for Newton personally, then the assumption will be that he had insider knowledge. Or if another lawyer in Mr. Griffin's firm made similar investments with both attorneys selling within the same period, then the assumption will most likely be collusion. In that case, they'd both go to prison."

"And if neither situation is true?"

"Then we go to court to fight over the money."

"So I lose, if he's innocent."

"Not necessarily, but you will certainly lose if he's guilty. The FCC will demand full recovery of any profits made from insider trading."

"Does the FCC always investigate?"

"No, not usually," he says. "The truth of the matter is that the FCC rarely investigates unless someone with inside knowledge of a crime comes forward. Usually disgruntled employees or scorned lovers."

My face warms from hearing the category *scorned lovers.* Is that who I am now? Pitiful.

"I'll do more digging and find out who represented Newton. If Mr. Griffin had anything to do with it, he won't want a trial to bring attention to his claims to the money. He won't want the Feds looking closely at this account."

Paul tells me to make an appointment with the receptionist for next week, which I do right away. I shut off the tape recorder and note the time: 10:55. Can I trust him? He seems competent enough—direct, drop-dead serious, knowledgeable about the Feds, no unsavory body odors to speak of, only a tasteful hint of aftershave. Why did Jason recommend him? What if Jason handled the Newton account? What if Jason and Ralph colluded to make money? I think of Karen having a baby, how happy she is with her new life, her wonderful husband, their new house one block away from where she grew up—the baby's room of teddy bear sailors and boats.

I want to believe in Paul Anderson, but deep down something stops me. It is the same feeling I had signing the papers that gave Ralph signatory over the investment account. I arrive at my office and try to shrug off thoughts of money and fraud and betrayal. I put on my lab coat and become the doctor who examines patients from the bottom up. And at the end of the day, after the last patient leaves, I am left with uncertainty.

36

The following week, I am back inside Paul Anderson's office waiting to know who handled the Newton account, dying inside out to know it. He enters with that fleeting smile, tells me to have a seat, and reaches for a package his secretary hands him. He opens the large brown envelope and glances briefly at its contents before handing it to me.

"These are all the documents you've given me thus far," he says in a particularly formal tone. "I'm afraid I'll have to remove myself from your case, Dr. Faulkner."

"What? But why?"

"I did some investigating and found that a friend of mine is involved in your case after all. And as a policy, I stay away from cases that have to do with co-workers and friends."

"Who, Jason Ashby?"

"Jason is a very good friend of mine," he says matter-of-factly. Suddenly, I remember where I saw him. He was at Karen and Jason's wedding.

"So where does that leave me? What does Jason have to do with my case?"

"I would rather not go into any specific details, except to say that I can't do the best job for you and protect my friend, too, unless you should decide to quietly settle with Mr. Griffin."

There, he has finally said it. *Settle.*

"No, I'd rather find another attorney," I say sharply, standing to leave. "Tell me something, Mr. Anderson, does Karen know about your *friend's* involvement? Is that why she gave me your card?"

He clears his throat and says, "Apparently so."

Apparently. Karen is on my mind all the way to the office. I think about her pregnancy, her idyllic marriage and baby on the way, and wonder how long she has known Jason is involved. How could she do this to me? Apparently, she wanted me to be grateful to get Paul Anderson's card. I wonder how much money Jason made selling his stock before Newton filed for bankruptcy. Millions? The thought of Karen and Jason being involved turns my stomach.

An hour slips by with me sitting inside my car, parked on the lower level of my office building. My mind spins with what to do—call Karen, confront Ralph, contact the FCC? Am I willing to lie and cheat to save a friend? What happens to Karen's perfect life if I don't settle quietly with Ralph? What about *my* life? Get another lawyer, Lenita Mae, devil be damned; let the chips fall where they may. Rule 5. I will not risk my life to save anyone's reputation.

Birds echo inside the parking garage. I feel as if trapped in a cave. My pager goes off, and when I phone Kelly, she says, "Dr. Faulkner, the patients are getting backed up and one is threatening to leave."

"I'm on my way." I hurry up to the office and see patients for the rest of the day. I hear of bouts of dizziness, depression, and guilt. Mostly the mothers who work all day and come home to a house full of children and laundry and dirty rooms feel guilty. They are guilty of not listening, of not being at the school to pick the children up on time. They are guilty of complaining that it all falls on them.

There is nothing left of me at the end of this day. I have no more advice to give. My bag of tricks is empty. Usually I thrive on helping my patients solve their problems. But since leaving Paul Anderson's office, my usual energy burst, which pushes me from the moment I get to the office each day, has dissipated. The thought of being betrayed by Karen feels like death.

Tonight as I lie in bed contemplating the day's events, I open the book Ernest Hemingway gave me and read the section on forgiveness.

37

The smells of lavender and lilac and jasmine combine to tease the senses like a delicate perfume, an herbal bath, or tea. Water trickles by like a tranquil river. There is nothing better for the mind than being here in Ernest Hemingway's garden.

"Breathe deeply," he says, "relax your shoulders, breathe deeply and relax your pelvis and thighs and legs, breathe deeply and relax your arms and hands and feet." His voice is as firm and steady as a bass guitar playing the blues. *Breathe.* My eyes are closed and I hear and feel what Mama used to call the breath of God. A gentle breeze blowing the sheets above Rosetta and me was the breath of God and knowing this explanation made running between them all the more special, all the more necessary.

Ernest leaves me alone in his Garden of Eden. He is somewhere, pruning fruit trees, clipping away the old to make room for next spring's new. Last night while I was on call, I performed a two-hour C-section and a four-hour emergency hysterectomy, receiving barely enough shuteye to deliver a baby early this morning. Here and now, the weight of the world lifts and I am floating high above it all—above Karen and Jason and Ralph, above getting married and having babies. I think about the book Ernest gave me to read. *Lessons of the Lotus.* I am a beautiful spiritual being, with many blessings, and by living consciously, I will become aware of them.

After meditating, Ernest and I have dinner at a tiny vegetarian restaurant on Virginia Avenue.

"I'm enjoying the book you gave me," I say.

"Good, Lenny. I've stopped feeling guilty about Amy. I still miss her every day, but I'm beginning to focus more and more on life without her."

"That's wonderful, Ernest."

"It's a start," he says.

"That's all we can do, isn't it? Start over when we're knocked down?"

"You've been knocked down lately?"

"Worst than that," I say, feeling fire behind my thoughts. "Karen's betrayed me."

"Karen? That's incredible." Ernest leans forward in his chair, an elbow propped on the edge of the table, his fist holding up his bearded chin, transforming himself into *The Thinker.*

"Her husband's involved in an insider-trading scheme with Ralph that may cost me most of my money. She has to know. How could she not be in on it, too?"

"Friends are hard to come by."

"Don't I know it?"

"You're not absolutely sure about Karen, though, are you?"

"Not absolutely, a hundred percent. But Jason's her husband. How could she not be in the middle of this?"

"Weren't you living with Ralph?"

"Yes, but . . . I get where you're going with this, Ernest."

"Where am I going?"

"I'm not sure about Karen," I say, diverting my gaze away from Ernest. He takes my hand firmly in his.

"Is the risk of being wrong worth losing a friend?" he asks.

"No." I gaze into Ernest's eyes, which had seemed the saddest of the sad not so long ago and are now honorable and safe. I feel safe here with him now, like how I would imagine a baby must feel being cradled by a loving, nurturing parent.

"Lenny," he says softly, removing his hand from mine. "Why don't you call her?"

9:00 A.M.

Christina Dennis, return visit. Weight: 135 lbs. Height: 5'11". History: previously diagnosed with advanced case of endometriosis. Patient suffered severe pain in her abdomen. Complained that she was unable to work. Rec-

ommended oophorectomy after utilizing various treatments unsuccessfully over the past three years. Patient refused surgery.

"How have you managed, Ms. Dennis?" I ask, surprised to find her sitting straight in her seat, graced with a pleasant expression.

"Never better, Dr. Faulkner," she says.

"What happened to bring about this change? The last time you were here, I worried that you wouldn't make it to the parking lot."

"Well, I'm glad you asked," she says, and I expect a sheet of paper to instantly materialize in her hands, one of her infamous lists of questions. But instead, she crosses one leg over the other and proceeds to tell me about her Guru herbalist, her Chinese acupuncturist, her yoga classes, and daily Buddhist meditations. She has learned to channel the energy of her womb.

"Energy of your womb?" I say, suspecting that she has finally flipped her wig.

"Yes, Dr. Faulkner. You see," she says, standing and twirling in place a time or two. "I'm cured. I can't remember ever feeling this good."

"Let's have a look," I say, instructing Kelly to escort Christina Dennis to the first available exam room. Minutes later, I enter Room Three with Kelly as my witness. We give Ms. Dennis an ultrasound, and I spend more time than usual searching for tumors. I am at a complete loss for words, befuddled, amazed at this patient's clean bill of health.

"What happened?" I whisper, scratching my head as if a logical explanation will pop into it. Kelly shrugs. She is as confused as I am. There are times when endometriosis may go into remission for some women. However, I have never seen a case where tumors as advanced as hers, multiplying inside the pelvis and enshrouding both ovaries, suddenly vanish in a few months without the benefit of some kind of medical treatment.

"I wonder if it's permanent," I say.

"I'm completely cured," she says, confidently adding, "I learned to use the energy of my womb to heal it. That's why I'm here. You thought you had all the answers because you're a doctor. Western doctors are trained to know everything."

"I didn't know any other way to cure you, except surgically," I say, feeling smaller for having been arrogant during Ms. Dennis's last visit. "I'm sorry I was unable to help you."

"When I left your office, Dr. Faulkner, I had planned to never return. But then I remembered how willing you were to listen. You have potential. Anyone who listens can learn."

Kelly signals the time on her watch.

"Tell me the history of your new treatment," I say to Christina, ignoring Kelly's fingers one and four. It occurs to me that Ms. Dennis is onto something, and I am more interested in learning than rushing off to see the next patient. "Tell me about the energy of the womb."

"Women have been taught through the ages that our gifts are evil; our spiritual influence was eliminated from most religions. We have forgotten how to heal ourselves. Why? Is it because men don't have wombs? They don't have the instincts that women have? They don't understand?"

I shrug, clueless.

"Most doctors are men," she says. "Is there little wonder that they are willing to cut and remove what they can't cure?"

"But what is this healing energy of the womb and how are women to use it, Ms. Dennis?"

"It's the same energy we're born with. What mothers pass down to their daughters. Something all women have, but have been trained over the centuries to disregard, or to regard as evil."

"So how does it go from your head to your abdomen?"

"It doesn't have to move from one part of the body to another," she says. "Energy is from your head to your feet. The tingle on the back of your neck when something extraordinary rings true, the creation of life, the yearning in your heart for love, our instincts. There are some women whose big toes tell them whether it will rain or snow."

"I understand," I say. Mama could smell rain coming days ahead. I glance down at my watch, and say to Kelly, "Tell the patient in Exam Room One I'll be right with her."

When Kelly leaves, I ask Ms. Dennis a final question. "How do you get this energy to heal?"

She smiles calmly, and says, "You must first become aware."

"I'd like to examine you again in six months."

Tonight, I read about awareness in *Lessons of the Lotus,* and I realize how unaware I have become. Disconnected from my spirit. Out of balance. My chakras are unaligned. I spend each day filled with my own thoughts—

thinking, pondering, questioning, and listening, my brain in a constant state of babble, like a symphony playing out of tune. I breathe deeply, as I have done in Ernest Hemingway's garden. I imagine his trickling pond and herbal scents permeating the air. I envision thick, white clouds crossing a deep blue sky, and before long, time loses its significance. My eyelids become heavy. I imagine Ernest holding my hand. We walk hand in hand through the dark woods at the end of the jogging path. Soon, I become aware that I am falling asleep.

38

11:45 A.M.

Angelina Finley, routine pregnancy visit, 20 weeks gestation. Weight: 120 lbs. Complaint: exhaustion; food cravings. Blood test indicates anemia.

"I believe that cravings are Mother Nature's way of encouraging pregnant women to eat the nutrients they need," I say, after measuring the size of Mrs. Finley's womb. "You have iron-defiency anemia. Maybe that's why you eat spinach waffles and steak every morning."

"But it's nasty," she says. "I can't believe I eat that stuff. And I can't pass the ice-cream parlor near my job without stopping."

"Ice cream has calcium and vitamin A."

"And fat," she scowls. "Look at me, Doctor. I've gained twelve pounds already."

"You were too thin before. I don't want you to worry about your weight. Follow your instincts about food, especially those rich in iron."

Kelly attaches the fetal heart monitor to Mrs. Finley's stomach. She flips the switch on. We listen to mother and child heartbeats.

"I'm going to start you on a prenatal vitamin with a higher dosage of iron than the ones you're using now," I say.

"I ate a whole jar of pickles yesterday," she says.

"There's little harm in pickles. They have zero calories and provide carbohydrates that your fetus needs in order to grow properly. But try to eat more leafy green vegetables, and we won't worry about the ice cream."

"And there's one more thing, Doctor," she says, twiddling her thumbs over her burgeoning belly. "I'm from Cuba and my husband is all-American, you know. So I was wondering about this genetics thing. See, in my family back in Cuba, we have multiracial blood. My great-grandmother was as dark as you, but you'd never know it to look at me."

"And your question is . . ."

"If my baby comes out looking black, let's say, would that be unusual?"

"Very," I say. "Is the natural father black?"

Ms. Finley's face reddens. "My husband is white," she says. I repeat *natural father* and she shrugs. "Black, I think. Maybe."

"There was a case several years ago in South Africa, during apartheid, when two white parents were forced to move because their child was black."

"How was that possible?"

"I believe it was the child's paternal grandfather who confessed that his grandmother was black."

"So if my child comes out looking like my great-grandmother, there's nothing we can do about that."

I meet Stella for lunch at the diner across the street. She has gathered all the data necessary to begin setting up our home for pregnant girls. She makes a few notations in her notebook and says how excited she is that everything is falling into place.

"That's great," I say, briefly scanning her list of preliminary cost figures.

"All we need is a name," Stella says.

"I have the perfect name," I say, "Linda's Safe House."

"Linda?"

"In honor of Linda Jenkins, the girl who died after giving birth."

"Oh, yes, she was your inspiration for wanting to do this," Stella says.

I glance back at the costs for housing, supplies, salaries, utilities, and education, among various others. I think about Ralph's lawsuit against me. I cannot lose the money, not now. I can't.

"You think we'll have enough money ten years from now?" I ask.

"We should. I've applied for several government grants and invited some very successful women in town to sit on our board, including Norma Scott, heiress to the Calico Oil fortune. She owns an old house I've got my eyes on."

"What about staff?"

"I've interviewed candidates for three part-time social work positions and a full-time secretarial job," she says.

"What about a nurse?"

"No one has answered my ads so far."

"I wonder why? Isn't the salary attractive enough?"

"Money's not the problem," Stella says. "A qualified nurse can earn as much as eighty dollars an hour examining and educating our girls."

"Then we should be turning them away."

"There's a nursing shortage everywhere, Lenny."

"Well, I see nurses all the time," I say. "I'm sure I can find at least one who'd like to join our staff."

"Good luck," Stella says, smiling wisely. "But there's one more thing we'll need: a license to operate. Plus, a lot of legal work needs to be done before we get started."

"I know just the lawyer who can help," I say, before considering the fact that Paul Anderson has just declined to represent me.

After work, Ernest calls to invite me out to hear House Rocker Johnson at the House of Blues. It is Friday night. I am not on call, and very much in need of a friend.

"I'd love to go," I tell him. An hour later, we're sitting front and center, watching the lead guitarist play like a man half his age. A kinetic energy flows through the room like ripples in the middle of a pond, waking every pore and corpuscle. I think about what Ms. Dennis said about the energy of the womb, and I feel the sway of my hips corralling it as I dance in place.

When the set ends, Ernest teaches me more about the blues and how it began in the Mississippi Delta. The names of famous blues musicians—W. C. Handy, Charley Patton, Joe Dockery, Robert Johnson, Howlin' Wolf, Blind Lemon Jefferson, B. B. King, Muddy Waters—peel from his lips like months of the year, and I try holding onto each name. I remember only one: Muddy.

"I'll play his music for you," Ernest says as we leave the club.

"You have many of his recordings?"

"A few. But that's not what I mean. Come to the Corner Grill two weeks from tonight."

"I'd like that," I say, wondering what he means.

Ernest drives me home and escorts me to my front door.

"I had a wonderful time," he says.

"Come inside and have something to drink," I say, not wanting to be alone just yet.

"No thanks, Lenny, I'd better go on home."

"But why? You don't have to work in the morning."

"No, but I don't feel up to more fun right now."

"You feel sick, or something, Ernest?"

"No."

"Oh, I see, you're missing Amy."

He shrugs. "Good night, Lenny."

I watch Ernest walk down the driveway to his car, and just before he opens the door, I call out to him, "I'm glad we're friends!"

"Me, too," he says.

10:30 A.M.

Karen Ashby, return pregnancy visit, 28 weeks gestation. Weight: 162 lbs. Complaint: back and hip pain.

"I started to call you Friday," I say, leaning over Karen on an exam table. "But since you were coming this morning, I decided to wait and hear in person your real reason for giving me Paul Anderson's card."

"My real reason? You needed a lawyer, and he's as good as it gets."

"Come on, Karen," I say, eyeing her skeptically.

"All right, all right. He dated Mikayla before Ralph. He's a nice guy and he didn't deserve what she did to him. I thought you two would hit it off."

"Paul was with her at your wedding, wasn't he?" I ask, feeling for her baby's head, the pain in her pelvis, back, and hips—understandable at this point. Karen's body is loosening up in anticipation of the big day.

"Why didn't you tell me, Karen?" I ask. She sucks in her plump, pregnant cheeks, reminding me of a squirrel stashing nuts away for the winter.

"I'm sorry I didn't say anything about it before," she says remorsefully. "Poor Paul lost Mikayla at my wedding. I feel partly to blame for what happened to both of you."

"So it had nothing to do with Newton Technologies?"

"I don't know what you're talking about, Lenny," she says, perplexed by the sudden hostility in my voice.

"Come on, Karen. You expect me to believe you don't remember purchasing Newton Tech stocks for Ralph?"

"Do you remember every patient?"

"The ones who stand out."

Recognition lights up in her eyes. She does remember.

"That's the stock that made all that money," she says, her know-it-all finger tapping her bottom lip.

"How much of the stock did you purchase for Jason?"

"For your information, Dr. Faulkner, another firm handles our investments. We have a blind trust account because my husband wanted it that way."

"Then who told Ralph about Newton? Somebody at *your* husband's law firm had that company as a client. And somebody at *your* husband's law firm told Ralph when to buy and when to sell."

"Well, it wasn't Jason."

"How else would Ralph have known to sell his shares two days before the company filed for bankruptcy?"

"I don't know anything about who somebody is or what somebody did," Karen says testily. She bats those big, brown eyes of hers that never lie, and I know she is telling me the truth.

"Oh, Karen, I'm sorry, I should've known."

"What, Lenny? What is Paul telling you?"

"He said he can't represent me anymore. He said a friend of his is involved in my case."

"And you suspected me and Jason?"

"I didn't know what to think. When I asked Paul Anderson if you knew about it, he didn't deny it."

"When did this happen?"

"On Thursday."

"Five days ago. I see. That's interesting. I must've left at least half a dozen messages for you since then. Why didn't you call me back?"

"I told you, I knew you'd be coming this morning."

"Why are you avoiding me, Lenny?"

"I'm not," I insist.

"Then why don't we have lunch anymore?"

"Because," I say, hesitating to add words I might regret. I take out my measuring tape and scale Karen's womb, preoccupying myself with figures. How many centimeters from here to there. Comparing them to the normal-growth chart. "Looks like he's seven pounds already."

"Lenny?"

"You're having a very big boy."

"I need you, Lenny," she quavers, taking hold of my hand. I turn away to avoid her watery eyes. "I don't want to lose my best friend."

I swallow hard, biting back tears, and my heart stops for a moment. A painful influx of shame shoots through me. The truth of the matter is I am jealous because Karen has a baby swelling inside her belly.

"I love you, Karen, and I'll love your baby, you know that," I say, exploding into sobs. Karen pulls herself up and reaches out for me. We embrace like long lost friends who finally, after many trials and tribulations, meet up again, and share a big cry.

"Girrrrrl," she trills, wiping away last tears, "this little boy is on his way."

"One terrifically hard labor coming up," I say jokingly, a lighthearted attempt to regain my composure.

"Forget that back-to-nature stuff," she commands. "Give me something to knock me out as soon as I go into labor."

"And miss the show you'll put on?" I laugh. Kelly enters the exam room and signals to me.

"Excuse me for a minute, Karen," I say, before joining Kelly by the door.

"Mrs. Jenison in Exam Room Two is almost hysterical," she whispers.

"She's always almost hysterical," I whisper back. "She's fine. Ever since her pregnancy, she practically hangs out in the hospital emergency room. She thinks something's wrong with her baby."

"What should I tell her?" Kelly asks, exasperated.

"Ask her to count how many times she feels the baby move."

"But she can't possibly feel much now."

"I know, but it'll give her something positive to focus on until I get there. I have to check on the lab results for another patient first."

I turn to Karen, and say, "We have to talk more."

"Lunch tomorrow?" she says.

"Let's."

11:30 A.M.

Susan Jenison, return pregnancy visit. 20 weeks gestation. Weight: 184 lbs. Complaint: nausea, gas, bloating. Blood test indicates abnormally high serum glucose level.

* * *

"I see you've gained twenty-three pounds in less than four months, Mrs. Jenison."

"The baby," she says.

"It's important to eat healthy, well-balanced meals, but—"

"I'm very careful about eating the right foods."

"Cakes and chips and ice cream? The right foods, my eye," Mr. Jenison interjects.

"A little sweet now and then won't hurt the baby," she says.

"Oh, yes it can," I say. "Mrs. Jenison, your blood sugar is a bit high. We need to be concerned about gestational diabetes. I'm going to advise you to cut out all sweets, with the exception of fruits and other foods with natural sugars. I'm referring you to a dietitian, who will put you on a low-carb diet."

"But I really don't eat that much," she whines.

"Yes you do," Mr. Jenison says.

"What? Are you watching every little thing I put in my mouth now?"

"I don't have to look far, since you devour everything in sight."

"You take that back, Alan, or else," she growls.

"I want what's best for the baby," he says.

"You just want to annoy me," she says.

After Kelly puts a new film cartridge into the ultrasound machine, the four of us watch the image of the fetus materialize on the screen. I zoom in on the baby's pulsating heart. Normal. With a point and click, marking an *X* here and there, I am able to measure the approximate size of the head. Normal. I measure the length of the arms and legs. Normal. The fetus does a 360-degree turn and Mrs. Jenison gasps as if in fear for her own life.

The fetus turns again, kicking and peddling his arms.

"Oh, no," she groans. "It's starting already."

"What's starting, honey?" Mr. Jenison says.

"Circles," she says. "I told you it would happen."

"How do you know the baby's not hyper because of all them cookies you ate before we got here?"

"You don't know what you're talking about."

"And neither do you."

The fetus draws its tiny hand up to its mouth and there is a collective sigh from the parents over how cute it is.

"He's got his daddy's head," Mrs. Jenison says, gleaming with pride. Mr. Jenison takes hold of her hand.

"I hope it has your beauty," he says, kissing the back of her plump hand. "You mean the world to me, Angel Face."

"We'll have a wonderful son like his daddy," Mrs. Jenison says as if she had not insulted him seconds ago. They seem lucky to have each other. Surely there is a man in this world that I will fall for, who will love me, no matter what, one day—sooner rather than later. There has to be a man somewhere who is willing to kiss away my flaws and settle for my best qualities.

"Mr. and Mrs. Jenison, you should expect a daughter," I say, smiling.

They watch the screen cooing at every jerky little movement their female fetus makes; every flip is now an acrobatic feat. I reach for Mr. Jenison's hand and place it on his wife's belly. He giggles like a schoolboy when he feels a slight vibration. Kelly checks her time, and whispers, "Rush hour is worse at six than at five."

I think about the Jenisons as I head home from work—how at odds they were in the beginning of their visit and how loving they turned out to be. At the core of each of them is an intense set of emotions that can surface as gently as a smile, a word of sweetness, respect; in contrast, they can flow as heatedly as hot lava, pulling apart a marriage that hangs by a thread. Maybe love itself is a paradox, a figment of our collective imaginations—what we think a couple's primary interest should be but seldom is.

Deep down, I am still bitter over all that Ralph has done to me. My throat tightens as soon as I arrive home. From the street, my house looks foreboding, with its dark windows, shrubs flailing in the wind, and tall grass needing to be cut. Ralph tended the lawn when he lived here. He took care of the "manly" chores around the house: the plumbing, repairs, and whatnot. As I enter the house, I smell mildew seeping through the floorboards and closets, places where Ralph used to spray with a bleaching concoction he made himself. Ralph knew a thing or two about killing mildew. I don't. I don't even know where to begin. I notice that the far wall in the kitchen is warping from water spilling inside from the overflow of the gutters. Ralph used to clean the gutters. I am afraid to go out on the roof, afraid of falling. I feel the same way I did the first time I ran around a track—alone, vulnerable, and afraid.

Well, there is no man around here anymore, Lenita Mae Faulkner. Maybe there never will be. Face it. No man will be doing the manly stuff now—you will. I tell myself these things as I change into my jogging attire. I stretch and go for a long run. The wind in my face feels liberating after an hour. There is no time for me to do much around the house, an hour here or there to fix anything. It is a matter of priorities, isn't it? A matter of spending time or money. I can either do the work myself, or hire a man to clean the *damned* gutters, another one to repair the *damned* kitchen wall, and still another to replace the *damned* pipes that bang and rattle loud enough to wake the dead whenever I turn on the hot water.

I think about the garden in Ernest's backyard and how peaceful it feels being there. I want to feel peaceful again. I want to be happy and less alone. As I round the corner of Chestnut and Valemont, I stop to watch the distant light in Ernest's front window. Without forethought, I walk up to his door and ring his doorbell a few times before he answers.

"Lenny," he says, bewilderment furrowing his brow. He stands before me wearing bedroom slippers, wrapped in a striped robe, his hair untamed and feral.

"I was jogging by, on my way home, and I thought about something you . . . the book . . . said . . ."

"Would you like to come inside?" Ernest asks politely.

"For a minute," I say, hesitating before entering as waves of doubt and misgiving wash over me. The air is lightly scented with herbs from his garden—lavender, sage, basil, and rosemary—and from candles burning on the mantel above his fireplace. We pass through his living room, with its antique-white walls, a comfortable chestnut wool colored sofa, a wooden upright piano against the far wall, and a coffee table made of an old leather suitcase, stacked with books and magazines. A wooden rocker sits next to the fire. A book is left on the seat and an afghan rests over the arms. I imagine Ernest sitting there, reading for pleasure.

"I hope I'm not disturbing you," I say, gazing briefly at the painted portrait of a pale brunette with large hazel eyes and lips like rose petals.

Amy, I know it. I feel like an intruder who made the wrong choice. Go home to the dark emptiness, and dwell.

"How about some tea?" he asks.

"Sounds good." Ernest has a warm, cozy nook, a home where every square inch is tended and loved—every eclectic piece of furniture, every brightly colored painting, the bookshelves filled with books, and the uniquely splayed curtains, like rainbows across each window. I follow Ernest to his kitchen, and when he gestures for me to sit, I find myself admiring the beautifully handcrafted table of deep oak with its polished grain, and run my palms over it.

"I love this table, Ernest." Ernest picks up a teakettle from his stovetop and pours hot water into two mugs. I watch him add tea bags.

"I made it years ago in a woodworking class I took. From a single oak tree."

He hands me a cup of ginseng tea and sits across from me at the table. I notice a heart, with AMY carved in the center, and an awkward silence thickens between us.

"You made this table for your wife?" I ask, the two of us staring at the heart.

"We used to sit under the oak tree it was made from, before we were married. We'd dream about the family we were going to have. Amy called it our talking tree. Sometimes we'd sit under it and talk things out for hours. It died the same year we were married. I gave this table to her for our first anniversary."

"I bet she loved it."

"She did, but now, looking back, it seems more like an omen."

The sadness I notice in his eyes, there since the first time we met, might always endear Ernest to me. There is something about his faithfulness to Amy, even after death, that is both admirable and disheartening. What kind of woman can evoke such boundless love? A name etched forever in his heart, her picture greeting all perspective lovers, her flawless white skin, and things, a constant reminder of what they meant to each other.

"Amy was lucky to have had you, Ernest."

"Lucky? No," Ernest scoffs, shaking his head deniably. "I was glad she was sickest during the summer, when I didn't have to lose any work to stay by her side. And when she died, I was angry with myself for thinking it—wanting her to die on schedule, before the school year began. I was angriest with myself, until recently."

"What's helping you get through this, Ernest?"

"My work, I suppose. I love teaching. I count my students as my greatest blessings . . . and . . . my friendships."

Ernest pats me lightly on my arm at the word *friendships.* I wonder what he would do if I suddenly kissed him. Run. I am his good friend, his buddy to pal around with from time to time. Yet, I cannot help feeling more than what I am supposed to feel—something more than friendship but less than passion.

"My friendships are blessings, too," I say nervously.

"Karen's still in the picture."

"Yes, she and Jason didn't have anything to do with Ralph's insider-trading scam after all."

"I had a feeling."

"You did," I agree, "but I'm still angry about Ralph. Don't you feel at least a tinge of anger about losing Amy?"

"No, not anymore. Now I'm . . ."

"Now you're what, Ernest?"

"Lonely. That's the label my friends and family have heaped on me anyway. I don't know, maybe they're right. I rarely go anywhere because I generally feel out of place in public, and I don't date. I'm not ready for that yet. I try to stay busy around here."

"Doing what?"

"I always have papers to grade, the lawn and garden, books to read, my music . . . plenty to do."

"Music? Your blues, you mean?"

His face lights up with a boyish grin, an infectious giggle bubbles out, and we both break into laughter as if remembering the same source of amusement. What?

"My blues," he chuckles. "Nobody owns the blues. Didn't I teach you better than that?"

"You know what I meant," I say, as if offended.

"Are you coming to the Corner Grill next Saturday?" he asks enthusiastically. "I'll have a surprise for you."

"What kind of surprise?" I ask, glad to see Ernest happy. "Will there be a wonderful man waiting to whisk me away?"

"Better than that," he says.

"You're finally going to shave your beard." I laugh.

He rubs his chin and says incredulously, "You really want me to get rid of it?"

"What can be better than that?"

Diary notes:

Still reading Lessons of the Lotus. Must remember that I am a beautiful, spiritual being with many blessings. Must live consciously, and stop worrying about the money. Remember Rule 3: I will follow my dreams, no matter what.

Paul Anderson is surprised by my unannounced visit. "The office is usually closed by now," he says. "I just happen to be here."

"You owe me an explanation, Mr. Anderson," I say snippily. "You led me to believe that Karen and Jason were involved in Ralph's insider-trading scheme. And I don't appreciate being misled by someone I've hired to tell me the truth."

"I never said they were involved."

"*Apparently.* You didn't deny it," I say, overemphasizing the word that led me to falsely accuse Karen.

"Apparently."

"It was Mikayla Roberts, wasn't it?"

"Jason mentioned Newton Tech to me over a golf game, and I happened to mention how well the stock was doing to Mikayla." He narrows his eyes, sucks his bottom lip, and sighs heavily. "I had no idea that she and Ralph Griffin would act illegally."

"That's a good explanation for what happened, Mr. Anderson. But I'm still being sued for a million-plus dollars, and because of you, I've completely lost all faith in lawyers."

"Unforgivable of me, I suppose." Paul retrieves an official-looking document from the corner of his desk and hands it to me. I read past the fine print, the case number, *wherefore* and *heretofore.*

"Griffin versus Faulkner, dismissed?"

Paul nods his confirmation.

"But what does it mean? What happened?"

"It means that after a brief phone call to your friend, Mr. Griffin, in which I explained that if he chose to proceed with his case against you I would be obligated by oath and conscience to bring a matter of insider trading to the FCC and the FBI."

"You called Ralph?"

"His lawsuit against you was dropped this morning, Dr. Faulkner."

"You mean it's over?" I exclaim.

"Yes, and I doubt you'll hear anything further from Mr. Griffin," he says. "So am I forgiven?"

"Only if you agree to something."

"Something?" he says.

"I can overlook the egregious way I've been treated if you agree to handle the legal paperwork for a home for girls I'm trying to help start." I remove the materials Stella gave me from my bag. He carefully examines each page.

"Not my area of expertise," he says matter of factly. "But I'll get to work on it as soon as I can."

"I appreciate anything you can do, Mr. Anderson."

He says nothing, and in the awkward silence, my mind flip-flops over the strong features of his face, his flared nostrils and proud chin, the smile that comes uneasily.

"Paul," he says.

"Pardon me?"

"Call me Paul."

Mrs. Stein greets me with, "Hello, stranger." She hands me a letter that came to her house by mistake.

"I'm glad that foolish postman got mixed up. It's been a long time since I've seen you at home."

"Come in, Mrs. Stein," I say. I lead her to the kitchen, where I make us some tea.

"The neighborhood has changed so much these days, Lenny. When Ezra and I moved here, we were the first Jews for miles. Now there are as many coloreds as whites. After the sixties, a lot of my old neighbors moved away. They didn't want to live around different people."

"Coloreds?" I ask, the word clinging to my throat.

Mrs. Stein nods in agreement, unaware of any negative connotation the word carries from the Old South. "Ezra got a lot of flack for teaching at a colored college. But he did it anyway."

"Is that right?"

"Even some of our Jewish friends were uncomfortable about it. Ezra was told many times to get a job at Emory or Georgia Tech. But he liked where he was. He never regretted staying at Morehouse."

I pour more tea into her cup. "Was it love at first sight for you?" I ask.

"When I met Ezra again after all those years, I admired him. I had compassion for how he'd suffered. He was intelligent and kind. But I didn't feel romantic toward him back then."

"And you married him anyway?"

"He was a patient man. In time, I came to understand the meaning of what love really means."

"And?"

Her eyes twinkle as if watching a beautiful memory unfold. She puckers for a sip and says, "Love is not something that happens. It's a choice one makes. I'm convinced of it. I trusted that my Aunt Gertie, who died a horrible death, had been right. This was the man for me. And he was."

We finish our tea and I regret not having baked cookies or some sweet delicacy to add.

"I should've made brownies. I'm good at that."

"Oh, don't worry yourself about it. True friends understand these things. Why don't you come for dinner at my house next Saturday night? I'll have a surprise for you."

"A surprise?"

"There's a wonderful man I want you to meet, Lenny." Her face lights up with excitement. I want to tell her that wonderful is nice, but romance is closer to the top of my list just now.

41

It happens naturally. First we speak over the phone while I'm at the office. About Linda's Safe House, and how the legal paperwork is going. "Shouldn't take long," he tells me, but then he phones later that night. Paul Anderson has pulled some strings and expedited the process of our getting a license. I meet him for lunch the following day. And today, Saturday, I cancel dinner with Mrs. Stein to spend the evening with him—Paul. Paul and I have dinner at a quaint restaurant downtown, not far from my house.

After dinner, he drives me home and comes inside for a drink. Paul drinks very little wine before kissing my hand, then my cheek. My face burns, and I fear falling in love too quickly. We are like two racecars on the speedway, revving our engines, raring to go. He embraces me and I see the two of us off at a distance. Paul and Lenny. Lenny Faulkner Anderson. Lenny F. Anderson. My biological clock tick, tick, ticking.

The phone rings, the spell broken as my answering machine records a message from Ernest. "Lenny, I came by earlier to take you to the Corner Grill. Sorry you missed your surprise."

Paul nibbles my neck and below, to the fleshy, exposed part of my breast, where he has miraculously unbuttoned my blouse.

"I can't, I'm sorry," I say, breathlessly, pushing him away from one tremendously hot spot.

"It's all right, Lenny," he says, standing to leave. "Join me for a ride next Sunday in the country."

"I like Sunday rides," I say.

"You'll love my horse, Mickey."

"Mickey? A horse?"

"You do ride, don't you?"

"Of course I do," I lie.

Paul arrives at two o'clock to drive me to his horse farm in the country.

"How long have you owned Mickey and Pickey?" I ask, laughing at the names of Paul's horses. A boy no more than thirteen or fourteen brings them from the stables to us. I surmise from his ruddy complexion and sun-bleached hair that he spends most of his days working outside.

"That there brown quarter horse's the biggest one," the boy says.

Paul takes its reigns and holds him steady while the golden palomino, Mickey, is presented to me.

"She's a sweet one, ma'am," the boy says, helping me to mount her. "You don't have to worry about Mickey."

Paul hops on his horse and we trot toward a trail at the edge of a large corral.

"It's been ages since I've been on a horse," I say as my butt bounces like it has the hiccups.

"That right?" he says with an amused glint in his eyes.

"I'll try not to make a fool of myself."

"You're doing fine," Paul says, and bows his lips in a devilish grin. "HAW!" He lightly whips the horse's backside. It breaks into a faster pace, galloping along a trail that enters the woods, with me following closely behind. Mickey has a mind of her own, however. I am doing nothing to steer her from the trail as she races dangerously between trees and leaps over deep watery ditches. I hold onto the reigns as if my life might end at any moment. My knees grip the sides of the horse like forceps.

"Stop. Slow down, Mickey. Heel, girl!" I try to remember what Roy Rogers said to make Trigger stop. "Whoa! Whoa, girl! Whoa."

Mickey picks up her pace.

Ahead of me, Paul has a steady stride. He and Pickey are one, gliding through the woods as if by magic. He rides with his head high with a rhythm reminiscent of an old Western. I follow behind him like a jack rabbit on speed. Not once does he glance back at me, and for that I am grateful, because my mouth is frozen open as Mickey gets horrifyingly close to the trees. It is as if she is sending me a message. *One wrong move and you're off my back.* She switches to the other side of the trail and my left arm hits a tree. I almost scream because it feels broken. Impulsively, I kick her. She darts to the other side and tries to rub me off her back. My right leg smacks against a tall oak.

"Yoooou bitch!!!!" I scream, and she tries to throw me off her back.

Oh, why did I lie? I have never been on a horse in my life. Paul stops and turns to see me, barely hanging on. He grabs my reigns and pulls back to make Mickey slow to a soft trot.

"You all right?" he says. I force a smile; my body aches all over. I spit dead bugs.

"I'm fine," I say, grateful to be alive. We reach the end of the woods and ride across a huge open pasture covered in timothy and clover. Paul dismounts and helps me down. I slide to the ground feeling beaten up and scared witless. My feet are unsure of the ground as we guide the horses to a nearby creek. I rub my arm, which isn't broken after all, and sit beside the trickling water. It invites me to remove my boots and cool my feet for a short spell, which I do. Paul sits beside me but keeps his black riding boots buckled. I see this as an opportunity to know more about him.

"Where are you from, Paul?"

"Philadelphia," he says, and when he asks me, I tell him the truth. He laughs, and says, "Madoosa County isn't on the map, is it?"

"It's the dot just before the state of Florida."

He laughs again, and says, "I bet you couldn't wait to get out of there."

"Madoosa County wasn't a bad place to grow up," I say.

"Really?" he says like he doesn't believe me. I remember something Karen told me once about men, that they are turned off permanently by a woman who talks about herself too much. Karen, the expert, believes that a woman can have a man eating from the palm of her hand if she plays the mating game right. I ask Paul if his family still lives in Philadelphia.

"My father died a few years ago, but my mom and sisters are there."

"What was your dad like?"

"Hardworking."

"And?"

"That's mostly all he did. My father worked all the time."

"What about your mother?"

"She took care of the family."

"Is that what you want in a woman, Paul?"

"No," he says. Paul stands and dusts himself off. I cover my cold, wet feet with socks and slide them back inside my boots. When he reaches for me, I hesitate. Karen's advice whispers inside my head. *Men like Paul only respect women they can't control.* I grab hold of his hands and pull up. I turn my head away when he attempts to kiss the side of my face. *Keep him guessing.*

"I want a woman who isn't afraid to go after what she wants," he says.

"And I have a rule that requires me to follow my dreams," I say. We take the reins of our horses and begin to walk across the creek. The water is lowest along the path I choose, where the sound of it reminds me of Ernest Hemingway's garden. I close my eyes and sniff the scent of dark earth and honeysuckle. Mickey jerks and I yank the rein. She cranes her neck around and looks me dead in the eye. I lose my balance when she nudges me, sliding butt first across a slippery rock. The horse hates me.

"Hah, Mickey," I yell, standing with my legs spread wide apart. "Hah." I yank the reign as hard as I can and she gets to stepping. I wonder if she once belonged to Mikayla. Mickey. *Mikayla. Paul.* Of course, there has to be a reason why the horse hates me. Paul snakes an arm around my waist and guides me across the creek. When we get to the other side, he kisses me lightly. I am afraid to open my parched, gritty mouth. Maybe he thinks I'm playing hard to get.

"How many rules do you have?" he says. I swallow whatever it is at the back of my throat, telling myself bugs are extra protein with legs. Dead bugs can't kill me.

"A few," I say.

"Rules for how to keep a man guessing?"

"No, rules for life."

"I see," Paul says. He steps back and helps me mount Mickey. His face goes blank, eyes darting away inscrutably. I find myself guessing about what he thinks of me. Will this be our last date? Did I say too much? He hops on Pickey and we're off again—across the field of timothy and clover, back through the woods where Mickey reminds me that my life is hanging by a single thread—a hard-enough smack against a strong-enough tree, and I'm a goner. At the end of the trail, it is only by the grace of God that I've survived.

Later in the evening, Paul drives me home. Every part of my body aches as if I have been beaten with a bat. I proffer my cheek, which Paul lightly kisses. He gazes into my eyes as if longing for something more substantial, more stimulating than the heavy petting of a few nights ago. I unlock the front door. He raises an eyebrow sexily, and I go for it, sucking his lips like there's no tomorrow. There's a loud smack at the end.

"Thank you for a lovely afternoon, Paul."

He looks at me with an expectant glimmer. "Does tonight have to end so soon?"

"I have rules, remember?" I say.

"Yes, but what rule says I have to go home?"

"The one I'm going to write tonight." I step inside the house, telling him good night, slowly closing the door in his face.

I'm falling faster than Rome over Paul Anderson. And it scares me. My heart can't take another betrayal. How can I be sure that it's time to take our relationship to the next level? When will I know he's worth it?

Rule 8.

I won't make love unless it feels right.

Diary notes:

Two weeks have passed since I've heard from Paul. I must remember Rule 4, and stop waiting for his call. I am a beautiful, spiritual being with other blessings in my life to consider besides him. Will go out to Corner Grill with Ernest tonight.

It is shortly after seven o'clock when Paul phones. "So, what are you doing tonight?"

"I've just finished taking a bath, and now I'm lying across my bed with my feet propped up on the headboard."

"Sounds relaxing," he said.

"It is."

"Have you had dinner yet?"

"No, not yet. I wasn't planning to eat much. A sandwich, maybe."

"Would you have dinner with me tonight, Lenny?"

"I suppose," I say, pretending that I am not excited enough to jump up and down on the bed. I pretend that I am not relieved to hear his voice. After we say good-bye and hang up, my mind goes aflutter, and I cannot think straight about what to wear, what to do with my hair, what to say when I answer the door. The phone rings. Ernest.

"Ready to go?" he asks.

"Oh, Ernest, I forgot. I can't tonight. Something's come up."

"Another time, then," he says, sounding disappointed. I think about his carved heart for Amy, and I feel ashamed of myself for taking our friendship for granted. Ernest cleaned my gutters last week and left a note saying, *Just doing my duty as your friend.* Tomorrow, I will make things up to him. Make chili and take him a bowl. Better yet, I will invite Ernest over for chili and beer. We can watch a basketball game, his favorite team, whatever it is. I think about his large collection of books. Tea. Ernest is an herbal tea lover. I will invite him to dinner and tea.

An hour later, the doorbell rings, and I know from the moment Paul smiles that tonight will be special.

"It was really thoughtful of you to invite me out, Paul," I say. He escorts me to his car, and tells me he was surprised to find me available.

"I've called you before and you weren't home," he says.

"Next time, leave a message."

Paul parks in front of a five-star restaurant, the kind with valet service. Once seated, I quietly listen to him talk about his day. He tells me that he has filed a class action suit that is taking up most of his leisure time.

"Who's being sued?" I say.

"It might be of interest to you," he says, leaning back in his chair. "The manufacturers of a birth-control device."

"Oh." I am tempted to debate with him. I know he is suing the company that makes birth-control implants. I have inserted many into the arms of young women desperate for a simpler way to prevent pregnancy. Many lawyers exploit a few cases where a medical treatment has failed or works improperly; they dangle these cases in front of the media, and before long, patients who never had a problem before are convinced they are dying.

"Aren't you concerned that such lawsuits may stop researchers from developing safer methods of birth control?"

"No," he says, glancing down at his menu. The waiter returns to our table and Paul orders the blackened trout. I order smoked sea bass, and he says, "Trout's better."

"Better for *you,* maybe," I say.

"It's better because it's fresher."

"But I want bass," I insist.

"The bass has been frozen for months."

"I don't care."

"That's odd," he says. "I had the impression that you did."

"What do you mean I did?"

"Cared about what you ate."

"Paul, let's change the subject before you cause me to break one of my rules."

"Which rule is that?" he says, surprised.

"The one that tells me to suit myself."

"I see," he says softly. "When do I get a copy of these rules?"

We go to a dance club after dinner, where the inside is dimly lit. There are clouds of gray smoke from one end of the room to the other. After an hour, I smell like a tobacco factory from head to toe. I am on the verge of suggesting that we leave. But when a slow song is played, Barry White crooning deep and sexy, I want Paul to ask me to dance. I pretend I cannot hear something he says, and lean closer until our bodies meet.

"Can you put up with this?" Paul asks, planting a passionate kiss on my willing smacker.

"I don't know," I say, closing my eyes, bracing myself for another kiss.

"The cigarette smoke's burning my eyes," he says.

"Mine too." I sigh, watching him rub his eyes.

Paul takes me home and escorts me to my door. He pecks me on my cheek.

"Good night, Lenny," he says.

"Good night, Paul."

After preparing for bed, I write in my diary

What's not to like about Paul Anderson? He's tall, dark, and handsome. Successful and intelligent. A great kisser. Yet, there is one flaw that bothers me. A petty flaw, perhaps. But one that agitates my brain like a head cold I can't quite shake. He actually told me what to eat. He insisted that I change my order. Is this the beginning of a control issue? I have to stand my ground. Rules are not made to be broken. Rule 1. I will not allow anyone to control me. Rule 2. I will only change to suit myself.

The following morning, I awake to the sound of distant church bells and think about Mama. *Be the first to ring the bell, Lenita Mae. Be the first. Be the first.* I picture our family walking home from Waycross Baptist, Mama with Bobby held tightly in her arms, like a bundle, Daddy with his hat in his hands, wearing his only suit, the one in the picture, and Rosetta pulling me along, her hand moist from wiping away her tears, days after word came that Joseph was killed in action. Mama ambles slowly along, almost passively, each step leaden with grief. *Be the first, Lenita Mae. They won't have nothin' to tease you 'bout no more.*

I get out of bed and set about cleaning the house, an attempt to change the focus of my mind from gloomy reminiscences, the deaths of loved ones, to what I am doing now—staying conscious, scrubbing the toilet, the sinks, mopping the floors in the bathrooms, the kitchen. After changing the beds, I go for a run along Peachtree and back, stopping momentarily at the corner of Chestnut, where I ponder whether or not to knock on Ernest's door. He has painted it a lively blue. I knock.

"Lenny, what a surprise!" Ernest exclaims.

"I noticed you painted your door."

"Oh, yes, that. Just brightening things up around here," he says giddily. "Come in, Lenny. Come in."

"For a minute," I say, entering his warm, cozy home, with its smell of apples and cinnamon brewing in the kitchen. "I really came by to thank you for cleaning my gutters."

"Nothing to it." He shrugs.

"Come have lunch with me later, Ernest," I say. My stomach growls loud enough to be heard, like a lion lusting after a meaty antelope.

"Stay and eat something now," Ernest says, grinning.

"A little bite," I say, embarrassed. "I haven't showered. Just finished running. My hair's a mess."

"You look great," Ernest says. I relax and follow him to the kitchen, where in the middle of the room, on the other side of the small island, I notice a woman hovering over his stove, humming happily. She glances up at me and smiles. I freeze. She is the spitting image of the picture over the fireplace mantel, the woman I assumed to be Amy.

"You must be the doctor Ernest has been telling me about," she says, "Hi, I'm Genevieve." She extends her hand and I step forward to shake it.

"Hi. Call me Lenny, please," I say, nervously.

"He's told me how great you are, naturally," she says.

"Really?" I say, confused. Ernest said he wasn't ready to date again. He said he didn't get out much, didn't feel comfortable in public. But here stands this woman, Genevieve, quite at home, cooking, no less.

"Genevieve's my sister-in-law," he says. "She's been here on business all week."

"Oh, I see."

"I'm leaving in a few hours to go home to San Francisco, Lenny, so you must stay for breakfast. I want so much to get to know you better. Ernest doesn't seem to have any friends here, other than you, and to be honest, I'm worried about him turning into a hermit."

"He definitely has that potential." I laugh.

"Give me a break, you two," Ernest faintly protests.

Genevieve serves her specialty, Belgian waffles with stewed apples and a dollop of sour cream. While we eat, I notice how she purses her lips when she chews—like budding roses—and wonder about the picture over the mantel.

"So, that's you in the painting?" I ask, pointing in the direction of the living room.

"Oh, that painting was actually a self-portrait Amy made around the time she was first diagnosed with the cancer."

"She was quite an artist," I say, stunned by how uncanny the resemblance Genevieve has to the painting. My stomach tightens. Amy surrounds me with her decorative touches, her name carved in the table, and now I feel as though she is here in the flesh. The air feels thick with her presence. I can hardly breathe.

"Ernest has too many reminders of Amy in this house," Genevieve says. "It's been almost two years now. Still, he mourns like it was yesterday."

"She was my wife," Ernest hastily objects.

"Of course, she was," Genevieve says, taking a sip of tea. "And please, don't get me wrong, Lenny, I miss my sister terribly. We were close friends as well as sisters. But the way Ernest is living isn't healthy."

"I'm fine."

"There's no room for another woman. Don't you agree, Lenny?"

"I . . . I . . . can't answer that. It's up to Ernest. He's got to decide when he's ready to move on with his life."

"You sound like a true friend," she says, smiling wisely, her eyes narrowing as she carefully scrutinizes me.

"She is," Ernest says, "I told you so."

"You didn't believe him?" I ask. "That we're friends?"

"I don't believe in platonic relationships between men and women," Genevieve says. "Eventually, they either split apart and never see each other again, or become something more."

"There're always exceptions," I say.

"That's what Amy used to say," she says, candidly. "Before she married Ernest."

Later, Ernest comes over, and we have chili and tea.

"Hope you weren't offended by Genevieve," he says.

"No, of course not."

"She means well."

"I can tell she cares a lot about you."

"Aside from Genevieve's husband and daughter, I'm the only family she has."

"That's nice," I say, thinking how I never liked Rosetta's husband. Larry was ignorant and mean. He knocked out my sister's front tooth. "You're like a brother to Genevieve."

"You've heard of father figures, right? Well, I'm her brother figure."

We laugh.

"It didn't bother anyone in Amy's family that you're black?"

"In the beginning, it bothered her father a great deal, but he gave us his blessing shortly before he passed away." Ernest gets up from the table and helps himself to another serving of chili. The phone rings and the answering machine records a message from Paul. "Lenny, I'd like to take you for a ride in the country tomorrow. In a car, this time."

I jump up to answer the phone, too late. The line is dead when I pick up.

"Who's Paul?" Ernest asks.

"We're seeing each other," I say.

"Oh, is he Mr. Wonderful?"

"Mr. Wonderful?"

"The man who'll whisk you off your feet?"

"I don't know, Ernest," I say. I think about my history with Paul. He had a relationship with Mikayla, and led me to believe Karen and Jason were involved with Ralph. His horse, Mickey, almost killed me. He did not call for two weeks.

"What don't you know, Lenny?"

"Paul works too much."

"Not a good sign."

"But he has his good points, too."

"Good points?"

"Well, he helped me in my case against Ralph, he seems to respect me, and hasn't gone too far."

"That's it?"

"Isn't that enough to build on?"

"You didn't say he cares about you, Lenny. Caring makes for a strong foundation in a relationship."

"Maybe he does."

"Maybe he doesn't care for you as much as I do."

My mind goes blank. Part of me wants Ernest to leave. The other part wants him to hold me.

"I shouldn't have said that," he says. "I'm sure this Paul's a wonderful guy."

43

The following day, Paul and I drive to Lookout Mountain and hike along the bluff. We watch hang gliders twirling through the air, one after the other lighting on a spot that appears the size of a pen point from where we stand. Sailing at greater distances, they resemble large, black hawks. I envy the freedom they must feel. From another point along the bluff, I am able to see seven states through a telescope. Paul calls out, "North Carolina, Virginia, Ohio, Arkansas, Georgia, Alabama, and Mississippi." He leans close to me, pointing out where I should look. I breathe in his manly scent like I am sniffing for fresh air. I consider what Ernest said yesterday. Does Paul care? He turns the telescope, and tells me that Ohio is at ten o'clock.

"But where's Arkansas?" I say. Paul wraps an arm around my shoulders and turns the telescope to the left.

"Off in that direction," he says.

"Oh," I say, gazing up at him. At this moment, I would not mind him kissing me as he did last week at the dance club. Passionately. Even with a few tourists waiting to use the telescope, I would relish him holding me close. But Paul decides it is time to take me home, as sunset fades into darkness.

We say good night at the door, but when he kisses me until my body becomes rebellious and unwilling to play by my rules, I invite him inside. The night is chilly and he makes a cozy fire. For the first time in months, my house feels warm and full. We have a few glasses of wine while sitting in the dark with a flickering light emanating from the fireplace. He does not pick up the remote control to switch on *the game*—unlike Ralph. His strong arms envelop me in a long overdue hug. He does not ask me to fetch the beer.

Paul pours more wine into my glass. I take a sip and we begin to neck on the sofa. Rule #8 sneaks into my head. *I won't make love unless* . . . Paul stands, reaches for me, and before long, we're in bed.

It is after ten o'clock in the morning when I awake alone. Paul has dressed and left without a note or a good-bye kiss. I feel cheap and used. He could have said good-bye. I broke rule #8 like it didn't matter. Haven't I learned? Didn't nine years with Ralph teach me anything? I remember Ernest asking, "Does he care as much as I do?" Karen's voice rolls around inside my head, saying, "You're too available, too easy."

Why did I do it? Hell, I was better at sticking to rules when I was eleven. *You're a foolish, foolish woman, Lenita Mae.* Paul probably thinks I am all talk on the surface and horny as hell underneath.

A few weeks pass and I cannot help calling him. I dial his office, half hoping he won't answer. I watch Kelly pass my door on her way out. Once again, I am the last doctor to leave.

Paul's receptionist answers and transfers my call. My stomach churns. I hate worrying about convention: whether or not I am playing the game properly. I hate the unwritten rule that tells women to wait for *him* to call first. Paul answers.

"Lenny, how've you been?" he asks, as if pleasantly surprised.

"Fine," I choke out.

"Well, I've been thinking about you."

I do not believe him one iota. What to say? What to say? What to say?

"Oh. Well, I've been wondering about the rest of the legal work for Linda's Safe House." I lie through my teeth. I hate lying when the truth should be easy.

A brief pause follows and I imagine a serious, thoughtful expression coming over his face. I want to see him. Why can't I say so?

"Oh, yes, I completed all that over a week ago, Lenny," he says. "I'll have my receptionist send copies of everything to you immediately."

"I can come by to pick it up," I say, before I can stop myself.

"It won't be necessary," he says. "The appropriate papers have been filed and there's nothing here you'll need right away."

"Oh. Well, thanks for everything, Paul," I say.

"I was glad to do it, Lenny."

We exchange a few pleasantries before saying good-bye.

Paul phones at the end of the week.

"I have tickets to see the Falcons play," he says, sounding confident. "How'd you like to come along tonight?"

Here I am, lying in bed like a sack of potatoes, after wasting a lot of energy waiting for this call, breaking rule #4. *I will never again put my life on hold for a man.* Something about which Paul is completely oblivious. He is a workaholic like his father, I'm sure of it.

"Can you make it?" he asks when I don't answer right away.

"No, I'm sorry. I'm on call this weekend."

"What about next Saturday night?"

"I can't."

"Can't?"

"Something's come up."

"Oh." He sighs. "The rules."

"Yes."

"I'm sorry, I should've called sooner," he says, his voice an octave higher. "I've been preoccupied with my work. I had to go out of town. My clients are all over the country."

"Are you apologizing, or making excuses?"

"I'm sorry," he says. "Can we start again?" I think about this for a moment. I shouldn't have gone to bed with him. I'm worth more than a quick-and-easy roll in the hay. I won't give in to desire next time.

"I'll think about it," I say, but after we hang up, I ponder whether or not I should. I phone Karen and complain.

"Give him a second chance," she says.

"But I'm not a holiday, a man's night out, a good-time girl for when he happens to be in town."

"I know, girl, but he's a good man. He'll change if you play the—"

"I'm so done with games, Karen," I say abruptly, cutting her off. "I can't go through another Ralph, I can't. I have to be me and if I'm not enough for Paul Anderson . . . If he'd rather work around the clock than spend time with me, then I don't want to see him again."

"Every man's not Ralph, Lenny. You've got to stop thinking like that. Give him another chance."

"I'm scared, Karen," I quaver. "If I get in any deeper, Paul could break what's left of my heart, and I might not recover."

"But you can't spend your life avoiding love."

"You're right," I say.

"Of course I am," Karen says, "You're a strong woman, Lenny. It's not like you need him."

"No, it isn't."

"Call him tomorrow," she says, enthusiastically. "Tell him he's got one chance to prove himself to you, and if he fails he's got to deal with me."

I laugh at what threat Karen might pose with her burgeoning belly. Later in the night while lying in bed, I remember how hard it was to function after Ralph left me. A broken heart is the worst kind of pain. It lingers elusively, sometimes hiding beneath the surface of other things—work and other preoccupations. But when the silence comes, the doom and gloom of being home alone ascends like the night, and I recollect the sweetness of his breath. My heart aches all over again. I cannot allow myself to go through this with Paul.

Before going to bed, I take out my diary, and write

People make time for what they want. If Paul wants to see me, he knows how to reach me. There's nothing complicated about us getting together more than once a month. He has to take time to eat, go to the bank, get groceries, work out, or go to the toilet once in a while. Why not time for me? I have to do something besides waiting for us to get started. Do something, Lenny. Remember Rule 4: I will never again put my life on hold for a man.

24

At two in the morning, I receive a page from the hospital emergency room. Shaniqua Davis has been in an accident. Her water has broken. "She's hemorrhaging," the nurse says urgently. Paul mutters, "What time is it?" He's half asleep, so I avoid disturbing him further by dressing in the dark, stub my big toe, and mute the scream. *Holy crapola.* In no time, I'm on the road heading for the hospital in a treacherous downpour and fog so thick in places I can hardly see. My car slides into the parking lot. *Dear God, let her be all right.*

Shaniqua is only two centimeters dilated, with massive blood loss from trauma to the abdomen. The emergency team works frantically. A nurse tells me the baby is experiencing decelerations, the fetal monitor beeps faintly. A flashback of Linda Jenkins strikes like lightning, and I panic. It can't happen again. I can't lose another young patient. Shaniqua is having a placental abruption; her placenta bursts and must be removed immediately.

She is already prepped for a C-section. Shaniqua is put to sleep, and I surgically remove the baby as quickly as possible. The infant boy calls out in a tiny whimper when I lift him from his mother. I swaddle him tightly in a warm, cotton receiving blanket, holding him close to my heart. I reflect on his mother not wanting him. "I don't want no boy."

The baby begins to turn a rosy brown as he opens his eyes and searches my face; his quivering bottom lip pulls at my heartstrings. I pass him off to the neonatal nurses, who rush him to the neonatal intensive care unit. And I commence putting Shaniqua back together again.

★ ★ ★

"What happened last night?" I ask Shaniqua Davis later that morning in ICU.

"I fell," she says weakly.

"No, Shaniqua, you couldn't have sustained these injuries during a fall. You almost lost your baby. How did it happen? Did your mother get angry? Did she beat you?"

"No, I fell, Dr. Faulkner," she insists. "I took the wrong step off the front porch, and fell like I said."

Ms. Davis enters the ICU, and sits in the chair next to her daughter's bed. She ignores me.

"Congratulations on becoming a grandmother, Ms. Davis," I say, with forced cheerfulness.

"Mmmm-hummm."

"There's a problem we need to discuss, Ms. Davis," I say. "Shaniqua and her baby's well-being. Her injuries could not have been caused by a fall. She didn't misstep and end up with this much trauma. I think she was beaten."

"If Shaniqua said she fell, then that's what happened," she says, annoyed.

"At two in the morning?"

"I don't care if it was three or four in the morning. If she says she fell, she fell. And you can't prove any different."

"Look, Ms. Davis, I don't want to fight with you," I say, softening my tone.

"Then hush."

"Hush? I will not hush. A baby's life is at stake here. Suppose Shaniqua is holding her baby and falls like that again?"

"She won't, Doctor," Ms. Davis huffs, rolling her eyes at me. "Now I don't have anything else to say to you."

"Then I'll have a talk with Ms. Parker about this."

"Mmmmm-hummmm. Good-bye."

The following day, I return to the hospital to check on Shaniqua. She is wide-eyed when I enter the ICU, fretting over the pain in her abdomen. Moaning. I pull back the sheets and examine her stitches, but it is the sight of red welts and purple bruises sprawled across her belly that captures my attention. I noticed this atrocity the night I did her C-section, and now it looks even more swollen. She could have lost her life and her baby.

"Your mother did this, didn't she, Shaniqua?"

"No, I fell," Shaniqua says softly.

"I'm sorry this happened to you," I say. "But we can't let this happen again, Shaniqua. You know that, right? We've got to protect you and your baby."

"I just wanna go home."

"You can't go home right now. You can't live with your mother after what's happened."

"But what am I supposed to do?"

"I've spoken to Ms. Parker and she's made arrangements for you," I say. "Temporary shelter for you and your baby."

"Mama said you don't have the right to take me away. She said as long as I say I fell, you can't make me do anything. I wanna go home." She puts her thumb in her mouth like a bawling toddler and rolls over to face the wall. A child having a child. Another statistic. I wonder if she understands that she came within seconds of death.

I visit Shaniqua's baby in the intensive care nursery, retrieving him from his incubator at the first whimper; his quivering bottom lip makes me weak all over. Tubes run into his tiny nostrils and into his delicate, frail body. It's unfair, damned unfair that he has to suffer. He is innocent and helpless. He had no say in how he would enter this world.

The baby gazes into my eyes as if searching for his mother, and my heart melts. I have never felt like this before, this desperate need to nurture a baby I've delivered. A big part of me feels responsible for his well-being. I have to know he is going to survive.

I spend hours here, volunteering to feed and hold Shaniqua's son, crooning nursery songs from my lips as I gently rock the baby to and fro, my finger stuck in his tiny hand while he struggles to breathe.

45

Shaniqua's baby has been in intensive care for two weeks now. I visit him every morning before going to work and every evening before returning home. Paul is in New York on business, again. I miss him less when I am with Tajuan, his tiny body cradled in my arms, filling the need I have to nurture. Shaniqua, on the other hand, rarely visits Tajuan from a shelter only a few blocks away. She named him Tajuan, after the two boys who might be his father, either Tazwell or Juan.

I run into Stella early this morning, after making rounds.

"What brings you here?" I ask.

"I'm investigating another child-abuse case."

"It never stops, does it?"

"New cases every hour."

"Well, I've fallen in love with Shaniqua's baby," I say, smiling wide at the thought of him. "I love holding that boy."

"You're probably the reason he's survived so miraculously," she says. "The neonatalogist told me he should've died."

"Why doesn't Shaniqua spend more time with her son?" I ask.

"She's in shock, Lenny. It's normal for these young mothers to separate themselves from the reality of their circumstances."

"The reality is that her mother needs to be prosecuted," I say bitterly.

"Beating a pregnant woman is a much more serious crime than abusing a teenage daughter. But the problem is, we can't prove it."

"She almost killed her grandson," I say. "How much proof do you need?"

"We needed Shaniqua to tell us that, but she refused."

"Can't she remain at the shelter, until she does?"

"No, Lenny, Shaniqua's sticking to her story that she fell. Now that she's had a baby, she's legally considered an adult. She's free to go home, and is doing so as we speak."

"And the baby?"

"He leaves for home when he's well enough, probably in a few days."

"But Shaniqua said she doesn't even want a boy."

"A lot of girls say that at first. They don't usually mean it."

"But her mother almost killed Shaniqua and the baby. Suppose she loses control of herself again."

"Lenny, there's nothing else we can do."

A few days before Thanksgiving, Karen is my last patient. She complains about her weight, her cravings, pain in her back, her swollen ankles.

"I might die from exhaustion, Lenny," she cries, begging me to induce her.

"You have at least six weeks," I say, measuring the size of her womb to be sure. "He's going to be huge!"

"I'm so tired, Lenny," she moans. "He kicks and punches me all night long. I can't get comfortable no matter how I sleep. I wish I had a mattress with a big hole in the middle."

"I wish I had a dollar for every patient who says that."

"I can't take it anymore," she says, pouting.

"The baby will be here before you know it, Karen," I say, stroking her forehead. "Just hang in there."

She sighs heavily. "I'm not talking about the baby," she says. "I'm sick and tired of Mother telling me what to do." She mimics her mother, saying, "You're eating too much, Karen. It'll take forever to lose that weight."

"Cut the cord, Karen. It's long overdue. As long as you allow your mother to treat you like a child, you'll never have to take responsibility for what goes wrong in your life. You can always blame her."

"I can blame her for driving a wedge between me and Jason. He sides with her every chance he gets."

"But you stand for it, Karen."

"I know," she says helplessly.

"Sammy is going to need you to be his mother, not her. He won't understand it when Grandma tells him not to do what you say."

"She'd never do that," she says.

"She wouldn't?" I ask skeptically.

"Oh, Lenny, come to dinner with us on Thursday. With you there, I'll have the nerve to do it."

"Come for Thanksgiving? To your mother's house? I don't think so," I say, conjuring up an image of Karen's mother holding me by the elbow. *It's a shame you're not pregnant, too. I wish you were married. Have you considered lightening your skin?*

"I have other plans," I say.

"With Paul?"

"I haven't decided."

"He hasn't invited you yet, has he?"

"No, but he might call tonight."

"Lenny, it's too late. Two days to turkey day. Don't accept an invitation from him now. He'll take you for granted. Play the game and assume he isn't going to ask."

"I've told you, no games," I say adamantly. "I have my own rules."

"But you don't have a how-to-get-him-and-keep-him rule," she says.

The phone rings. My heart skips when I answer it.

"Haven't seen you in a long time."

"Ernest?"

"Yours truly," Ernest says, cheerfully. "Did you get my invitation?"

"Invitation?"

"My house . . . Thanksgiving dinner," he says. "Unless you have other plans."

"Other plans?" I say, thinking how alone I will be if Paul does not invite me to Philadelphia with him. I refuse to wait any longer. No more breaking of the rules. "Why no, Ernest," I say. "I'm not doing anything at all."

"Great then," he says. "My parents are coming, and I want you to meet them."

"I'll be there, Ernest," I say quickly, before I change my mind. Soon after our conversation, I fill with doubts. What if Paul calls tonight? I sleep with the phone next to my head. It does not ring until morning, when Rosetta calls to invite me to her house for Thanksgiving, the house she inherited from Mama.

"Bobby and his family's gonna be here," she says, excitedly. "You oughta see what we've done to Mama's old place. It looks so good, Lenita Mae. You won't recognize a thing."

"Oh, Rosetta, I wish I could, but I'm on call the next day."

"That's too bad, Lenita Mae. You know, ever since the funeral, I been seeing how I held myself back all these years, depending on you and Mama to always bail me out. I got the notion after you left that there ain't no reason I can't do better for myself."

"I'm glad to hear that, Rosetta," I say.

"I quit my job and turned Mama's place into a restaurant, Lenita Mae. Lots of home cooking. Folks from all around been coming."

"You quit your job!?" I'm stunned.

"Yeah, well, I didn't want you to know until I knowed I could do it. I feels proud of myself."

"Then I'm proud of you too, Rosetta," I say. "But how did you get the house painted? And what about the junk out front?"

"Bobby done it all," she says. "He even give me the money to fix things up inside. We're partners, Lenita Mae. Me and Bobby is gonna make do."

"I'm glad for both of you," I say, feeling uplifted by her news. I tell Rosetta that I will come down when I have more time off from work. "Maybe I can help you expand. Maybe I can become a partner, too."

At four o'clock, I walk over to Ernest Hemingway's house for Thanksgiving dinner. I imagine Paul sitting at his mother's dining-room table with his sisters seated around him. They know him better than any other woman can. They will get him to laugh and behave foolishly. He won't have a thought about me.

Ernest is standing on his front porch, waiting to greet me. "Glad you could come," he says, giving me a quick hug and a kiss on the cheek.

"Thanks for asking me," I say, just before an older version of Ernest appears from behind him, smiling.

"This lovely young lady must be the doctor," he says. Ernest beams as he introduces me to his father, Dr. Ernest Hemingway.

"Ernest?" I say, surprised. "You're Ernest Hemingway, too?" His mother, Lydia, an attractive, dark woman, peeks out from the kitchen.

"People always assume Ernie was named after the writer," she chimes in. I follow them to the dining room, where a large oak table is set with Oriental hand-painted pottery dishes, crisp white dinner napkins, and flowers clipped from Ernest's greenhouse.

"Everything's lovely," I say. "Can I help do anything?"

"No, no, dear," Mrs. Hemingway objects enthusiastically. "Now that you're here, we're all ready to eat." She brings out one dish after another, while Dr. Hemingway carves the turkey and Ernest selects music for us to listen to while we eat.

"This next one's Duke Ellington's version of 'Satin Doll,' " he says. The lilting swing of trumpet and bass combine with the fragrant meal spread across the table to create a special satisfying mood.

"I like it," I say. Midway through the meal, I observe the way Dr. Hemingway cares for his wife.

"Honey, do you need more salt?" he asks.

"A little more water," she says, preparing to stand.

"Don't get up, Honey Bear, I'll get it." He hurries off to the kitchen, and returns with a full pitcher of ice water. "Anyone else?" He pours his wife a glass.

"No thanks, Dr. Hemingway," I say. He places the pitcher at the end of the table.

"Anything else, Honey Bear?"

"No, Sweetness."

Dr. Hemingway sits, after seeing to it that she wants for nothing. Ernest is just like his father: kind, loving, and patient.

"Mother and Daddy," Ernest says, tapping his wine glass with his spoon. "I'd like to make a toast to our illustrious guest."

"Illustrious?" I say, incredulously.

"Lenny's one of the best doctors in this city."

"Oh, Ernest, stop," I protest.

"It's true," he says with pride. "Without naming names, let me say that I hear many women teaching at my school rave about her."

"I could tell that about you, Dr. Lenny," says Dr. Hemingway.

"Here's to Dr. Lenny Faulkner, one of Atlanta's finest."

They clink their glasses, I hesitantly add mine, secretly counting my blessings. *Thank God for this wonderful meal, and for the fine company who prepared it. Most of all, thank God for my dear friend, Ernest.*

★ ★ ★

Back home alone, I pour myself a gin and tonic, some of the booze Kevin left behind. Three glasses later, I philosophize about fate. If the Indians hadn't helped the colonists survive, they would have died and there would have been no need for slaves. I would probably be the eighth wife of a village chief with a few babies tugging at my wrap. There would be no concern about romance. There would be no expectations of a phone call from Paul. I would get my day of the week to be with His Highness, and that would be that.

Another glass, and my head spins. At one point, before Tajuan left the hospital and I lost contact with him, I had a glimmer of hope that somehow Shaniqua would not want to take him home. I pictured myself adopting him, and Paul falling in love with both of us. Love, the paradox I continue to yearn for in my life. I had an illusion of forming a family. But illusions are tricks on the brain. My body goes limp when the phone rings. I fumble to answer it. Paul says hello twice. I don't respond.

"I should've called last week," he says apologetically.

"You've got that right, Buster. I oughta throw the book at you."

"I'm sorry, Lenny. But you know I've been working up here in New Jersey off and on for two months. This morning I drove a rental car to my mom's house."

"Good for you," I say, slurring, "Ssssooo what?" as the room begins to spin again. Paul asks if I've been drinking. I ask him if he knows what they call a turkey with a briefcase. He ignores my question.

"My flight leaves here in an hour," he says.

"They call him a lawyer," I say, chuckling. I fall back across my bed. Paul's voice becomes distant and minuscule. The phone goes dead and I drift into a deep sleep. When I awake, it is morning.

The sun streams across my face. Paul is sleeping next to me. He snores. I don't remember him coming over. I don't remember opening my front door and inviting him inside. But here he is. God, my head aches when I try to lift it. I prop it up with a hand long enough to view the clock on my nightstand. I have to be at rounds in half an hour. I blow into the palms of my hands and sniff. My breath stinks. I am no drinker. I hope I did not make a fool of myself last night. Hope I did not break Rule #8: *I won't make love unless it feels right?* I don't even know what we did.

46

The Christmas buzz hangs excitedly in the air. The hospital lobby displays expensive artificial trees as well as giant wreaths and garlands. All my due patients beg to deliver before the big day. Some want the tax deduction this year. Others believe their lives will be made easier once they squeeze six to ten pounds out of their little keyholes. Karen is one of the latter. These days our conversations begin with *please. Please, Lenny, take it out.* The baby, now the nameless *it,* has been turning Karen's body against her. *Get it out, please.*

Early this morning, I phone Paul, and a woman answers. I immediately hang up, believing I dialed incorrectly. I dial again and his answering machine picks up. I reluctantly leave a message that Karen and Jason would like us to come over for dinner tonight.

"Page me," I say, before hanging up. His whereabouts become more mysterious with each day. I have only seen Paul twice since Thanksgiving. "The case keeps me busy," he says. The case takes him out of town. The case keeps him running "twenty-four seven," he says.

I drive to his apartment downtown after work. It is Friday and the traffic is especially heavy. I park illegally in front of his building, slip past the doorman, hop on the elevator, and begin to have doubts. My heart races when I reach the twenty-second floor and head toward Paul's apartment. *Why am I here?* I ask myself, standing outside his door. Yet I knock because I am dying to know who answered his phone.

Paul opens the door. His brows arch and eyes widen in more than surprise. "Lenny, what . . . what . . . what are you doing here?"

"I'm glad to see you, too, Paul," I say, crossing my arms over my chest. He lingers at the threshold before inviting me inside.

"Come in, Lenny," he says.

"How long have you been home?" I say. He is wearing his bathrobe. My nostrils take in the steam rising from his shower. Paul's face is clean shaven; the scent of soap emanates from his neck when he hugs me.

"A few hours."

"Did you get my messages?" I say.

"No, not yet."

"Oh. Well, Karen and Jason want us over for dinner tonight. They have something special to tell us."

"Sounds great," he says, smiling. Not a genuine show of pleasure, though. His eyes are trained on me. We enter his roomy living room with its oversize chairs, contemporary tables, and decorative art. Two empty wineglasses sit on the coffee table next to a half-empty bottle of wine.

"Care for a drink?" he says.

"A club soda, if you have it," I say, wanting Paul to go behind his bar while I have a look around. A black baby grand piano faces a large bay window. In the few times I have been here, Paul has refused to play a single note. Now I wonder if he plays at all. From way up here, I see out over the city, its bright lights sprinkled like stars in the dark. When I turn around, Paul is watching me again. He smiles and I smile back. He approaches with my glass of club soda. My eyes drift to the piano and the picture on it, a new picture, one that was not there before. It reminds me of the picture on his desk the first day I met him, the one facing him, the one I could not see. I reach for the framed eight by ten.

"Lenny, don't," he demands.

"Mikayla," I say calmly, satisfying my curiosity—dying inside. Her big, perfect teeth gleam with delight, her eyes cunning and superior. A door closes down the hall, and I know she's here. Once again, Mikayla Roberts is at the center of my betrayal. A closer look, and I see that the initials on the sheet music on the piano are MR. Paul grips me by the arm.

"It's not what you think, Lenny."

"Let go please," I say, clenching my teeth. "How do you know what I think, Paul?"

He promptly withdraws his hand. Paul looks guilty, not as expert as

Ralph in the art of cheating. I recollect the night I followed Mikayla in my car, when she pointed me out to Ralph with a smirk on her face. The humiliation I felt returns to me, and I push Paul back. He stumbles as I race down the hall, my senses keen enough to track even the slightest sound. I open a door and find her standing in Paul's bedroom in front of a mirror, clad in her underwear. She screams.

"Aren't you engaged to someone else?" I hiss.

"Lenny, don't!" Paul exclaims. I turn around to face him, finally seeing him for what he is. He follows me to the front door, awkwardly reaching around me to open it. "I'm sorry," he says.

I inhale deeply, and extend a hand to shake his. "Nice knowing you, Paul Anderson. Good-bye," I say. Very civilized. No scene to regret later. A quick glance back at his bedroom door, and I smile. Paul Anderson is a workaholic, just like his father was. Mikayla deserves him.

Karen and Jason want Paul and I to be godparents to their son.

"I can't speak for Paul," I say, "but I'm honored you've asked me. Really, you don't know how much." I become weepy.

"I'm so very lucky you're my best friend," Karen says.

"Where's Paul?" Jason asks.

"He's preoccupied with his work tonight," I say. "He can't come."

"That's too bad," Jason says.

We have a quiet dinner, just the three of us. Later, Karen and I clean the kitchen while Jason sits in the den watching television. I whisper that Paul seems to be back with Mikayla.

"Nooooo!" she exclaims, dropping a spoon on the floor. I bend over to pick it up. Karen is barely able to rinse a plate and put it in the dishwasher. Her tummy is enormous. She stares wide-eyed, standing in the middle of the kitchen floor with her mouth open.

"I am not believing this," she says, dumbfounded. "Ralph and Mikayla's wedding is in two weeks."

"I saw her at his apartment tonight."

"But . . ."

"She was in her underwear."

"Nooooo!" Karen pats me on the back. "He'll not be godfather to *my* baby. Not now." She shakes her head sympathetically. "Girrrrrl, you have the worst luck with men."

"I know. But I'm not angry anymore. Mikayla did me a favor. Ralph and Paul are the kind of men I don't need."

"Your composure amazes me, Lenny."

"Comes with practice," I say, laughing. "One of these days, I'll get it right."

47

While jogging I glance up at the crystal blue sky, with its thick, nebulous clouds resembling those in biblical paintings—the ones where sunlight beams through them as if God is sending a message. I think of the baby Karen and Jason are going to have. My godson. I think about Tajuan and how much I still miss him. Nearly two months have passed since I held him in my arms and smelled his precious baby scent.

When I reach approximately two miles from home, I turn back. At the corner of Chestnut, I notice Ernest standing on a ladder, removing an object from a large elm tree off to the side of his house. I wave when he sees me and stop to see what he is doing. He climbs down and carefully removes the roof of a brightly colored birdhouse. I peer in to see a bluebird hiding inside.

"How cute!!!" I exclaim. "Shouldn't he be farther south about now?"

"You'd think." Ernest shrugs.

"He's waiting for the right mate to come along."

"You know something about birds, too, Doctor?"

"A female bluebird won't move in with her mate if she doesn't like his house," I say, something I learned as a child growing up in the country.

"Something's wrong with his house?" Ernest asks, chuckling. He hangs the birdhouse back in the tree and shudders slightly from the cold. "I never knew female bluebirds were so picky."

"Well, they are."

"What about you, Lenny? Could you see yourself settling in with Paul?"

"No, we're not together anymore."

"Maybe I'm calling him the wrong name."

"No. I'm over with Paul."

Ernest gives me a sincere, questioning look. "You sure?"

"Yes, I truly am."

"Are we still on for tonight?"

"Oh, yes. And you're supposed to have a surprise for me."

"I always try to keep my word."

Ernest and I leave for the Corner Grill around eight. We sit at the same table by the window as the first night he brought me here. "The Professor" makes a hand gesture to "Old Man" before standing. Ernest heads for the bandstand.

"What can I get the lady?" Old Man says, while Ernest unassumingly sits at the electric keyboard in the center of the room, joining an electric bass player, an electric guitarist, drummer, and a female vocalist whose sassy phrasing draws me in. Before I think twice, I am up on my feet, dancing in place.

They perform a variety of tunes by artists from Bessie Smith to Etta James, Walkin' Blues to the deep-down Mississippi Delta—light, risqué, intimate, smoldering. The audience loves them. They love Ernest especially. Chords flow from his fingers like rushing water channeling through him. He becomes a different man. His head rolls with the tide, shoulders hunch and relax, eyes close, and at one point he focuses on me.

Ernest comes out front to the microphone at the end of a piece and says, "We dedicate this next song by Muddy Waters to a very special lady." He points to me. "Dr. Lenny Faulkner, the best woman, best doctor, and best friend."

He uses an acoustic guitar to play "Honey Bee," strumming and singing like there's no tomorrow—no more troubles, no other considerations. I am still standing, swaying to the beat. Here and nowhere else. At the end of the song that Ernest has put so much of his heart into, he leaves the bandstand and comes over to me.

"Are you having fun, Lenny?" he says, wiping sweat from his brow.

"Yes, Ernest," I say. "You didn't tell me you could play so spectacularly . . . in a band, no less. You didn't tell me you could sing."

"I can't tell you everything all at once," he says with a wink. "Otherwise I won't be able to impress you later."

"You've impressed me plenty tonight, Ernest. What a surprise!"

Diary notes:

I've put Mrs. Stein off long enough. She's invited me for dinner a total of three times in the past two months. So tonight, on the eve of my thirty-fifth year on the planet, I have accepted. Who knows? This guy she wants me to meet might not be so bad.

I think a lot about turning thirty-five. It is one of those landmark ages. Like eighteen, when I was so determined to shape up that I lost the size of a person from my body. That year, I also voted in my first presidential election. Twenty-five was the year I ran in my first race, purchased my house, and met Ralph. Thirty was the year Frank O'Connor hired me to work at Women's Health Choice. The year Ralph moved in with me. Most of his things were at my place by then, and it seemed natural for us to live together, even natural for him to control my money. I have learned quite a few lessons since then, about what men are capable of—but more about myself. Now, when a relationship is not working, I have no qualms about ending it, no looking back with regret.

Thirty-five should be my biggest year yet. I read once that a woman at this age stands a better chance of being struck by lightning than finding a husband. I wonder if a man can tell by looking at me that I'm in the "strike zone"? I walk over to Mrs. Stein's house for dinner.

"Dr. Faulkner, please come in," she says, greeting me at the door. "I'm so glad you could make it. Meet my daughter, Sonya."

"I've heard so much about you, Doctor," Sonya says. She is a slender woman with attractive, dark features. She extends a hand, and I am immediately impressed by how soft it is.

"Call me, Lenny, please," I say. We enter the living room, where I meet the other guests: Sonya's husband, Jeff, Mrs. Stein's brother, Albert, and his wife, Estelle. Mrs. Stein's son, Randolph, sits in a chair by the fireplace and chats with his cousin, Michael. And last, I meet Randolph's wife, Leslie, and a single woman named Margot, standing in the entrance to the kitchen.

Mrs. Stein pulls me aside and whispers, "The man I wanted you to meet isn't coming."

"Oh?" I feel suddenly out of place.

"Dinner is being served," she announces, lifting her hands in a grand gesture. "Let's eat."

Everyone heads into the dining room, taking seats, which seems a big task for me. *Where to sit? Where to sit? Where to sit?*

"The young man had a conflict this evening," Mrs. Stein whispers discreetly.

"Oh, well, you tried," I say, swallowing my disappointment. I sit next to Mrs. Stein's nephew, Michael. Dr. Michael Cohen. Margot sits on his other side. I get the impression that they are being put together, scientifically matched like Mr. and Mrs. Stein were. I catch Mrs. Stein's knowing glance at her sister-in-law, Estelle, and the nods and winks flowing between them.

"I've seen you at the hospital several times," Michael says to me, oblivious to what is expected of him and ignoring the woman he is being matched with. He is a tall, handsome man with black, curly hair. I don't recognize him at first, but then he says, "I guess it's about time we've met. Timing is everything, isn't it?"

My face drops.

"It was you!" I exclaim, flabbergasted, straining to be discreet as I recollect the morning after Linda Jenkins's death. My mad dash to the locker room in my underwear, when a man's voice had emanated from the doorway of one of the on-call rooms. "Timing is everything." I am too embarrassed to speak. His gaze bores into the side of my face. I eat and can't taste the food. When I glance over at Michael, he winks. If I could, I would bury myself in a hole. Margot peers around him to say, "What kind of medicine do you practice, Dr. Faulkner?"

"Obstetrics and gynecology," I say, an octave above my normal range.

"I need a new gynecologist," she says. "Do you have a business card?"

"Sorry, I don't. But I'm listed."

I try to focus on most of the dinner conversations. They splinter off into pairs in one instant and come back to the group in another. Estelle confides that Albert has been having trouble with kidney stones lately.

"So he shouldn't eat so much salt like he's doing, and he definitely shouldn't have that second piece of meat on his plate. Wouldn't you agree, Dr. Faulkner?" Albert's eyes narrow reproachfully. He drops his fork onto his plate and grunts.

"Well, a single meal won't cause kidney stones," I say diplomatically. Michael laughs aloud. When I turn to look at him he winks again, and my mind goes blank. Later, as the guests leave, Mrs. Stein reminds me that my coat is in the hall closet. I wait for Albert and Estelle to squeeze past me before I reach inside the closet. A voice startles me. I turn to see Michael.

"Please, let me help you," he says, taking my coat and helping me into it. His coal black eyes send goose bumps up my spine.

"Can I see you again?" he whispers.

"I don't think so," I whisper back.

"Why not?"

"Because you've seen too much of me already."

Mrs. Stein calls out from the end of the hall. "Did you find your coat, Lenny?" she says.

"Have dinner with me tomorrow," Michael says.

I do an about-face and head toward Mrs. Stein as if I missed what he said. He follows close behind, and whispers, "Please, meet me for dinner."

I say good-bye to Mrs. Stein. She leans closer as if to divulge a top secret.

"How are you planning to celebrate your birthday tomorrow?" she asks. "I could make a call. *He* might be available then."

"No thanks," I say, blushing. "I have other plans."

"I won't stop trying," she says.

"I know."

Outside, the air is frosty and cold, and grayish clouds float like chimney puffs that block out part of the moon. It is an eerie night, black and foreboding, the kind that feels most lonely. I have a career I love, great friends, excellent health, and more money than I ever thought possible for a single woman like me. But there's no one to share my life with, no one waiting for me to come home. Maybe this is a sign, my intuition telling me I don't need to have a man anyway. I don't need to have a child. I don't need to have a family of my own.

I turn at the crunching sound of footsteps following me across the frozen grass between Mrs. Stein's house and mine. Michael Cohen seems taller in his black overcoat, his charismatic face illuminated by houselights.

"Is it yes that you'll have dinner with me tomorrow?" he says.

"Yes," I say, without hesitation.

49

I missed the first board meeting for Linda's Safe House because of a delivery. The second I missed because my last patient of the day had a seizure. The third, I delivered a set of twins one hour apart. The fourth, I was still seeing patients after it ended. Stella calls me at the office to remind me of the one today.

"Glad I caught you before you had a chance to get away," she says. "Tonight's meeting is very important. You really need to come to this one."

"Oh, Stella, I'm kind of backed up at the office."

"Come, or I'll pay someone to break both your legs," she jokes.

"Stella, you know I'll be there if I can."

"I really need your support this evening, Lenny. The board will vote on salaries. And as you know, I've turned in my notice to the Department of Social Services. My job with them ends in ninety days. For me to effectively run the home, I'll need to do it full time, and earn the same salary."

"Stella, for what you do, you deserve twice whatever they're paying you."

I hurry my appointments along and arrive at the meeting on time. Mary Moore, the board's secretary, reads the minutes from the last meeting. "Renovations on the newly acquired house are almost complete." Next, Mona Desmond, a tall, thin, stylishly put-together woman covers old business; her report, a tedious droning of soft, feathery words, causes my eyelids to become heavy. Norma Scott, the wealthy oil heiress, calls for new business, and just as my eyelids are about to close, Carolina

Smelling, a short, broad woman with a throaty voice, stands and announces the proposals for staff salaries. Stella excuses herself and exits the room so that we can vote.

"I object," I say, right away raising my hand.

"Object?" Carolina asks, her brow furrowed in bewilderment. "But we've researched this extensively. These are fair wages."

"I think Stella should earn more," I insist.

"How much more?" Norma Scott pipes up.

"Thirty percent more than what you're proposing," I say. "I've known Stella a long time, and what she does is worth twice as much. We're getting a bargain, any way you look at it."

At the end of the meeting, after all the board members have left, Stella says, "You said something to them about my salary, didn't you, Lenny?"

"Something," I say, nonchalantly.

"You're the best," she says.

A few days before Christmas, the spirit of "Deck the Halls" and "Jingle Bells" finally sinks into me. It is in every song on the radio, every building I pass. Nothing is left undecorated—even the hospital has wreaths, trees, elves, and mechanical Santas on every ward. And here, at my medical building, where I spend the bulk of my time, there are angels made of lights greeting me at the door, eight mechanical leaping reindeer, a mechanical Santa playing hand bells, and a humongous tree that must have taken an army to decorate. Frank O'Connor's wife must have gone way over the Christmas budget once again.

After seeing my last patient, I receive a phone call from Stella.

"I just wanted you to know how grateful I am for your contribution," she says in a warm, sincere tone.

"Thanks, Stella, but I was more than glad to do it."

"Without you, Lenny, none of this would've come about. You've turned a girl's tragedy into a wonderful memorial, and I assure you that I'll do everything I can to make Linda's Safe House a success."

"I've no doubt."

"Everything's coming together nicely," she says.

"You're an excellent businesswoman, Stella," I say. "I'm in awe of the way you finessed getting that house from Norma Scott."

"She was born in that old house."

"She sold it to us for less than half its value because you made her feel good about our cause. You made that old woman want to contribute a heck of a lot more than she had planned to. She practically gave us that five-bedroom house, with all the amenities."

"Indeed. We've been lucky so far. I've been lucky to know you, Lenny. You're the one who started it all. Now we're almost ready to open."

"What's the date?"

"The fifteenth of January," she says, hesitating before adding, "You really need to come to our next board meeting, Lenny."

"I'll try my best."

"You work too hard," Stella says sharply. "Why don't you take some time off and go over to the house? It's only a few blocks away from your office. There's no excuse for your not seeing it."

"I've been busy here," I say.

"I know, Lenny. But you need to see how your money's being spent. Go over there and have a good look around. Maybe you'll see something the rest of us on the board haven't."

"I'll do it," I say. Stella tells me where to find the key—under a rock, ten paces to the right of the front porch. I drive to an old Georgian home, probably built shortly after reconstruction, the outside recently painted a pristine white. I go inside and find one room after another, brightly painted in cheerful, welcoming colors that draw me inside.

The nursery takes up the entire basement area, the walls painted with ballerinas, teddy bears, and clowns riding on red and white ships, sailing across a royal blue sea. Upstairs, I stand in the middle of the airy, yellow kitchen, with windows that open to an abandoned garden, and I feel the energy of my spirit return. I hear it telling me that this place is part of my purpose. I imagine girls learning about pregnancy and parenting. This place *will* make a difference.

I go outside into the backyard, which is overgrown with weeds and thickets, and full of scattered stones and abandoned patches of dirt. A vision of Linda Jenkins comes to mind, her sad look transforming into a smile, her last words swirling inside my head. *She'll live, won't she, Doctor? Live. The baby. She'll live.* This will be the spot for a vibrant garden.

Once home, I take the time to finally send Christmas cards that may not arrive before Christmas. I reminisce about Venita Perry and Laura Ruth, the good times we had in college, how accepting they were of my weight. I miss them. Life has a way of getting in the way of friendships. They, like other friends I have had over the years, move in other directions after marriage and babies. From the moment that first baby arrives, women are inundated with new responsibilities, from nursing and feeding to play groups and PTA meetings, soccer practices, swim lessons, piano. Their lists seem to go on and on. Soon Karen will join this legion of old friends I rarely see. I write inside her card

May all your future Christmases
be blessed with little feet and laughter.

I think about Tajuan. I see his little face, and the quiver of his bottom lip grabs me by the heart. I wonder if he is being properly cared for, if Shaniqua is getting the kind of emotional support she needs. I have an overwhelming desire to hold him again. What excuse can I use to see him? *Gifts.*

Christmas lights are all over the neighborhood as I head back out into the frosty cold. I drive to Lenox Mall, and once inside head straight for FAO Schwarz, where I pick up a stuffed bear, a toy truck, and a thingamajig with buttons that make various animal sounds when I push them. My spirit lifts as I wind my way through massive hordes of shoppers, stopping at one shop for a cute little coat, and another shop for perfectly soft suede booties. I buy a small three-foot tree.

Back home, I wrap each item, including a sweater for Shaniqua and perfume for Ms. Davis. I mount my small tree on a table in the front window and go to bed exhausted, soon dreaming of what Tajuan will look like with more hair, bigger cheeks, fatter thighs. We stroll through my neighborhood and I wave at Mrs. Stein. She runs a hand gently over Tajuan's face. We stop to visit Ernest, where the bluebird has a mate and three bluebird babies. Mama waits for me at the front door, standing there without her cane, more meat on her bones, and says, "Having my grandbabies is worth more than all the money in the world."

The alarm goes off. I awake in a cold sweat. The dream had seemed so real, Mama standing at the front door. Within an hour I am dressed for work and heading out to the office, the bag of gifts stored in the trunk of my car. At the office, I pull Shaniqua's chart and look up her phone number. I call her house, allowing several rings. No answer. Kelly peeps into the doorway.

"Patient ready in Room Three."

9:10 A.M.

Marsha Dingle: 46-year-old white female, return patient, 39 weeks gestation. Weight: 182 lbs. Height: 5'8". Gravida/para—pregnant with twins. Birth control: none. Fertility methods to initiate pregnancy. Complaints: Constant backache. Little sleep.

"We're almost there, Marsha," I say, smiling. Marsha Dingle is a first-time, over-forty mother. She gives me hope that I still have time to have babies.

"I can't wait," she says, excitedly. "How much longer, Dr. Faulkner?"

"You're three centimeters dilated, and that constant backache, that throbbing that you feel off and on, is actually contractions."

"Really?" Marsha's mouth drops. "I thought they'd be more obvious. Sharper."

Kelly hooks Marsha up to the fetal heart monitor, and I begin examining the printout strip for each contraction. The baby's heart quickens with pressure from the mother's womb clamping down on it, the sound of the heart races louder, and then grows soft and steady.

"Every woman is different," I say. "You're the kind of woman who might deliver in the backseat of a cab or in the bathroom of a department store and not feel much of anything."

"Surely not," she laughs.

"Happens all the time." The contractions are closer and closer. "Marsha, are you ready for two new additions?"

"I think so. . . . No, not yet, Dr. Faulkner. My husband's away on business."

"I'm afraid if he doesn't get back here immediately, he might miss everything. You're in first-stage labor." I glance at Kelly, making notes in the patient's chart.

"Arrange for transport for Mrs. Dingle to the hospital, please, Kelly," I say.

Kelly leaves the exam room. Soon an orderly from transportation appears with a wheelchair. The hospital is less than a block from our office.

"Ready, Mrs. Dingle?" Kelly says.

"Oh, my God, it's happening!" Marsha declares.

"See you in a little while," I say, as Kelly and the orderly roll her away.

I sign off on Mrs. Dingle's chart and stop by my office to place another call to Shaniqua. The phone rings eleven times. Still no answer. I see the patient in Room One, who complains of a vaginal yeast infection; the patient in Room Two needs a pap smear; and in Room Four, I detect a lump in the armpit of a twenty-six-year-old woman, Ms. Carol Jeffries.

"It may not be anything," I say to Carol, "but, as an extra precaution, I'm sending you for a special ultrasound, and possible biopsy, depending on the results."

"I thought it was a boil," she says. "My mother always got 'em."

"Does your mother still get them?" I ask.

"She died of breast cancer six years ago."

Breast cancer. The sound of it stings me to the core. I breathe deeply, make a note in Carol Jeffries's chart, and say, "We'll know something soon."

My beeper goes off after I leave the exam room. I check the time. It is now 10:45. Almost two hours since I first phoned Shaniqua. I return the page from labor and delivery. "I'm on my way."

I run helter-skelter through the halls, out of the building, down the sidewalk. I speed through the emergency room door of the hospital and take the elevator to labor and delivery, where I catch my breath. Marsha Dingle is panting between contractions, the nurses instructing her not to push.

"I'm trying not to," she says. "My body has a mind of its own."

I quickly wash, slip on a pair of latex gloves, and place my fingers into the patient's vagina. I feel the first baby's head. An instant later, Marsha pushes, and a tiny human pops out.

"My, my, right on time," I say, holding the slippery flesh. Little gray eyes peer up at me, and the pink skin gets even pinker as the baby breathes in a new life, not once crying or screaming. She is born even tempered. She coos.

"Is it all right?" Marsha asks between continuing contractions, her brow furrowed with needless worry.

"You've a healthy daughter," I say, just as Mr. Dingle bustles into the room.

"I came as fast as I could, honey," he says, laying eyes on his beaming wife and newborn baby girl. One more to go.

I leave the hospital and call Shaniqua's house again from my cell phone. As it rings, my mind conjures up a series of pictures: Tajuan being left alone. Shaniqua slitting her arms, bleeding to death in front of her son. Ms. Davis beating Shaniqua for having a baby that cries all night. The phone rings several times, but there is no answer. I call Stella's office from my cell phone as I drive aimlessly through town.

"I'm worried about Tajuan," I tell her. "Stella, what if something's wrong with him?"

Stella releases a heavy sigh, and says, "I know at least part of what you might be feeling because I've been there, Lenny. I've been alone for the holidays, over thirty, and desperate for a child I didn't have."

"It's more than that."

"Is it, really?"

"Yes, Stella, haven't you ever known something was true before it happened? Haven't you ever wished you'd followed your instincts before?"

"Many times."

"I don't want to regret not doing something because all I had was a gut feeling." I picture Tajuan's quivering bottom lip. "Please, Stella, help me do something. I have to know he's all right."

"I was on my way home to begin my Christmas vacation, but I suppose I can make a detour."

"Oh, Stella, will you?"

"I suppose I can think of a cockamamie excuse to give Ms. Davis for why I'm dropping in."

"Thank you, Stella, you don't know how much it means to me."

"I'll call you later at your home," she says, "but in the meantime, I don't want you worrying for nothing. Go out and try having fun for a change. You work too hard, Lenny."

I need to believe Tajuan is healthy and loved. I need to hold on to it and get on with my life. I decide to take Stella's advice about having fun, and invite Michael to join me for Karen and her parents' annual Christmas party, hoping that the knot in my belly from worrying about Tajuan will go away.

The Roberts home is splendidly turned out for this festive occasion: waiters dressed as elves serving cocktails and a piano player performing one holiday tune after another. Mrs. Roberts hired a professional decorator just to put up the tree, Karen told me. I introduce Karen to Michael, and she introduces him to Jason, her parents, and so on. I had expected at least a few people to be put off, or at least surprised that I am dating a white man. But no one seems to notice.

On the night of my birthday, Michael took me to my favorite restaurant, the Purple Peach. He was very attentive, very charming, and very handsome. He gave me a single rose, which made me happier than I ever was with any of the jewels that Ralph gave me. It was like poetry, the way he placed it inside my hand, careful to avoid pricking me with its thorns, telling me how lucky he was to share my day. I don't think of Michael as different from me, except that he is a man I very much want to know better.

Karen whispers in my ear, "Where'd you meet him?"

"It's a long story," I say, watching Michael while he isn't watching me, captivated by his dimpled smile. He seems content to listen to Christmas songs and off-tune singers, laughter and jokes that may or may not be funny. He is genuinely polite. I could fall for a man like him. Michael Cohen. Lenita F. Cohen. Drs. Michael and Lenita F. Cohen. Goes together quite well.

After an hour or so, I have had enough of cocktail-party talk with people I hardly know, of meaningless jokes, of listening to Karen gripe about her pregnancy and Mrs. Roberts go on and on about her future grandson and what he will mean to their family. I think about Tajuan and my heart begins to ache, the festive singing and laughter swirling around me like a hurricane, becoming too much to endure. I whisper to Michael, "I'm ready to leave."

He takes me home, and I invite him inside. We sit on the sofa where he plants a first kiss on my cheek. I offer him tea.

"That's all I have," I say. He smiles.

"I'm not thirsty," he says. "I wanted to dance with you at the party, but nobody danced."

"Christmas music is hard to dance to."

"Oh, yeah, Christmas."

I get up to light the logs in the fireplace. A steady yellow-blue flame roars and crackles, cutting the chill in the air. Michael tells me he wants to dance.

"Humor me," he says, taking me in his arms, my head resting on his shoulders as we slowly maneuver across the floor. He hums an unfamiliar melody next to my ear, a sweet-natured tune, maybe one he makes up as he goes along. His heart beats like a drum against my chest, its cadence becoming wild and frenetic. I feel him getting excited. He stops and takes my face in his hands, meeting my lips with his.

"I've never kissed a Jewish man before," I say breathlessly.

"Neither have I," he says. I laugh. His eyes gleam with anticipation. I wonder how a white man as eligible as Michael can be attracted to me. Surely, with all the available white women who must be after him, he can have any woman he wants—beautiful, sophisticated-looking women, like Margot from Mrs. Stein's dinner party. Why me? What if he wants me to be his flavor of the month? Chocolate this month, vanilla the next. How can I be sure? He attempts to kiss me again, but I withdraw, my hands pushing him gently away.

"I can't," I protest.

"What's wrong?"

"I'm not in the mood for this," I say, and I tell him briefly about Tajuan, and my worries about his safety. "I'm sorry."

"Don't be sorry for caring about a child," he says, gathering his overcoat. "I respect that." He heads for the door, glancing back to say, "I'll be in touch." When the door closes, part of me wants to rush after him. I don't expect to see him again.

Karen calls before my head hits the pillow, saying, "I just want to know one thing. . . . How? What? When? And where did you find him?"

I tell her everything, her appetite, as usual, insatiable in matters of love. "He seems to like me," I say, unsure.

"Seems! He couldn't take his eyes off you all evening."

"You think so?"

"There's one thing I'm never wrong about. . . . I saw it in his eyes."

"What in his eyes?"

"Want."

Want. He wants me, he wants me not. Karen and I exchange good nights.

A lonely feeling comes over me, and I think about Michael in the wee hours of Christmas morning, wondering if I should wait for his call. Should I make big plans for myself today? Take myself out on the town? The phone rings, and I am instantly drawn into a conversation with Stella.

"Tajuan's doing well," she says. "I spoke with his pediatrician, Dr. Mitchell. He said Tajuan was normal on his last visit."

"But did you see him?"

"No. I stopped by Shaniqua's house a few times, but no one was home. Ms. Davis has family in Tennessee. She probably took Shaniqua and the baby to visit them."

"What if she didn't? What if something's wrong, Stella?"

"Will you stop worrying? As soon as I know anything at all, I'll call you. But for now, try to enjoy the holidays. It's Christmas, Lenny. Give it a rest."

"I'll try." After saying good-bye I think about how pointless it is to worry. Here I am, a thirty-five-year-old woman, home alone on Christmas day, with packages beneath my Charlie Brown-like Christmas tree for a baby I might never see again.

I take a chance and invite Michael over for dinner. He agrees to come, and I spend the morning poring through old cookbooks for what to serve him. I find a grocery store that's open and race to it before it closes. Back home, I try very hard to follow the recipes. I consider what Mama once said about cooking, that you have to find your way around the kitchen with your nose. *If it smells right, use it. If it tastes right, then you've got the right amount of ingredients.* Mama never used a recipe in her life.

At five o'clock, Michael arrives with a bottle of Pinot Grigio, my favorite, and I serve grilled seafood, gazpacho, risotto, garlic bread, and a mixed green salad. Nat King Cole croons "White Christmas" in the background, and we eat by candlelight.

"Beautiful," he says after a few mouthfuls.

"Thanks. It was easy to make."

"I meant you're beautiful."

"Oh." My face warms. I look over at my small Christmas tree, which sits in front of a window.

"It being Christmas, I should've brought something in addition to the wine," he says.

"You brought yourself, that's more than enough," I say, gushing like a bashful schoolgirl. A slow romantic melody plays and he gazes seductively into my eyes. Or maybe I'm hoping I'm not the only one with lust on the brain.

"Am I going slow enough?" he says, leaning toward me. My mind races a mile a minute when he kisses me long and sensuously.

Oh, God, let me be strong tonight. He pulls me to my feet and we slowly dance.

"How lovely . . . how pretty," Michael purrs into my ear. His hands trace the outline of my back. When he cups my bottom firmly in his hands, my inner voice recites, *Rule #8. I won't make love unless it feels right. I won't . . . I won't . . . I won't.*

"I can't," I say.

"Please, Lenny."

"Nooooo," I say firmly, startling myself by pushing away from him. "I mean, I've just gotten out of a serious relationship, three bad relationships really, and I don't want to rush into something I'll regret later."

"You're afraid I might hurt you?"

"Yes."

The doorbell rings, and I excuse myself to answer it. I think how shocked Mrs. Stein will be to find her nephew here if she's standing at the door.

"Ernest?" I say, shocked to see him.

"This is for you," he says.

"You shouldn't have." I take the silver-wrapped gift in my hands, admiring the large white and silver bow.

"I'm on my way to Ohio for Christmas," he begins to say, before stopping mid-sentence at the sound of Michael asking where the bathroom is.

"Two doors to the right," I say.

"I see you're busy," Ernest says disappointedly, a hurt-boy look appearing in his eyes. "I wanted to invite you to dinner tonight, before I leave. I left you a message last week."

"Ernest," I say, feeling perfectly lousy. "I'm sorry."

"Merry Christmas, Lenny," he says.

"Ernest, listen, I . . ." Michael comes up from behind. He takes possession of my waist. This is very awkward, indeed, the three of us standing in the doorway. Ernest and I are friends. Good friends. I do not understand this tension between us, but it is palpable, like frost in the air.

"Everything all right, dear?" Michael says.

"Michael, Ernest. . . . Ernest, Michael," I say, stupidly introducing them. They shake hands, mumbling their nice-to-meet-you's, very civilized, very gentlemanly, very rigid.

"Good-bye, Lenny," Ernest says.

"Merry Christmas." My voice carries like a dog bark in the darkness. I wish I had given Ernest a present. I should have returned his call. A light goes on inside Mrs. Stein's kitchen. I wonder if she sees, wonder if she knows.

50

"I received your mail again yesterday," Mrs. Stein says, handing me an envelope while standing in the doorway. I glance down at the obvious Christmas card from one of my colleagues. I forgot to send Christmas cards this year. I invite Mrs. Stein inside.

"I have something for you," I say.

"No, you shouldn't have," she says, shaking her head. I scurry over to my paltry little tree and retrieve a present with her name on it.

"Open it, Mrs. Stein," I say.

"You know I don't celebrate Christmas."

"It's an early birthday gift," I say. She opens it, mumbling that her birthday isn't until April. She pulls out a book titled *From Holocaust to Segregation,* a collection of short stories about Jewish people who came to America and taught at black colleges and universities throughout the South during and after the Holocaust. She flips through until she comes to Ezra Stein.

"Oh, my," she says, nervously touching her dead husband's black-and-white picture and running her fingers over it. "I didn't know there was a book." She marvels at how perfect a gift it is. She can't know about Michael and me. "I'll treasure this always. Thank you, Lenny."

She gives me a gentle squeeze before returning to the book. I toss the Waxlers' Christmas card onto a pile of other Christmas cards collecting on the coffee table. I glance at the one gift for me under the tree, from Ernest, and wonder what it might be. I tear off the wrapping and find a note attached to the gift box that reads

Dear Lenny,

It's been a while since we've gotten together. I miss our talks and seeing you run past my house. It meant so much to me having you in the audience that night I performed for the first time since Amy passed. I'd like to play for you again. Don't be such a stranger, my friend.

Merry Christmas,
Ernest

Inside the box is a crystal replica of a birdhouse. A pair of porcelain bluebirds brace themselves at the door, with wings drawn back as if ready to fly. *Ernest.* I think of the day he chased me for a mile or more just to give me a few letters and purple tulips, how he put brass numbers on my mailbox and cleaned my gutters, expecting nothing more than friendship in return. I picture him playing his heart out at the Corner Grill, us sitting together in his kitchen having tea, and the day he found a bluebird that needed a mate. An ache grows in my gut from missing him. I consider what Genevieve, Amy's sister, said about platonic relationships, how they never last. The thought of losing Ernest hurts me to my core. I am conflicted over him. I interrupt Mrs. Stein's concentration on her new book by tapping her shoulder.

"Tell me, Mrs. Stein, how did you know Mr. Stein was the right one for you?" She glances up from her book, snapping it shut, a pensive faraway look in her eyes.

"Well, let's see." She sighs, trying to recollect events of nearly sixty years ago. "I was living in New York when, one day, as I was crossing the street, a coal truck charged from nowhere and struck me."

"Mr. Stein saved your life?"

"No, Ezra wasn't there when it happened. But he visited me every day in the hospital, always coming at the same time, with a book or a newspaper. He read to me, you see."

"Sure, but did you feel a spark go off?" I press on.

"No sparks. True love is deeper than that, dear. There was another fellow at the time, and I don't remember his name, but he could make me swoon just by saying 'Hello, sweetheart.' This fellow only came to visit me once in the hospital."

"I know the type very well."

"I trusted Ezra. It's easy to fall in love with a man you can depend on." Mrs. Stein does not mention the man she wanted me to meet. Fact of it is she hasn't tried to get us together since the night of her dinner party. I wonder if she has changed her mind. Maybe she really does know about Michael and me. She turns back to her husband's page in the book and says wistfully, "He read to me. I'll never forget it."

Of course she knows about Michael and me, I think to myself. His car was parked in my driveway last night. It wouldn't be like Mrs. Stein to miss a thing like that.

Michael and I chat in the kitchen over coffee as I shuffle through a stack of mail left piling up on the countertop since before Thanksgiving, junk mail mostly, an occasional bill, a few holiday cards, and one belated birthday card from Laura Ruth, including a picture of her family: husband, two sons, and one baby daughter. There's a note explaining that Venita Perry just had a bouncing baby girl.

I think about Tajuan and begin to weep.

"What is it, Lenny?" he says. "Did I say something? Did I do anything wrong?"

"No, no, it's not you, Michael. I was just thinking about Tajuan."

"The baby boy you're worried about?"

"I feel like something terrible has happened to him," I say.

"You're connected to this child like a mother," he says.

"I just want to know that he's safe. He's become a part of my life, and I miss him so much."

Michael stands behind me like a warm buffer from the chill inside as we stare out the kitchen window. A car skids dangerously close to the curb. It stops abruptly, then slowly creeps out of sight.

"It hardly ever snows," I say.

"Lucky us." Michael says, holding me tighter.

"I've known you less than a month," I say.

"Is there a maximum allowable time for falling in love?"

"In love . . . with me?"

"Anything wrong with that, Lenny?" The way he says my name melts my heart. Michael covers my face in wet, intoxicating kisses. I ask myself *What if he only thinks he loves me? What if he's just saying that he does?* He leads me to my bedroom, and we lie across my bed. I close my eyes. Am

I being naïve or just plain stupid? His hands work fast to remove my clothes. I want the light to flow through me, and my intuition to tell me what to do. Michael's flesh merges with mine. He is a part of me now. I recollect Mama's voice begging me to run. *Run, Lenita Mae. Be the first to ring the bell. Run, or you'll miss the truck. Rule 8: I won't make love unless it feels right. Oh, God, what am I getting into?*

The snow has vanished completely. It is always temporary here in the South, rarely lasting more than a day. Michael dresses and prepares to leave. But there are things I want to discuss with him, like where do we go from here? Are we officially together? I am about to say, "Do you love me more or less now?" But he gathers his belongings quickly; an emergency awaits him at the hospital. So I say nothing other than good-bye, my instincts warning me to be careful.

51

My mind drifts back to the feel of Tajuan in my arms as I enter and exit each exam room in my office suite. I recollect his wee fingers and the smooth bottoms of his feet, his supple body resting in my arms like a stuffed doll, the way his eyes rolled back as he drifted off to sleep. I feel protective and responsible, a myriad of emotions welling up inside me. Stella said Tajuan appeared to be in good heath when she finally visited him and his mother. *They appeared to be adjusting well.* Appeared. I know about appearances. Ralph appeared to love me for nine years.

At home, I enter the room I have not opened since my mother's death. I have been afraid to do it until now. Strangely, I am drawn here by runaway thoughts of Shaniqua's baby clouding my mind. I could make a nursery with sailing ships and baby fluff. I want to adopt Tajuan. An open adoption would allow Shaniqua to remain active in his life, as active as we agree would be in Tajuan's best interest. A strange, joyful sensation pulses through me. I phone Shaniqua's house, and when her mother answers, I identify myself.

"What do you want, Dr. Faulkner?" Ms. Davis asks pointedly.

"Ms. Davis, I'm calling to see how your daughter is doing," I say.

"She's fine."

"May I speak to her, please?"

"About what?"

"Well, she didn't return for her six-week postpartum visit. And as you know, a C-section is major surgery."

"She's fine, Doctor. Shaniqua's got a lot of catching up to do at school. We haven't had time to come in yet."

"I'd like to ask her a few questions, if you don't mind," I say.

"I do mind," she snaps. "Last time Shaniqua talked to you, that social worker came snooping around here and put her in a nasty old shelter. I oughta sue both of you."

Thoughts of what to say pass through my mind so quickly, I cannot grab hold of one . . . *open adoption . . . best interest of the baby . . . Shaniqua . . . her education.*

"I just wanted to ask—"

"Don't call here again, Dr. Faulkner. Remember, I work for a law firm. I know what harassment is. And right now, you are harassing us."

I attempt to focus on the here and now, instead of looking beyond one day to the next. I try not to think about Shaniqua again, and to ignore the tugs at my heartstrings, Tajuan's face appearing like afterthoughts. On New Year's Eve, Michael phones to say he will not make it to my house before midnight. He is on call and has two emergency surgeries. I decide to surprise him.

Around nine o'clock, I slip a negligee inside my overnight bag. I stop at the liquor store near the hospital to pick up a bottle of champagne on sale. Michael and I will start the New Year in style.

When I enter the hospital, I page him and he calls me back on my cell phone.

"How's it going, Dr. Cohen?" I ask coyly. "Have you finished both surgeries yet?"

"One more to go," he says. "I'm lying here in one of these lonely call rooms, counting down the end of the year with Dick Clark."

I take the elevator up to the fifth floor. "If it makes you feel any better, I'm all alone, too."

"Well, sweetheart, as soon as I can get away from here, I'll see what I can do about that."

"Sounds worth waiting for."

"I'd better run now, I'm getting beeped. I'll call you back as soon as I finish."

I retreat to the locker room, where I change into the negligee, check myself in the mirror, and give it the once-over. I wrap up in my overcoat and head toward the call rooms. There is one occupied room. A Top Ten rock 'n' roll hit plays above the sound of my knocking on the door. I hear

Michael's voice and open the door to find, spread out like sheaves of wheat on a narrow hospital bed, Michael and Dr. Lui, nakedly entwined. I stand frozen when the woman shoots me a glare with her dark eyes.

"What the fuck are you doing here?" she growls. The bottle of champagne slips from my hand, crashing to the floor. *Four . . . three . . . two . . . one. Happy New Year.*

"Lenny!" Michael exclaims, shock distorting his features. He looks evil to me now. I run to escape further humiliation. It would be intolerable to hear him say "I'm sorry." After leaving the hospital in a daze, I find my car and sit in the cold parking garage for a long while. Am I expecting too much? Is it impossible for a woman like me to find true love? And what is true love anyway? How gullible I was to believe Michael loved me, how easily I threw myself at him. I start the engine and drive past party revelers leaving buildings—men dressed in tuxedos and women sporting fashionable dresses and gowns. Why did I have to come out tonight? *What a foolish, foolish woman you are, Lenita Mae.*

Once home, I fall across my bed, stunned by the events of the last half hour. Why wasn't I enough for him? I take out my diary and write

The New Year is shaping up to be just peachy so far. I didn't stick to the rules. I wasn't ready to make love, but I did it. Why didn't I keep my legs closed? I wanted to believe Michael loved me, but it turns out he's a philandering cheat. I won't take him back even if he begs. He's not worth it. Today's mantra—Rule 6: No man is worth suffering over.

52

4:55 P.M.

Pamela Tucker-Jones, post-operative visit. Weight: 220 lbs. Last normal menstrual period: November 10. Is hopeful that missed period in December indicates pregnancy.

A sigh escapes me when I think how hard today has been. I've tied tubes, found tumors, discovered herpes, gotten a positive AIDS report on an ambitious, young, professional woman, and determined paternity. I test Ms. Tucker-Jones's urine and find that she is pregnant. She is indeed going to have a baby after all. I am amazed.

"Looks like you're having a baby," I say brightly as I enter my office where she is sitting across from my desk, her meaty legs crossed.

"Yeah!" she exclaims, clapping her hands. "I knew it wouldn't take much longer. I knew it! I knew it! I knew it!"

"You were right, Pamela," I say, dismayed.

"And those nurses at the hospital thought I couldn't do it," she says haughtily. "They didn't know how hard I'd try."

"You're incredible," I say. Pamela Tucker-Jones knows what she wants and goes after it. She is not afraid to fail. I watch the way she sticks her chest out proudly, with shoulders back and head erect. She wears a conspicuous red silk dress that accentuates the curves of her body. Her overall demeanor says, "This is who I am—fat, positive, and sexy—now deal with it."

* * *

After Ms. Tucker-Jones leaves, I shut my office door and phone Stella.

"I called Shaniqua at home," I say.

"I know, Lenny. Why did you do that?"

"I want to raise Tajuan, Stella," I cry.

"Let him go, Lenny."

"I can't, Stella. I love that boy."

"Ms. Davis phoned me yesterday," she says gravely.

"For what? Because I was concerned about her daughter?"

"Don't call her again, Lenny. *Please.*"

"Shaniqua didn't come back for her six-week visit. I worried that something happened to her or the baby."

"She's seeing another doctor now."

"But Stella—"

"Why don't you visit the home you've helped build, Lenny? Linda's Safe House needs you. Give us some of your free time."

Silence floats through the house like a ghost, surrounding me with an empty feeling that will not go away by reading a book or flipping channels or eating a microwavable dinner. I sift through the mail and find a postcard from an old friend from medical school. Hilda Gentry. We used to go hiking and mountain climbing together. She writes

> *Just made the top of Kilimanjaro. Wish you were here. Hope you still climb.*
>
> *Hilda*

The thought of climbing even the highest mountain pales in comparison to the thought of bringing Tajuan home to live with me. But that will not happen. I need to face this fact. He is not my son. He belongs to his mother and her mother. They belong together. They. Not us. Not me and Shaniqua Davis's son. Stella was right. I need to let go.

I suit up for a run, sprinting most of the way. The cold stings until I reach two miles. I try not to think about Tajuan and how much I love him. I try not to remember loving him at first sight, caring for him, feeding him, his tiny heart pulsing inside his chest. When I reach the woods, I stop to consider how my mother changed after Joe died, how she grew cold and distant, far different from the woman who used to smile and rub salve on my knees after a day of picking strawberries. It was as if a big chunk of her heart broke off. She must have ached at least as much as I ache now for Tajuan.

My nostrils begin to freeze, and I head back to my house. I shower before going to bed. While lying awake, I listen to the tempestuous wind as it whips across the eaves and overhangs. I think about what Mama said the morning she died, that she would send me a man from heaven, God willing. One I deserved. One who would be kind and considerate. Why is it so hard? Haven't I been a decent person? Do I want too much—a husband who loves me, and a child of my own?

Before I enter into the deep cycle of my sleep, my pager goes off. Labor and delivery. The responding nurse tells me that Karen Ashby's water has broken. "She's in labor," she says. "Five minutes apart."

Six hours later, Karen's cervix is nine centimeters dilated. Her contractions are two minutes apart. I tell Jason to give her ice when she needs it, to rub her lower back until the epidural kicks in to paralyze the pain.

"Whatever you say," I whisper, "don't tell her she can do it."

"What?" he says, puzzled. He lifts Karen's hand and is about to kiss the back of it when she claws his wrist.

"Oh, God!!!!!" she screams.

"Breathe, Karen," Jason says.

"God!!!!"

"You can do it, Karen. That's my girl." Jason gently rubs his hand up and down his wife's arm.

"Don't you touch me!" she screams. "DON'T YOU EVER TOUCH ME AGAIN!"

Within seconds, Karen is fully dilated and pushing through a major contraction. The nurse counts ten seconds. The vulva stretches wider. Karen takes another deep breath and pushes for another ten seconds. The uterus relaxes, then hardens abruptly. She repeats the deep breaths and the pushing with all her might through six more contractions.

"You're so brave Karen, I admire you so," I assure her. She is worn and vulnerable. The baby's head pushes through without tearing. I suction its nose and mouth while Karen gathers enough energy to push the rest of him out—a bouncing baby boy, big enough to sit up at the table. One more thrust, and he falls into my hands, his spirit sifting through my fingers, like thick, warm steam. There can be no greater feeling than baby breath. A brand new soul reaches beyond its tiny boundary to touch all the other souls around it. My heart is full when I hand Karen her first child, and she collapses back against the birthing bed relieved, saying, "Thank God!"

53

This morning, before going to work, a sharp pain digs into my stomach so dramatically that I drop to the floor, doubled over, clutching the spot and applying pressure to it. A vivid image of Tajuan comes to mind. I see blood spilling from his lips. His screams fill my head, and I wonder if I have gone mad. I recollect how Mama was before she was told of my brother's death. She knew as I now know. My premonition of Tajuan has to be right. Something awful has happened. Immediately I phone Stella at her home and beg her to once again visit the Davis household. "Make sure Tajuan and Shaniqua are safe."

"This will be the last time, Lenny," she says. "I won't bother the Davises again."

I go through the rest of the morning in a fog, until Stella stops by my office at half past eleven to tell me that she found Tajuan abandoned at home while his grandmother was at work and Shaniqua was at school.

"He was left in a playpen," Stella says. "I heard his screams and opened the front door. It wasn't even locked. Anyone could have gone inside. I found him cold and wet from a soggy diaper. Anyone could have taken him."

"I knew it, Stella."

"Yes, you did, Lenny, and there's more," Stella says. "There were bruises on Tajuan's legs and back, a miserable diaper rash, and critical weight loss. He weighs two pounds less than he should."

"I didn't want to be right," I cry.

"I've filed an emergency report with the court and had Tajuan taken immediately into custody. He was placed in foster care."

"Foster care? Why not me? I want him."

"Be patient, Lenny."

Patient. The next day, Stella stops by my office and says, "Ms. Davis was arrested but released, and no charges were filed against her."

"But, Stella, you know it was her fault. Shaniqua wouldn't have—"

"Shaniqua beat him, Lenny. *She* did it."

"Oh, my God!"

"She was supposed to take her son to a baby-sitter's house on her way to school, but he wouldn't stop crying, she said. A voice inside her head told her to kill her son, that he'd be better off without her. Shaniqua says she can't remember hitting him or leaving him alone. She was in shock."

"She has postpartum psychosis," I say. "Shaniqua's severely depressed." I contemplate her last visit to my office, the self-inflicted cuts and lacerations on her legs and arms.

"Stella, I think of the faraway look in Shaniqua's eyes after she delivered Tajuan . . . just as helpless as Linda Jenkins's face the night she died. How did I miss it? How did I miss the opportunity to do something?"

"You warned Ms. Davis, and so did I."

"But . . ."

"I've filed a petition with the court to have Shaniqua's parental rights terminated," Stella says, handing me a copy, which states *Due to the severity of the abuse, it is my professional opinion that it is in the best interest of the child for the mother to lose all contact permanently.*

"What happens to her now?"

"She'll probably get probation. Maybe counseling."

"I want to help her, Stella. What can I do?"

"If Shaniqua's case goes to court, you can testify on her behalf."

"How long before I can file for adoption?"

"It could take several months for Shaniqua's rights to be terminated. Depends on how soon it takes the review board to meet and make their recommendation. Then, of course, a judge has to review it and make a decision. Some judges postpone the decision because they want the mother rehabilitated. They feel a child is better off with its natural parent."

"They want him to die next time?" I say bitterly.

"Lenny, I'm on your side, remember?" She takes her copy of the petition from me and files it in her briefcase.

"I'll do anything to get him," I say.

"I want you to prepare yourself for the possibility that Tajuan goes back to his mother, Lenny. It happens far too often."

54

I must wait patiently for Shaniqua's rights to be terminated; there is no other choice, no shortcuts through the process of adopting Tajuan, no common sense in the court of common laws. I testify at a hearing, insisting that Shaniqua began showing signs of severe depression before giving birth. I add that Shaniqua's mother wanted her pregnancy to be difficult. *She undermined my treatment of her daughter.* I glance at Shaniqua, noting her blank stare and her unkempt appearance—the image of the girl I used to be. There, by the grace of God, go I. She is given probation and mandatory psychiatric counseling. No decision is made about her parental rights.

Waiting to become Tajuan's mother is as unsettling as when I waited for Mama to die, except that instead of mourning, I am hoping. I hope for the day I can enter my house to find my son there, ready to greet me.

Stella has made arrangements with his foster parents, Mr. and Mrs. Corbin, for me to visit him at their home after work. This evening when I arrive, Tajuan is sitting on Mr. Corbin's lap, and the old man tickles his feet and the folds of plump flesh under his arms. Tajuan flails his arms wildly and giggles.

"What a good-looking boy," Mrs. Corbin says, standing next to me with a towel draped over one of her broad shoulders, scenting the air with baby powder and sour milk. She reminds me of Mama—homespun, her hair worn back in a country bun, a pair of fuzzy house shoes adorning her feet. Mr. Corbin is thin with sharp features that become birdlike when he laughs aloud. He lifts Tajuan up in the air, and when I reach for him, two tiny teeth appear suddenly, his mouth gaping into a wide grin.

"He's always happy to see you," Mr. Corbin says.

"That little fellow knows you're his mama." Mrs. Corbin chuckles. I pick Tajuan up and hold him tight.

I take him for a walk, slowly pushing his stroller in front of me as we canvass the neighborhood, and when we return, I give him a bath and put him to bed, lulling him to sleep with a nursery song. *Sleep my little one. Sleep my pretty one. Sleep.*

"You don't look like a woman who wants to meet a man, Lenny," observes Karen over lunch. "Your hair is all over your head. Get a hair relaxer, girlfriend, or get it braided . . . something, anything. And your clothes. . ."

"What's wrong with my clothes? They're comfortable."

"They look *too* comfortable."

"I won't dress to please a man," I insist.

"You've given over half your money away to that home for girls you're supporting, and don't get me wrong, Lenny, I think it was an admirable thing to do. However, the other half is still more than most people will ever see, and it's growing, but it's not working for you, girlfriend."

"What are you saying, Karen?"

"There's plenty of money for shopping, Lenny. And it's time."

Reluctantly, I let her take me to Lenox Square Mall, Perimeter Mall, the Mall of Georgia. She waits while I get my hair done—a mildly relaxed curly 'do.

"Now you're ready to meet Mr. Right," she says, beaming.

55

I phone Ernest and leave a message on his answering machine. "Just thinking about you," I blurt out. "Call when you can."

In a way, I am relieved he did not answer. Part of me is still not ready to face Ernest. The possibility exists that I might feel more than I should for him. And Ernest, being a very perceptive man, would know immediately that I am ready to cross our friendship boundary. It could mean the end of us, another failure. The worst failure would be to lose Ernest as my friend.

Later, I go to the bookstore, and while perusing the self-help section, a man taps me on the shoulder. I turn to face him, startled.

"I can't imagine you'd need any answers as together as you seem," he says, smiling.

"That's because you don't know me," I say, off-center. He has smokers' breath and brown stains on two of his front teeth, but otherwise this man staring me eye-to-eye is not bad to look at—just bold. He invades my personal space. I take a step back.

"I'm Glenn Chavis," he says.

"Lenny Faulkner."

"Well, Lenny, I'd love an opportunity to know you better."

I hesitate. Glenn wears an Afro—a perfectly square one.

"I sell real estate, if you're ever in the market for a new place," he says.

"That's nice to know."

"We can talk more about it over dinner," he says. "What about tomorrow night? You pick the place."

I try to think of a graceful escape.

"How about Pirate's Cove," he says, snapping his fingers. "For the best seafood in town. I've been wanting to go there for a while now."

"I . . . I'm . . ."

"What about seven? I'll pick you up, just give me the address. I know Atlanta like the back of my hand."

I stare at his extended hand, his map of Atlanta.

"I'll meet you there," I say, too quickly.

The following evening when I get home from work, I listen to my messages—one from Karen, telling me Sammy's getting his front teeth. "You've got to come see him," she says. I skip past a few telemarketers, to a message from Ernest. "Sorry I missed your message. I'll call back." I call him immediately and leave another message.

"Please call me later tonight, Ernest."

Oh, Ernest, where are you when I need you? I go to the Pirate's Cove Restaurant to meet a man I hardly know.

"Well, well, well, you're looking mighty fine, woman," he says, grinning.

My stomach tightens when he slips a hand around my waist. I casually push it away, as the hostess guides us to a table. I check the time on my watch before we sit. Seven-fifteen. I quickly look over the menu.

"What're you ordering?" he asks.

"Salmon, I think."

"Don't be foolish, get the lobster," he insists. "It's the best."

"Grilled salmon," I say to the waiter, rolling my eyes at Glenn. I cannot stand being told what to eat.

"I'm paying," he says. "I can afford to buy you lobster."

"I have a rule against eating lobster tonight," I say.

"What are you? A Seventh-Day Adventist, or something?"

"No, I'm a follower of the rules."

After dinner, he asks if we can see each other again. I tell him no, "It's against my religion."

A few days pass when I have received no other messages from Ernest. I pick up the phone and put it down several times, a lump in back of my throat, my heart racing like a schoolgirl. *Rule 4: I will never again put my life on hold for a man. Rule 6: No man is worth suffering over.* I call Ernest and leave a final message.

"I hope I get to see you sometime this year, Ernest . . . ha . . . ha. I miss our talks. Call me, please."

The following week, I meet Avery Thomas, an up-and-coming businessman. We meet while standing in line at the supermarket. He seems nice enough, invites me out for drinks. He tells me that he is tired of the single life. "I'm looking for the right woman to marry," he says.

"Really?"

"I want a woman who is intelligent, has a career that she enjoys, and is ready to start a family."

"I'm waiting to adopt a child," I say proudly. "A beautiful baby boy. His name is Tajuan and I adore him."

"Why are you adopting?"

"Because I want to. I'm ready to be a mother."

"I think you should reconsider. I'd think long and hard about taking on the responsibility of raising someone else's child. Children cost a lot of money these days."

"I can afford to care for my son without anybody's help," I say defensively.

"Oh, yeah?" he says, smoothing it over with, "I bet there's nothing you can't do, doctor." But by now, my view of Avery has been tarnished. I don't think I like him very much. Yet, when he invites me to dinner on Friday night, I willingly give him another shot. Maybe I have judged him too harshly.

Avery takes me to a pretty expensive restaurant in Buckhead, with valet service. He opens my door, escorts me inside, and once we are seated, he tells me to order whatever I want. Wine from a pricey wine menu, appetizers starting at twenty bucks and up, mahi mahi flown in this morning, and chocolate roulade.

"The prices are really up there," I complain.

"Don't worry about that," Avery says. "You're with me."

At the end of the meal, when the check comes, he looks at me funny, pats his pocket like Bobby just discovering he is low on cash, and says, "I can't find my wallet, Lenny. I must've . . ."

"I'll take care of it," I say, annoyed, doling out of my purse to cover it. Then, to make matters even worse, before the credit card receipt comes back for me to sign, Avery caresses my arm and leans closer.

"I have something that might interest you," he says.

"Oh, really," I say, more annoyed.

"An investment opportunity of a lifetime. I'm talking megabucks. Import/export. Products purchased from Indonesia and sold here in Atlanta as well as other parts of the country for huge profits."

"Sounds like a business deal *you* won't want to miss."

"Only one thing," he says, sliding his hand next to mine. "I require a few thousand more dollars than I can presently get my hands on to fund this business venture."

"Is that right?" I ask, clutching my purse.

"We can pool our resources," he says charmingly. "I'll make us a fortune."

"I'm sorry, but I can't," I say, signing the credit card receipt. "I have control issues around money."

"Control issues?"

"Yeah, I have to be in control." I slide the receipt inside my purse and stand to leave. "Good-bye and good luck."

I laugh about what happened during a phone conversation with Karen. She says, "Meeting Mr. Right isn't easy, Lenny girl. You've got to keep dating. It's a numbers game. You go out with ten and one is bound to be better than that fool who asked you for money."

"I don't know, Karen. Maybe I'm over the dating hill."

"Oh no you're not. You just need to invest more hours in your social life. It takes time to meet the right person. Finding a husband is at least as important as having the right career. And besides that, when your adoption goes through, you're going to need more time to spend with your son."

"Maybe you've got a point. I do spend most of my life caring for patients. I enjoy it. The challenge of solving medical problems adds adventure to each day. And I cannot imagine wanting any other career."

"That's not what I'm saying, Lenny. You'll be a mother soon and every mother has to prioritize her life and make career choices."

"Well, I'd never want Tajuan or the next man I happen to fall in love with to feel neglected."

"Maybe it's time you cut back on some things."

The following morning, I arrange an impromptu meeting with Dr. Frank O'Connor, stopping him in the hallway, coaxing him into my office where I explain that I need to reduce my patient load by a third.

"A third?" he says incredulously. "You'll make a third less salary."

"I'm not worried about the money, Frank. I need more time. I'm adopting a baby." He raises his brows in utter dismay. I would not dare add that my love life needs a few extra hours a week. Frank says he has to talk it over with the other doctors, and after a day or so, he agrees, saying, "You're the first to make such a request."

"I'm the only doctor in the group who doesn't have a wife."

During a Saturday morning run, Ernest drives past me with a woman sitting next to him, a white woman with long, flowing dark hair. I cannot see her face, or determine how pretty she is, or isn't. I wonder if she might be light-skinned, as if her racial classification would really make a difference to me. I would feel no better about Ernest being with a green woman from Jupiter. He turns onto Peachtree and a feeling of inadequacy comes over me; the little girl taught to despise her own dark skin and kinky hair lingers beneath the surface like a disease. In my mind's eye, Mrs. Roberts takes me by the arm, and says, "Lighten your skin if you want him." I imagine her pointing out her daughter, while Karen stands in a picture perfect pose with her husband and newborn. *Jealousies.*

I watch Ernest and the woman as they vanish into traffic, grateful not to have been spotted as I cross the street, and take off down the running path, soon chanting to myself. *I am a beautiful, spiritual being. I am beautiful. I am . . .*

56

With my workload reduced, I manage to spend more hours each day with Tajuan at the Corbins' home, located less than five miles from my house. I usually take him for long evening walks. Sometimes I read to him. But always, the day ends with me putting him to bed. After eight o'clock is the time I have allotted for dating. So far, nothing, until Karen and Jason invite me to dinner.

Tonight, I wear the short black dress, the one that best shows off my figure, and a pair of spiked, black heels. The dinner is an obvious set-up, with my blind date being Lonnie Daniels, a man slightly shorter than me, and stout with broad shoulders. During the meal, Karen whispers in my ear that Lonnie is an investment banker. "He's divorced. Eligible."

Lonnie, the investment banker, is not bad to look at, just arrogant as hell. He spends an hour discussing his favorite topic—himself—and says, "A man in my position has to be careful about the women he dates. There are so many sisters out here after my money."

"That must be a blow to your ego," I say.

"I don't mean it that way," he says. "I do have other qualities that attract women."

"Really?"

He laughs as if I had intended to be funny, and says, "By the way, what kind of work do you do?"

"Well, I don't need your money," I say pointedly. "If that's why you're asking."

"She's a physician," Karen blurts out.

"A doctor," he says, smiling as if amused. "How'd you like to have dinner with me tomorrow night?"

"I can't, I'm busy."

Over the next few weeks, I refuse a total of six dates with him. But I relent after a little prodding from Karen, and agree to go out for dinner. He picks me up promptly at seven Friday night, and we have a lovely evening together. But when I tell him about Tajuan, how I cannot wait for him to come live with me, Lonnie says he has all the children he wants.

"Child support payments to two women," he complains. A damper is put over the rest of the evening. I *really* do not like him. And only God knows why I agree to a second date.

The following Saturday night, Lonnie takes me out to a downtown dance club. He drinks heavily, slurring his words, and his demeanor becomes aggressive.

"It's time for me to go home," I say forcefully.

"One more dance," he demands, pulling me onto the dance floor, twirling me around, and causing both of us to crash into people. At the end of the torturous ordeal, I snatch his car keys from his loose grip.

"I'll drive home," I say, annoyed. "I'll take a taxi from your house."

"Fine with me," he agrees, wrapping an arm around my waist. Once outside, we get into his car, going no farther than a few blocks, when he begins to fondle me, pulling at my blouse.

"Cut it out," I demand. In a matter of seconds, his hands are all over my body as if I were a car at the carwash, only navigating through town.

"You know you want me!"

"Stop it!" I yell. Finally, I pull into a well-lit gas station, bolt from the car, and phone a taxi. I watch him through the glass-plated walls, passed out in the passenger side of his car. Why didn't I follow my instincts about that creep? An hour later, after I finally get home, I shower the feel of his paws off my body and settle into bed with my faithful diary. For today, I write:

My intuition told me not to go out with him. I knew Lonnie Daniels spelled trouble as soon as he opened his mouth. I should've listened. The next time my inner voice says don't go, I'll stay home.

Rule 9.

I will heed the warnings of my inner voice.

57

9:00 A.M.

Badalele Mobutu, 23-year-old West African woman, 38 weeks gestation, return pregnancy. Gravida—1 para—0. Weight: 162 lbs. Complaints: Because of her circumcised vagina, she is worried about having a huge amount of pain or dying during delivering. History of present illness: Her sister died while giving birth.

"I know I've asked you this before, Ms. Mobutu," I say, while examining her vagina, "but I failed to make a note of it. Please tell me again how old were you when you were circumcised?"

"Twelve."

"Twelve," I repeat, looking closer at the purplish vulva mushrooming over the opening to the vagina. The sight of this deformity is appalling. I have wanted to ask her *why* since her first visit a year ago, before she became pregnant by her professor husband at a local university.

"It must have been terrible for you," I say.

"No, Doctor. Where I come from all the women in my village are circumcised. It is customary. Hurts a lot at first, but that's all. You don't think about it much after that."

"But why?" I ask. My index finger barely makes it through the opening of her vagina, so that I cannot determine how much her cervix has dilated. Ms. Mobutu's delivery might end up being a disaster. "Why in the world?"

"In my village it is a sacred ceremony," she says, and I can tell by the tautness in her voice that I have offended her. "It is done to keep women pure. You see, we do not believe, as American women do, that mating is to satisfy sinful thoughts and urges. For us, it is strictly to bring new life into the world."

"Too bad it doesn't have the same effect on circumcised men. The birthrate would plummet, I assure you." I explain to Mrs. Mobutu that in order for me to help her bring new life into the world, I will have to make an incision from the opening of her vagina up to the clitoris and cut away all the scar tissue in between.

"That will take away the pain?" she asks.

"No, unfortunately there will be pain. But after you heal, you won't be circumcised anymore because unlike other female circumcisions I've read about, your clitoris was left intact."

"I won't be circumcised anymore?" she asks, incredulously.

"For you, Ms. Mobutu, after your delivery, mating will never be the same."

Kelly knocks on the door at the end of the day and sticks her head inside my office.

"Can I have a word with you?" she says.

"Sure," I say, glancing down at my watch. "You know it's almost five o'clock? I thought you'd be home by now."

"That's just it, Dr. Faulkner, because you've cut back your hours, I'm having to work less and earn less money. And I don't think it's fair."

"I'm sorry, Kelly, but when I decided to cut back my hours, I had no idea that it would affect you, too."

"I really need to earn the same salary," she says.

"Well, I know how you might be able to do it," I say. Kelly's eyes light up. She sits in a chair in front of my desk, leaning forward as if afraid she might miss a detail.

"There's an opening for a part-time nurse at Linda's Safe House," I begin, before removing two pennies from the weight cup and sliding them into the gumball machine.

I tell Kelly about how Linda's Safe House was named. "After Linda Jenkins, our patient who died after delivering her baby."

"I remember her," she says.

"The purpose of Linda's Safe House is to help girls who decide to keep their babies. Provide them with a good place to live. Teach them to become good mothers. Encourage them to finish their educations."

"And keep them healthy," Kelly says, smiling. We chew our gum and talk about what young mothers need. She shares her perspective as a woman ten years younger than me, and I feel a connection with her for the first time. Rush hour comes and goes, and for once, Kelly does not complain about the time.

58

Tajuan is six months old and my doubts about getting him grow like a cancer. I try to keep busy doing other things with my new free time, even spending at least five hours a week at Linda's Safe House—examining the girls, teaching them about their bodies, and answering their questions, no matter how redundant or ridiculous. With help from the pregnant girls living there, we planted an herb and flower garden. We dug and planted, pulled weeds, and organized beds, transforming the backyard into a beautiful place to contemplate our lives. There are days when I find myself waiting for Tajuan, while watching the flowers bloom.

Near the end of spring, I take a short weekend trip to Madoosa County to keep my promise to Rosetta. But really, what I yearn for is the sense of family I had after Mama died. No matter how positive I try to be, Tajuan remains in foster care, and I go home to an empty house at the end of each day.

"Be right with you, Lenita Mae," Rosetta says, before hustling out of the kitchen. She and Bobby work quicker now, the dinner hour nears as they diligently stir dishes that warm atop gas burners, and intermittently baste meat in a smokehouse where the back porch used to be. I watch them drape tables with impeccably white cloths and set them with real plates and silverware in the old living room and single bedroom that once smelled dank and mildewed.

"Now," says Rosetta at half past three in the afternoon. She sits across from me at a butcher-block table in the small kitchen where steam spilling from pots and pans warms my face.

"Everything looks great, Rosetta," I say, marveling at how the old place has been spruced up, varnished, rebuilt, refurbished, with new ovens added to look like something out of *Country Living* magazine.

"Well, just let me get a look at that boy you's about to adopt," she says, grinning wide, no longer covering her smile. When I remove a pack of newly developed pictures I've taken of Tajuan, Rosetta cackles boldly.

"He's yours all right," she says, studying each snapshot carefully. "Looks just like you." I peer over her shoulder to glimpse the one of me holding Tajuan on my lap.

"You think?" I say, close to tears.

"Yes, he does," she positively asserts.

"But what if I don't get him? You know the state hasn't terminated Shaniqua's rights yet. Suppose she gets him back?"

"You can't think like that, Lenita Mae. Lord knows, you ne'er would've got through college and medical school and doctoring training thinking like that, now would you?"

"I needed to hear that, Rosetta. He is mine," I say wistfully. Bobby comes in and picks through a few pictures.

"He's definitely all yours," he says.

"I don't like his name, though," I say. "A name should mean something, don't you think?"

"You oughta change it, first thing," Rosetta says.

"He should be named for greatness," I say, beaming proudly.

"I always wished I'd named one of my boys after our brother," Bobby says, checking the time on his watch, less than an hour before dinner guests begin trickling in. I don't recognize my little brother anymore, a man who waits tables instead of waiting to be served.

"Joseph Allen Faulkner's a fine name," he says.

"I'll consider it, Bobby, thanks." I glance down at a picture of Tajuan with one of his winning smiles. How much longer must I wait to bring him home? What if the adoption fails?

The herbs and flowers at Linda's Safe House are in full bloom. A few of our girls had their babies. One put hers up for adoption and returned home to live with her mother. It was during this same season, with the scent of natural perfumes hanging elusively in the air, that Shaniqua voluntarily relinquishes parental rights to her son.

"What brought on this change of heart?" I ask Stella, after she phones me at my office.

"She truly believes it's in her son's best interest."

"I hope it was Shaniqua's idea, and not her mother's."

"It's what she wanted, Lenny. Ms. Davis had nothing to do with it. And the best part of it is that she wants you to raise him."

"She actually said that?"

"Insisted on it."

"Oh, Stella," I say, bursting with joy.

"Just thought you'd like to know why a decision's about to be made on your petition for adoption."

"Oh, thank you, Stella, you're an angel."

"That makes two of us."

After exchanging good-byes, I run ten miles without stopping. I receive a notice regarding the adoption in the mail the following day, and the following week, I am in court. All the waiting seems like seconds compared to now. Ninety days after the court reviewed my petition to adopt Tajuan, he officially becomes my son. *Me, a mother at last.*

This morning, I rummage through mail while he sleeps, and open a letter from Annie, the hospice nurse who cared for Mama. She writes that she saw my ad in the paper looking for a nanny, recognized the address, and wants the job.

> *I've grown tired of caring for the dying. Now I'd like to take on a newborn for a change. I know your mother would be proud of your baby.*
>
> *Yours truly,*
> *Annie*

Goosebumps sprout across my arms. Timing really is everything. I call her right away.

"When can you start, Annie?" I ask.

"First thing in the morning," she says.

On the very day I bring him home, I change my son's name to Joseph Allen Faulkner, in honor of my deceased brother. This morning, after dressing him, I take him outside and he reaches for the sun. He babbles and points out a bird flying overhead. "Bird," I say. He coos, "Da . . . da."

I put Joseph in his jogging stroller and we take off. Fast. We cross Peachtree and cruise along the path running parallel to the road, where wild wisteria bloom close to the edge, and the perfumed scent of the vernal season fills us both with anticipation as we enter the woods for the first time. The path that winds through the close-knit trees is smooth and worn, the air cool and crisp, with sunlight trickling between the leafy branches overhead like sprinkles of gold.

Joseph's tiny voice trills in the wind. I slow to a trot and name everything within his tiny sphere that is either big or brightly colored. I talk to him as if he understands completely.

"Did I tell you about my brother?" I ask, as we turn down Chestnut, and at the corner of Valemont, I hope to glimpse Ernest at work in his garden. I am ready to face him now, and for him to meet Joseph.

"Did I tell you how brave my brother was?" I singsong to Joseph. "Are you paying attention? Are you listening to me?"

Joseph's round eyes narrow as a gentle spring breeze stirs around him, lulling him to sleep.

"Joe had big dreams for himself, but he died protecting our country. Now it's up to you to dream big."

Across the lawn and up a slight hill, I spot Ernest. I wave and yodel like any proud mother might, "Helloooo, Ernest, looo."

He stares curiously at me before removing his gardening gloves. Astonishment slides over his face as he makes his way across the lawn to meet me. I notice that his hair is neatly trimmed and handsomely shapes his face that is now beardless, showing off a chiseled jawline.

"You've shaved!" I burst out.

"I have," he says nonchalantly, smoothing a hand across the side of his face. "Did it over the Christmas break. It was time, don't you think?"

"Yes, you look . . . you . . . you've changed, Ernest."

"Well, what have we here?" he says, bending awkwardly to better see Joseph. "Yours?"

"My adopted son, yes," I admit proudly.

"Very handsome young fellow," Ernest says, kneeling for a closer look when Joseph wakes up and whimpers. "May I?"

"Sure."

Ernest gently removes Joseph from his restraint, holding him face-to-face. It occurs to me that Joseph will need a father figure soon. There may come a time when I, the mother, am not enough.

"Come inside, Lenny," he says, taking Joseph up to his house. I follow them inside, surprised to see the decorative changes. The small foyer is off-white, and abstract Jacob Lawrence prints meet the eyes above the fireplace in the bright red living room, where everything appears to be more modern. I notice an overstuffed white sofa with glass end tables. I wonder if the redhead I spotted riding in Ernest's car redecorated, if she encouraged him to get rid of the beard. We head inside the bright yellow kitchen, where the windows look bigger and are curtain-less. The table is covered in red oriental fabric, blocking the name AMY from sight.

"You've changed things," I say.

"It was time," Ernest says. He sits with Joseph on his lap, and I sit across from them, watching him peel a banana.

"Can he have a piece?" Ernest asks.

"Sure," I say, pleased. Joseph gobbles greedily. I think about the christening ceremony for Karen and Jason's son, how Jason held Sammy up to the light afterwards, very *Roots*-like, everyone watching a traditional display of affection between father and son, the women especially beaming, silently cheering them on.

"Ernest, I wonder if you might like to consider being my son's godfather?"

"Godfather?" he says, stunned.

"Well, you don't have to commit just yet. It's not like a real christening or anything. And there's no financial obligation on your part. I just thought . . ."

"I'm honored," he says graciously. "But why me? Why not the man you're involved with?"

"I'm not involved anymore," I say. Ernest offers Joseph another piece of banana and looks thoughtfully at me. I quaver, "But if the person you're involved with has a problem with it, I understand."

"I'm not involved, Lenny," he says.

"Well, I just thought . . . I mean, I saw you with someone . . . and figured you were . . ."

"I'm getting on with my life."

"I understand, Ernest," I say, feeling foolish.

"Anyway, it's nice of you to think of me," he says. "I'd be happy to do it."

"Really, Ernest?"

"I don't make idle promises."

"I know, Ernest Hemingway. You're just like your father."

He smiles. "That's one of the nicest things anyone's ever said to me."

"It's true."

After returning home from our walk and visit with Ernest, I put Joseph down for his nap. It occurs to me that my son will probably come to think of Ernest as his father, the way Genevieve thinks of him as her brother-figure. I write in my diary for today.

We are another way of forming a family, without the boundaries of blood and familial history, without the same roots or expectations of marriage. We are here because we truly want to be. Here and nowhere else. Committed, Ernest and I, to this beautiful child I have chosen. What would it be like to have a relationship with another man? Where would he fit in our picture? How would it affect Joseph? I would never want a relationship that threatens the emotional stability of my son. If I ever fall for another man again, something has to be made perfectly clear in regards to my priorities.

Rule 10.

My son comes first.

The Finish Line

An ambulance pulls up to Mrs. Stein's house. The warning peals loud and shrill. Red lights twirl around like Christmas. Transfixed by the horror of this moment, I hold Joseph in my arms as paramedics rush inside. A few cars stop in the street. Passersby stand in my front yard, watching. What on earth? I keep saying this, thinking it. She was fine yesterday. We were going to have tea. What on earth?

Minutes later, they remove her body on a stretcher, a sheet covering her head. My heart sinks to the pit of my stomach. Mama used to say that death comes in threes. I wonder if Mrs. Stein knew death was coming, if she had the slightest inkling. We are all going to die, I know. Everybody knows. From the time we are born, we are living to die. Yet, I cannot imagine life without Mrs. Stein. She was one of my dearest friends, and it seems like only yesterday that she first brought me the mail. Who will return my lost mail now that she is gone? Who will introduce me to the man Mama wanted me to have? The man sent from heaven. The man I deserve.

I take Wednesday off to attend Mrs. Stein's funeral, held at a small synagogue on Clairmont Avenue. I sit three rows behind her immediate family. Michael Cohen and Dr. Liu sit in the row in front of me. The rabbi stands before the temple of mourners and eulogizes Mrs. Stein. I wish I had the nerve to tell them all how she read the Torah to Mama, and how Mama heard God speak to her. I wish they all knew how special she was.

After the service, I leave the synagogue and come face-to-face with Michael and Dr. Liu.

"Dr. Faulkner," he says.

"Dr. Cohen," I say, an ache growing at the base of my throat. It is tough seeing the man who cheated get on with his life without a hitch. There should be consequences, accountability. He should have suffered, too.

A hand taps my shoulder, and I turn to find Ernest Hemingway standing next to me.

"Ernest? How'd you know, Mrs. Stein?"

"We kept getting each other's mail," he says.

"That's right," I say, remembering the evening Mrs. Stein mentioned meeting Ernest and his wife.

"Mrs. Stein would come by and admire my garden on her morning walks. She got to know Amy before she died. Was really sweet about reading to her near the end."

"Oh, yes, she was good about that. She read to my mother."

"Amazing, isn't it, how we all got to know each other?"

"Yes, Ernest, it really is."

He chuckles softly to himself, saying, "She had a nice lady she wanted me to meet."

"Oh?" I say, surprised, the hairs standing up on the back of my neck. Ernest was the mystery man, the man Mrs. Stein studied and found most suitable for me. A stream of light flows from my head to my heart.

"Hope you meet her, Ernest," I say.

"I think I already have," he says, arching his brows. Ernest smiles as if secretly amused, without parting his lips, his eyes turn into veiled slits that see through me, and I have the feeling he has always known I was the chosen one. We walk silently together across the breezeway toward the parking lot, as reflections of all that has changed in a year appear like snapshots in my mind—Ralph's deception, Mama's death, Linda Jenkins's suicide, and now Mrs. Stein being laid to rest. A profound sense of loss comes over me, like the grayness of winter. It is temporary, I know. Sadness is not something to run from because it passes on its own, like it passed for Ernest, now getting on with his life. For me, it always passes in spite of the enormity of the pain, passes when it is ready. So I allow my sudden downheartedness to ebb and flow with each solemn step, until I reach my car, where the sun bears brightly down on Ernest and me.

"Life is funny, isn't it?" I say.

"You might say that," he says.

"One minute the world comes tumbling down around you, and in the next, it's in the palms of your hands. Maybe not as funny as it is profound."

"I suppose that's true as well."

"Really, Ernest, I have so much to be grateful for."

"I understand," he says, standing next to my car.

"So many blessings."

Ernest nods in agreement.

"When I think about all Ralph did to me, and how I ended up with all that money because of it, I mean, it makes me think that God is not only just, but has a heck of a sense of humor."

Ernest folds his arms and leans against my car, listening intently.

"All I wanted was a family of my own," I say, averting my eyes away from him. For however long it takes, I know he will listen to whatever I have to say. Ernest is a patient man who cares.

"Now you have a beautiful son," he says.

"Yes." I fumble with my car keys, accidentally dropping them when I prepare to unlock the car door, and when they ping against the payment, Ernest immediately stoops to retrieve them. I imagine myself climbing to the top of Kilimanjaro with him following close behind, and Joseph, as an older boy, struggling to keep up with us, holding on, each step made easier because we are together.

"Lenny?" Ernest says, concerned. "Are you all right?"

"Yes, thank you," I say, unaware of how long he has been waiting for my daydream to end. I reach out to hug Ernest, no longer conflicted about my feelings for him, knowing with certainty in my heart as I draw him closer and closer.

"I love you, Ernest Hemingway," I whisper, without a single forethought or premeditation.

"Oh, Lenny," he says, burying his face in my hair. His arms gently envelop me, the reserve between us dissipating like snow melting, his hard body relaxing into mine. "I've wanted you . . . but I was afraid."

"Afraid?" I ask, lifting my face to his.

"Yes, of losing you."

"I'm here." I kiss Ernest, his mouth covering mine, his warm breath becoming my breath, intoxicatingly. Footsteps cross the parking lot, and voices grow louder. Doors open and close.

"I'm so fortunate to know you," I say, breathlessly.

"No more than I," he says sweetly. "Lenny, you came along at my darkest hour and brought light back into my life. I'll always love you for that."

Love. Ernest unlocks my car door, but before I climb inside, he stops me with a tender kiss to my cheek. The air is filled with unspoken passion, words we are not quite sure of, and commitments we are unprepared to make. He helps me close the door after I get inside the car. The sound of it shutting has a permanent cling to it, like titles—doctor, friend and single mother. My life is so much more than any one thing. It feels bigger. I feel bigger. I feel as though I have climbed the highest mountain. I am standing on top of Kilimanjaro.

Ernest taps my window as Old Faithful's engine bristles and hums. I quickly roll it down.

"You're not alone in this, you know," he says. "I won't take my role as godfather lightly. I'm here whenever you need me."